Zane Radcliffe was born in  1969. After graduating from moved to London in 1994 to writer. He is now a Creative good advertising agency in E

His first novel, *London Irish* (2002), earned him the WHSmith New Talent Award. This follows the success of his first short story, *My Dog* (1974), which was awarded a B+ and a Big Red Tick by Miss Hassard at Ballyholme Primary School. *Big Jessie* is his second novel.

Praise for *London Irish*:

'Very fresh, very funny. I laughed until I stopped'
Colin Bateman

'Brilliant, shocking and very, very funny'
Irish Tatler

'A fast-paced, darkly comic thriller'
Irish News

'Radcliffe's writing is technically skilled, evoking . . . the image of a child playing with bits on a bomb site'
What's On In London

'Madcap comic crime in the vein of James Hawes or early Colin Bateman'
Bookseller

'There have been some outstanding débuts this summer, but in the comic thriller genre *London Irish* is undoubtedly the best new title of the year. It rocks!'
Daily Record

www.**booksattransworld**.co.uk

Also by Zane Radcliffe

LONDON IRISH

and published by Black Swan

BIG JESSIE

Zane Radcliffe

BLACK SWAN

BIG JESSIE
A BLACK SWAN BOOK: 0 552 77096 5

First publication in Great Britain

PRINTING HISTORY
Black Swan edition published 2003

1 3 5 7 9 10 8 6 4 2

Set in 11/13pt Melior by
Falcon Oast Graphic Art Ltd.

Black Swan Books are published by Transworld Publishers,
61–63 Uxbridge Road, London W5 5SA,
a division of The Random House Group Ltd,
in Australia by Random House Australia (Pty) Ltd,
20 Alfred Street, Milsons Point, Sydney, NSW 2061, Australia,
in New Zealand by Random House New Zealand Ltd,
18 Poland Road, Glenfield, Auckland 10, New Zealand
and in South Africa by Random House (Pty) Ltd,
Endulini, 5a Jubilee Road, Parktown 2193, South Africa.

Printed and bound in Great Britain by
Cox & Wyman Ltd, Reading, Berkshire.

Papers used by Transworld Publishers are natural, recyclable
products made from wood grown in sustainable forests. The
manufacturing processes conform to the environmental
regulations of the country of origin.

For Natalie

CHEERS

All at Transworld, notably Simon, Prue and Claire. Jonny Geller, as always. The Leith Agency, especially Gerry. Those hugely talented and not unattractive people at Newhaven, especially Gareth, Ken and Jonathan.

I administer an overdose of thanks to Nurse Liesel Radcliffe who informed much of this book. And I would personally like to thank everyone who voted for the first one. But that would take a long time and you'd probably feel uncomfortable if I just turned up on your doorstep, unannounced.

1

I stood in the silt, buck naked and covered head to toe in my own excrement, as my classmates sang:

Whoa-oh Big Jessie (Bam-ba-Lam)
Whoa-oh Big Jessie (Bam-ba-Lam)
Big Jessie is a fat (Bam-ba-Lam)
Ginger twat (Bam-ba-Lam)

Seventeen of them, laughing and guldering till the spittle leapt from the corners of their mouths. Rabid wee gobshites the lot of them. They wouldn't let up, not for a second, not even when a passing Viking long-ship gunned its engine on Lough Erne. The replica boat ferried people round the Fermanagh lakes, tracing a figure of eight round Crom Castle and Gad Island lookout tower. Loaded with tourists it was. Every one of them took a snap of my shivering, shit-smeared behind.

As if this wasn't embarrassing enough, my brain chose that moment to despatch a cruel and in-voluntary electric signal to my groin, summoning my first truly memorable erection. I was ten. It was 1977 — the Year of the Wookie. It would go down as the year the Queen enjoyed her Silver Jubilee, the year Elvis enjoyed his last cheeseburger, the year Ram Jam had their hit (Bam-ba-Lam), and the year Jessie Black shit himself and got a hard-on in front of *everybody*.

I would never live it down.

I cursed myself. I had suspected the school trip was a bad idea from the moment Mr Swain had told assembly it involved water sports and one of the big boys (Kirk McClaren) bleated, 'That'll be Jessie Black wetting his bed, sir.' Cue schoolboy laughter. From Mr Swain.

The poster outside the assembly hall had initially seemed inviting enough. It promised an activity weekend on the Ulster Lakes, canoeing, caving, biking, climbing, and abseiling. If I wasn't already persuaded, then Kirk McClaren sealed the deal. He told all the first years that if you didn't go on the trip you were gay. This became the last desperate thrust of my argument when trying to prise the £10 deposit out of my dad.

'But if I don't go, I'll be gay,' I said.

My dad considered my predicament. He thumbed the stray straggles of Three Nuns tobacco into the bowl of his pipe and, displaying characteristic empathy, said, 'This fella – McClaren is it – judging by his surname his forefathers were Scottish. They wore kilts. No man in our family ever wore a dress, you tell him that. We'll see who's gay then.'

'But Dad, he'll punch my lights out.'

Dad sucked the flame off a Swan Vesta and tossed the spent match onto the hearth. It missed. He looked me up and down and proffered one last piece of sage-like wisdom. 'Son,' he said, 'you got to feel sorry for Scottish transvestites. In a country whose fiercest warriors dress in tartan skirts, any fella who dolls himself up in the full Shirley Bassey won't be taken seriously unless he invades Poland.'

'Dad.'

'Jessie.'

'The carpet's on fire.'

As my father stomped on the burning match my hopes of visiting the Ulster Lakelands were extinguished with it. No canoeing or archery for me. The only activity I could look forward to would be a bout of bare-knuckle boxing with McClaren in the school quad.

I sought sanctuary in the kitchen. Mum was polishing Dad's shoes with a pair of his Y-fronts. When she saw me, she rinsed her hands under the tap. She moved to the cupboard and reached down a biscuit jar. I informed her that a biscuit wasn't going to make me feel better. Not even a fancy one, like a Taxi or a Wagon Wheel. She allowed her hand to form a snake and slid it into the jar. She produced a big, orange note, a tenner, and handed it to me. She nodded towards the living room and made a *shush* sound, putting a stained finger to her lips. This was between her and me.

And so I found myself not being gay at the Lakelands Activity Centre. The huge complex dominates the tiny village of Kesh, which sits buttonholed to the northern lapel of Lower Lough Erne. For some reason Lower Lough Erne is actually above Upper Lough Erne on the map, a fact I queried with Mr Swain. He was sharing a seat at the front of the Ulsterbus with Miss Blundell, our new student supply teacher. Miss Blundell was wearing leather trousers like Suzi Quatro. Mr Swain had his hand on her knee. I guessed he must have been checking the leather was real.

'Sir, why is Lower Lough Erne above Upper Lough Erne?' I asked.

Swain whipped his hand off Miss Blundell's

trousers and adjusted his wedding ring. He was beetroot.

'What do you want, boy?'

'Why is Lower Lough Erne above Upper Lough Erne, sir?'

Mr Swain gave me exactly the sort of considered and informative answer a child expects from his Head of Department, alerting my young mind to the lively possibilities of physical geography. 'Why is your mouth above your arsehole, Black? It's to stop you talking shite. Now get back to your seat before I skelp ye.'

I made my way back down the bus to a chorus of jeers and a *rat-a-tat* of coins hitting windows. The weekend had started badly and from there on it deteriorated.

The words 'activity weekend' and 'fat kid' do not sit happily in the same sentence. I had been looking forward to the abseiling right up until the instructor made everybody wait while they searched for an adult-sized harness to accommodate my considerable girth. We went rock-climbing. I was forced to ascend last, my classmates refusing to come up behind me for fear the rope wouldn't cope. My weight didn't inhibit my enjoyment of the archery. That activity only became physically demanding when I became the target for the other kids' arrows. I wanted to do the biking but anticipated that McClaren and his cohorts would be out of sight before I located the gears on my Grifter. Not wishing to eat their dust, I took the safer option of horse-riding. Bad move. I was the only boy partaking, forced to don my riding helmet among a gaggle of giggling girls. And barely one mile into the trek my pony – Sherpa – had to be retired after experiencing some sort of cardio-respiratory murmur.

The instructor assured me the horse was getting old and his wheezing was in no way connected to the large ginger load on his back. Whatever, I had to dismount and suffer the indignity of walking Sherpa back to the centre.

I was told to spend the rest of the afternoon playing table tennis with Miles Huggins, the school asthmatic. I had never really spoken much to him until that afternoon. We hadn't really had the chance to form a friendship. He was always missing school because of his illness. He was as thin as a liquorice pipe with skin the colour of sweetie mice. One of the lenses on his glasses was permanently frosted.

He thumped me 11–9, 11–7, 11–1.

Miles tried to cheer me up by turning his eyelids inside out and saying *ah-so* like a Benny Hill Chinaman. He knew how to make me laugh. I asked him if he wanted to be my friend and he said *sure* and gave me a go on his inhaler.

So it wasn't a totally miserable weekend. Miss Blundell even took us on a tour of the lough. We cut a trail through the barbed gorse and bejewelled brambles, Joanne (for Miss Blundell had told us her name) indicating this and pointing out that with the unflagging enthusiasm of a student supply teacher. She took us to the Marble Arch caves, an underworld of rivers, waterfalls, winding passages and lofty chambers. When we emerged, we witnessed a flock of Canada geese skimming the water like bouncing bombs. Joanne told us that somewhere at the bottom of the lough there lay a squadron of Catalina flying boats, used in the Second World War to locate Germany's deadly U-boats in the Atlantic. It was a Catalina from Lough Erne, she claimed, that spotted the *Bismarck* in 1941. A day later, the warship literally went down in history.

13

I loved Miss Blundell and I hoped that she would get a full-time job at our school. Mr Swain seemed similarly impressed. He was always complimenting her and he even made the effort to go to her room after lights out to help her prepare her syllabus.

We were due to spend the Sunday on the water, canoeing, sailing and windsurfing. The prospect filled me with dread, not least because we were all to wear wetsuits. They're not the most flattering of garments even on a slim fella and, sure enough, I emerged from the changing hut encased in rubber, looking like a snake that had swallowed a sheep.

Before we got changed, the instructor had made us all laugh by saying that professional divers liked to pee in their wetsuits to keep themselves warm. This seemed to activate the malicious gene that was irreparably written into Kirk McClaren's DNA. I had just managed to force one leg into my wetsuit when he collared me.

'Oi, Jessie, I hope you're going to pee in that when you zip it up,' he said.

'No, course not.'

'What are you, a poof? If you wanna be a pro, you got to pee in your wetsuit. Did you not hear the instructor?'

'Have you peed in yours?'

McClaren was conscious of the other boys gathering round him. Flies to a turd. He upped the ante.

'Peed in it? I've done more than that. Have you heard of free divers?' he asked.

'Course,' I said, even though I hadn't.

'Then you'll know those boys are the business. They can hold their breath underwater for hours. They can stop their heart. They dive so deep they get crushed to a third of their size. And it's cold down there. Minus

14

fifty-seven. And do you know how they keep warm?'

I nodded. Hadn't a clue.

'That's right, they shit in their wetsuits. It gets squished all around them and keeps them warm. So that's what me and the guys are doing, isn't that right, Steeky?'

My fellow first years gazed up at Stephen Meeks. He was the school's head boy yet he preferred to be relegated to the role of McClaren's right-hand man. Meeks bent slightly on his knees and concentrated his expression like a baby filling its nappy. He grunted. He straightened. Then he hopped up and down, windmilling his arms. 'God, that feels good,' he said. 'Aye, it's like a sauna in this here suit, so it is.'

'See, Jessie. That's what real men do. They shit in their wetsuits. Or perhaps you aren't a real man?'

'Course I am.' As if to emphasize the point, I tucked my dick into the rubber suit and hauled the arms over my shoulders. I slowly zipped it up, taking care not to catch a roll of fat or an errant nipple.

'Are you sure you're a man? Isn't that a wee pair of girly tits you've got on ye? You should be changing with the girls. They tell me you like riding ponies.'

Again, the laughter rattled the rafters. But I wasn't going to let him beat me. Not this time, not in front of everybody. For once I was going to do the right thing.

'Course I'm a real man. I can prove it.'

I braced my guts and, thanking the Lord that I'd eaten thirds at breakfast, I began to empty my bowels into the suit. That the sensation was both warm and unexpectedly pleasant only confirmed that McClaren wasn't winding me up. A huge grin erupted on Kirk's face – like the Joker – and he endorsed my manly act by patting me on the back. I had done the right thing.

I had been validated and vindicated. I was one of the lads.

Apart from one near-death experience while performing capsize drill in my canoe, I quite enjoyed the water sports. It aroused in me a previously dormant aptitude for windsurfing. Indeed, I contrived to stay upright on the board for longer than anyone before falling ingloriously into the soup some distance beyond a safety area that had been marked out, inadequately I thought, by half a dozen fluorescent pink buoys the size of spacehoppers. When the instructor dashed for his jet ski and fizzed urgently across the mile and a half of lake to retrieve me, I thought he was coming out to offer his congratulations. Instead, he hauled me onto his vessel, screaming hysterically. I couldn't make him out because my ears were full of water, but I guessed he wasn't saying that I'd be presented with the windsurfing medal at the end-of-trip prizegiving.

But if I was disappointed at that, I was mortified when I returned to the changing hut. All the lads were already inside. They had peeled their wetsuits down to their waists and were exhibiting a collection of clean, porcelain-white torsos. That familiar grin had spread itself across McClaren's face, though now I saw it in an altogether different context. The Joker laughed. I felt ill. I knew what was coming.

'Get them off, Big Jessie.'

I tried not to cry. I really tried. You didn't argue with McClaren, not when he had an audience. I duly unzipped my rubber suit and my poo-greased belly popped out like a pea from a pod. I looked like someone had varnished me with iodine prior to a Caesarean.

The hut became filled with a loud mixture of laughter, derision and disgust. So much hollering that the windows fogged up. Even Miles Huggins was laughing and he had a hole in his heart.

'Get them *right* off,' said McClaren. He was clearly enjoying His Finest Hour.

I extricated myself from the wetsuit as fast as I could, pausing only to gag against the stench.

'Big Jessie's on a dirty protest,' yelled Huggins. He had tried to hide himself behind the big lads, but I clocked him. Fucking turncoat.

'This is Kesh, not Long Kesh,' goaded McClaren.

'What are you, a Taig?' asked Stephen Meeks.

'Well, he's got ginger hair,' said McClaren, completing the one-two with Steeky.

I felt immediately cold. Meeks had opened the cabin door. My thin coat of shit no longer provided insulation from the October air.

'There's no shower in here, shitface. You're going to have to make a run for the lake,' goaded Meeks.

The head boy was right. My only option was to dash for the water. I searched for a towel to cover myself, but someone had hidden my sports bag. Huggins turned his eyes to the ceiling (at least, he turned the one that was visible through his single clear lens) in an expression of mock innocence. I wanted to cut him and watch him bleed.

Meeks and McClaren started the slow handclaps. They had six years on the rest of us. They were supposed to be looking after wee lads like me. Instead they rejoiced in picking off the weak. Fucking cowards, the pair of them.

There was nothing for it. I cupped my hands over my balls and made for the lake.

I had scarcely run the length of a canoe when I realized that the girls had not yet retired to their hut to get changed. They were still collecting pebbles at the water's edge. I froze in front of them. You could have heard a pin drop. And several handfuls of pebbles.

And then the singing started. McClaren and Meeks emerged from the hut, leading their choir in a radical reworking of 'Black Betty'.

I felt a familiar heat rising up from my cheeks, bringing the water in my eyes to a low boil. That's the problem with being fat, pale, and ginger. Embarrassment *shows*. There's no masking it. The blood races to your chubby little cheeks, engorging the capillaries till you look like you're storing two shiny red apples for winter. The slightest twinge of embarrassment and my face and neck would go crimson, then bright vermilion, before plumping for deep damask. To the nickname 'Big Jessie', my young detractors often appended the title 'Red Cheeks of Ulster'.

I was human litmus paper.

I stood shivering with the blood filling my cheeks and the silt filling the gaps in my toes. Unfortunately my facial capillaries weren't the only things becoming engorged. I could no longer contain my stiffening penis in my cupped hands.

I wanted to die.

Then an angel appeared. She opened her wings of brilliant white and accepted me in their embrace. Rather, Carmel McCaffrey appeared. She opened a soft, white towel and wrapped it round me.

I don't know why she did it. Why would she be bothered with me of all people? I never had the nerve to speak to girls, certainly not Carmel McCaffrey. She was way too intimidating. She was the tallest person in Year 1 and the only Catholic. While most of us were ten, she looked about twelve. She had tits. She smelt of sweat.

On the first day of term Carmel had stood in front of our class and told us how she was shot before she was born. Back then, her pregnant mother had marched from Belfast to Londonderry. She had set out with eighty marchers from City Hall and it took them four days to reach Derry's walls. But when they got there, the marchers were attacked by some off-duty B-specials and Carmel's mum was shot in the stomach. Mother and baby survived, but the bullet had lodged itself in Carmel's unformed leg. Her toes hadn't yet separated. She showed us the X-ray on the classroom window. It was mad. The bullet was a wee black spot no bigger than a wine gum. Carmel said that the doctors saved her life and so, when she grew up, she was going to become a nurse.

I guessed that was why she put the towel round me and walked me to the medical room in the activity centre.

I was shown to a shower so powerful that it near peeled the skin right off me. I was given antiseptic shampoo that smelt exactly like the stuff Mum used on Midge, our spaniel. It stung my eyes and got in my mouth but I didn't care because I had decided two things:

Carmel McCaffrey was going to be my best friend for ever.

And McClaren, Meeks and Huggins were going to suffer. Even, as it turned out, if it took me twenty-four years.

2

Six oranges sat in a wooden bowel on a table draped with a Union Jack.

The backdrop to this still life was a floor-to-ceiling window that held a scene both expansive and expensive, the view from the first million-pound apartment in Northern Ireland. The River Lagan ran across the glass like a seam of coal. On the far bank, a light sugar dust of snow picked out the city and Black Mountain beyond. To the left sat the Markets, the Hilton and the ultraviolet Waterfront Hall. To the right, the redeveloped docks, the Odyssey arena and the two yellow ship cranes that famously bookend Belfast. Only a fortnight earlier, Madonna had switched on the city's Christmas lights. They now formed low constellations against a whisky-coloured sky. Belfast was a winter wonderland. All that was missing was a Disney fairy.

'It's just like Beirut,' I joked.

'I think you've got something there, Jay. That'd make a cracker slogan. *Belfast – It's just like Beirut*. It might just keep the tourists away, stop this place turning into another bloody Dublin.' Diggsy adjusted the height of his tripod, keeping his eye glued to the viewfinder of the attached digicam. He shifted the focus a whisker and tiptoed back from it. 'Right,' he urged. 'Have another look. Tell me if you see anything different.'

I looked into frame. 'Nope. Same as yesterday. Same as the day before yesterday. And the ten days before that. It's still six oranges in a wooden bowl sitting on a table draped with a Union Jack. And Belfast behind them, looking like Never-Never Land. Or, if you're a staunch Paisleyite, a Never-Never-Never Land.'

'So you don't notice anything different about the oranges?'

'Nope.'

'They're not starting to rot?'

'Nope.'

'Are you sure? One of them's definitely on the turn. I can see the mould from here. Is the camera not picking it up?'

''Fraid not, Diggsy. Your oranges are in fine fettle. The Man from Delmonte, he say *yes*.'

'Rallacks. It's too cold in here. The air's preserving them. I'm going to have to leave the heating on full blast, till the end of the week if needs be. Long enough for the fruit to decompose.'

'You're forgetting something. I pay our leccy bill,' I said.

'This is art, Jay. You can't put a price on art.'

'Yes you can. Van Gogh's *Irises* – twenty-seven million.'

'Philistine.'

'Non-practising,' I corrected.

'I'm creating a contemporary video installation here. I'm making a statement.'

'And what would that statement be? *I own half a dozen oranges*. Profound.'

Diggsy sighed. He knew I was winding him up and

was refusing to play ball. He unclipped the three clothes pegs attached to the sleeve of his *Taxi Driver* T-shirt and used two of them to fix a semi-opaque filter over his largest spotlight. The spare clothes peg he returned to the front of his T-shirt, pinching De Niro's cheeks.

Of course, I knew all about his latest 'statement'. Diggsy had talked about little else for a fortnight.

Belfast was buzzing, he had belatedly observed. The initial scepticism over the paramilitary ceasefires had, for the most part, receded. By the end of the Nineties, with the Good Friday Agreement agreed and a Northern Ireland Assembly assembled, the city had taken its first tentative steps towards peace and prosperity. With the advent of a new millennium it was now taking giant, giddy leaps. Every week another bar, hotel or entertainment complex seemed to sprout up and open its doors to an eager public. Money was being pumped into the province from all over the globe. You could have been forgiven for thinking they'd discovered oil under City Hall.

The effect on the city was as invigorating as it was rapid, like an egg in a microwave. In a little under five years Belfast had exploded into a bustling and colourful metropolis. It even boasted its own ice-hockey team. Occasionally, they won.

All this was grand but Diggsy wasn't so sure. He retained an unhealthy scepticism about the peace process. Diggsy retained an unhealthy scepticism about most things. *I didn't float down the Lagan in a bubble*, he would say. He was convinced that Belfast's bubble was about to burst.

Why? Well, for one, the Northern Ireland Assembly had just been suspended. This followed the Unionists' steadfast refusal to sit at a table with Sinn Fein while the IRA held on to its arms. Diggsy (that is, 'The Morose And Terminally Pessimistic Diggsy', to give him his full title) thought he saw a correlation. He believed that just as the city was flourishing, the Unionists were floundering. The two things were inversely proportional. While construction was taking place all over Belfast, the Unionists were ensuring that nothing constructive happened at Stormont. They met the irresistible force of progress with immovable objection. *Never, never, never. No, no, no.* Their politicians had become dinosaurs and their institutions, particularly the Orange Order, had become increasingly outmoded and irrelevant. And Diggsy (that is, 'The Artist Diggsy') felt compelled to make his statement.

Hence the video installation: a time-lapsed, fixed-rostrum shot of six oranges rotting to a blue-black pulp in a wooden bowl placed on a Union Jack while, in the window behind, Belfast propels herself into the twenty-first century at a dizzying pace. He had given it the working title *Orange Disorder*.

Diggsy flagged off a reflection in the window.

'I was thinking about my plans for this piece. I have a few ideas,' he said.

'Don't tell me. Tate Modern? Saatchi Gallery?'

'Seriously, Jay. I may need your help. You being the big arts journalist and all.'

'A *music* journalist. I'm a music journalist. The last bit of art I reviewed was a mural painted on the gable of our old terrace on the Cregagh Road. It depicted a UDA gunman with a head too tiny for his body, and two left hands. I found an aerosol and sprayed my critique underneath it – Three out of ten. Must try harder.'

Diggsy wasn't listening. He navigated his way across the wide expanse of our living-room-cum-photographic-studio and headed purposefully for the open-plan kitchen. He shucked open a Harp culled from the walk-in fridge.

'I need you to call that DJ fella, David Holmes. I want him to mix a soundtrack for my film,' he said.

'Yeah, like I have David Holmes's direct line.'

'Come on, Jay. You know everyone who's anyone.'

'Course I do. Tell you what, Diggsy, why don't I flick through my little black book of rock-star chums and see who else I can get to score your home videos. What about my old mucker Sting? On second thoughts, he'll be too busy teaching tantric sex to indigenous tribespeople. Damon Albarn's a possibility. Ah, but didn't he just do a soundtrack with Michael Nyman? And the theme for Danny Boyle's new film. And some project with that cartoonist friend of his. He's a busy boy, is our Damon. Tell you what, I'll give Thommy Yorke a bell, see if he has a window.'

'Jay?'

'Uhuh.'

'Cut the sarcasm. I'm serious. David Holmes is a Belfast lad. He might want to help out a local, cutting-edge video artist. It depends how you pitch it to him. Don't tell him the subject matter, just give him a blank canvas. Tell him he can loop the finished film and project it at one of his gigs.'

'OK, OK. There is a *slight* possibility I *might* know his manager.'

'Cool.'

'Whoa there. One condition. I need a favour too.'

Diggsy leaned across the breakfast bar. 'Name it,' he said.

'I'm heading down the Limelight tonight. The Harlots are headlining.'

'The who?'

'No, they've split up. The Harlots. Belfast's bright young indie hopefuls. Their debut EP's just been released on Ugly Duckling. Lamacq loves them.'

'Sorry, Jay, can I have that in English?'

'Look, I'll be reviewing their gig and I need you to take photographs.'

Diggsy burped the first word of his reply. 'No. No photos. I'm a *video* artist. I don't do the still image. It imposes too many constraints. I only use my SLR for reference.'

I knew Diggsy was prickly on this subject. He believed that life was a flux, an organic, malleable entity. The still image was therefore an unrepresentative, dishonest image. The camera always lies, or so he believed. Taking his philosophy to its illogical conclusion, he declared that photobooths were the work of Satan. Having consulted my passport photo I was inclined to agree with him.

I wouldn't have asked Diggsy to blow the dust from his lens cap, were I not in a real fix. Simon, my regular snapper, had phoned to say he'd come down with 'a mystery bug'. His wife had cooked him a dodgy leg of lamb and Simon reckoned he'd contracted foot and mouth. I asked him if it was Northern Irish lamb, reassuring him that the epidemic had not yet reached our shores. He asked me how to check if the leg was Northern Irish. I told him to look for the bullet-hole through the knee.

So now I was in the schtook.

I decided to make the gig sound more attractive to Diggsy. Film buff that he was, I knew he had a particular weakness for Russ Meyer chick flicks.

'The Harlots are going to be big fish,' I announced. 'Well, big fish in the small, deoxygenated pond that is Northern Irish indie rock. I've got three columns to fill

25

in Saturday's *News Letter* and a large white space which, I hope, will be occupied by a stunning photograph of Scarlet Harlot, six-foot-one of ample-breasted, perspiring frontwoman.'

The Harp can sank slightly in Diggsy's fist, a Pavlovian response, a sign his palm had become suddenly moist.

'Sorry, Diggsy, did I not mention that The Harlots are an all-girl outfit?'

He rested his tinnie on the granite worktop.

'So,' he said. 'Will I ah, like, get paid for this?'

'Let me see, David Holmes's manager? I *thought* I had his number.'

'OK, OK. I'll photograph these girls for you. But I'm not happy about it.' Diggsy exited the kitchen, unbuttoning his fly as he went.

'Where are you going?'

'Shower, shit and a shave.'

I grabbed his Harp and fed a slice of Stereolab into the CD player. I threw myself onto the couch and cracked open that morning's edition of the *News Letter*. I checked my column for typos and was pleased to count only four. Something bothered me about the page though. It wasn't quite right, like something was missing. It took me a few seconds to work it out. A stock mugshot of my good self would normally be positioned within the masthead at the top right-hand corner of the entertainment page. But in that morning's edition it had been positioned elsewhere, on top of a photo of The Corrs. My head and shoulders had transplanted themselves onto Andrea Corr's body. Though I may often have fantasized about having Andrea Corr's body (a scenario in which I would *never* leave my apartment), the creature the paper had conjured was not a pretty one. The boys in paste-up had clearly been having a laugh.

As my editor was fond of reminding me, the Ulster *News Letter* is Britain's oldest daily. Cutting edge it isn't. The last time the *News Letter* got a scoop was in 1776 when it became the first newspaper anywhere in Europe to publish the American Declaration of Independence after the ship carrying it to England took a piss stop in Londonderry. In two and a half centuries the *News Letter* had become less of a newspaper and more of a pro-Unionist fanzine. How successive editors must have rued that the paper was first printed in 1737, forty-seven years too late to cover the Battle of the Boyne.

For such a staunch, stick-in-the-mud rag to employ a music hack was as astounding as it was incongruous. Imagine *Angler's Monthly* hiring a fashion writer. Just as he or she would be penning endless articles on a limited theme ('This season's hot look – It's got to be Waders!' or 'Knee-length Waders – Do you dare to bare?') so the Ulster music scene offered a journalist little in the way of inspiration. Sure, Northern Ireland has produced the odd musician of note. It is a canon that includes Van Morrison, SLF, The Undertones, Therapy?, Divine Comedy, Ash and David Holmes. But such stellar acts appear about as frequently as comets. And for every Ash, we have to endure an Energy Orchard.

Week in, week out, I watched small bands play small venues to even smaller crowds, all over the province. I was allocated just one page a week, in the *News Letter*'s Saturday edition, and at times I was pressed to fill it. In such weeks a large photo of The Corrs was always a good standby.

The paucity of my journalistic remit did have its compensation in that I only had to show my face in the office twice a week. On Tuesday mornings I attended the weekly editorial powwow, and on Friday nights I put my page – Jay Black's Soundz (sic) – to bed.

Soundz with 'z' was not my idea. It wasn't even the work of a mischievous paste-up artist. The 'z' was appended at the insistence of Rupert Aziz, the paper's hirsute, Anglo-Turk owner. He thought the 'z' was 'cool'. He was fifty-eight years of age. Christ, he still used the word 'cool', a sure sign that he was not the arbiter of what is and what isn't. The 'z' became the bane of my life for the same reason I avoid 'nite' clubs and 'all-U-can-eat' restaurants. I asked my editor, Harry Clegg, to give me one good reason why he allowed Rupert Aziz to hurl his zeds willy-nilly into my column. He said nothing and instead produced a sheet of A4 on which he wrote: *Becoz he payz our wagez*.

Still, the job had its moments. Just occasionally, an internationally recognized artist would be brave enough to include Belfast on the back of their tour T-shirt. They would fly in to the province, do the gig, and fly out again, all in a matter of hours, and I knew that if I could somehow blag an interview, there was a chance I could syndicate it to one of the nationals – *NME*, *Melody Maker*, *Hot Press*. The artist would become my quarry and I enjoyed the thrill of the chase. I had to devise increasingly inventive ways of getting close to them. Writing for the *News Letter* doesn't exactly guarantee you that exclusive tête-à-tête. I was journalistic plankton, bottom of the food chain when it came to getting access to the stars. You don't tell Madonna's people that you're from the *News Letter* and suddenly find yourself granted three hours in her boudoir discussing the role Catholicism has played in her music, while snorting cocaine off her thighs.

Unfortunately, for all their hard-ass, cock-rock posturing, most groups remained too scared to touch down at Belfast International. And even when they did fly in for a gig, it wasn't always a given that the *News Letter* would cover it.

I once had the misfortune of sitting through three hours of Elton John at Stormont Castle and somehow summoned the will to write a thousand words on the experience. But the review never made it into the paper. Harry Clegg, a tub-thumping Prod with a face like a burst cushion, decided to ditch my page altogether. Circumnavigating the fact that he hadn't attended the gig, Harry wrote the Elton John review himself. He slapped it on the front page under the emboldened headline: 'SODOMITE AT STORMONT'.

The paper fanned its pages in my lap, a butterfly effect from the apartment door having been opened. Karma fell into the hall, keys between her teeth. She was lugging fistfuls of bloated carrier bags. She had more bags than she had fingers to carry them with, and from the names on their glossy flanks you'd have sworn they belonged to other people – Penny's, Clarks, Ann Summers, Easons. She dumped the lot where she stood and slammed the door with her bottom.

'Christmas is a Christian festival,' she said. 'So tell me this, where exactly in the Bible does Christmas shopping appear? Did God prescribe it as some sinner's penance?'

I turned the music down.

'Do you want a hand?' I asked.

'No, Jay, you're all right.'

Karma peeled off layer after layer of clothing: coat, scarf, body warmer, jumper. It reminded me of one of Diggsy's B-movie videos – *The Incredible Shrinking*

Woman. She reached a cardigan out of one of the carrier bags and threw it on over her nurse's uniform.

'I'm going to wet a pot. You still white and none?'

'Got a beer, thanks.'

Karma stuck the kettle on. 'It's mayhem out there. So much for the peace process. Violence was erupting in every store I went into. Still, I think I've got everybody's present, except yours. You're so difficult.'

'No I'm not. Just buy me something expensive that I don't even need.'

'Good idea . . . what about silicone implants?'

'Ha bloody ha.'

'Seriously, Jessie, if that's what you want I'll have a word with one of our plastics boys up at the Royal.'

Karma returned to the hallway and rifled through her coat's many pockets. She removed a small paper bag.

'Here,' she said. 'I already got you a wee present.' She lifted something colourful out of the bag and threw it at me. It smacked me in the crotch.

'Bullseye!' she shouted.

I examined the offending object.

'A lighter?'

'Aye. A bloke outside Markies was selling them.' She thickened her Belfast accent: '*Thee liders fra poun.* I got one for each of us. You, me and Diggsy.'

'But what do we want with cigarette lighters? None of us smokes.'

'Uch, I know. But sure, they were only a pound.'

It was a peculiar logic, but one you couldn't argue with. Not least because Karma didn't look like she had the energy for an argument. She had just come off a twelve-hour shift at the Royal Victoria Hospital. She looked knackered. She wearily lifted the milk carton out of the fridge. You would have thought it was a brick, the way her arm sank.

Karma joined me on the sofa. Something was eating her. She dunked a ginger snap into her mug. When she lifted the biscuit out, the bottom half was missing, like there were piranha in her tea.

Karma sucked on the biccie, all wall-eyed.

'Everything all right?' I asked.

'Huh? Oh, aye. Everything's fine.'

'Hard day at the office?'

'Usual malarkey. We'd a kid in with half his scalp missing. Wee toerag had hitched a ride on the back of a gritter on the Glenn Road. Showing off he was. His buck-eejit mother was cheering him right up until he lost his grip. Honestly, what would you do with them.'

I never knew quite what to say to Karma when she came in from a shift. I always felt so uncomfortably guilty. There was I, getting paid three times as much as her for doing sod-all squared. I'd be writing three paras on some precious sub-Velvets wannabes, while she'd have to summon the words to tell a single parent their one and only had died. And the things she'd seen. I don't know how she dealt with the half of it. Yes, she used humour. She would often come in cracking jokes, but rarely were they accompanied by a knowing smile or a twinkle in the eye. Nurses can be the blackest of comedians. From bedpan to deadpan without breaking stride. Perhaps this was how she coped.

'Then we'd a punishment beating in from Poleglass. They broke into the guy's flat wearing Santa masks and trussed him up with the fairy lights from his tree. They beat him so hard one of his teeth had imbedded itself in his knee. His five-year-old found him and called the ambulance. Apparently the scum that attacked him left a Christmas card on his mantelpiece. *Happy Christmas and be out by New Year*, it said. Oh, here. That reminds me.' As she often did, Karma abruptly changed tack. She unzipped her purse and handed me some amateur-looking business cards.

On the first card, crotchets and quavers were floating round the words: *JESSIE BLACK, Music Hack. Groupies may Access ALL Areas*. The second card contained a graphic of a clapperboard, with the legend: *PETE DIGGS, Film Director. Weddings, Christenings, Wakes*. On the third card, a violent red pulse line formed a border round the copy: *CARMEL McCAFFREY, Naughty Nurse. Kiss-o-gram meets Cardiogram*.

'A hoot, aren't they,' she said. 'I made them up on one of those wee machines in the Castle Court shopping centre.'

'Karma, I thought you'd stopped doing the Kiss-o-grams.'

'I have,' she said, a little piqued. 'It's just, well, I've lined up half a dozen gigs before Christmas. Office parties. Nothing seedy. I need the extra money.'

'If you need money, I can sub you. You're taking on too many hours at the hospital as it is. You're going to kill yourself.'

Karma snatched the cards out of my hands. 'Jesus, Jay, don't you start. I'm my own woman. I can do what I like.'

'Don't I know it.'

And I did. I was her closest friend. I knew her better than anyone.

Carmel McCaffrey is, like the song says, an Independent Woman. Her relationships with men rarely lasted beyond the first back-to-mine coffee. The guys came and went (literally), Karma subsisting on a diet of one-night stands and I'll-call-you-tomorrows. Not that it bothered her. It suited her. For one, her shift work wasn't conducive to sustaining anything long-term. And she had assured her mother that if she hadn't found Mr Right by age thirty-six, she would defrost a sample from the hospital freezer and impregnate herself with a turkey baster (unsurprisingly, Carmel's mum still declines to come to ours for Christmas dinner).

Karma took her empty mug to the kitchen and rinsed it.

'Oh, here. You'll love this,' she giggled. She walked to the front door and retrieved the Ann Summers bag. She removed a single garment from it and held it to her chest. It was a nurse's uniform, in blue PVC.

'Well, I suppose it's practical,' I said. 'It'll wipe clean easily after you get puked on in triage.'

'Fuck me,' said Diggsy as he re-entered the room. 'Is that outfit standard issue in the Royal these days? Quick, somebody break my legs.'

'You blokes are all the same,' said Karma. 'Sex, sex, sex.'

'Don't be so simplistic. Diggsy and I aren't governed by our loins. We're complex, multidimensional creatures.' I grabbed my jacket.

'Where are you off to?' she asked.

'Down the Limelight to check out some Harlots.'

3

She emerged from a flurry of wind-blown rose petals, her pale skin interrupted at regular intervals by bands of red: scarlet bob, scarlet lips, cropped scarlet top, scarlet mini, scarlet knee socks, scarlet boots. She looked like a barber's pole, or a lolly that *had* to be licked.

And, slung about her hips, a twelve-string guitar. She didn't strum it. She seemed to pluck it, with nails the colour of cocktail cherries. Her chords *bristled*.

Scarlet briefly surveyed the thick, undulating carpet of sweaty heads that spread out beneath her, before emitting a high-pitched yelp. Any higher and her vocal contortions would have been reserved for the sole appreciation of dogs. It was this glass-popping howl that announced 'Acid Dropout', The Harlots' opening number and the first track of four on their *Rhubarb Rock* EP.

The Limelight was heaving. I stayed at the back and propped up the bar with the other old farts. Well, I was thirty-four. My days in the mosh pit were well behind me.

I had lost sight of Diggsy. The only indication I had that he was doing his job was the occasional blue-white flash from the front of stage. Not two numbers in, he emerged from the melee looking like someone who'd accidentally got sucked through a car wash. He was sweating so much you could see his nipples through his T-shirt. He set his camera on the bar.

'Fuck me, I reckon I've lost a stone in there,' he said.

'What are you having?'

'Pint of anything, as long as it's cold and wet.'

I was handed two ready-poured pints from a long line on the bar. The glasses were plastic. They wobbled when I grabbed them, displacing their frothy heads over my hands and down my sleeves.

'Did you get any good shots?' I asked.

'Not sure,' said Diggsy. 'It's mayhem in there. I could barely focus the camera before I got shunted six yards to the left or right. Your feet don't touch the ground. Still, the kids seem to be enjoying it. There's one lad has his dick out and he's pressing it into some wee girl's ass. She's none the wiser.'

'The girls look stunning, don't they? That was some entrance Scarlet made. You must have rattled off a couple of corkers.'

'As I said, not sure. I'd taken six or seven shots when I realized the lens had a rose petal stuck over it. I'll go in again when it calms down.'

Diggsy and I sank a couple more pints and enjoyed the set. He seemed more taken with the film being projected onto the band's backdrop than he was with their music. It was one of those old information films they used to screen in schools in the Seventies. Filmed on Super-8, the footage followed the whole process involved in the manufacture of a stick of rock. It cut from an angry lava of bubbling red goo, to a machine squirting out long scarlet cables of molten sugar, to men in white coats and hairnets rolling thick slabs of the stuff into sticks the size of redwoods. This was interspersed with blipvert close-ups of the wobbly red writing fossilized into cross-sections of rock. But in place of the familiar names of seaside towns (Blackpool, Skegness, Paignton), each stick of Harlots' rock was infused with a random word: Starburst, Soda, Cosmo, Orange, Ariel, Sun. It read like someone's shopping list.

I had reviewed The Harlots once before, when they played support to another of Belfast's finest, Go Commando. The girls weren't ready for it back then and it showed. Go Commando blew them off stage. But in Scarlet Harlot, you knew they had a star. That voice. She used it as an instrument, scattering indecipherable outbursts like hundreds and thousands over a richly textured sound. Sometimes you thought you caught a word or a hint of a phrase, but it rarely made sense. It didn't matter, because you were seduced not by what she was singing, but by the *sensation* of what she was singing. As the rock-manufacturing film suggested, she could well have been reciting her shopping list and it would still have sounded celestial.

Diggsy didn't get it.

'Why is she singing in Klingon?' he asked.

'The same reason you talk in Shite,' I countered. 'Now get yourself up there and take some photos. This is their last number.'

The Limelight is probably unique among rock venues in that the band are forced to exit via front of stage and make their way through the crowd to get to their dressing room. That the girls managed it without getting their clothes torn from their bodies by the mass of baying adolescents was largely down to a posse of security guards that even George Dubya would consider excessive. These guys were huge. They looked like they were on day release from the primate house at Belfast Zoo.

I asked the barman where the Limelight got their security.

'What, you mean the Jungle VIP?' He nodded at the entourage. 'They're not our boys. They must be with the band.'

I was confused. What would a poxy little indie band be doing with that level of security?

I tapped the largest bodyguard – the King of the Swingers – on the shoulder. Actually, I couldn't reach his shoulder and inadvertently poked him in the stomach. My finger concertinaed on impact.

''Scuse me, mate. Jay Black. *Ulster News Letter.* Any chance of an interview with the band?'

'No,' he said. He had tattoos on his teeth.

'Come on, man. I only need five minutes.'

'I'll give you one minute.'

'Well, I suppose it's better than nothing.'

'One minute . . . to get out of here before I insert two fingers into your nostrils, my thumb into your mouth and I bowl you into the traffic on the Dublin Road.'

'Oh, right. I see what's happened here. I think you're confusing me with an opportunistic fan. I'm Jay Black. I write the music page in Saturday's *News Letter.*'

'Fifty-nine, fifty-eight . . .'

I didn't pursue the point. Rather, I pursued Diggsy. I found him by the exit, chatting up the young girl selling Harlots merchandise from a makeshift stall.

'Come on, Diggsy, let's go.'

'Houl yer horses, Jay. I'm talking to Eithne.'

The young girl gave me that look that I sometimes get when people recognize me from the mugshot in the paper. She didn't look *at* me, so much as *over* me, scanning me like a photocopier. I knew the image had registered when a nervous smile forced its way onto her face.

I pulled Diggsy to one side.

'Listen, mate, if we don't get out of here now, we're dead men. So just buy your Harlots T-shirt, your Harlots mug, pen, ironing-board cover or whatever you're after, and let's scoot.'

'I can't.'

'You can.'

'No. I can't.'

'Why not?'

'Because Eithne here was *about* to tell me where the band are going for their post-gig shenanigans. Weren't you, Eithne?'

I wasn't confident that Eithne knew what a post-gig shenanigan was. She looked about twelve. She sipped amateurishly from a Bacardi Breezer. She wore a plastic daisy clipped to her hair and her breasts made little impression on the Harlots vest that covered them, like a small child punching a curtain with both fists. Still, she seemed to speak with some authority when she said that the band was heading to Bar Baca, a new joint just off Donegal Place.

'It's their opening night,' she said. 'I'll never get in. It's over twenty-ones only. Youse can have my ticket, so youse can. It's a plus one.' She made to hand Diggsy the ticket, but quickly retracted it. 'Ah, wait. Only if yer man gives us a snog, like.' She pointed at me.

I didn't have time for this. Realizing that I would now be placed on the Paedophile Register, but desperate to get to the band, I leaned over and offered the wee girl my lips. She put her hand round the back of my head, pulled me towards her and burped hotly in my face. It smelt of watermelon.

Then she collapsed.

I bent to the floor and prised the ticket out of her hand.

'We can't just leave her,' said Diggsy. 'She's only a youngster.'

'What do you suggest – that we take her home and raise her as one of our own?' I hauled him out onto the street.

It was a ten-minute trudge through the snow to get to Bar Baca. Diggsy wouldn't let up. It was too cold, he said. He didn't have a jacket. His sweat would freeze and he'd develop hypothermia. And why did I try and snog Eithne? Couldn't I see he was 'well in'?

'She was twelve, Diggsy.'

'Sixteen.'

'Is there a difference?'

'In the eyes of the law, there is. Thatch on the cottage, grass on the pitch.'

'I despair.' I hawked and spat. It was that cold I expected my saliva to shatter on impact.

Diggsy hugged himself. You could hear his teeth. 'It's always you they go after, isn't it? Mr Rock Journo. I never get a look-in,' he said.

'Oh, dry your eyes. Stop feeling sorry for yourself.'

'If I didn't feel sorry for myself, nobody else would.'

Five years ago you would never have found a place like Bar Baca in Belfast. Ostentatiously designed to a Moroccan theme, it was all dark woods and vivid silks in natural dyes of saffron, umber and indigo. Bottled beers were set on a brushed steel bar-top beside bowls of toasted cashews. People sat in huddles, perched in cross-legged uncertainty on the many voluptuous floor cushions. Falafel, stuffed vine leaves and red-pepper hummus were ushered between tables by pencil-lean girls clad in aubergine linen. It was a world away from the spit'n'sawdust, old-soak-in-a-duncher Ulster pub of yore, and testament to how eclectic this city had become. There was a day not long ago when the people of Belfast thought a korma was something you slipped into after the Provos gave you a good hiding.

Diggsy eyed the label on his lager with some suspicion. 'I think this is written in Arabic,' he said.

'It can't be. The Arabs don't touch alcohol.'

Diggsy took a sip and immediately winced. 'Jeez, now I know why,' he said.

I didn't indulge him. I had spotted my quarry. Scarlet Harlot (vocals, twelve-string), Kate (bass), Derbhla (rhythm guitar), and Mags (drums) were occupying a candle-lit alcove adjacent to the bar. I checked for the Jungle VIP – nowhere – and made straight for Scarlet.

'Are those cushions taken?' I asked.

'Help yourself,' she said.

I waved Diggsy across and we sat ourselves, lotus-like, at the end of their table. As a welcoming gesture, Kate offered Diggsy a dish of dried apricots.

'Can't eat those things,' he declined. 'They go through me like a Porsche.'

Kate immediately looked uncomfortable. She withdrew the apricots and edged herself as far away from Diggsy as she could. The girls returned to whatever it was they were talking about.

'Well done, mate,' I said. 'You really broke the ice there. Have you considered a career in the diplomatic corps?'

'I can't eat dried fruit, OK,' he barked. 'It's not my fault I have a narrow duodenum.'

The girls glared at us.

I looked directly at Scarlet and, for some unfathomable reason, I said, 'Narrow duodenum.' In a lilting, Southern Irish brogue. I accompanied this with a tut and a playful roll of the eyes. Bejaysus.

For any aspiring journalist, this set piece can be found on page one of *How to get an exclusive interview with a Rock Star*, in the 'Don't' section. Look it up. It's right under 'Don't swallow your beer the wrong way and sneeze it over aforementioned Rock Star'. Which is precisely what I did next.

I attempted to recover some dignity.

'Scarlet. I'm Jay Black, *Ulster News Letter.*' I offered my hand.

She declined to take it, preferring instead to wipe the beer from her knees. 'I know who you are,' she said.

Scarlet looked even better close up. For the first time I noticed two ruby studs set into her left nostril. She sipped a strawberry daiquiri, her front teeth pinching her bottom lip as she swallowed.

'I enjoyed the gig,' I said. 'I'm going to stick a review in Saturday's paper. I was hoping I could grab a few words with you.'

'What do you want to know?' she asked.

This threw me slightly. I had been so preoccupied with engineering an opportunity to speak to her that, now the opportunity had arisen, I realized I hadn't thought what to ask her. Schoolboy error.

Scarlet ran a long strand of red hair behind her ear. She had changed into a fresh top, red with white dots, like a cartoon toadstool. Its wide neck allowed her scarlet bra straps to show.

I thought of a question.

'What's your favourite colour?' I joked.

'Are you wise?'

'OK, so what's with all the red – the hair, the clothes, the daiquiri?'

41

She looked at me like I was stupid. 'Red is power. It's the colour of domination. Think about it. Stop lights. Warning signs. The matador's cloak. The Devil. It's the same in sport. Ferrari. Manchester United.'

'Swindon Town?'

She ignored me.

'It's no coincidence that the Nazis chose a pre-dominantly red flag,' she said.

'Are you saying Alex Ferguson's a Nazi?'

'I'm saying that I wear red because it puts me in control. People notice red. They respect it. They yield to it.'

I believed her. I was already yielding.

'But calling yourself Scarlet. Isn't that a bit extreme?'

'You're assuming that I've changed my name.'

'You haven't? I mean, Harlot, it's not the most common surname. Are you one of the Lurgan Harlots, or one of the Harlots from Magherafelt?'

'You're funny,' she said. 'But that doesn't mean I'm going to tell you my real name.'

'Come on, what name would be so embarrassing that you'd have to change it to Scarlet Harlot? Betty Swallocks? Michelle Suit? Ann Widdecombe? Tell me, tell me.'

Scarlet shook her head. But she was smiling. My charm offensive was starting to work.

'Your wee friend seems to be getting on with Mags,' she said.

True enough, Diggsy was engaged in a bout of verbal sparring with The Harlots' drummer. You wouldn't have fancied his chances in an arm wrestle with her, though. Mags had the sort of forearms that only sprout when you neck a can of spinach.

'Jesus, he's even laughing,' I said.

'You sound surprised,' said Scarlet.

'I am. Diggsy rarely laughs. He was born with a cartoon cloud over his head. Peter Diggs and the world don't see eye to eye. He vowed that on his twenty-first birthday he was going to buy a Harley and ride it at speed into a brick wall.'

'What age is he?'

'Twenty-eight,' I said. 'He's always been a bit of a nihilist. When he was a kid, his father tried to charm him by telling him that Smurfs were real. But it only made him more depressed.'

'How come?'

'He lived out the rest of his childhood dreading that one day he would find one of the wee blue fellas caught in a mousetrap.'

'Aw. That's so cute.'

'Cute? It's sad, that's what it is. And conversely, Diggsy has never believed in Santa Claus. Not since his uncle, an engineer at Shorts, explained the facts.'

'The facts?'

'The facts. Diggsy happily reels them off to revellers each festive season. But as he's otherwise engaged, let me do the honours. I hope you're sitting comfortably because this can take some time.'

Scarlet leaned in a little closer and propped her drink on her knees.

'The facts,' I announced. 'No known species of reindeer can fly. There are two billion children in the world. Even discounting Muslim, Hindu, Jewish and Buddhist children, Santa would have to visit ninety-two million homes. That's assuming there's at least one good child in each of them. With only thirty-one hours of Christmas to work with, thanks to different time zones and the earth's rotation, Santa would have to make something like eight hundred and twenty-five visits per second. Diggsy's uncle wrote all this down for him. His calculations explain that Santa would only have, like, point zero zero one seconds to park, hop out of his sleigh, shimmy down the chimney, drink a glass of curdled milk, scoff a mince pie, leave a Connect Four and a satsuma by your bed, kiss your mother and get the hell out of there before you wake up. And remember, Diggsy's uncle was an engineer. He was able to inform his disbelieving nephew that Santa's total trip would exceed seventy-five million miles, meaning his sleigh would be doing a healthy six hundred and fifty miles per second, three thousand times the speed of sound and twice as fast as Michael J. Fox in a DeLorean. And, as even a kid knows, a conventional reindeer can only run, tops, fifteen miles per hour.'

Scarlet allowed herself a chuckle. Diggsy's borrowed Christmas message was getting me somewhere. Well, I decided, if it ain't broke . . .

'Assuming that each child receives no more than a medium-sized Scalextric, or a couple of Furbies, Santa's sleigh would be carrying a payload of roughly three hundred and twenty thousand tonnes, not counting Santa himself, who is invariably described as being overweight. To pull it would require about two hundred and twenty thousand reindeer, thereby increasing the payload to over three hundred and fifty thousand tonnes. Now it shouldn't need an aeronautical engineer to tell you that three hundred and fifty thousand tonnes travelling at six hundred and fifty miles per second creates enormous air resistance, heating the reindeer up like a shuttle on re-entry. In short, Rudolph and his chums would burst into flames creating vast sonic booms. And, as Diggsy's uncle gladly explained to him with the aid of some horrific doodles, the entire reindeer team would be evaporated

44

in, like, point zero zero four two six seconds. And a sixteen-stone Santa, which seems optimistically lean, would be pinned to the back of his sleigh by something like four million pounds of force. Happy Christmas, nephew.'

'God, that's terrible. How can someone do that to a kid? Children need to believe in magic. It's a wonder your friend isn't a manic-depressive.'

Diggsy laughed at something Mags had said. She had to grab his sleeve to stop him from falling off his cushion.

'Well,' I offered, ''tis the season to be jolly.'

Scarlet had finished her drink. I volunteered to go to the bar but she waved me away. 'You're all right. I'm not staying,' she said.

She stood up and threw her arms into a fur coat. I guessed the fur wasn't real because it was a vibrant signal red. That is, unless the coat was fashioned from slaughtered Muppet. I hoped not. For if Diggsy's father had told him Muppets were as real as Smurfs, then Scarlet's coat would send him spiralling into the black abyss.

I put my hand on her arm.

'You can't go. What about the interview? I haven't asked you about the new EP. Or your lyrics. Or your influences. I know, it's my own fault. I talk too much. I don't listen. Not great qualities in a journalist. But please stay. I haven't even asked you what your most embarrassing moment was.'

'What was yours?' asked Scarlet.

'It involved a wetsuit.'

'Sounds kinky.'

'Yeah, well.'

Scarlet pulled her hair into a ponytail and slid the lot under a woolly hat. 'You stay here and the girls will tell all you need to know about the band.'

That wasn't my point. I wasn't interested in the other girls. I was interested in Scarlet. She *was* The Harlots. In the way Limahl *was* Kajagoogoo.

For someone who needed the exposure, Scarlet seemed curiously shy of it. She pocketed her Embassy Reds and hugged each of the girls in turn.

'Mags, you're sure the van's sorted for Dublin?' she asked.

'Aye, Scar. And it's a Merc. Damien found it burnt out on the Twinbrook estate. He's had her in his garage three months. Says he's got her purring like a kitten.'

'Nice one. Right, girls, see youse all Friday morning outside Magdalene's. That OK, Mags?'

The drummer nodded.

Scarlet turned to me. 'Mr Black, I look forward to reading your review. I trust you're going to say lots of nice things.'

I wanted to say lots of nice things. Sweet, simple things like, *you're the most beautiful woman I have ever seen.* And *that thing you do with your bottom lip, you know, when you sip your drink, that's perfection.* And *when you sing it makes me feel like anything is possible.*

I wanted to say these things but I couldn't. The words were there but my mouth wouldn't form them. And me, the journalist. Me, who was never short of something to say. If I'd had my laptop I could have typed her a glowing eulogy right there and then. But without my trusty weapon with its delete key and its spellcheck facility, I felt disarmed and exposed. Any word I uttered – spontaneous, unchecked and unedited – would be vulnerable to attack. So instead I said nothing.

It had been this way all my life. As soon as I found

myself genuinely attracted to someone, the old foe embarrassment got the better of me and I'd clam up. Yes, I'd had girlfriends, but they were never the real deal. They were nice, or funny, or pleasant, or pretty, or interesting, or highly sexed, or kind, or keen, or convenient. With none of them did I experience that peculiar nausea associated with real attraction, like someone's taken an ice-cream scoop to your guts. None of them put me off my food. And none of them ever forced me to lose sleep. Except the highly sexed one.

I let Scarlet shimmy past me. My cheeks had turned the colour of her hair, her lips, her name. I watched her exit the bar and disappear into a black taxi.

I couldn't stomach the rest of my beer.

4

The snow had compacted on the pavements, turning them to glass. My mother would have described them as treacherous, as if they would somehow betray you. And, in a sense, they did. Just when I thought I'd got a sure footing, the black ice deceived me and splayed my legs like a newborn foal.

I had left Bar Baca on my own. I made sure I removed the film from Diggsy's camera before I left. Not that he noticed. He was too busy trying to remove something from Mags's ear. I think it was his tongue.

I tried flagging down a taxi but each one that passed was full. It was nearly Christmas. Empty cabs were as scarce as Buzz Lightyears. I wondered how Scarlet had been able to breeze straight into one on leaving the bar. It was a black cab, so it was unlikely that she'd booked it. Then again, who wouldn't stop for Scarlet?

The Dublin Road Multiplex was showing *It's a Wonderful Life*, a digitally remastered cut. On the steps outside, some enterprising youths were re-mastering their skateboards. They had unscrewed the wheels, turning them into makeshift snowboards. Each car that passed was pockmarked by snowballs, hinting at seasonal revelry further up the road.

Underdressed girls with raspberry ripple legs huddled outside takeaways, guarding hot fistfuls of cheesy chips and chicken pakoras. A young guy stood unsteadily at the bus stop with his arm round a Wise Man, forcing me to suspect that the Nativity scene outside City Hall was missing a statuette.

I walked past all of this in the absolute certainty that I was being followed.

I had spotted the man the moment I left the bar. He stuck out like the proverbial thumb. He was wearing one of those long, puffy coats that have replaced the sheepskin as the de rigueur winter wear of the modern-day football manager. He was sitting on the bonnet of a Vauxhall Cavalier, a sleeping bag having a smoke. When he saw me he extinguished his fag and stood bolt upright like a thickly padded rugby post. He couldn't have been more conspicuous if he'd been on fire. As he wobbled after me, negotiating the icy pavement, you could almost hear Stuart Hall cackling, *Here come the Belgians*.

Stupidly, I waited until I'd reached the law courts, until the crowds had thinned out to nothing, before I turned to confront him.

'Listen, mate, this isn't going to be worth your while,' I reasoned. 'I've only got about a fiver on me. And my watch was a freebie with petrol.'

Ignoring the freezing conditions he opened his long coat and, just as I was about to congratulate him on becoming Britain's bravest flasher, he instead pulled out a sawn-off shotgun. He must have been keeping it warm.

'Easy, tiger,' I said, raising my hands before I was told. 'Take the watch. And look, if you rifle through my wallet there's enough tokens to get yourself a set of six sherry glasses. They're yours.'

'Shut the fuck up and walk.'

The gun-toting football manager indicated the entrance to an underground car park. A shutter prevented entry. But you had to walk down a steep slope to reach it and I knew this would render us invisible from the street above. It would provide all the cover he needed. I imagined the man from NCP finding my lifeless, watchless body when he opened up on Monday morning. How would they be able to estimate the time of death? The ice would delay the decomposition of my corpse.

Happy thoughts then, as a shotgun nudged me down the slope.

'Please. Whatever it is, it's not worth killing me for. Christ, my trainers are only Dunlops.'

'I'm not after your fucking trainers. Or your watch. And nobody's going to get killed, so long as they do as they're told.'

He threw me against the metal shutter. Shards of ice fell onto my hair and neck. Cold tributaries traced their way under my collar and ran down my spine as the ice melted.

'Who are you and what do you want with Scarlet?' asked Mr Sawnoff-Shotgun. The monicker was appropriately double-barrelled.

'Jay Black. *Ulster News Letter*. And I don't know Scarlet. I was reviewing her gig for the paper.'

'You're not to lay a finger on her. Is that understood?'

I nodded. I tried to memorize his face, to make life easier for the police artist, but it was dark and each time he spoke his features got lost in plumes of condensation.

'Stay away from her, or the only Scarlet you'll be seeing will be pouring out the holes in your head.' He nudged the gun onto my forehead and then followed up with three more jabs, making the sign of the cross. Spectacles, testicles, wallet, watch.

I could no longer tell whether the water running down my back was ice cold or scalding hot.

'Right,' he said. 'Take your shoes off.'

'I thought you weren't after my trainers.'

'I'm not. I've got taste. Just be a good boy and give us your socks and shoes.'

Jesus, I thought, who is this guy? And why was he so keen for me to stay away from Scarlet? Was he a jealous fan? Hardly. He couldn't have looked more unlike the fey, rose-tossing indie boys who had earlier populated the gig. Was he an overprotective roadie? I doubted it. If this guy was a roadie, he would have threatened me with a pen-torch before securing a list of his demands to the pavement with gaffer tape. And as far as I could remember, no boyfriends were mentioned in the biog faxed through to me by The Harlots' record company. There was nothing in it to suggest that Scarlet dated a green-eyed, gun-toting maniac.

I handed him my Dunlops with the socks balled into them and another possibility occurred to me. This guy was a shoe fetishist.

'You have been warned,' he said.

He pushed my shoes through the gaps in the car-park shutter, well out of my reach. They looked even more stupid in isolation than they did on my feet. Like I'd spontaneously combusted.

He made his way back up to street level. I waited a beat, then climbed the slope with bare hands and bare feet. I made the ascent in just enough time to see him smash the window of an abandoned Hyundai. The rear tyres spat slush into the air, turning the snow into a black marzipan, as the car spun clumsily out onto the road.

The ungodly hour, the inclement weather and the resultant lack of taxis meant I had no choice but to walk the last mile and a half to the apartment barefoot.

I passed an old soak curled up in a doorway. His feet poked out from under a sheet of cardboard. His brittle quilt had the word 'Tayto' written across it in exuberant yellow and red. His shoes had no laces and they looked two sizes too big. He was out for the count and would have been none the wiser if I'd slipped them off his feet. Then I remembered a nursing text-book that Karma had showed me, full of photographs of ugly, suppurating chiropody, and all temptation quickly receded. I pitied the poor bugger and folded my last fiver into his pocket. It was, I realized, the season of goodwill to all men. And I had, after all, just escaped with my life.

I'd never had a gun pointed at me before. Not a real, living, breathing gun. I had often imagined what it would be like to look down a loaded barrel. I used to believe that the gun was only as dangerous as the person pointing it. In other words, I thought I would fear the gunman and not the gun. If a guy in a balaclava broke into my bedroom and put a gun in my face, I would abdicate all control of my bodily functions, digestive, urinary or both. However, if Diggsy put a gun in my face, I'd expect to lean over, pull the trigger and light a cigarette from it.

But the experience didn't correspond to the theory. Looking into the sheared figure of eight sawn at the tip of that shotgun, its barrels whistling like pan pipes in the chilly wind, I had realized that it didn't matter who was holding it. All that mattered was the physiology of the gun itself. What size were the cartridges? With what velocity did the bullets leave those metal tubes? How little pressure was required to sink the trigger and release them? Over what distance would the sound be heard?

He had ordered me to stay away from Scarlet. But how could I? I hadn't given up on that interview. I never gave up on an interview.

Before leaving the bar, Scarlet had asked Mags about a van. They had arranged to meet up on Friday morning. I had probed Mags more thoroughly, though not as thoroughly as Diggsy's tongue. The band was intending to travel down to Dublin in the van. They had two gigs scheduled for the coming weekend. On the Friday night they played main support to PJ Harvey at the Point. On the Saturday night, they were headlining Filthy McNasty's. The gigs were designed to officially launch their debut EP. It was due for release the following Monday, but preview copies would be sold at both venues. Half the music industry was on Saturday's guest list.

This was the opportunity I was looking for: the opportunity to get close to Scarlet. Shoes or no shoes, I wasn't about to pass it up.

I told Mags I wanted to shadow the band on the road. I said I wanted to get to know the real Harlots as opposed to the Harlots the public sees on stage. She punched me for that, with one of those impressive forearms. Then Diggsy intervened. He told Mags he would tag along to compile a photo diary of the band. He promised them a spread in *NME* and, Bob's your auntie's live-in lover, Mags agreed to pick us up first thing Friday morning.

I caught sight of the Albert Bridge. I was nearly home. My feet were completely numb, which actually made it easier to walk. It prevented me feeling the jags and the cuts of the ice on my soles. How long before my feet turned brown with frostbite? How much further could I go before they became the colour and consistency of shredded duck?

The Hilton Hotel loomed large above me. I considered getting a room, but I was only five minutes from my apartment. I *had* to get to my apartment. It had two advantages over the Hilton. It wasn't £140 a night. And it came with an en suite nurse.

At my back, I heard a squelching sound gradually increasing in volume. A police Land Rover slowed up alongside me, moving at a snail's pace through the slush and grit. It was checking me out, like the camera car at an Olympic walking event. I felt like the race leader on my last legs, with the crowd in my ears and the stadium in my sights. Only three more minutes until I cross the threshold of my apartment and collapse in a heap. Three minutes until Karma removes a Union Jack from under a bowl of oranges and throws it over my victorious shoulders.

The Land Rover was really bugging me. I tried to look into the passenger window but it was as black and impenetrable as a wet roof slate. The van had the number of the Confidential Telephone painted on the side. This number had been used by thousands of informants over the course of the Troubles. I considered keying it into my mobile and telling them to piss off and leave me alone. But they wouldn't be able to act on the information as they'd be obliged to respect my anonymity.

The Land Rover revved its engine and scuttled some distance ahead of me. Then it came to a leisurely halt. Two policemen discharged themselves from the back doors. With almost comic synchronicity they covered their bald spots with their green, broad-peaked hats. They slid their fingers into leather gloves and made spans with their hands as they marched towards me. The taller of the two blocked my path.

'Are you Jessie Black?' he said.

Scottish.

'I am. What's happened?' It's Dad, I thought. It's got to be Dad.

'Mr Black, we need you to accompany us.'

'Jesus, what is it? Stroke? Heart attack?'

On my last visit to my parents' house, I had to finish digging over Dad's rose beds for him. He had complained of a pain in his shoulder and Mum wanted to call a doctor. Dad told her to quit worrying, there was nothing wrong with him that a hot port and lemon couldn't cure. I wished she had called a doctor.

'Please, Mr Black. Follow us over to the van.'

'No. Not until you tell me what's happened to Dad.'

The smaller copper lost his patience.

'Nothing's happened to your da. Now get in the back of the wagon, asswipe.' His leather gloves squeaked as he wrestled me onto the road.

'What is this? What have I done? Is walking barefoot an arrestable offence? Shouldn't you be out catching armed shoe fetishists?'

I tried to prise myself away from him, ducking my upper body under his arm. But my feet could no longer support me. My head hit the tarmac, hammer-hard.

I felt weightless, like a marionette, my arms and legs suspended on wires. I realized I was being carried. The tinnitus caused by the fall only disappeared when the Land Rover's doors slammed shut behind me, causing my ears to pop.

A bag was put over my head. I couldn't make out the colour, but if the outside was anything like the inside, it was very, very black.

5

After about fifteen minutes the Land Rover jolted to a halt. I tried to estimate all the places that were fifteen minutes from Belfast by meat wagon. Carrickfergus? Lisburn? Bangor?

I was made to get out with the bag still over my head. My shoeless feet touched virgin snow and as I walked I could feel the icy fronds of frozen grass underneath. I was in a field. Well, that narrowed it down, I thought. Ninety-five per cent of the surface area of Northern Ireland is carpeted in lush green grass. It's one big field. I could be anywhere.

But there was an unmistakable sound in the middle distance – the metallic whine of jet engines. I remembered that Aldergrove was fifteen minutes north-west of the city. I was somewhere in the vicinity of the international airport.

As if to confirm my location, my ears were immediately assaulted by a deep, penetrating boom. The bag whipped violently about my face like it was trying to free itself. A helicopter's rotor had cracked into life not fifteen feet from where I was standing. I was shepherded on board.

I waited until I could feel our ascent levelling out

before I asked any questions.

'What's the in-flight movie?'

'Shut it, wise guy.'

'I don't think I've seen that one. Is it Martin Scorsese?'

No response.

'Listen, there's something you should know. I have a nut allergy. So, if it's OK, no dry roasted peanuts with my complimentary G and T. Cocktail savouries are fine.'

Again, silence. That's the trouble when you fly economy. They don't want to know you.

My feet were burning with the cold. I asked my captors for a pair of those slip-over socks that airlines like to provide, but they remained resolutely mute.

I couldn't hear them, I couldn't see them and it wasn't long before I began to lose all faith they were even there. Had they bailed out and left me alone in the back of a helicopter, on autopilot, heading for the upper reaches of the ozone? I wasn't a good flier at the best of times. I hate the complete abdication of control, your life in their hands and all that. Multiply that fear by ten and you still don't come close to the terror of being trapped in an unmanned helicopter with your hands cuffed and a bag over your head. I couldn't have been more scared had I been a blind man with vertigo trying to negotiate my way along the edge of Tor Head without a stick.

I heard a voice crackling over the radio. Thankfully it was met by a response from our pilot. As he spat back some meaningless co-ordinates, I was reminded of the old joke about the Aer Lingus plane coming in to land at Shannon airport. The control tower asked the pilot to state his exact height and position. He replied, *I'm six foot two and sitting in the front seat*. Humour in adversity. I was learning from Karma.

Don't ask me where we touched down. I guessed it was another fifteen minutes from Aldergrove, but I was not acquainted with helicopters and I had no idea how far they travelled in that time. I had been unable to unravel the pilot's co-ordinates and there were no further clues to the location as I exited the chopper.

Well, there was perhaps one clue. The next vehicle I was forced into had no windows. The bag over my head could not prevent the icy breeze from numbing my face as we moved off. And strangely, I could hear no engine. Whatever I was travelling in, it was powered by battery. I narrowed it down to a golf buggy or a milk float. My feet had again felt grass before I stepped into it and we were now moving over undulating terrain, so I plumped for the golf buggy. I mean, what would a milk float be doing on a golf course?

More to the point, what was *I* doing on a golf course?

For some reason, I thought of Diggsy. He hated golf. He couldn't understand why grown men would dress like Rupert the Bear, hit a ball across a field with a stick, and then spend four hours repeating the process while towing their luggage. As my buggy negotiated drumlins and skirted bunkers, I was also reminded of the television pictures I'd seen from the Garvaghy Road that July. The Orangemen had been engaged in their annual stand-off with the RUC. Every Loyalist thug within a 100-mile radius had turned up to swell their numbers. The Garvaghy stand-off had become more of a festival than a protest, like Glastonbury with bowler hats. And, this year, the protest had attracted an altogether better class of Loyalist thug. For, when tensions reached breaking point, they didn't issue the traditional volley of sticks, stones and petrol bombs at the police. Instead they produced golf clubs and plastic buckets from the boots of their cars and began to chip, fade, slice, rib, draw and hook range balls at the RUC. I remembered the headline in the *Irish News*: 'TIGER HOODS'.

I was driven in silence. All that could be heard above the low hum of the battery was the ominous rustle of trees. Large trees. Either this was a mature golf course or we were entering a forest. I didn't have to wait long to find out.

My vehicle stopped and the bag was immediately removed from my head. My eyes had become so accustomed to the pitch black that I was blinded by what little moonlight filtered through the dense canopy above me. At first I couldn't fully discern the trees, but I could smell their sap. This was a pine forest. It had a sweet, cloying smell, far removed from the pine fragrance they fob you off with in your toilet freshener. In whatever direction I looked an impenetrable wall of stout trunks barred my way.

'So, guys. What do you want? I assume you haven't brought me here to select my Christmas tree.'

'Down the steps,' said Scotland, undoing the cuffs.

I couldn't see any steps. Not that I expected to. Not in the middle of a fucking forest. I was about to ask for directions, but they were forced upon me. In the same way adults guide small children round by placing a hand on the top of their heads, a leather glove landed on my bonce and ushered me towards an opening in the forest floor. Sure enough, there was a set of concrete steps. I counted nine before we came to a metal door. Scotland knocked on it with a leather fist and we were admitted.

There was a welcome blast of warm air as I entered, the same thing you get when you walk into M&S on a wet and windy Wednesday. Only there was no lingerie in sight. Instead, I was led through a warren of windowless, pictureless corridors with security cameras mounted at every turn. They recorded us entering the first door we came upon.

The room behind it was unexpectedly plush. Like the Oval Office, only square. It was dominated by an impressive mahogany table. This sat on a pristine carpet with a Harp and Crown woven into it, and a golf ball rolling over it. The golf ball caught the rim of an empty brandy glass, spinning it on its side. It came to rest at my feet.

'Jessie Black,' said the man clutching the putter. He unbuttoned his golf glove and offered me his hand. 'It's been a while,' he added.

I was standing in a concrete bunker under a forest, near a golf course, fifteen minutes by helicopter from Aldergrove Airport, shaking hands with the Chief Constable of the RUC, Stephen Meeks.

'Steeky. You haven't changed a bit,' I said. 'Still the same shit-eating grin.'

'Can't say the same about you,' he said. 'You've thinned out. What was it, liposuction, jaw-wiring or stomach stapling?'

'Puppy fat,' I said.

'And what happened to the carrot top? Do you dye it?'

'No. Inside that ginger boy there was a strawberry-blond man waiting to get out. To what do I owe this displeasure?'

'Uch, sorry. I'm a lousy host. Do take a seat.'

My old head boy directed me to one of the leather chairs that flanked the long table. It was the sort of table that wars were plotted on. He sat directly opposite me. To the attendant officers we must have looked like two grand masters robbed of their chessboard.

The Chief Constable dismissed one of his sidekicks. 'Andy, run out and grab us some coffee,' he said. 'And a few biccies. Do you still like biccies, Jessie?'

'Please, call me Jay.'

'You never liked your name, did you? I can't blame you. Big Jessie. What were your parents thinking?'

'They liked their Westerns. Jesse James. My mother unwittingly added an "i" when she registered me. For thirty-four years my dad's been saying she did it because she lacks finessie. Still, it could have been worse. Back then Dad was seduced by Julie Christie in *Far from the Madding Crowd*. If I'd been born a girl, he would have christened me Bathsheba.'

'You got off lightly.'

Stephen Meeks hadn't changed. He was the youngest Chief Constable in the seventy-nine years the RUC had been in existence. I had kept an eye on his progress since the day he left school. It was a task made easier when I took my first job as a cub reporter on the *News Letter*. Meeks was rarely out of its pages.

He was seventeen when he followed his high-ranking father into the constabulary. He was precocious and ambitious and was winning promotions while his contemporaries were still trying to work out which end to hold their handguns. Meeks quickly became the glamorous face of the RUC. He was the golden boy of the force. Dynamic, fit and handsome, his profile was deliberately raised in an effort to attract young recruits into the green uniform. He was cynically planted onto the shoulders of the Chief Constable and his deputies at every photo opportunity. It was unashamed PR and it worked. Recruitment went through the roof. Meeks was on his way up.

He was fast-tracked to the top job in 1996 when his three immediate superiors perished in a Chinook that came down in fog over the west coast of Scotland. He inherited a police force whose morale was worse than at any time since the traumatic events of August 1969. There was pressure to radically reform the force, to change its name or disband it altogether. Meeks made no secret of his emotional attachment to the RUC and its traditions. At his inauguration he committed himself to resisting all attempts at reform. He believed that the RUC was being used as a political football and he was determined to defend his men against what he saw as the emasculation of their force. In a statement that the *News Letter* proudly splashed across its front page, Meeks said he was against reform because he believed the very word implied that what had gone before – 12,800 men and women in service, 260 giving their lives – was to be discredited and disowned.

But despite the rhetoric and his professed loyalty to the constabulary, word had it that Meeks was being groomed to lead the Metropolitan Police, Interpol, or to head up a new anti-terrorist unit in Britain. There were also whispers that he was receiving backhanders from certain Protestant paramilitaries. He had gone on record to say that any allegations made against him were part of a witch-hunt heavily stimulated and manipulated by Sinn Fein.

Did he have a different agenda to the one he paraded in public? I wasn't sure. But if the RUC had its bad apples, I suspected that Stephen Meeks was the fermenting, wasp-riddled Bramley at the top of the tree.

'What do you want with me, Steeky?'

'Stephen.'

'Why have I been abducted and transported by helicopter to the Black Forest?'

'Transported by my *private* helicopter, no less. I thought I'd give you the full presidential treatment.'

63

'Are you saying that when Clinton came to Belfast you chauffeured him round with a bag over his head?'

Two cappuccinos arrived. Lord knows where the officer got them. Starbucks had already conquered our cities and towns so perhaps they were moving into our forests and awarding franchises to squirrels.

'I apologize for the bag,' said Meeks. 'I have to protect the identity of this location. It is possibly our last completely secure refuge in the province. The IRA have managed to pinpoint our other bunkers.'

'Bunkers? Why do you need bunkers? Have the Provisionals gone nuclear?'

'Of course not. But we need these places in times of crisis.'

'And this is a time of crisis?'

'As of six o'clock this evening, it is.'

'I'm sorry, Stephen, I don't follow.'

'Custard cream?' he offered.

'No, ta.'

'Good man. Got to watch that figure,' he said. He used his spoon to ladle the chocolate off his coffee, depositing the powdered froth into an ashtray that looked like it had never been used. It was only then that I noticed how physically fit he was. For a man who spent a lot of his time in a concrete burrow, he radiated health. I figured that the golf played no small part in it. Three holidays a year I guessed – Gleneagles, La Manga and Valderama. His face had the healthy glow of a single-handicapper. His skin was taut as a drum. Bastard.

'So, what's the big crisis and what have I got to do with it?' I asked.

'You are already aware that the Northern Ireland Assembly is suspended.'

'I am.'

'Well, at six o'clock this evening, George McCrea, leader of the Ulster Unionists, informed me of his resignation as First Minister. It is his last, defiant protest at the failure of the IRA to commence decommissioning of its arms. He goes public tomorrow. The whole peace process is about to collapse. That, me old china, is the crisis.'

'China Crisis. Where are they now?'

'Have you been listening to a word I've said, Black? This is serious. No decommissioning and none of us has a future.'

'Well, I'm sorry to disappoint you, Stephen, but I can't help. I hold no sway with the IRA. I have a few contacts in the Tufty Club, if that's a help.'

'I'll pretend I didn't hear that. Look, we both know that the only person who can secure decommissioning is Sinn Fein numero uno, Martin O'Hanlon. But he's a bit like you, Jay. He claims he can't influence the IRA.'

'Yeah, right.'

'I know, I know. Of course O'Hanlon could do his bit to break the impasse, but why bother? As it stands, the British and Irish governments have until Christmas Eve, when a new First Minister must be elected, to forge a deal on arms. If they don't, McCrea won't put himself up for re-election and the Unionists may abstain from any vote. In that event, there is a real danger that Martin O'Hanlon will be elected First Minister by default. And he'll have the mandate of the people firmly behind him. Remember, it was the people of Northern Ireland who voted for an elected assembly. It was the people of Northern Ireland who voted for engagement. Martin O'Hanlon believes in engagement. He isn't the one walking away from the table.'

'And what can I do about it?'

Meeks pushed his chair back and rose to his feet. He

swung his left leg like a Ping, putting golf balls along the carpet with his foot.

'O'Hanlon has been repackaged by his party. They have succeeded in rebranding him as a champion of democracy, a champion of the people. He has managed to secure the support of even the most moderate Republicans. Christ, some of the Protestants in his constituency are prepared to go on TV to say what a swell guy he is. If O'Hanlon becomes First Minister the consequences for the union, not to mention my force, will be catastrophic. O'Hanlon wants total de-militarization of the province and that includes dismantling the RUC. I will not let that happen. Did you know that Interpol classified Northern Ireland as the most dangerous place in the world to be a police-man – twice as dangerous as El Salvador?'

'You mean we're world-beaters? I haven't felt this proud since Spain '82.'

'I'm serious, Jay. The record of awards to the RUC for bravery and gallantry is unequalled in war and peace by any other police force. Yet Martin O'Hanlon is still pushing for an alternative, unarmed, community-based policing to replace us. I'm sorry, but the alternative *policing* currently being peddled by those who resort to violence and intimidation is unaccept-able. O'Hanlon and his IRA cronies masquerade as protectors of the community when in reality they corrupt and exploit it. Kangaroo courts, knee-cappings, racketeering and self-appointed thuggery will become a grim advertisement for our country if O'Hanlon becomes First Minister.'

'I agree, but what can I do about it? I'm a two-bit music hack. If you'd wanted shrewd political advice, or a bit of spin, you should have abducted John King, our home affairs correspondent. In fact, do me a

66

favour and abduct him anyway. He's an arrogant asshole.'

'I'm not looking for advice, Jay. I'm looking for action. I want you to go to work on O'Hanlon. I want you to do whatever you can to discredit him. I want you to embarrass him in the most public and humiliating way you can dream up. Yes!'

The Chief Constable had kicked a golf ball straight into the brandy glass.

'Whoa there, Tiger. What makes you think I can embarrass O'Hanlon?'

'I know a lot about you, Jay. You're forgetting that we go back a long way.'

'Trust me, I have a long memory.'

'Yes, I'm sorry about all that teasing business at school. Kids can be so cruel. But hey, it was character-building. You've turned out OK, haven't you? Done quite nicely for yourself, or so I hear. What are they paying you at the *News Letter*?'

'Wee buttons.'

'Wee buttons? But wait, don't you live in a pent-house apartment on Gregg's Quay? Must be seven figures, a pad like that. I'm obviously in the wrong job.'

'Oh, I don't know, Stephen. What are those clubs in the corner – Calloways? You're not doing so badly yourself.'

'I don't think anyone would begrudge me a little danger money. It comes with the job. On the other hand, some might question how a *two-bit music hack*, as you put it, can afford such a palatial abode. Oh wait a minute, you can't. It was given to you, wasn't it? A freebie from my old pal Kirk McClaren.'

I could feel the heat in my cheeks. After all these years, he still knew how to get to me. He knew how to put me on the spot. But how could he know about McClaren? Nobody was supposed to know about McClaren. I had been given the apartment by McClaren on the one condition that nobody found out about McClaren.

'Yes, Jay. I know all about you. I know you didn't start out as a music hack. Then again, that's common knowledge. Two years into your career at the *News Letter* and you were the most notorious journalist in Ireland. And how did you gain that reputation? By embarrassing people, that's how. You built a career on naming and shaming the great and the good – politicians, clergy, rock stars, sportsmen, business-men. You've broken scandals on hospitals, councils, schools – you've even had a stab at the RUC in your time. You seem to have a nose for these things. And you embarrassed Kirk McClaren Properties into hand-ing you the keys to the show apartment in the Y2K development on Laganside. That is why I can think of no man more capable of bringing Martin O'Hanlon to his knees.'

'So you want me to embarrass Martin O'Hanlon. You want me to try and discredit a man who has already been imprisoned for murder and other acts of terrorism and yet still he enjoys the popularity of a saint. Impossible.'

'I don't believe it is. Yes, people know about O'Hanlon the Terrorist. And yes, he has recast himself as a great orator, a deal-broker, a compassionate man, a family man, an all-singing, all-dancing, all-Irish fucking hero. But everyone has skeletons in their cupboard.'

'Aye, but O'Hanlon's skeletons are buried in unmarked graves somewhere over the border.'

Meeks ran his hands over his temples and into a

thatch of black hair that, even at forty, was flecked with grey. It was perhaps his only physical imperfection and a sign that he had spent his life checking under his car every time he got into it. He was right. I didn't begrudge him his danger money.

'You've got to dig deeper,' he said. 'Get creative if you have to. You've got to find a way to humiliate this guy. Or at least get something on him so *I* can threaten to humiliate him, so I can force him to kick-start the decommissioning of IRA arms. There must be something you can dig up. O'Hanlon's got too much to lose – his reputation, the support of his people, his place in history.'

'I dunno, Stephen. I gave up the gutter-hack bit years ago. And anyway, O'Hanlon's too dangerous. I'll be way out of my depth. As my sweet old grandma always told me, *don't fuck with the IRA.*'

'Don't you worry. My boys will be watching you all the way. If things get hot we'll get you outta there before you can say Divisional Mobile Support Unit.'

'And what if I say no?'

Meeks returned to his seat. Like the grand master he made his move.

'Kirk McClaren wasn't the only one of our school chums that you exacted your particular brand of revenge on, was he, Jay? McClaren wasn't the only one you sought to embarrass. We both know that I was on your list. And who knows, you might have got to me if you hadn't cocked it up big-time with Miles Huggins. Would you like your readers to know about Huggins?'

He could have been bluffing. But given our history, I knew that he wasn't.

'No need, Stephen. My readers can be spared that exclusive.'

69

'Thought as much. So we have a deal then. You've got till Christmas Eve, one week, to get something on O'Hanlon. Otherwise, I'll be reopening the investigation into the death of Miles Huggins. See, you and I know it wasn't just some tragic accident that you just happened upon. In fact, if I remember rightly, there's enough meat in that little sandwich to stick you with a manslaughter charge. Eh, Big Jessie?'

6

Haven't we all felt the caustic sting of embarrassment at some point in our lives?

For most of us it's an embarrassing haircut, or a dubious passport photo that betrays us for ten years. It's our mothers forcing us to wear hand-me-down clothes or the wrong trainers to school. There's the embarrassment of our first fumblings with bra straps and knicker elastic. There are embarrassing illnesses and afflictions. And there are all manner of social faux pas that can litter our lives like landmines.

There's that innocent, everyday embarrassment and then there's the other kind – humiliating, soul-crushing embarrassment. The sort that stays with you. The sort you cannot forget.

In an attempt to rid myself of my demons, I confronted them. I immersed myself in the study of what makes people like me embarrassed. As a cub reporter I had already developed a thirst for research and I had the resources of a national newspaper at my disposal. But the Internet hadn't been invented back then and the *News Letter*'s microfiche wasn't exactly a user-friendly research tool, at least, not the vast catalogues they kept in a cardboard box next to a main radiator.

The small sheets of film had melted and only served to provide a rather warped view of history. So I spent long evenings stowed away in the Linen Hall Library, a former linen warehouse opposite Belfast's City Hall. I would pull all the files and books I needed and sit in the same spot, right beside a display cabinet containing, among other chronicles of the Troubles, a Republican children's alphabet book – *A is for Armalite, B is for Balaclava*.

It didn't take me long to understand that if you have the power to embarrass people, you are very powerful indeed.

The Japanese are the masters. They have invented the *sokaiya*, people who make a living from embarrassment. The sokaiya have variously been described as corporate extortionists, shareholder activists and yakuza mobsters. They prey upon the Japanese desire to maintain at least the outward appearance of harmony and avoid public humiliation. Essentially, the sokaiya specialize in digging up dirt on major corporations. They then demand hush money from them, threatening to turn up at the shareholder meeting and ask all sorts of embarrassing questions. Part of the reason they thrive is that companies in Japan don't release nearly as much information to shareholders as businesses do elsewhere. After a couple of top-notch performances at a shareholder love-in, a sokaiya can hope to receive an annual brown envelope through the post by simply declaring his *intention* of turning up at a meeting. He gets paid not to come, not to embarrass everyone, and can sit quietly at home watching *Richard and Judy* or their Japanese equivalent (Reiki and Judo?).

The Japanese are not alone. Indian eunuchs, it seems, have got in on the act. The eunuchs, or *hijras*, have been a cultural feature of India for centuries. Where once these castrated men guarded the harems of Indian princes, they now live in isolated groups, ostracized by society. They make a living by dancing at ritual occasions such as weddings and births. The eunuchs tip up uninvited, decked out in gaudy jewellery and trowelled-on make-up, and perform clownish imitations of Bollywood song and dance extravaganzas. And they have the gall to demand money for it. But I was more interested in the role the ever-enterprising Indian banks had devised for these outcasts, as generators of embarrassment among debtors. If you get behind with that loan repayment, the Indian bank no longer writes you a pompous letter demanding non-receipted monies. They send the eunuchs round.

Imagine the scene: you're at work, keeping your head down, trying not to offend the boss, doing your daily best to put a roof over heads and shoes on feet, when in troop the eunuchs, swirling their saris and beating their drums. A Hindi dance spectacular ensues, right between you and the water cooler. It seems the eunuchs are considerably more likely to collect on the spot than the normal bank official who serves you a polite, manila-bound request.

Well, something clicked in the young cub. I decided I wanted to be like the Japanese sokaiya and the India hijra. Well, perhaps not the Indians. I was still quite attached to my meat and two veg.

I realized that I could extend their practices to Northern Ireland, a country more used to threats of violence than threats of embarrassment. I knew that if I had the power to embarrass people, I could get what I wanted. What use was violence? We'd had twenty-five years of it and nobody had got what they wanted.

73

See, people have egos and reputations to protect. They'd rather have their legs shot to pieces than be publicly humiliated. A few plates, pins and screws, and legs heal. OK, so you don't look great in swimming trunks, but the damage can be repaired. A broken ego is beyond repair.

You need something more powerful than violence to get your way in Ulster. And, right up until the death of Miles Huggins, I had it.

Chief Constable Meeks was right. In the early Nineties I had quickly gained a reputation as the young Turk of Ulster journalism. I would do whatever I could to embarrass those in authority and bag an exclusive. I had the uncanny ability to get close to these people, close enough to dig their dirt. I knew all the tricks. I would root through their bins (people really should shred important governmental despatches, even at home). I would pose as their estate agent (it's amazing how ready some people are to hand you their house keys), or their financial adviser (and how willing they are to tell you where their money goes while furnishing you with printed, indefatigable evidence). I have even cut their hair (the surest way there is to find out all you need to know about someone). I have acted as their friend or, on one notable occasion, their lover. (I had been investigating Fiona O'Keefe, Ireland's all-conquering Olympic swimmer, who was suspected of taking performance-enhancing drugs. The relationship didn't last long because of my failure to perform in the sack. I couldn't keep up with her. Lord knows where she got her stamina.)

I didn't entirely enjoy what I did, exposing these people, splashing them all over the paper. Sure, most of them deserved it, but it all felt a bit sleazy. There is little dignity in sifting through someone's household waste and, in the end, what did I achieve? The odd front-page byline in 14-point upper case, and the knowledge, among other things, that some Northern Irish breakfast-show host uses waxed dental floss, has tuna on his pizza and, strangely for a bachelor, goes through two pairs of sheer black tights a week.

To put it another way, I wasn't something my mother liked to brag about at her bridge night.

But then I got thinking. What if I could apply my skills in another way? What if I sought ways of embarrassing those people who really had it coming? All those bastards who'd made my life a misery. Yes, you could call it revenge. Yes, you could call it blackmail. I was going to humiliate these people to get my own way. As the Japanese and Indians have proved, it's a lot more civilized than baseball bats in back alleys and bullets in bones. And a lot more effective too.

So I looked up Kirk McClaren's name in the Yellow Pages.

It was '95 and peace had broken out. Businesses were expanding, new companies wanted to establish themselves in the province, and people were flocking into Belfast to fill all the new jobs. Thing was, the city struggled to accommodate them. There simply wasn't enough property. Belfast was fit to burst. The Northern Ireland Executive came up with a solution. They awarded planning permission on vast tracts of Belfast wasteland to anyone who could demonstrate they had the capital and the manpower to develop it. The order went out to build, build, build.

In this spirit, NIE awarded Kirk McClaren Property permission to develop Gregg's Quay on the eastern bank of the Lagan.

It was a contentious decision. Right up until the final presentations to Belfast City Council, a rival company – Laganvale Developments – were expected to be awarded the land. They had earmarked the site for two state-of-the-art office blocks with conference facilities. As part of Laganvale's pitch, two American businessmen took to the chamber floor promising to fill the proposed buildings the second the plaster was dry. Their companies – IPK Technologies and Baltimore Life – would create in excess of 1,100 jobs between them. They promised to invest heavily in the local community and to improve transport links to the redeveloped East Side of the city. As a gesture of goodwill that could in no way be interpreted as a bribe, they had already contributed towards the expansion of the nearby City Airport.

Kirk McClaren, by contrast, was proposing to build luxury penthouse apartments overlooking the river. His presentation included a virtual tour round the flagship Y2K apartment block, set to an appropriately visionary Brian Eno soundtrack. At one point the voice-over described Y2K as 'an eyrie, perched administrant over Belfast's new horizon'. This clearly wasn't the much-needed housing for nurses, teachers and blue-collar workers that the city was crying out for. Nor was it a means of creating 1,100 jobs. Kirk McClaren wanted his apartments to attract Belfast's 'new elite'. His market researchers had identified this group of Celtic Tigers, young professionals who were apparently prepared to part with one million plus for the privilege of bestriding the city like colossal wankers.

In short, it was a done deal. Laganvale Developments had it sewn up.

Only it wasn't. And they didn't. And I knew why.

Within two minutes of closing those Yellow Pages and lifting the phone I had secured a job as an electrician working for Kirk McClaren Property. It wasn't the most thorough interview I had ever endured. McClaren had been awarded planning permission on condition he had the apartments up and ready by 1 January 2000. He needed all the help he could get, so new employees were not subjected to the closest of scrutiny. He asked me my name (I gave a false one). He asked for my National Insurance number (I insisted on cash in hand). And lastly he asked: *can you wire a plug?*

The job was mine.

I did my best to ingratiate myself with McClaren whenever he appeared on site. He certainly didn't recognize me. I had thinned out. My hair was more sandy than ginger. And I was no longer 4'8" with a girl's voice and a blazer full of football stickers. In fact, we became such good pals, he invited me round to do a spot of wiring in his home, McClaren Towers, a mock-Tudor monstrosity in the Holywood hills. That's Holywood, County Down – with one 'l' and even fewer stars.

McClaren was right to trust me alone in his home. I did a good job. Not only did I wire in four telephone points and an aerial socket, I even rigged up a hidden camera at no extra cost. At least, I didn't let it show on the bill.

I didn't have to wait long to get what I wanted.

McClaren, it emerged, liked to host pool parties at his Holywood home. Men-only pool parties. The camera captured it all – Kirk McClaren sucking a cock that belonged to one Reverend Ian Crawford MP.

It seemed that in order to acquire his prime slice of undeveloped Laganside land, McClaren was screwing the prominent Unionist politician, ordained minister, Belfast councillor and platinum-selling balladeer,

77

Ian Crawford. Ironically, this reverend/ councillor/ MP/troubadour* (*delete as applicable) was notorious for his public and outspoken outbursts decrying the unchristian practices of promiscuity and homosexuality. 'The only solution to homosexuality in Ulster,' he famously proclaimed, his voice rising to a crescendo, 'is a good LYNCHING!' Then he grabbed his guitar and warbled a track from his latest cassette, available from all good Christian bookshops across the province.

It didn't take a genius to work out that the Reverend Crawford would be somewhat discredited if it emerged that he enjoyed it 'up the Gary'. Nor did it take Stephen Hawking to deduce that Belfast Council would never have awarded Kirk McClaren planning permission if he hadn't secured William Crawford's casting vote. And I had the video evidence explaining how that vote was secured. In other words, I had Kirk McClaren by the short and curlies. As did Ian Crawford at the point I switched the video off.

I doorstepped McClaren and confronted him with the evidence. He threatened to have me shot. When he spied Diggsy sitting in a van not ten metres away with a video camera trained on him, he quickly whipped the offer of execution off the table and replaced it with the slightly more generous offer of ten grand in cash.

But I wasn't interested in his money. I wanted to hurt him. I wanted to embarrass him in the most public and humiliating way I could. I wanted to destroy his business, his reputation, his marriage. It was the least I could do.

And then he offered me the apartment. And if Diggsy hadn't just been kicked out of his parental home and Carmel hadn't so recently been attacked on the steps of the nurses' quarters at the RVH, I might have laughed in McClaren's face. I would have enjoyed that moment more than anything because I would have known how he felt. How many times had he put me in that insufferable, utterly powerless position?

But instead, Carmel McCaffrey, Pete Diggs and I moved into Northern Ireland's first million-pound apartment, on the condition that nobody found out about McClaren. On the condition that his business, his reputation, and his marriage remained intact.

I wasn't letting him off that easily, though. I only decided to accept the apartment the moment I realized that, by doing so, I was sentencing McClaren to a life lived in abject and consummate fear.

To this day McClaren knows that at any time I could hand my keys back and go public. Call it the Sword of Damocles or the Pen of Black, a great dark threat hangs over him. In the way Meeks has to check under his car every time he gets into it, McClaren cannot perform even the most rudimentary, everyday function without feeling this omnipresent threat. He cannot enjoy his business, his reputation or his wife (though given his sexual predilection, the latter is hardly a great loss). He cannot enjoy all these things because he knows that at any time he may lose them. His life is governed by uncertainty. And that uncertainty is dictated by me.

I am the sokaiya to McClaren's fat cat. I own him.

Six years on and the Chief Constable of the RUC gives me one week to do the same to Sinn Fein leader Martin O'Hanlon. I only agreed to it because I had to. I only agreed to it because, after the thing with Miles Huggins, Meeks owned me.

I guess it's just a microcosm of how the world

operates. None of us are free. In a sense we are all property. We are owned by our partners, our parents, our children, our pets. We are owned by our bosses, our banks and our mortgage lenders. We are owned by the television that incapacitates us and by the newspaper that governs our opinions. We are owned by the books that grip us and the songs that inspire us, by the clothes that label us and the accent that stereotypes us.

Armed with the right tools, anyone can own anyone.

My task was to make Martin O'Hanlon my property. I had to start rifling through his bins.

7

'Aaaaagh. That hurts.'

Karma had my feet in a basin of God knows what.

'Shut the fuck up and keep them in there,' she scolded.

'I like your bedside manner,' I replied. 'Is that how you talk to all your patients?'

'No, only big babies like yourself. Christ, I've had four-year-olds with bleach burns who make less noise than you.'

The soles of my feet were cut to ribbons. The combined effects of alcohol and black ice the previous evening had succeeded in numbing the pain. It hadn't occurred to me to rinse them under a warm tap before I fell into bed. Frankly, it was the last thing on my mind, some distance behind Scarlet, a sawn-off shotgun, a death threat, an abduction, an RUC Chief Constable, a Sinn Fein leader and blackmail.

'How on earth did you let your feet get in this state?' asked Karma. She lifted my left foot out of the hot water and sponged it with diluted Dettol.

'Aaagh – I don't know. I must have been sleepwalking.'

'Sleepwalking? Where . . . across the Arctic? They're all cuts and lumps.'

'How callus of me.'

'Ha bloody ha. You won't be smiling if you lose a couple of those toes.'

'Is it that serious?'

'No, you'll survive. But I'd lay off the Irish dancing for a while.' Karma left me with my feet immersed. 'I'll grab a couple bandages from my room. Don't be sticking your fingers into any sockets while your feet are in the water.'

I paddled in Dettol and looked out over the city. The low winter sun could only make a half-hearted attempt at a thaw. It took a passing helicopter to dislodge huge mattresses of snow from the roofs of the East Belfast tenements.

I had decided to go into the *News Letter* offices. I needed to start digging on Martin O'Hanlon. I wasn't up to speed on the prospective First Minister. Harry Clegg, my editor, would want to know why I was again so interested in politics. He employed John King to handle the political stuff. He wouldn't want me treading on King's toes (not that I was in a state to tread on anything). He'd tell me to stick to writing about all those bloody bands with daft names and no tunes. And for good measure he'd recommend that I try listening to Sinatra: *Now that man had timing. That man could fuckin' sing.*

Karma fashioned two white boxing boots onto my feet from bandage and gauze. Sadly, the side effect of this was not an ability to float like a butterfly and sting like a bee. Rather, it was an inability to squeeze my feet into anything other than a pair of slippers. A pair of oversized, hairy monster slippers. They had been a joke present from Karma the previous Christmas.

'I can't walk into the office in comedy slippers.'

'Why not?'

'Don't be silly. I write for a national newspaper. I walk into the office looking like a bloody Hobbit and I'll lose all credibility.'

'You have credibility?' asked Karma.

A thought occurred to me.

'What size is Diggsy?'

'Five foot eleven.'

'His feet?'

'I've never seen them,' she said. 'But if it's true what they say and they're in proportion to your manhood, I'd guess he's a size twelve.'

'I'll go and wake him.'

I slid my bandages along the floorboards, turned 180 degrees, and moonwalked into Diggsy's room. The room was bright. The curtains were open. A poster of a scantily clad Carrie Fisher presided over his pristine duvet. Strange, Diggsy was never up and out this early. He was rarely up and out at all. Then it dawned on me. His bed hadn't been slept in. He hadn't come home. I had a flashback of Bar Baca and Mags. Who'd have thought it, Diggsy the Groupie?

I rummaged under the bed for shoes. Unfortunately, Diggsy was no Imelda Marcos. I only managed to retrieve two battered Converse All-Stars, spilling a stack of chronologically ordered *Empires* in the process. Thankfully the All-Stars fitted, but only if I left the laces undone.

I was in business.

I took Diggsy's scooter through the city and Shaftesbury Square, towards the Lisburn Road. The gritters were out, much to the chagrin of two Methody schoolgirls dressed in hockey gear whose legs got pebble-dashed by a passing lorry. I took the bike down Tate's Avenue, a steep decline that afforded a stunning view of Cave Hill and the rocky outcrop known to locals as Napoleon's Nose. The hill was snow-capped, like Napoleon had sneezed his cocaine all over it.

I sped past Windsor Park and a snowman sporting a Linfield FC bobble hat. One of the wee hallions building the snowman plucked out one of its eyes and chucked it at my front wheel. I resisted the temptation to shout 'Up the Glens!' and turned onto the Boucher Road and into the industrial estate where the *News Letter*'s two prefabricated buildings sat.

One of the buildings had no windows. It thrummed and clacked and spat out vans inkily loaded with papers. This building contained the printing presses. It was known as Production.

The second, slightly smaller building housed the newspaper offices. The offices were open-plan and were laid out over two floors. The upper floor was entirely occupied by advertising sales, giving you some idea as to the ratio of ads to actual content in the paper. On the ground floor sat the editor, his deputy, the writers, the designers and the paste-up artists. Actually, the paste-up artists rarely sat. They stood at three long banks of drawing boards, angled at 45 degrees and covered in rubber. The drawing boards, that is, not the paste-up artists. This building was referred to as Editorial.

Production didn't like Editorial and the feeling was reciprocated. A strange sort of sectarian divide operated between the two camps. Production thought Editorial were a bunch of overpaid, jumped-up, arrogant arseholes, who didn't do proper jobs. Editorial looked down on Production because they ate bacon sarnies with inky fingers and because they still felt it necessary to consult topless calendars from as far back as 1984. How the paper ever got produced on time, twice a day, six days a week, was a miracle to rival any weeping Madonna that Catholicism had to offer.

The moment I walked onto the Editorial floor, panic ensued. My colleagues slapped their watches with looks of utter incomprehension. One pretended to dial the speaking clock.

'Fuck me,' said Harry Clegg. 'I thought today was Thursday. Paste-up, what's the date on the fuckin' masthead?'

'It says Thursday. My fuckin' mistake,' shouted Davey Clegg, Harry's son. He used his scalpel to unpick the masthead and made a show of replacing it with Tuesday's.

'Very good. Just because I only work a Tuesday and a Friday doesn't mean I can't pop in whenever the notion takes me.' I pressed a button on the coffee machine, more out of habit than desire.

'I'm not paying you fuckin' overtime, Jay.'

Harry's eczema was playing up. His brow was raw red. When he rubbed it the skin flaked into the air like old paint stripped from a lintel. I stuck a protective hand over my coffee, fearing contamination, and found my desk.

Our Home Affairs correspondent, John King, was sitting opposite me, forking fried rice into his moon face. He had invented the 'Home Affairs' title in a transparent attempt to make himself sound a little more like Kate Adie and a little less like a camp inadequate with an odour problem who still lived with his mum.

'Bit early for shrimp fried rice, isn't it, Nosmo?' I asked.

The boys called him Nosmo King because he liked to tell you what you could and couldn't do. Cigarettes were his big no-no.

'Ah, Jay. Are you here to do some real journalism or have you just popped in for your crayons so you can draw? Wait, don't tell me, Harry's giving you something juicy, something challenging. He wants fifty words on Dana in *Mother Goose* at the Grand Opera House.'

'If I told you I was researching the life and times of Martin O'Hanlon, would you believe me?'

Nosmo laughed loudly, spilling his fried rice. The little brown 1s fell down between the Us, Vs and F4s on his keyboard. 'Sure, what would you know about Marty O'Hanlon? You think Sinn Fein is a term used in football to describe a player faking a leg injury.'

I ignored him and fired up my PC.

I knew a lot about Martin O'Hanlon the 'reformed' terrorist and Sinn Fein head honcho, but I knew very little about Martin O'Hanlon the man. I knew he was married to Caitlin and their daughter was a musical prodigy of some renown. In fact, Edel O'Hanlon was almost as famous as her father, having done for the harp what James Galway did for the flute. Or what Marty O'Hanlon did for the Armalite.

I typed the name 'MARTIN O'HANLON' into the Internet search engine and it brought up results 1–8 of 812. Out of curiosity, I keyed in 'GEORGE BEST' and got results 1–8 of 505; 'HIS HOLINESS THE POPE' – results 1–8 of 1,076; 'SCARLET HARLOT' – results 1–8 of 8; and 'TELETUBBIES' – results 1–8 of 1,228. From this I drew two worrying conclusions: one, Martin O'Hanlon was an even more popular figure than Chief Constable Meeks imagined; and two, the Teletubbies were bigger than Catholicism.

O'Hanlon's popularity was nothing short of a phenomenon. O'Hanlove, I christened it. And it had all happened so fast. Before his election as Sinn Fein leader and his appointment onto the Northern Ireland Executive, Marty O'Hanlon's only real Internet presence was as a bit-part player in grim news archives and dour political theses posted on the Web. But the moment he became party leader a curious thing happened: the jokes started. Spoof websites and viral e-mails began to clog the information super-highway. It was perhaps the first move in an unconscious and subterranean propaganda war: the process of making one of the most feared architects of terrorist atrocities in modern times into a celebrated cult. And this triumph of PR was instigated, not by Irish Republicans, but by an altogether scarier army: Net nerds.

I immediately found a website devoted to serious consideration of Martin O'Hanlon's attractiveness to women. I was invited to scan in my own mugshot to be displayed, in quick succession with others, next to a picture of Marty. With a click of the mouse, surfers could then vote as to whether I was 'Hotter' than the former terrorist or 'Not'.

On other sites, computer-generated mock-ups cel-ebrated him further. I was particularly taken by an image of Marty O'Hanlon's face superimposed onto the body of a Teletubby (they get everywhere). The accompanying caption read: *Tiocfaidh ar Laa-Laa*. I made a mental note to e-mail it to Nosmo's desktop and set it as his wallpaper when he wasn't looking.

Online gamers could thump O'Hanlon, shoot O'Hanlon, stick a penalty past O'Hanlon, or watch O'Hanlon perform the YMCA dance to a chorus of '*I'm I-R-A*'. You could even order O'Hanlon bog roll.

Each sheet carried his face and the words: 'Wipe out terrorism'.

The more sites I entered, the more I considered whether it was all in bad taste. Perhaps it wasn't. We have always lampooned our bogeymen on the principle that if we laugh at what we fear, we diminish it. What better response to a terrorist – who perhaps still hopes to terrorize – than to laugh in his beardy face? During the Second World War Adolf Hitler's programme of genocide didn't prevent short-trousered comedians in school playgrounds the nation over from raising a grubby finger to the upper lip, shooting out an arm in a Nazi salute and performing a comedy walk.

But the fun subsided the deeper I delved. I began to refine my search terms and the Internet did what it does best. It cut to the chase.

O'Hanlon: arrested in Bundoran with 250 lbs of gelignite and 2,666 rounds of .303 ammunition under the rear seat of his Ford Granada. O'Hanlon: imprisoned for eight months in Long Kesh for membership of Oglaigh na Eireann. O'Hanlon: provided the ideological foundation for the Provisionals for the next twenty years. O'Hanlon: 'the armed struggle is a necessary and morally correct form of resistance.' O'Hanlon: 'it will remain an armed struggle while the enemy is armed.'

The more I searched, the more the pattern of the man began to emerge. O'Hanlon's rhetoric had become much less confrontational over the years. As party leader, he now wore the mantle of a very personable, intelligent, articulate and self-disciplined man. It was precisely these qualities which made him so dangerously effective. This was a man who had risen from the ashes of Republican terrorism to inspire his party to thirty-two seats on the Northern Ireland Assembly,

entitling them to three seats on the executive government of Northern Ireland. He had masterminded a
remarkable transformation, taking Sinn Fein into the
mainstream. And he'd done it without the IRA having
to give up so much as a spud gun.

No wonder Meeks was hacked off.

The closer I got to result 812 of 812, the more I
appreciated what a charmed life O'Hanlon had led, for
numerous attempts had been made on it. On one
occasion a Loyalist gunman sent to murder the Sinn
Fein leader accidentally shot himself and was caught
by passers-by. I followed links to accounts of jammed
guns, getaway cars that failed to start, and the incredible story of a team planning to bomb O'Hanlon in
his local pub, who arrived without a match to light
their crude device.

How could I hope to bring this man down? He was
impregnable, indestructible, untouchable.

And then I found something. It appeared on one of
those amateurish, single-page, home-made websites
that the Net often sucks you into against your will.
Typed in iridescent green against a black background
was a potted biography of Martin O'Hanlon. It looked
like someone had started to write it before realizing
that they didn't know how to build a second page onto
the website. So they gave up mid-sentence. Thankfully
there was enough to interest me within the two surviving paragraphs that were hanging around forlornly
in this lonely outpost of the World Wide Web.

The biography began with O'Hanlon's student days.
I adjusted the colour on my monitor until the
migraine-inducing green became sober grey, and read
how the young Marty once had journalistic
pretensions of his own. He attended Queen's
University in the late Sixties, where he became editor

of the student newspaper, *The Gown*. And that, according to this website, was where The Life of Martin O'Hanlon began and ended.

It might have been nothing. But if, as I had observed, O'Hanlon's rhetoric had become less loaded and more guarded over the years, then there was just a chance that his guard might have slipped earlier on in his life. Students are always embarrassing themselves. Most of them haven't quite managed that transition between dependent child and responsible adult. It's not that they let their guard slip, rather, they haven't yet learned to be guarded.

I resolved to take a trip down to the university, maybe grab a few back issues of *The Gown*, just to see what the young O'Hanlon had been writing. If I was to pierce his formidable armour then this looked as good a start as any.

'So, did you get what you wanted on O'Hanlon, or are you just playing online pool?' bleated John King, all satisfied with himself.

'A bit of hush, Nosmo. I'm concentrating here. I'm just putting a bit of e-chalk on my cyber cue before I address my virtual white.'

'You do know he'll be down in Dundalk on Saturday, at the Sinn Fein Ard Fheis? Harry's sorting me out with a press pass.'

Dundalk. North of Dublin. Today was Thursday. Tomorrow I would be heading down to Dublin. I could kill two birds: travel down with the Harlots on Friday, check out the PJ Harvey support gig, nip up to Dundalk on Saturday afternoon for the Sinn Fein Circus Sideshow, and I'd be back in Dublin that evening to see Scarlet and the girls headlining.

I needed to get that press pass before Nosmo got his sticky fingers on it. If Harry's eczema was an indicator of his mood, getting the pass was going to be as easy as stealing a joey from the pouch of a boxing kangaroo.

I approached with caution.

'Why the fuck do you want to go to a fuckin' Sinn Fein Ard Fheis? You write about fuckin' pop music. Sinn Fein Ard fuckin' Fheis, he says. Are Westlife doing a fuckin' PA at it?'

Harry's skin erupted. He had blotches on his blotches.

'Close,' I said.

'What do you mean, fuckin' close?'

'I heard a rumour Ronan Keating's speaking at it.'

'You're tellin' me Ronan fuckin' Keatin's speakin' at a Sinn Fein conference?'

'It's only a rumour. But take a look at this. The guy has political aspirations.'

It was desperate, I know, but I had remembered that Ronan Keating once claimed in an interview that he saw himself as a future Taoiseach. I had located the piece on the Net, printed it off and now held it under Harry's nose.

'As I said, Harry, it's only whispers. But what if he shows? It'll be massive.'

'Jay, I'm not fuckin' stupid. There's as much likelihood of Ronan Keatin' addressin' Sinn Fein fuckin' delegates as there is of me winnin' the Nobel Prize for fuckin' ballet dancing.'

'There isn't a Nobel Prize for ballet dancing.'

'Exactly.'

'Oh, right. Point taken.'

I retracted the article and folded it into my back pocket.

'Houl on there a fuckin' minute,' said Harry. 'I haven't finished. Listen, I don't know what it is you're up to, Jay. I don't want to fuckin' know. We've been down this road before. You're fuckin' lucky you're still in journalism after that footballer died. Don't go gettin' yourself into anythin' you can't get out of, do you hear me?'

'Loud and clear, Harry.'

'Right. Now give me your hand.'

Harry grabbed my wrist. He pressed something hard and green and plastic into my hand. The press pass.

I was about to thank him but he shushed me.

'You're only gettin' it cos that wanker Nosmo dunked my last fag in cold fuckin' tea.'

8

The main Queen's University building is a triumph of mid-nineteenth-century architecture. It sits in a pleasant, self-contained and bustling little area, half a mile south of the city centre. A regal carpet of flat green lawn is customarily rolled out in front of the grand old dear, but an uncouth December had replaced it with a thick white shag-pile of snow. I arrived at Queen's via Belfast's Botanic Gardens, which fan out behind her like a flamboyant royal train. In better weather, the gardens were home to spring-term scholars, cider drinkers and spontaneous, life-threatening games of hurley.

The students' union building stands opposite its alma mater, caught in her disapproving glare. The two buildings are separated by a road, a set of traffic lights, and over a century of architectural hubris. The union's beauty is not so much aesthetic as anaesthetic. The only redeeming feature of this concrete carbuncle is the cheerful reflection of its illustrious parent in its ugly, grubby windows.

I made my way up the concrete steps, doing my best to blend in with the file-carrying, lecture-dodging hordes. But the moment I entered the largest of the union's three bars, I felt like an outsider. I was being eyed with suspicion, not because these students somehow knew I was on a mission to bring down the leader of Sinn Fein; they eyed me because I was so obviously not one of them – wrong age, wrong hairstyle, wrong walk, wrong newspaper, wrong sodding trainers. A couple of girls looked at me like I was some sort of sex case, probably because I was subjecting them to a scrutiny unbecoming of a gentleman (either the women I was attracted to were getting younger, or I was getting older).

I needed to find the *Gown* offices, but I couldn't resist the promise of 'Guinness – a pound a pint' that fluttered from bunting above the bar. Such are the joys of subsidized imbibing. Was it any wonder student grants were stopped? All they do is piss 'em up a wall.

I found a table beside an empty dais in the middle of the Speakeasy. The bar was packed. It had barely gone midday, yet already tall, frothy stacks of empty Guinness glasses were being unsteadily erected on tables all around me. Thursday lunchtime and they were all hammered, this educated elite, this top 10 per cent, the bridge-builders, politicians and neurosurgeons of our future. God help us if there's a war.

An earnest-looking chap with a shaved head and John Lennon specs threw a photocopied leaflet at me. On it was printed a photo of an earnest-looking chap with a shaved head and John Lennon specs. His face was all pinched and panda-eyed. As my mother would have commented, he had no meat on him. This guy could've hidden behind a Belsen escapee.

'All right there,' he said, his voice drained of enthusiasm. 'I'm Rory McConnell.'

Not according to his leaflet he wasn't. According to his leaflet he was Ruadhraigh Mac Connaill.

'That's my manifesto. I'm a candidate in the Student Sabbatical Elections. I'm going to be your new Entertainments Officer,' he mumbled, in monotone.

A waspish girl stood beside him, joined at his hip. She punched me on the collarbone. I was about to counter with a deft uppercut when I realized she had merely assaulted me with a sticker. I unpeeled it from my jacket. It read: 'Vote for Ruadhraigh, End of Story'.

Shame he couldn't have come up with a catchier slogan, I thought, something that rhymed.

'So, you could be my next Ents Officer,' I said. 'How do you propose to entertain me? Can you juggle?'

'Read my manifesto. I've got loads of experience. I went to the same school in Derry as Neil Hannon out of Divine Comedy. I've been backstage at Spiritualized, Dandy Warhols *and* JJ72. Oh, and I play the bass. At least, I'm learning to.'

'And that qualifies you to organize a year's worth of entertainment for twenty-three thousand students? What experience do you have of handling money, I mean, I'm assuming you'll be in charge of a large budget?'

'Well, I worked the door when my mate's band played in Auntie Annie's. I was in charge of a large cash box.' He self-consciously flicked his fringe out of his eyes, even though he didn't have one. 'Go on, mate. Vote for me. Everyone thinks I'm great craic.'

'Who's standing against you?' I asked.

'Gavin Patterson. But you don't want to vote for him.'

'Why not?'

'He's a Prod.'

'And that affects his ability to provide quality entertainment?'

'He's going to axe the Folk Night. He's invited the Sandy Row Regal Flute Band to do a residency on

Wednesday afternoons. And he says he's going to cancel the Union's subscription to Setanta, so the bars can't show live Gaelic football. He wants to subscribe to Rangers FC TV.'

'And this is all set out in his manifesto?'

'Well . . . no. But we're telling people that's what he's going to do. It's a sure-fire vote-winner. Apparently Patterson was seen wearing a Remembrance poppy when he canvassed the halls.'

'Did you see him?'

'Not me, personally. But you can believe it, can't you? He's a Brit, so he is.'

'Well, I'm convinced. No way can we have Patterson on the Student Executive. Next thing you know, he'll be objecting to the Union's bilingual policy. He'll be insisting that the signs for the toilets aren't just written in English and Irish, but French, Japanese, Urdu and, Lord help us, Welsh. Tell you what, Rugrat, or whatever your name is, you've got my vote. But only if you can point me in the direction of the *Gown* office.'

'You want to be a journalist?'

'Yes, I do. When I grow up.'

I located the *Gown* office in the bowels of the union building. I would never have found it had it not been for Ruadhraigh's directions: 'Turn right at reception, walk past the bookshop, the hairdresser's and the launderette and you'll come to a bloke sitting in a bath full of baked beans. He's listening to Steps for twenty-four hours. He'll tell you where it is.'

I didn't bother to knock. There wasn't a door. The *Gown* office could have better been described as the *Gown* cupboard. It contained a filing cabinet, a sofa that had seen more use as an ashtray, and an old school desk, the sort that comes with an integral inkwell. As if to emphasize the redundancy of the inkwell, all the graffiti etched enthusiastically onto the desk was written in biro.

What little wall space they had was plastered in *Gown* front pages. The design of the masthead had been restlessly rejigged every third issue, an indication that the editorship had changed with similar frequency. The pages on display were culled from as far back as 1967. Together they formed a potted chronicle of student unionism in Northern Ireland, their headlines starkly highlighting those stories that cut to the very heart of what it means to be a student in Belfast: 'QUEEN'S GIRL GUNNED DOWN IN GIBRALTAR'; 'QUB GAA ARE UVF TARGET'; 'PAISLEY JR JOINS ALUMNI'; 'HARP LAGER HALF-PRICE ALL SEPTEMBER'.

I was just advancing towards the filing cabinet when I heard a loud American voice. It was the aural equivalent of a shepherd's crook, for it abruptly hauled me back.

'Coming through.'

She was a plump girl, with a tightly cropped mop of dyed hair. I could tell it was dyed because the henna had stained the tops of her multi-studded ears. She barged past me, lugging a breeze block of pristine papers. She thumped them down on the sofa and ripped one from the top of the pile.

'Lookie here, my first issue as editor. Take it.' She handed me her *Gown*, the first of an inconsiderable print run. She explained, 'It's a special edition, focusing on the pro-life, pro-choice debate that confronts many pregnant women in Ireland. I've subtitled it *The Abortion Issue*. Neat, huh?'

The ink was barely dry on the front-page headline: 'STAY AND DELIVER OR YOUR MONEY FOR A

LIFE?' The question mark was formed from a graphic of a curved umbilical cord with a balled-up foetus impersonating the dot at its base. Understated, I thought.

'So what are you,' I asked, 'pro-life or pro-choice?'

She looked at me like she'd just stepped in me.

'Pro-life, of course. I've organized a picket this afternoon, outside the Well Woman Centre on the Lisburn Road. They've been operating a counselling service, handing out advice on abortion. It sucks. We're gonna get us some eggs and hurl 'em at any woman going in or coming outa there. One of our girls lives on a farm out in Ballycastle. She's got hold of some eggs that contain undeveloped chicks. That's gonna make 'em think.'

'Jesus. Isn't that a bit extreme?'

'Abortion is murder. We're campaigning for a civil rights issue here. A few eggs is nothing. I was a member of RESCUE back home in Ohio. We used to spray the clinics with piggies' blood.'

'Don't pigs have rights?'

'I'll tell y'all about rights. Women's rights.'

'What, like a woman's right to choose whether she gives birth or not?'

I shouldn't have said it. I shouldn't have stoked her fire. She was off on one.

'Whoa, there. Acceptance of abortion is a rejection of the womb's function. It's a betrayal of the feminist cause. Of all the things which are done to women in order to fit them into a society dominated by men, abortion is the most bloody, violent and degrading invasion of their physical and psychic territory.'

'What, and spraying them in pigs' blood isn't?'

She whipped the *Gown* out of my hands.

'Listen, fella, I'm busy. I've got me a paper to distribute and a protest to organize.'

98

She opened the filing cabinet and removed a chunky Magic Marker and a roll of posters. She threw them on the floor and fell to her knees.

'Sorry, I'm Jay Black. *Ulster News Letter.*'

She ignored me and unfurled the posters. They all appeared to advertise student union gigs that had long since passed – the Mission, the Wedding Present, EMF. She took a poster and flipped it over, exposing its glossy white back. She markered a pro-life slogan onto it in angry, blood-red letters. For the first time, I noticed a wigwam of canes propped in a corner of the office. She was making placards.

'Jay Black? *Ulster News Letter*?' I reiterated. 'I've heard good things about the student newspaper. My editor has sent me down here to offer a work placement to one of your writers. I was wondering whether you could recommend someone?'

She dropped her marker and quickly hauled herself up from the floor. Her face was flushed. She extended her hand. 'Tammy Hudson. Editor of *Gown*. It'd be really neat to write for you guys.'

Oh, you're my friend now, I thought.

'Well, before I award you the placement, I'll need to see some of your writing. Do you keep back issues?'

'Sure. Thirty-five years of 'em. They're filed away in there, y'all.' She indicated the battered filing cabinet. It was covered in stickers representing every cause known to man, woman and beast.

'Perhaps I could browse through them, Tammy? I promise not to disturb you. Seriously, you finish your placards, warm up your egg-throwing arm, or do whatever it is you have to do.'

'Actually, I've got to get me up to the bar to start handing out these papers. You help yourself to the old *Gowns*. My stuff's in every issue from May '99 onwards. But take a look at October 2000. I wrote a great piece in it about student prostitution.'

'Sounds a laugh. I'll check it out.'

She struggled to lift the large bundle of papers. I would have offered to help, but I would have only been imposing a dangerous masculine prerogative on her, further subjugating her womanhood. Or something.

Tammy left me in the office with only a desk, a sofa, a filing cabinet and my thoughts for company.

I had never really considered where I stood on the whole abortion thing. So many times in my youth I found myself wishing I hadn't been born. The teasing, the bullying – it could all have been avoided if my mother's scans had picked up that I would be born fat, ginger and useless. There was a time when I actually believed that; a time when I blamed my parents for bringing me into this world, for subjecting me to everything I had endured.

It was Karma who got me through those black days. Carmel McCaffrey – who took a bullet before she took her first gulp of earthly air. How hard the doctors had fought to save her in that punctured womb. How greatly her fragile life was valued and how joyously her birth was celebrated. Carmel made me appreciate my life. She helped me understand that what happens in your past only makes you a stronger person in future. She was the living, breathing embodiment.

Carmel gave me perspective. Carmel gave me karma.

And then I remembered the gun in my face not twelve hours ago and I was reminded that life is fragile at whatever stage. I considered my city, its terrorists and characters like O'Hanlon who for thirty years had presided like judge, jury and executioner over all of its people. And I came to the conclusion that in Northern

Ireland it is as if your religion is some sort of birth defect that, if identified, can result in your termination.

I pulled papers from the cabinet. Many of the older issues had yellowed, like they'd been pissed on. Their newsprint smelt as sour.

Martin O'Hanlon's name appeared in the earliest editions of the *Gown*, circa 1966. His first articles never amounted to more than a quarter-page. But even the most insignificant of his stories were imbued with his politics, which were both left-wing and extreme. By 1969 he had graduated to co-editor and allowed himself the luxury of a double-page spread on the People's Democracy, an organization he had formed with fellow Queen's students to champion civil rights.

But it was another DPS that caught my eye, bang in the middle of an issue dated May 1967. Spread across the centre pages was a series of photographs from that year's PolySoc Ball, an end-of-year formal for Queen's University's politics students.

The photos were a revelation in more ways than one. Even in his early twenties Martin O'Hanlon was distinguished by that thick black beard. His hair was longer back then, stopping just short of his shoulders. Hairy hands protruded from the cuffs of his tux. He looked not unlike the hirsute lover illustrated in Alex Comfort's *Joy of Sex* book, though O'Hanlon's contemporaries could not have teased him about the similarity until the early Seventies.

Virtually every photograph pictured O'Hanlon with his co-editor, Kate Rogers. Or so the captions attested. Judging by the cut of them, their relationship clearly went beyond what is considered professional in the field of journalism. O'Hanlon and Rogers were all over each other. In one shot, he appeared to be taking her temperature with his finger. Not that Kate Rogers's face gave any indication she was ill.

I looked more intently at the girl in the Alice band with the smile as broad as a Cheshire cat's. I knew that smile. I had seen it in newspapers many times. In the nationals, too. And in more recent years that smile had been credited not to Kate Rogers, but to Kate Owen, Secretary of State for Northern Ireland.

I carefully removed the centre spread, taking care not to damage the paper so brittle with age. I neatly folded it into a novel that Tammy had left on the desk (by Toni Morrison, whoever he was). I tucked the book into my inside pocket.

This could be big.

9

'I'm thinking of giving up alcohol,' said Diggsy.

It was 7 a.m. and we were standing on the Albert Bridge, cold and hungover. Neither of us had managed to grab much sleep the previous evening. Karma had gone out on her night shift, leaving us to babysit her ten-year-old. Her ten-year-old bottle of Bushmills, that is.

'You'll feel better when you get a bit of brekkie into you,' I said. 'I'm sure Mags won't mind stopping for a sausage roll.'

'No, Jay. I'm serious. I can't touch another drop. See, I believe that each and every one of us is allotted a quantity of alcohol that we can drink over the course of our lives. And I've drunk all mine very quickly.'

'Aye, and it's turned you soft in the head. I'm telling you, abstinence is not the solution to your problem. Not unless it's smothered in brown sauce and rammed in a bap.'

The traffic slowly started to fill the bridge as workers from Cultra, Helen's Bay, Bangor, and Newtownards made their way into the city to occupy offices and populate production lines. But no work would be done today, the last Friday before Christmas.

These people had office parties to go to. They had worked diligently all year and now it was payback time. This was their one chance to loosen that blue collar and enjoy free Buck's Fizz, a dry turkey dinner and a forlorn fuck in the stationery cupboard.

Thankfully, the *News Letter* had planned something a bit different for our annual office do. The guys on the Sports desk had organized the usual overpriced meal, but this was to be preceded by an afternoon of 'corporate boxing'. These organized bouts, adhering to all health and safety regulations, are designed to give office workers the chance to pound their bosses into oblivion. Similarly, they afford bosses the opportunity to keep underlings in check with a savage hook or well-placed shot to the ribs. The idea had proved surprisingly popular with our female staff, the majority of whom had signed up to fight Harry Clegg. This was in response to his suggestion that women shouldn't box because there'd be a catfight at the weigh-in when they questioned the integrity of the scales. He also suggested that you could award women a Lonsdale belt, 'but they'd only be wantin' a matchin' fuckin' Lonsdale handbag as well'.

I was almost sorry I was missing it. But I had a week-end with Scarlet to occupy me. And an opportunity to get O'Hanlon on the ropes.

The temperature had dipped overnight but not enough to freeze over the Lagan. An island of slush had formed close to one of its banks but it wasn't substantial enough to take the weight of a grey heron that tried valiantly to gain a foothold. I let my eyes follow an eight-man rowing boat as it scythed effortlessly through the water. It disappeared under my feet, before emerging from the west side of the bridge with the freedom and grace of a giant Pooh-stick. A border collie barked at it. The dog had been walking his owner along the towpath.

'How come murdered bodies are always discovered by people out walking their dogs?' I pondered. 'When someone goes missing, the police should dispense with televised appeals and mugshots on milk cartons. They should just ask us all to walk our dogs.'

'I don't *get* dogs,' said Diggsy. He leant his forehead on the handrail. 'Man's best friend, they say. Well, I'm sorry, but anyone who wipes their arse on my carpet and runs off with my bog roll is no friend of mine.'

My thoughts turned from dogs to brass monkeys. The wind coming in off Belfast Lough would have gone through you. The saline on my eyeballs had started to freeze. How Diggsy was surviving dressed in a suede jacket and a *Planet of the Apes* T-shirt was a mystery to confound all accepted cryogenics. We had been told to keep an eye out for a red Mercedes van, but our lift was late. Mercifully it arrived just moments before snow blindness set in.

Mags wound down the driver's window. 'Morning, boys. Hop in the back. The door's open.'

Kate and Derbhla were sitting up front beside her. Derbhla was sleeping while Kate was attempting to read a map by turning it upside down.

I slid back the side door of the van, throwing light onto Scarlet. Even at this early hour, she looked immaculate – red polo neck and ski pants, burgundy body warmer, Oxbloods, her scarlet hair scooped on top of her head and secured with a strawberry clip. When you looked at Scarlet you looked through rose-tinted glasses.

'Hi there,' she said, a little too loudly. It was then that I noticed two thin wires running out of her ears. She adjusted the volume on her Walkman, closed her eyes, and nodded her head in time to some anonymous, transcendental track.

Diggsy and I squeezed into the double seat immediately behind her. It was a tight fit. The van had been loaded to bursting with drums, high-hats, guitar cases and amps. We had no choice but to wedge our sports bags onto our knees.

This was going to be a long journey.

My apprehension was further compounded as the van pulled off. Diggsy immediately turned to me and announced his intention to 'boke'. Mags hit the brakes and seagulls instantly congregated on the Albert Bridge in anticipation of a hot lunch (reconstituted pasty supper in a whisky sauce).

We got him as far as Newry before we had to stop again. Diggsy hung his head out the van door and repainted the kerbstones, their green, white and gold becoming green, white and textured beige.

'Jesus, Diggsy, could you not have waited till we got over the border? It's only another couple of miles,' I said. 'Never shit on your own doorstep.'

'I'm not shittin', I'm throwin' my ring.' A dry heave bent him double.

'Are you OK, pet?' asked Mags.

'No,' said Diggsy. 'This T-shirt's ruined.'

He was right. Roddy McDowell had puke all over his little monkey face.

'Listen, I'll stop here,' said Mags. She killed the engine. 'I'll nip across the road and get you some water while you change your top. Anyone else need anything?'

'Chocolate,' said Derbhla and Kate.

'Ciggies,' said Scarlet.

'A bucket,' said Diggsy.

'Actually, I'll go with you,' said Derbhla.

106

'Me too,' said Kate. 'I need to stretch my legs.'

The three girls crossed the road.

Diggsy lifted his sports bag onto the pavement. He pulled his shirt over his head. An auld dear wheeling a tartan shopper stopped in front of him. She took one look at his naked, shivering torso and a sudden epiphany came over her. 'Holy Mary, Mother of God,' she said. 'I've forgotten my turkey.' She about-turned her bulging trolley and headed back down the high street.

Diggsy, unruffled by the septuagenarian, zipped himself into a trackie top and did his best to hand-wash his soiled shirt in the snow. He wasn't normally this interested in laundry. Not to the point of spontaneous improvisation, anyway. He seemed reluctant to get back in the van.

Then I realized he was trying to buy me some time alone with Scarlet. I was supposed to be shadowing her, getting under her skin, finding out what made this singer/songwriter tick. But I had barely got a word out of her since we departed Belfast. Those earphones had been plugged resolutely into her head the whole way down the motorway, long enough for her to have mastered Latvian from a language tape.

'What are you listening to?' I asked.

'Oh, sorry, twenty Embassy Reds,' she replied.

I motioned for her to remove the earphones.

'Ah, you're with us now. I was just wondering what you were listening to. You're still ordering fags, so I'm guessing it's not a self-hypnosis tape.'

'No, it's not. But that isn't such a bad idea. I really should quit smoking. It's not good for my larynx.' Scarlet tipped her head back and stroked her throat.

'Your larynx sounds fine to me. At least, it did the other night.'

'Why thank you,' she said. She pressed the eject on her Walkman and removed the cassette. 'I've been listening to this. It's all the tracks we've demoed for the first album. There's eighteen on here, but the record company wants us to whittle it down to a neat dozen. I'm having trouble deciding which six songs to kick out. I don't want to sound big-headed but they're all just too damn good to be relegated to B-sides.'

I took the cassette from her. This was gold dust. Eighteen Harlots tracks and all of them, with the exception of 'Acid Dropout', had yet to grace the ears of Joe Public. If I could sneak a wee preview I'd be guaranteed a half-page in *NME* no problem. So I chanced it.

'Why don't you bung it in the van's stereo and we can all vote on our top twelve tracks?'

'Piss off. This isn't the Eurovision Song Contest. Three years of my life is on that cassette. I will decide what gets on the album and what doesn't.'

I turned the cassette over in my fingers. The same two words were Tippexed onto both sides of the plastic casing: 'Red Guitar'.

'Is that going to be the title of the album then, "Red Guitar"?'

'It could well be,' she said, with a smile that suggested it was.

'You do know that David Sylvian had a hit with "Red Guitar"?'

Scarlet snatched back the cassette. 'I only said it *could* be. Nothing's decided yet.' She looked hurt.

I had crossed a line. I tried to restore some professional decorum.

'So, when do I get to interview you properly? There's a lot I want to ask you.'

And there was. I wanted to ask her where she got

that voice. I wanted to ask her who her influences were (though I had crossed David Sylvian off the list). I wanted to ask her about her lyrics because at times they were indecipherable and she reputedly refused to write them down. I wanted to ask her if she saw herself having children one day. And I wanted to ask her if she thought I would make a good father.

I wanted to ask her all these things, but I would have to wait. Mags, Kate and Derbhla had returned to the van.

'Get it down ye, big lad,' said Mags. She handed Diggsy his water. 'There's your ciggies, Scar. And we got a big bag of Smarties. Kate's gonna pick you out all the red ones.'

'Ta,' said Scarlet, catching her fags.

It was then I remembered Karma's little gift. I had my lighter primed before Scarlet unpicked the cellophane from her cigarette packet. I sparked up a flame, but I couldn't get the lighter to sit still. It wouldn't behave, not until Scarlet took my arm. She steadied my wrist with her gloved hand and sucked the heat right out of me.

We drove.

'I managed to get us some punts,' said Mags. 'They gave us our change in Irish.' She followed the signs out of town.

Newry's citizens are well placed to take advantage of any fluctuation in the exchange rate. Although they live north of the border, their proximity to it has led to two currencies being accepted in the town: the pound and the punt. And it was destined to become three, for the Republic was set to join the Single European Currency. There was likely to be a transitional period where the pound, the punt *and* the euro would become legal tender in the town. In such circumstances,

Newry would be distinguished as the only town in Great Britain where the euro was common tender. Newry would be an embarrassment to a British government that was resisting a move into Europe. The town would grow in notoriety. Tourists would flock to this feisty little outpost, this geopolitical and socio-economic quirk.

It's a pity, then, that Newry is such a hole.

My heart was cheered as the van climbed out of the town. We followed the main road round a snow-capped Slieve Gullion and over the western slopes of the Mournes.

This used to be one of the most notorious roads in the province, not because of its blind bends and its treacherous inclines, but because it provided the main gateway to the southern counties. If you wanted to cross the border, you had to drive your car along this road and take it through one of the largest and most heavily fortified army checkpoints in Europe. And until 1997, the checkpoint was fully operational.

The road was overlooked by a patrol base, constructed within a triangular fort, using a military principle inherited from the Romans. The idea was that two sentries could observe all three perimeter walls from two watchtowers, forty feet high. Waste pipes were installed in these towers so the soldiers could relieve themselves while on watch. Unfortunately, this would not prevent them shitting themselves during an RPG7 rocket attack.

The central building, or 'submarine', was a hardened structure designed to withstand even the most obstinate IRA mortar. This was reputed to house the most technologically advanced surveillance apparatus available to man, army or government. My father often drove my mother and me through this checkpoint on our way to Easter weekends in Wicklow. He would say that he hoped we were wearing clean underwear, for the army had special devices that could see through your clothes. When he said this, I would curl up in the back seat with my hands over my balls. My mum would tell him to stop being so bloody ridiculous and he would tell her to watch her language because the soldiers up on the hill could pick up every word she said. I remember being convinced they could read my thoughts as well. I always endeavoured to think nice things as we entered the south of Ireland.

The rusty watchtowers became visible as the Mercedes climbed the hill, their corrugated iron protesting in the wind. The patrol base may have been abandoned but it had not yet been dismantled. It was as if the army was merely on holiday and could move back in at any time. The building remained on the cold, exposed hill, down but not out – a statement of the British government's faith (or lack of it) in the peace process.

As we neared the old checkpoint I noticed that sections of concrete half-pipe had been placed on their sides all along the road. They were perhaps eight feet in diameter, plenty room for a soldier to dive into for cover. As it was, they formed an aqueduct for the melting mountain snow. Indeed, the thick blanket of snow had given the scene the apparent innocence of a Christmas card. But when you inspect the card closely, you notice that the robin is perched on a sandbag, and the red-berried holly has entwined itself round a machine-gun post, and you realize you're dreaming of a black, not a white, Christmas.

I had thought that we were the only vehicle on this

soulless stretch of road, but I was wrong. An army Saracen was parked up ahead.

'What is this? I thought they'd got rid of the checks,' said Mags. 'Shit, I've got dope.' She quickly reached across Derbhla and Kate. She whipped something out of the glove compartment and tucked it down the front of her jeans.

Our van was brought to a halt by an outstretched hand. Two armed soldiers stood in front of us. A third soldier remained connected to the Saracen by a long coiled radio cable. He was barking something into the mouthpiece.

Mags wound the window down.

'Licence?' asked the older of the two soldiers. It was amazing how someone could make one word sound so Scouse.

'Why are you stopping people?' asked Mags.

'Aye,' shouted Scarlet. 'Why don't you piss off back to England where you belong?'

I was shocked. I had got used to Scarlet exuding a cool detachment. But there was nothing detached about her now. She wasn't even semi-detached. She meant what she said.

Mags did her best to defuse the situation. She handed over her licence. 'I promise you that's me,' she said, indicating the photograph. 'I was only seventeen. I thought I was Siouxsie Sioux.'

The soldier didn't look convinced. He looked from the goth in the photo to Mags and back to the photo again.

'Is this your vehicle?' he asked. He couldn't mask the condescension in his voice. The thought of some-one younger than himself owning a Mercedes, and a woman at that, was more than the armed Liverpudlian could bear.

'It's my brother's,' said Mags. 'He does them up. I'm fully insured.'

'Where are you coming from?' he asked.

'A position of intolerance,' shouted Scarlet. 'I will not tolerate your occupation of my country.'

'Belfast,' said Mags.

'Where are you headed?'

'Towards a unified Ireland,' spat Scarlet.

'Dublin,' said Mags.

'We're supporting PJ Harvey,' added Scarlet. Somehow, she managed to make 'PJ Harvey' sound like a celebrated Irish rebel.

'Could I ask you all to get out of the van?' said the soldier.

'You can ask,' said Scarlet.

'Listen, darling, if you don't co-operate the only gig you'll be playing will be in a venue that's ten by ten with bars on the window.'

'They already are,' I said. 'It's called Filthy McNasty's. Doors open at eight, tomorrow night.'

The second soldier had made his way round the side of the van. He opened the door and politely invited us out. 'All of you. Get the fuck out. Now.'

'Such a gentleman,' said Scarlet as he held the door for her. She used all of her height to disconcert him.

We were instructed to step away from the van while they checked the band's equipment. The three soldiers made a show of opening every guitar case and examining every drum. They removed the backs from all of the amps. They seemed to be doing their damnedest to find something, *anything*, that might suggest these girls were Republican terrorists. Guitars strung with tripwire? Traces of Semtex under their plectrums? A bodhrán?

The six of us stood and performed our own

113

idiosyncratic rituals designed to stave off the cold. Scarlet lit a fag. Derbhla ate chocolate. Kate fought with her map. Mags threw snowballs at Diggsy. And Diggsy pissed his initials into the snow in hot yellow letters.

It occurred to me that he should be taking photographs. The blinding snow, the abandoned checkpoint, armed soldiers garrotting guitars and dis-embowelling amps – stick the girls front of shot, slap a headline on top suggesting they're destined to terrorize the charts . . . *et voilà*, The Harlots have their very first *NME* cover.

Why had the army set up a roadblock? Yes, Sinn Fein was due to hold their Ard Fheis in Dundalk, just over the border. I knew there'd be some sort of security presence, but I had imagined it would be a more covert operation. Three squaddies poking their guns up Republican noses would only enflame things. But why stop and search a vanload of girls on their way to a gig? I remembered my conversation with Chief Constable Meeks. He said his boys would be watching me all the way. Perhaps he had set this up in an attempt to reas-sure me, to make his presence felt.

But these guys were army, not RUC.

'Right, one at a time, I want you to get your hands on the side of the van.' The Scouser waved Mags across. 'Driver, you first.'

'You can't do this,' said Mags. One soldier placed her hands on the passenger window, while the Scouser frisked her. She stooped slightly, jamming her thighs together, steering her crotch away from him. 'What have I done?' she asked, terrified he'd get his hands on her dope.

'Leave her alone,' shouted Scarlet.

'OK, Little Red Riding Hood. It's you next.'

'Fuck away off.'

It took two of them to drag Scarlet to the van. One of the soldiers received an Oxblood to the ankle for his trouble. He held her hands on the window while the other soldier kept her calves rooted to the ground.

'This is illegal. It's a breach of my civil liberties,' screamed Scarlet. Her face was as red as the rest of her.

The Scouse squaddie frisked her with one hand, keeping the other on his rifle. He started at her shoulders and worked his way down. But the second his hand touched her bottom it kicked up in the air. It was if he'd touched a live wire. He was thrown backwards, onto the ground. He made no sound. He held up his hand. It was completely coated in blood, like he'd dipped it in a tin of pillarbox gloss. Two of his fingers were missing.

'Everyone down,' screamed his colleague.

We didn't need the encouragement. We fell to our bellies.

'I've been shot,' said Scouser.

When you hear someone say that line in a Western or a 'Nam flick, it always sounds so superfluous. An actor receives a gutful of lead and he says *I've been shot*, and you're very sorry for him and all, but he's stating the fucking obvious. He's wasting four of his precious last words.

But as the Scouser examined his stumps and repeated 'I've been shot' it was almost a question: *Have I been shot?* For there was no trace of a bullet. And none of us had heard a gun.

'Stay down, everyone. Soupie, I'll try and get to the radio. See what you can do about Weejee's hand.' The eldest squaddie started to haul himself through the slush in an attempt to reach his Saracen.

His uninjured colleague grabbed Derbhla round the throat.

115

'Give me your scarf,' he demanded.

She lifted her cheek off the snow, just enough to let him pull the scarf free. He wrapped it over Scouser's hand, tying it tight at the wrist. 'You'll be all right, Weej. We'll find your fingers. The snow'll keep 'em fresh. We'll get 'em sewn on, no worries.'

'You'd better,' said Scouser. 'It's my wanking hand.'

'Tosser,' said his mate. They shared a pally laugh. 'Now let's assess the situation. We've got a man down with a wound to the hand. Weejee, did you see anything or hear anything?'

'No,' said Scouser. 'I just touched the bitch's arse and my fingers disappeared.'

'Serves you right,' said Scarlet. She lay somewhere behind me and although I couldn't see her, I could sense her anxiety.

'This is the second top I've ruined today,' said Diggsy. While all of us had found snow, Diggsy had managed to dive onto dog shit.

'Are there fuckin' wolves in these hills or what?' he added.

'Shut it,' said the uninjured squaddie. 'There's no wolves out there, but there *is* a sniper, so for fuck's sake keep it down.' He angled his body towards the Saracen. His colleague had reached it. We stayed schtum while he radioed in.

I had fallen beside Scarlet. We lay with our backs to each other, top to toe. We were cold and our clothes were getting wet. The heat from our bodies was melting the snow beneath us. The capillary action drew icy water into our ribs and round our thighs. I wanted to say something to her. I wanted to tell her it was all going to be OK. But we couldn't talk.

I manoeuvred my head under my arm, trying to steal a look at her face. At the very least I could give her a nod or a smile, some bit of non-verbal reassurance. But her body was turned away from me and I could only make out the back of her head. Her hair was soaked. It had turned a darker red. It fanned across the snow like blood from an exit wound. Her shoulders were jerking. She was crying. I groped behind me, trying to find her hand. But I could only grab air and fistfuls of snow. I tried another tactic. I slid my leg back as far as I could, till twine started pinging from my hamstring. My foot met her shoulder and steadied it. In slow, steady increments, her jerking stopped.

And then I heard a familiar noise. The last time I had heard such a noise I had a bag over my head. It was unmistakable. It was a helicopter.

The soldier shouted from the Saracen, 'Soupie . . . Weejee . . . we've got cover. Let's get out of here.' He reversed his vehicle towards us.

'But what about my fingers?' asked Scouser.

'No time. Jump in.'

'You're not just going to leave us here,' I said. 'Not at the mercy of some sniper?'

Scouser looked incredulous. 'You think someone's trying to assassinate your band?' he asked. 'Christ, you lot must really suck.'

But before he could get away, Scarlet had something for him.

'Wait,' she said. 'I've found one of your fingers,' she said.

She raised one of her own, her middle finger, and held it to his face.

10

We drove through Dublin in silence.

Well, not silence exactly. Our ears had to endure a relentless assault by Public Enemy. Mags had kept the volume at 11 since the border. There had been little need to stop for petrol, the van could have bounced through County Louth powered by stereo alone.

But the six of us had remained silent.

I was becoming increasingly paranoid. What if that bullet had been meant for me? What if the IRA had somehow got wind that I was after O'Hanlon? What if they knew I was acting under instruction from the RUC Chief Constable? Had they despatched a gunman with orders to take me out? And what if the shot *was* an accurate one? What if the gunman really did mean to hit the soldier? Why not kill him? Why shoot his hand? The bullet had taken his fingers the moment they touched Scarlet's bottom. Surely not, I thought.

I had been warned not to lay a finger on Scarlet. I had been promised a bullet if I did. Was the same guy following us, the one who had threatened me? Would he shoot a soldier just because he brushed Scarlet's ass? Who was this guy anyway? Was he Scarlet's stalker? You read about nuts like that. One thing was certain, this nut had more advanced weaponry than the sawn-off shotgun he so prosaically brandished at me. This nut had silent, pinpoint weaponry.

I asked Diggsy to warn me the second he saw a red dot illuminating my forehead.

O'Connell Street was hiving. Shoppers remained undeterred by the cold snap. Not that you could gauge the temperature from the cramped comfort of a robustly heated van. Duffles, muffs and bobble hats provided the only clues to the cold outside. The pavements were bone dry. The sky was a flat, peacock blue. A watery sun gilded the city. This was summer diluted.

The tape cut out, triggering the van's radio. The dial straddled stations, seguing between the Gaelic footie and some religious broadcast: 'Our Lord Jesus *receives a hospital ball from Noel Mannion and as the Meath forwards pile in* the blood begins to weep from his hands and feet.'

Mags switched it off.

'Where am I dropping you guys?' she asked.

'Anywhere here will do. We'll probably grab a wee B&B near the train station. I've got to catch a return to Dundalk tomorrow morning.'

'Are you sure?' asked Mags.

'Yeah, because you could stay with us,' said Scarlet.

'No thanks. I'm too old to kip in student digs. I don't fancy waking up with my cheek glued to some sticky Rathmines carpet. And anyway, I didn't bring a sleeping bag.'

'No, but you did bring a box of wine,' said Diggsy. 'When you finish it, you can inflate the silver bag and use it as a pillow. No sticky carpet need grace your fair cheek.'

'What makes you think we're staying in a dive?' asked Scarlet.

'You're on an independent record label,' I replied. 'You drive yourself to your own gigs. In a stolen van. I'm just guessing here, but I'll bet your tour budget does not extend to the penthouse at the Clarence. No, I reckon you're kipping on floors. That's unless you're close personal friends of Bono or the Edge.'

'The Clarence?' laughed Scarlet. 'It's not plush enough for girls like us. Oh no, the place we're staying is far more ostentatious. Come on. There's plenty room. And it won't cost you a penny.'

'I'm not sure,' I said.

'Look, we're all a bit shaken up after this morning. We've got two gigs this weekend that could make or break us. I don't want to sound girly, because we women can handle ourselves, but I think we'd feel a bit better if we had a couple big strong guys staying with us.'

'Sorry,' I said. 'The adjectives *big* and *strong* do not apply to Diggsy and me. *Lily* and *livered*, yes.'

'Hold on,' said Diggsy. 'You're forgetting, I'm in the WWF.'

'Aye, you are,' I said. 'The World Wildlife Fund.'

Scarlet touched my shoulder. 'Don't make me beg, Jay.'

This was the first time she had used my Christian name. And she knew it, too. She knew exactly what she was doing.

'OK, then. But don't you lot already have security at your gigs? What about those gorillas in suits that you brought to the Limelight?'

Scarlet retracted her hand. 'Sorry, Jay, I don't know what you're on about.'

I let it go, but only because she had said my name again.

We seemed to be driving south-east of the city. I was

not that familiar with Dublin and I had to wait until we passed Lansdowne Road to get my bearings. We raced a DART through Sandymount, then Mags slipped the van into fifth and we hit the coast road. To our left, the Liffey spilled into the sea.

We drove another ten minutes along Dublin Bay until a sign welcomed us to 'Dalkey', '*Deilig Inis*' and '(Thorn Island)', like it couldn't make its mind up. Elegant Victorian terraces lined the sleepy streets, their names suggesting that the town's inhabitants harboured delusions of living on the Italian Mediterranean coast – Vico, Sorrento, Bellamarina. And who could blame them, for Dalkey enjoyed sea views to rival any in Sicily.

'Is anyone going to tell me where we're staying?' I asked.

We pulled off the main road and descended a steep hill that took us past the harbour. The Rosslare lifeboat was being repaired on the slip. Mags slowed the Mercedes like she was looking for a turning.

'This is it,' said Scarlet.

The van swung right, seemingly straight into a clump of close-knit trees. They concealed a private road. We trundled along it, our tyres crunching big chips of gravel the colour of minced meat. It quickly dawned on me that this was no private road. This was somebody's driveway. We must have travelled a good 200 yards before we arrived at a house straight out of Edgar Allan Poe.

'Shit,' said Diggsy. 'Are we staying with the Addams Family?'

'Welcome to my home,' said Scarlet.

'Your home?' I asked. 'But it has turrets. And a spire. Nobody lives in a house with a spire, not unless they drink blood.'

121

'Well, my parents do.'

'Your parents drink blood?'

'No. At least, not to my knowledge. This is our holiday home.'

'Your holiday home? Why can't you be like normal people and keep a rusty caravan in Millisle?'

'Stop complaining, we've got the place to ourselves. My folks are in New York for the weekend. They're doing their Christmas shopping.'

'Well, I hope they bring you back something nice. Like a diamanté coffin.'

Scarlet showed us inside. The sleeping arrangements were not discussed but I guessed we'd get a room each. The place was huge. You could have hit a seven iron down the hall. With only minimal conversion the fireplace that dominated the drawing room would've made a nice granny flat. The chandeliers were the sort you more commonly see Errol Flynn swinging from.

We carried our stuff through to the back of the house. I suggested we should stop halfway and set up camp for the night, to break the journey, but Scarlet insisted we soldier on. It was worth the hike. A modern extension had been sympathetically added to the rear of the old building. It was laid out on two levels, the lower level being entirely consumed by a swimming pool. The upper mezzanine afforded a vertiginous view out to sea. The water was framed by a blood-coloured Japanese maple that fell over the cliff at the foot of the garden. It presided over a small island, a solitary dollop of green in the foaming blue, from which a stone column appeared to periscope.

'That's Dalkey Island,' said Scarlet. 'If any of you fancy a swim, there are towels by the steam room.'

'Why would I want to swim out there? It's

uninhabited. All I can see is grass, a couple of gannets, and a big stone chimney thing.'

'The big stone chimney thing is a Martello tower. And I wasn't asking you if you fancied swimming out to the island, I was asking you if you fancied a dip in our pool.'

'Thank God for that. I was about to cover myself in goose fat.'

'Do we have time, Scar?' asked Mags.

'Yeah, our soundcheck's at four. The Point's only half an hour away in the van. So get your cossies on.'

'I didn't bring a swimming costume,' said Derbhla.

'Me neither,' said Kate.

'Well,' said Scarlet. 'Bra and pants it is. I'm sure the boys won't mind.'

'I do,' I said. 'No way am I wearing a bra.'

'I think we all need to get out of our clothes,' said Scarlet. 'We're all mingin' after this morning. Especially yer man.' She indicated Diggsy, adding, 'He's covered in wolf shite.'

I was wrong about the bedrooms. There were six of them all right, but her parents' room was strictly out of bounds. I had to double up with Diggsy. We changed out of our clothes, each of us making a conscientious effort to avoid catching sight of the other's penis. Diggsy reloaded his camera and counted his remaining film. He held up four rolls between the fingers and thumb of one hand.

'Do you think Scarlet would let me put these in her fridge?' he asked.

'So that's what they mean by freeze-frame photography,' I said.

'No, these are Ilford black and white. I need to keep them cool. And anyway, I don't want to take all my film out to tonight's gig. I'll only use it or lose it.'

Diggsy and I located the kitchen and opened the giant Smeg. He slid his film in beside a tall jug of cloudy red liquid. While we had been freshening up, Scarlet had been preparing Sea Breeze.

We found her by the pool. She had abandoned her wet ski pants in favour of a bikini and sarong that matched her cranberry cocktail. She could have starred in an ad for Special K.

Derbhla and Kate sat on the side of the pool with their legs in the flat blue water. Diggsy and Mags disappeared into the sauna. I shepherded Scarlet onto a bamboo sofa on the upper mezzanine.

'This is some pad,' I said, sitting myself beside her. 'What do your parents do?'

Scarlet chewed her straw, like it was a trick question.

'My dad's in the import-export business.'

'What does he trade?'

Again, it took her a moment to answer. I guessed she had been interviewed before. She may only have been on the cusp of stardom but already she had learned to choose her words carefully. Or perhaps she was just naturally aloof. Whatever she was, a pro or a natural, it dismayed me. Not because I hoped that she'd trip up and divulge something she shouldn't, but because she was treating me as a journalist and not a friend. In her head she had already defined our relationship and now she assumed her role.

'Whisky,' she said. 'He imports and exports whisky.' My attention was drawn to a sideboard lined with single malts. She elaborated. 'He imports the Scottish stuff and exports the Irish stuff. It's very lucrative.'

'Clearly,' I said, casting my eyes to the pool.

'Did you know there are over a thousand Scottish whiskies?' said Scarlet. She had picked up a bottle of Glen Scotia and was reading from the label.

'No, I wasn't aware of that. I only know two things about whisky. I know that no two whiskies are alike. And I know that ninety-nine per cent of whisky drinkers can't tell the difference between them. If you keep stating the first point while bearing the second in mind, you can sound like a right little connoisseur.'

'I don't touch the stuff myself,' she said.

'Not even Red Label?'

'You think I'm stupid, don't you,' she said. 'You think this red thing is all an act, an image, something I'll snap out of the second the band splits up. You think I'm a fake.'

I didn't know what to say. She was right. I had thought all those things. But the more time I spent with her, the more I struggled to imagine Scarlet being any other way. So what if she only wore red clothes, drank red drinks, ate red Smarties and smoked Embassy Reds? Big deal that she'd christened herself Scarlet and dyed her hair the eponymous colour. Who was she hurting?

'I don't think you're a fake,' I replied. 'I think you're . . . single-minded.'

'Single-minded?' She wrinkled her nose. 'Do I take that as a compliment?'

'Yes. It means you're strong-willed, intelligent, forceful, outstanding, unique. I don't think you're a fake. I think you're . . .'

'What's the matter, Jay, lost your thesaurus?'

'. . . stunning. I do. I think you're stunning.'

There was a moment of dead air. My cheeks grew hot. Scarlet smiled.

'Who's red now?' she asked.

She was right. Red is the colour of domination. She had got me where she wanted me.

'Don't be embarrassed,' she said. 'I really appreciate it. Nobody has ever complimented me like that. Despite appearances, I'm not as confident as people think. In one way this *is* an act – the clothes, the hair, the name. I like to project strength because deep down I've always lacked it.'

'Is that what all that stuff was back at the border . . . all that kerfuffle about an occupied Ireland?'

'No, that's different. That's politics. I've never lacked conviction in my politics.'

'You surprise me. I didn't have you down as a rabid Republican. Your songs aren't political, at least, not the ones I can make out. Hold on, your encore – "Dead Man's Hole" – is that a reference to a bullet hole, the hole through which the life of a gunned-down Irish rebel is allowed to ebb away?'

Scarlet laughed. She shook her straw and loudly vacuumed up the last of her drink. She giggled again.

'The Dead Man's Hole. It's a large pool that the sea has carved into the rocks just a mile round the headland from here. I used to go down there as a wee girl. On a clear day you could see Anglesey. My dad said it was named the Dead Man's Hole because it was bottomless. The locals believe that if you dived into it, you would never come up again. There were fish in it though . . . horny gobblers.'

'Horny gobblers? Sounds like one of Diggsy's dodgy videos.'

Scarlet narrowed her eyes. The girl wasn't to be interrupted.

'The fish would come up to the surface and I'd try to grab them, but their gills were covered in sharp spikes. So my dad made me a net. He emptied some oranges out of their bag and strung the netting round a coat hanger. He fixed it to the end of a tomato cane and with it I caught my first horny gobbler. I set the net in a smaller rock pool, so the fish could breathe, while I collected corks from the shore. When I'd gathered enough, I snapped the corks in two and stuck the broken halves onto the horny gobbler's spikes. Then I released him back into the Dead Man's Hole. And each time he dived for the bottom, he floated straight back up to the surface.'

'And that's what the song is about?' I asked.

'Sort of. It's a song for anyone suffering from depression.'

'A real air-puncher, then.'

Again, Scarlet did that narrowing thing with her eyes. Either her patience was withering, or her contact lenses needed changing.

'I'm serious,' she said. 'For some people, life can seem like a bottomless pool, one that they can't get out of. They let it drag them under. I know. I've been there. But the song offers hope. If you can allow yourself to be buoyed by those closest to you, you can rise above your anxieties and float to the surface, like my fish. The song is about survival.'

'What happened to your fish?'

'He starved to death. Refill?'

Scarlet took our glasses into the kitchen.

I found it hard to see what anxieties she could have suffered. She was intelligent, articulate and attractive. She really *was* stunning. And her family were comfortably well off. Her upbringing sounded idyllic, what little of it she had been prepared to share. And she fronted a rock band, writing and performing her own music. The girl had it all. Young women would kill to be her. Young men would kill to be with her.

And then it hit me. Would a gunman kill to be with her? Would a gunman kill to stop someone else being

127

with her? What if someone really was stalking her? And what if she knew it?

We had all been scared back there, back at the border. The collective silence as we hared it down to Dublin was testament to how much the shooting had spooked us. But Scarlet had seemed the most affected. While five of us had lain in the snow, stiff as boards, totally petrified, Scarlet hadn't been able to keep still. Her shoulders rocked and her body rolled as she fought some deeper, uncontrollable fear.

Maybe she knew. Maybe she knew that the bullet was meant for her, indirectly, as a message and a reminder. The message – *I am out here, watching you.* The reminder – *you belong to me.*

If this were true, and I wasn't just getting carried away on a Sea Breeze, then it explained her asking Diggsy and me to spend the night with the band.

And if Scarlet had a stalker, he would undoubtedly be contributing to the anxiety and depression she spoke of.

11

The Point opened its doors. A hundred teenagers raced to the front, every one of them satisfying the qualifying time for the Irish Olympic sprint team. They formed a crush front of stage, inexplicable given the fifty metres of empty hall behind them. The metal barriers branded waffle marks onto cheeks and chests. The kids had come to see PJ Harvey but it was likely they would starve themselves of oxygen by the time The Harlots took the stage.

I guzzled the saccharine dregs of a four-punt Sprite and kicked the cardboard cup along the concrete floor. I had left Scarlet and the girls in their dressing room, putting their faces on, psyching themselves up. They had only just finished their soundcheck. We had arrived at the venue over an hour late. Before we left Dalkey, Diggsy had insisted on shooting the girls by the pool.

The Harlots' equipment was already set up on stage. A roadie strutted round it, looking self-important. He enjoyed the notable distinction of being both bald and ponytailed. He lifted Scarlet's red Les Paul off its stand and threw the strap over his shoulder. He strummed it three times. He aimed a quizzical look towards the sound desk at the back of the venue. He strummed again. This time he acknowledged the desk with a confident thumbs up. I turned round. The desk was unattended. And the guitar wasn't plugged in. He positioned himself behind the microphone and spoke into it, listing a football tactic, a mobile telecommunications company, a university degree and an African archbishop: 'One-two . . . one-2-one . . . 2:1 . . . Tutu.' He then secured everything to the stage floor with gaffer tape – leads, cables, pedals, stands, amps, guitars, even his own foot at one point.

I had left the backstage VIP area in search of a phone. I was carrying my mobile and the reception was good, but I needed to find a payphone. I needed to call Meeks.

He had given me a number where he could be contacted 24/7. It was a Belfast number and he had made me repeat it over and over again until I knew it by heart. He had cautioned me never to write it down.

At first I thought he was giving me his home number. I was excited by the prospect of putting a crank call in to the RUC Chief Constable: *'Hello, Stephen, Chris Tarrant here. I've got your friend Martin O'Hanlon in the studio. With your help we can get him to £64,000. He's going to give you a question with four possible answers* (adopt clipped West Belfast accent) *– Hi, Stephen, which of the following devices is about to be thrown through your window . . . a petrol bomb, a nail bomb, a coffee-jar bomb, or a fizz bomb?'*

But from the protocol that Meeks had attached to the number, I guessed it was that of an intermediary. We had to assume codenames. Meeks suggested we adopt our old nicknames, as they were easy to remember. I had to dial the number from a payphone and give my name as Big Jessie. I had to ask for Steeky and state the number of the payphone. Then I had to replace the handset and wait.

I did as I was instructed and waited by a phone directly outside the venue. It wasn't the most private place to take a confidential call from the head of Northern Ireland's police force, but it was the only payphone I could find on Dublin's North Wall Quay. The place was crawling with ticket touts and their mumbled offers to 'buy or sell', like they were reluctant stock traders. Food vendors lined the quayside promising *'Minrils! Sangwidges! Alcayhalic bivridges!'* Scores of opportunists milled through the crowd peddling *'PJ Hairvey T-shorts! PJ Hairvey progrims! Hairlots bandannas!'*

The phone rang.

I answered it. 'Hello, Domino's Pizza.'

'You're funny, Black,' said Stephen Meeks. 'I don't have long, so let's dispense with the wisecracks. First things first, why are you on the end of a Dublin number?'

'I thought I'd come down for the weekend, visit the Book of Kells, do the Joyce tour, generally clear my head.'

'No wisecracks, Jessie. Remember, it was you that phoned me. I assume you wanted more than a chat.'

'OK, I'm down in Dublin doing my day job, interviewing a band. But it's not all work and no play. Tomorrow I've been invited to a Sinn Fein shindig in Dundalk. I get to wear my new frock.'

'You'll be at the Ard Fheis?'

'Aye. Front-row seat, right among the press pack. Apparently we're each allowed to ask Martin O'Hanlon one question. I was thinking of asking him where he got his hair done.'

131

'Listen to me, Jessie. You'd better get something on him and soon. Our recently resigned First Minister, George McCrea, flew over to Westminster this morning to confront the Prime Minister. He and his fellow Unionists threw their toys out of the pram during questions. As you know, the slimmest majority often decides voting in the House of Commons. The Unionists can often tip the balance. This morning McCrea threatened to turn his party's vote against the Government unless the Prime Minister postpones our ministerial re-election. He's trying to buy time to see if there's any move on decommissioning. He's losing face. He realizes his resignation could backfire on him. He knows that O'Hanlon could get in by default.'

'And what are the Government going to do?'

'Nothing. That's my point. They can do nothing. It would be unconstitutional. George McCrea's credibility has been blown out of the water. His resignation has achieved nothing. All it has done is open the door for Sinn Fein. And his threats are empty. The Government aren't listening to him. He cut a sorry figure on the lunchtime news. Headless bloody chicken. The *Irish News* is already hailing O'Hanlon as our new First Minister. It seems that nothing's going to stop him.'

'We'll see,' I said.

'Tell me you've got something,' said Meeks. His voice was a curious mixture of hope and scepticism.

'I might have,' I said. 'I think O'Hanlon had a sexual relationship with Kate Owen.'

'Jay, I've told you before, cut the wisecracks. This is serious.'

'No, really. Martin O'Hanlon attended Queen's at the same time as Kate Owen. I'm pretty sure they were an item.'

'How sure? I mean, this is massive. Marty O'Hanlon and Kate Owen ... fuck. Mind you, I've always thought Kate was a bit of a looker, an oldie but goodie. What proof do you have?'

'I've got a few photos of them at a university ball. I won't really know how damaging they are until I confront O'Hanlon. If things get hairy, I'll know the story's a good 'un.'

'I'll stick a couple plain clothes down in Dundalk. They'll see you're not harmed. You do what you have to do. But I'll need more than a few snaps. This is dynamite, Jay. You can't even begin to think of the implications.'

'Oh, I can. And listen, while I've got your undivided, I was going to ask you a favour,' I said.

'Fire away.'

'I've got a friend down here. She thinks she's being stalked. What's more, I believe her. I want a couple of your boys to check it out.'

'I don't run a charity, Jessie. If some dumb southern cow thinks someone's thieving her underwear from her washing line, tell her to take it up with the Gardai. Lord knows it'll give them something to do.'

'*Hey, mistor, horry up. I need to phone me ma.*' A girl's voice, behind me.

'Steeky, I've got to go. I'll call you tomorrow.'

'I'm expecting good news,' said Meeks. 'Remember, the file on Miles Huggins is in my top drawer. Even after five years it still makes interesting reading.'

'*Mistor. Me ma. She'll have me guts for feckin' gartors.*'

I turned round, handset primed, ready to wind it round the wee girl's throat.

'Carmel?' I put the phone down.

'Evening, Jay,' said Karma.

133

'What's with the accent? What are you doing here?'

'Uch, I've had it up to here with work. I need a break. I swapped shifts with one of the juniors. I knew youse boys were coming down for the gig, so I thought I'd join you. I was just about to call you on my mobile when I saw you on the phone.'

'How did you get down?'

Karma jingled her car keys. 'In the death trap.'

'Come on then,' I said. 'Diggsy's backstage.'

'Wait, I need to get a ticket.'

'No you don't. Access all areas.' I gave her my pass. 'I'll say I lost mine. They saw me go out. You can vouch for me. Just pretend to be a Harlot.'

'That's never been a problem,' said Karma.

It was a breeze. We were admitted through a rear door and were in The Harlots' dressing room in no time. There wasn't a soul inside. The room contained a couple cracked plastic chairs, a sink, and a table on which sat a half-empty bottle of champagne, four plastic cups (red lipstick kissed the rim of one of them), a set list, a dozen doubled-up fag butts and a litre bottle of mineral water that acted as a vase for a healthy clot of red roses. Every connotation of red out-fit – spangly, silky, stripy, spotty, sultry, skimpy and downright silly – was hanging from an exposed scaffold pole. The girls' bags were stuffed underneath, along with Diggsy's camera case. And on the large mirror someone had scrawled lipstick graffiti: *Go Girls – Polly x.*

Diggsy lurched through the door, sucking a bottle of San Miguel.

'Karma! How's about ye?' he said. 'It's fuckin' magic in here. Free booze and everything. I've just been neck-ing some cold 'uns with PJ's road crew. Nice lads. They're going to introduce me to her after the gig. You

134

never know, I could be directing the video for her next single.'

'You could start by directing me to Scarlet,' I said.

'She's in the wee girls' room. She took a panic attack.'

'Shit.'

'Shall I go and see if she's all right?' asked Karma.

'See if who's all right?' asked Scarlet. She led the rest of the girls into the room.

'Diggsy said you took a panic attack,' I said.

'I'm fine. I always get the butterflies before a gig. Hypertension. But I'm fine. Two glasses of champagne and a couple of these little darlings . . .' Scarlet held up a small brown bottle. She tipped two pills onto her palm and slapped them into her mouth. '. . . and I'm right as rain.'

'What are they?' asked Karma.

'Beta blockers,' said Scarlet. 'They help me relax.'

'You really shouldn't mix them with alcohol.'

'And who are you, my mother?'

'I'm a nurse.'

They had only just met each other and already there were sparks.

Funny how that sometimes happens with women. And funny how it almost invariably happens with Karma and the women I want to get close to. I'd always put it down to the same desire to protect me that she'd first shown by a cold Fermanagh lake. I guessed she didn't yet think I was big enough or ugly enough to get hurt. And maybe I played on this. Maybe I liked having a 'big sister' watching out for me, making sure I didn't trip up. God knows I've tripped up in my time. I've fallen arse-over-tit into cowpats laced with broken glass, on the odd occasion. I needed watching.

'Scarlet, this is Karma, my friend and flatmate. And

Karma, this is Scarlet, my . . . my . . . I'm shadowing her band.'

'I know who she is,' said Karma, a little tartly.

'I'd love to chat,' said Scarlet, 'but I've got to do my voice exercises.' She tipped her head back, took a deep breath and held her arms straight out in front of her, perpendicular to her chest. She opened her throat and sang a scale. Rather, she didn't *sing* the notes so much as *bark* them. Deep, guttural, emphysemic yelps. She barked her way up and then down an octave. This she repeated, while jiggling her wrists. It was a convincing impersonation of the madwoman in the attic, and very disconcerting.

'Woah,' said Diggsy. 'I've got to get a photo of this.' He asked me to hold his beer while he retrieved his camera from its case.

Mags, Kate and Derbhla seemed able to ignore Scarlet's St Vitus's dance. They were indulging themselves in their own rituals – drinking champagne, eating chocolate, rolling bad joints. Diggsy gauged the light and positioned himself on his knees in front of Scarlet. He aimed his lens, focusing and refocusing it. A smile appeared under it. Diggsy depressed his finger and – nothing. He examined the camera. 'Shit,' he said. 'There's no film in it. Somebody's nicked the film.'

'What do you mean, somebody's nicked it?' I asked. 'Are you sure you haven't just forgotten to load it?'

'No. Definitely not. I ran off half a roll this afternoon, by the pool. I was saving the rest of the shots for this evening.'

Scarlet stopped barking. The girls stopped eating and drinking and smoking. The horror had registered.

Kate was first to react. 'You mean someone out there has got photos of all of us in our underwear?'

136

'That's not all,' said Mags. Her face was a picture. 'At least youse lot were wearing underwear. Pete took photos of me in the sauna.'

Diggsy started to laugh. 'Oh, I get it. Point taken, Mags. Look, I'll give you the negatives. Now hand it over.'

'I didn't take the film, you daft prick.' She thumped his arm.

This was accompanied by a loud scream, but not from Diggsy. Scarlet's eyes were out of her head. 'Stop it! Just stop it!' She held herself, rubbing the tops of her arms. 'Someone has come into our dressing room. They've gone through our stuff. And they've got photographs of me . . . of all of us. How did they get in here? Who let them in? They've touched my stuff.'

Derbhla put an arm round her and lowered her onto one of the plastic chairs.

'That's right, Derbhla,' said Diggsy. 'You help your wee mate. Guilty conscience is it?'

'What?' asked Derbhla.

'Admit it. You took the film. I know you were uncomfortable being photographed in your undies, but you didn't have to steal it. Tell you what, let's call an amnesty. You give me the film back and I'll promise to scan your photos into my iMac and paint out all your cellulite.'

Diggsy got thumped again. By Derbhla, this time. But it could as easily have been me. This was serious. This was beyond a joke. Scarlet was in a right state. She sat forward in the chair, her red platform heels clicking against each other like there was no place like home. She placed a hand on her forehead, checking her temperature, fanning a cockatoo fringe.

'The Harlots?' A bubbly blonde danced through the door waving a clipboard. 'On in five, girls.' She pirouetted out again.

'Can you do this, Scar?' asked Mags.

Scarlet tipped the pill bottle onto her lips. She guzzled champagne.

'Aye,' she said. 'I can do this.'

She couldn't do it.

Two songs in and she froze. The dry ice could well have been liquid nitrogen. She stood catatonic in the UV glare. She held her throat. Her voice had deserted her.

The band struggled though three more numbers with Kate assuming vocal duties. It wasn't the same. They had become a Harlots tribute band. Each number sounded like it had been taken from one of those Seventies *Top of the Pops* LPs on which session musicians did their best (and their worst) to mimic the Top Ten artists of that year.

Scarlet pawed at her guitar strings, keeping her back to the crowd. Robbed of her voice, they were The Counterfeit Harlots.

We didn't hang around for PJ Harvey, much to the consternation of Diggsy who accused us all of blowing his career as a promo director. Mags promised him he could shoot a video for their next EP. It was the only way she could shut him up.

Scarlet had insisted on getting back to Dalkey. She was inconsolable.

We loaded the van.

Karma and I followed it down the east coast, tagging behind in the death trap – a prehistoric Datsun, commonly believed to be extinct. They no longer made the parts for her car, so if anything broke it stayed broken. The car lacked two hubcaps, half an exhaust and a rear door that opened. However, under

138

Karma's ownership it had gained a fluffy steering-wheel cover, a vanilla tree and a window sticker: *Nurses' pay makes me sick.*

The Datsun protested as Karma found top gear (third).

Each time a set of headlights bounced off the rear-view mirror and into my face, I thought it could be him – Scarlet's stalker. I asked Karma to slow down or speed up, trying to gauge whether the cars behind were hanging back or keeping pace. But the ones that slowed were simply turning off the road. And the ones that looked like they were about to ram into us, over-took us. As we neared Dalkey, our rear window became a blue-black void. We were not being followed.

'You like her, don't you?' said Karma.

'Who?'

'Don't, Jay. I've known you too long.'

'You mean Scarlet?'

'No, I mean Mother fucking Teresa. Of course I mean Scarlet. I see the way you look at her. You like her.'

'She's all right.'

Karma threw me a sceptical look, the sort of look a nurse gives to a guy with an orange up his ass who claims he slipped on the floor tiles while carrying a fruit bowl into his bathroom. She turned down the car's heating and directed the air off our faces.

'What are you doing that for?' I protested, turning it up again.

'Sorry, I thought you were hot. Your face looked flushed.'

She had known me too long.

'All right, you win. Yes, I like her. I like her a lot. I like the way she looks. I like the way she smells. I like

139

the way she moves, the way she talks, the way she sings—'

'Sings?' Karma laughed, choking on her Polo mint. The broken bits dropped onto her lap like she'd lost her baby teeth in one go.

'Yes,' I asserted. 'I love her voice. Tonight was an exception. You saw how nervous she was before the gig.'

'Are you sure *nervous* is the right word? Don't you mean *unstable*? She was wolfing those pills like they were Smarties.'

'No she wasn't. Scarlet only eats red Smarties.'

'Exactly. The girl's a fruitcake.'

The Mercedes slowed down and swung into the trees. As we followed it up the gravel drive, security lights illuminated the house.

'See,' said Karma, nodding at the stone building. 'I told you she's nuts. She lives in a bloody sanatorium.'

12

The seven of us attacked the Scottish malt.

We followed in the footsteps of Johnson and Boswell
and journeyed to the Western Isles. Our expedition
began on the eastern seaboard of Aberdeenshire.
'*Slainte mhor!*' we cried as we raised cut-crystal
glasses, their bottoms heavy with Lochnagar. From the
outset it was bracing, windswept and keen. We forged
on to Elgin, pausing only to bathe in the pure and
ethereal waters of the River Spey – known to locals as
Glenfiddich and Cardhu. We moved northwards
through Inverness, the golden blood of Scotia pump-
ing through our veins. Glenmorangie was our stern
and muscular guide. A temperamental ocean carried
us to the isolated Orkneys where we found solace in
Highland Park, that most northerly of outposts. Our
mood became stoical and our conversation phleg-
matic. It was time to press on. But only four of our
party made it to the brackish waters of Oban. We
swam to the Isle of Jura, we negotiated a seemingly
impenetrable Islay Mist and we warmed our bodies
round a Laphroaig fire. Peat filled our nostrils and seaweed filled our boots. Our journey ended in
Bruichladdich, the most westerly of westerlies. We

tore off our shirts, we beat the heather and we snatched black grouse from the air with our bare teeth. Nothing could stop us. We were bravehearts. We had tasted *uisge beatha*. We were filled with the Water of Life.

We were fucking hammered.

Scarlet, Mags, Diggsy and I were the last four standing. Karma had switched to water. Derbhla and Kate had gone to bed, with each other, one of many revelations that evening. The whisky was up to its tricks.

Scarlet inserted another CD – 'Bíum Bíum Bambaló', a darkly beautiful rendering of a traditional Icelandic lullaby by Sigur Rós. It said much about her. She uncapped another malt.

'This one's called Glenlivet.'

'Glenmiller?' queried Diggsy.

'No,' I corrected. 'If it was Glenmiller, it would come in a little brown jug.'

Scarlet filled my glass to the height of the design cut into it. I swirled the pale amber liquid and brought it to my mouth. The whisky cauterized my nostrils before my lips could even get to it. I sucked it through my teeth and trilled it on my tongue.

'Hmm . . . I'm getting lots of peat and a suggestion of damp tweed.' I swallowed hard. 'Uhuh . . . yes . . . pronounced notes of burnt cottage with sheep dip in the finish.' I propped the glass on my knee. 'God knows what I'll find when I floss tonight . . . midges, mice droppings, slivers of Highland granite.'

'This is much nicer than Irish whisky,' said Diggsy. He had made a Lazarus-like recovery from his Bushmills hangover.

'What's the difference?' asked Karma.

'Irish whisky is sweeter because no peat is used in

the kilns,' said Scarlet. 'Not that I would know, I don't drink the stuff.' She necked her sixth Scotch.

'That's ironic, isn't it?' said Mags. She lay with her head on Diggsy's chest. 'Ireland has more bogland than anywhere on earth and yet nobody thought to use the peat to make whisky. I'd call that an oversight.'

'Gosh,' said Scarlet. 'This one's older than me.' She had procured another bottle from Daddy's diminishing collection. She read the label. 'Scald Lochnadubh sotis.' She had started to slur her words. 'Least, I think thass how you say it. Says here iss fifty year sold.'

She set the dusty bottle on the floor, in the middle of our circle. She smoothed her skirt and sat down cross-legged. While everyone gazed in reverential awe at the bottle of Lochnadubh, this avatar of whiskies – kilned with prehistoric peat (formed from the compressed bodies of woolly mammoths and cut from a croft belonging to Rabbie Burns himself) – I too stared in breathless admiration. At Scarlet's scarlet panties.

She caught me looking and slowly closed her thighs, bringing her red knee socks together. She leaned across and opened the bottle. She filled her glass. As she sat upright she allowed her legs to relax again. She sipped her whisky, making no attempt to cover herself. She kept her eyes on me the whole time, her compound eyes, for they refracted through the crystal cuts in her multifaceted glass.

In other circumstances I might have interpreted this as a come-on, but Scarlet was high on whisky and low on self-esteem.

'Scarlet, I can see your knickers,' said Diggsy.

Scarlet clamped her legs together again. 'Can't,' she said.

'If I close my eyes really hard I can,' said Diggsy.

Scarlet curled her lip at him.

'Last time I told a girl that I could see her knickers,' said Diggsy, 'she looked embarrassed and quickly closed her handbag.'

Scarlet's head lolled forward, a cataleptic lunge. She was falling asleep. I grabbed her shoulder before she keeled over. I unpeeled her fingers from her whisky glass and set it on the carpet.

'I don't think you should be drinking that,' I said.

'And why not?'

'One, you're falling asleep. And two, it's probably about a hundred quid a sip. Your father already faces financial ruin after the amount we've drunk. Let's not compound his debts.'

'Fuckim. He can stick it up hissole. Fucker deserves all he gets.' Scarlet snatched the glass and knocked back half a grand's worth of Scotland's finest in one.

'He's right, Scar. You've had enough.' Mags got to the bottle before her pickled friend could steal a refill.

Scarlet was left grabbing air. 'Bitch. Smy bottle. Smy house. I can do what I want.' Her words were harsh and serrated, her body language capricious. This wasn't the Scarlet I knew. This was Scarlett O'Hara, with a skinful.

'Fuck the lot of youse,' she screamed. 'I'mway fra pee. Thassif I'm ALLOWED?' The moment she stood up she went as white as a church candle. All the blood had gone to her eyeballs. They fell on each of us in turn. 'Magdalene? . . . Diggsy? . . . Florence Nightingale? . . . Mr Black? . . . S'at OK? Can I go to the toilet?'

The CD stopped.

I nodded.

Scarlet snatched her bag and lurched unsteadily out of the room.

The silence was more than any of us could bear. We

144

did our best to fill it. Mags skinned up. Diggsy changed the CD, while Karma argued with him over his selection. I gathered up the whisky bottles and returned them to their rightful place.

Mags must have seen something in my face for she patted the carpet and invited me to sit down beside her.

'Just ignore her,' she said. 'Scarlet sometimes gets like this. Don't take it personally. She's taken her bag to the bog so I figure it's just a bad time of the month. And anyway, she's annoyed with herself, not you. She knows she screwed up tonight.'

'I thought you sounded great, considering,' I said.

'No we didn't. We sucked. But we have a chance to redeem ourselves tomorrow night. She seems to have got her voice back.'

'I'd wait till the morning before you say that. Whisky has this habit of dissolving your throat lining overnight. Tomorrow you'll hear her singing in the shower and you won't know whether it's Tom Waites or Barry White.'

Mags tore a strip of cardboard from Scarlet's empty packet of Reds. 'I blame all of us, really. We shouldn't have gone on stage tonight. You saw what she was like. That thing with the missing photos really freaked her.'

'Mags?'

'Aye.'

'This may sound stupid, but does Scarlet have any – how can I put it – any *overenthusiastic* fans?'

'How d'you mean?'

'Has she ever been followed? Does she ever get crank calls? Do things disappear from her washing line?'

Mags passed me the joint. 'You think someone's stalking her?'

'I can't be sure. But it might explain why she's so highly strung.'

'No. No way. If some pervert was harassing Scarlet, I would know about it. She would've told me. Scarlet tells me everything.'

'So you're absolutely sure that nobody's stalking her?'

Mags allowed herself a chuckle. 'The only person stalking Scarlet, Mr Black, is you.'

She had a point. Scarlet hadn't agreed to my accompanying the band down to Dublin. I had initially brokered the trip with Mags. Scarlet hadn't given me permission to follow her, so, in a sense, I *was* stalking her. Mags was right. I was hounding her, watching her every move, noting her every word. I had instructed Diggsy to take candid snaps of her. Christ, I knew she wore red silk panties with a cream lace trim. Who was doing the stalking?

I should back off, I thought. Tomorrow morning I would get up before Scarlet and head to Dundalk. Karma could drive me to the train station. And I wouldn't return to Dublin. I would give Scarlet some air.

'I think I'll turn in,' I said. 'Big day tomorrow. Tell Scar I said goodnight.'

'I'll clock off as well,' said Karma.

'Karma,' said Diggsy. 'You can take the other single in Jay's room.'

'Where will you sleep?' I asked.

'Loverboy's in with me,' said Mags. She slipped her hand up the back of Diggsy's T-shirt.

Karma and I moved to the kitchen and rinsed our glasses in the Belfast sink.

'Some place this,' said Karma. 'And you say there's a pool?'

'You haven't seen the pool?'

'Nope.'

'You haven't lived. Follow me.'

I led her towards the back of the house. The rear extension was almost totally shrouded in darkness. We stood on the upper mezzanine looking out to sea. The moon was full. It illuminated the silver surf. Dalkey Island surfaced from the water like a slick black whale. It regarded the house with an invisible, immutable eye. A long thread of white foam fizzed onto the beach and danced across its glossy stage, a chorus line of flotsam ghosts. Their transient spirits disappeared into the sand.

'Isn't that amazing?' said Karma.

'It's beautiful,' I said. 'If you stood here every night before you went to bed, you would surely say your prayers. Because if that view doesn't make you believe in a higher force, then nothing will.'

We stood in silent reverie and let the moon cool our faces.

'Right,' said Karma after barely a minute. 'Sod this for a game of soldiers, let's see the pool.'

My eyes had adjusted to the dark, so I was able to lead her towards the steps that would take us down to the lower floor. Green light wobbled round the walls as we descended, an indication that the pool's underwater lighting was on. It was also an indication that the water wasn't still. The liquid light boogalooed all over us, like we were walking into a Hockney. I approached the bottom of the stairs with some apprehension. Although I could hear no sound, I was convinced that something, or someone, was in the pool.

A cheese plant slapped my cheek as I walked out to the poolside. It had acted prematurely. You are

147

supposed to slap a person in the face *after*, not *before*, they receive a shock. The rubbery slap only made me alive to the reality of what I saw next: Scarlet, floating face down in the luminous green, her red hair pulsing like an anemone.

Karma was into the water before me. She lifted Scarlet's head, cupping a hand under her chin. She kicked backwards, pulling her onto a broad set of steps that rose grandly out of the water. I did what I could to help. I forced my hands under Scarlet's arms and locked them round her chest. I hauled her lifeless body onto the tiles.

Karma checked for a pulse. She couldn't find one in Scarlet's wrist. She pressed two fingers under her jawbone. Nothing. She tilted Scarlet's head back and opened her mouth. She held her hand above it. Not a breath. She pinched Scarlet's nose and commenced mouth-to-mouth. She tore Scarlet's shirt open. Red buttons skittered across the wet tiles and into the pool. Karma made a fist and hammered it down between Scarlet's exposed breasts.

'One hundred, two hundred, three hundred, four hundred, five hundred.'

Karma put her ear to Scarlet's mouth. She shook her head. She repeated the sequence, throwing all her weight onto Scarlet's sternum.

'One hundred, two hundred, three hundred, four hundred, five hundred.'

No response.

'Is she dead?' I asked.

'Yes,' said Karma. She was sweating. 'Technically, she's dead.'

'Technically?'

'Feel her,' said Karma.

I held Scarlet's hand. It was porcelain cold.

'Her body temperature has plummeted. But that's a good thing. Her brain will be cold too. If I can resuscitate her there's a good chance it won't be damaged. I've got to keep going.'

'Brain damaged?'

The possibility horrified me more than the thought of Scarlet dying. I couldn't bear to see this beautiful woman, this wonderful lucid being, condemned to some ignoble, vegetative existence. Robbed of her spark she would be no more than a hollow shell. Nobody deserves that.

Or is it that nobody deserves to *see* that? Were my motives selfish? If I couldn't get Scarlet back in one piece, did I want her back at all? Would I be as keen as Karma to pump her chest and fill her lungs with borrowed air if I thought she'd end up all distant and broken?

I didn't like myself for thinking it. But, as I watched Karma go to work on Scarlet, a part of me honestly hoped that she wouldn't revive her.

'One hundred, two hundred, three hundred, four hund—'

Scarlet coughed up chlorine.

'We've got her,' said Karma. She flipped Scarlet onto her side.

But her relief was short-lived. A milky fluid began to stream from Scarlet's nostrils. It bubbled round the edges of her ruby nose studs.

'Oh Christ,' said Karma. 'Not cocaine.'

'Coke? I don't understand. I knew the girls smoked hash. I didn't see any of them do a line.'

'Do you follow them into the toilets when they have so-called panic attacks?'

'No,' I conceded.

'There you go then.'

149

Scarlet's chest moved up and down. But each time she drew breath, we heard a soft, clicking sound. At first we thought it was her lungs. Then Karma spotted something in the pool. We looked down to see a small brown bottle bobbing in the water. It tapped against the ceramic flue. Karma fished it out. The bottle was empty. She immediately consulted the label.

'Shit,' she said. 'Sotacor. Sotalol hydrochloride. And she's had the lot.'

'I thought she was taking beta blockers.'

'These are,' said Karma. 'But Scarlet said she was taking them for hypertension. Sotalol hydrochloride is not designed to relieve hypertension. It depresses the myocardium and should only be taken if the patient is suffering from extreme ventricular arrhythmia.'

'You've lost me.'

'Sotacor slows the heart. It's for patients experiencing irregular heartbeats. If it is taken by someone with a normal heart rhythm it can have the opposite effect. It can throw the heart into irregular spasm.'

'Can it be fatal?'

'A dozen tablets, washed down with whisky and a cocaine chaser? I'd say that could be fatal.'

'What'll we do? Shall I call an ambulance?'

'No, we don't have time. You grab a duvet from upstairs. We'll wrap it round her and get her into my car. I'll drive her to a hospital.'

'But you can't, you've been drinking.'

'I've been drinking water, Jay. So shut your face and take her legs. We're going to carry her out to the death trap.'

'Let me go with you, to the hospital.'

'No, Jay. I'll be fine. I'm a nurse. They'll listen to me. Besides, drugs are involved and you're off your tits on whisky and dope. You don't want them thinking you put her in this state. The hospital may call the Guards. It's best you stay here. Oh, and just to be safe, I'd get the girls to flush all their drugs into the Irish Sea.'

We carried Scarlet through the hall. Karma despatched Mags upstairs to fetch a quilt. I forced Scarlet onto the passenger seat of the Datsun. I belted her in. Her head fell onto her chest. If Diggsy had taken a picture of her then, it would have looked like crime-scene photography from some grisly Mafia drive-by.

Karma remained in the house, searching for her keys.

I lifted Scarlet's head. I balled up my jacket and propped it under her chin. She was cold, but she wasn't shivering, like her natural reflexes had shut down. I pulled a lock of wet hair away from her lips. I could feel her breath on the back of my hand.

'That's it, Scarlet. Keep breathing. That's my girl.'

Now, more than ever, I wanted to tell her how I felt. All those things that I had been too embarrassed to say, I wanted to say them now. It would be so easy. I could speak my mind without fear of rejection. She was barely conscious. She would be in no position to protest. She would have to listen to me. She would have to hear me out.

But my words were nothing if she didn't pull through. I felt suddenly stupid. I was angry at myself. Why couldn't I have told her how I felt? Because I was embarrassed? Because I feared that she'd laugh in my face? You stupid bastard, Jay. Rejection is *nothing* compared to this.

I tucked her into the duvet, hoping, praying that she'd sit up and laugh in my face.

Karma ran out of the house arm-wrestling a fleece, keys in her teeth.

'You'll phone me, Karma. You'll phone me as soon as there's news.'

'Go inside, Jay. You're shivering.'

I watched the car crunch down the drive till it became one with the night.

'Do you think it was an accident?' asked Derbhla. She had brought in a tray of coffee. Kate followed with the biscuits. The two girls sat on the sofa and locked their legs round each other.

'You don't think she tried to kill herself?' asked Mags.

Diggsy handed her a mug. 'Careful, Maggie, it's hot.'

'Well, she'd had a lot of whisky,' I said. 'And we know she'd done a bit of coke, though none of you seem to know where she got it. I suppose she could have lost her bearings and fallen into the pool. Those tiles are slippy. But then there's the pills. She caned the lot of them. It doesn't look good.'

'No,' said Mags. 'I know Scar. No way would she try and kill herself. She's had problems in her life, but she got over them. The tablets were helping.' She gripped her mug tightly, trying to draw all the heat from it.

'How could they have been helping? According to Karma, Scarlet shouldn't have been prescribed those pills. Not unless those problems you mentioned were anything to do with her heart. Did Scarlet have a dicky heart?'

'I don't think so,' said Mags. 'Her problems were all to do with her father. You heard the way she cursed him.'

'Aye, I thought that was odd. Only this afternoon she was telling me how wonderful her dad was, how he told her stories about the sea, how he made her a fishing net from a piece of cane. They sounded close.'

'Well, I've never met him. But from the things that

152

Scarlet has said, he sounds like a right schizo. He'll take a length of cane and make her a net, but he's as likely to hit her round the legs with it.'

'Her dad abuses her?'

'*Abused* her. Past tense,' said Mags. She gulped down a good dose of coffee. She sucked on her neat tobacco roly. 'As soon as Scarlet hit her teens, her dad was all sweetness and light. All the abuse happened when she was a kid. It was never sexual. It was all physical. He was a violent man. She once told me about the time he bought the family a cruiser. The day it arrived, he took them out to the Isle of Man in it. Only they never made it. Scarlet was playing on the boat when she accidentally dropped her sunglasses over the side. Her dad went spare. And even though she couldn't swim, he grabbed her and threw her into the sea, you know, to get the sunglasses. She was only four. He even turned the boat round and pretended to leave her out there. So tonight wasn't the first time Scarlet nearly drowned. If her mother hadn't dived in after her, she wouldn't be here today. Course, her dad passed it all off as a joke. Sick bastard.'

Judging by their expressions, this story was as new to Kate and Derbhla as it was to Diggsy and me. Mags was clearly Scarlet's confidante.

'Is that why she's changed her name, to disassociate herself from her father?'

'No,' said Mags. 'She just likes red stuff.'

'Do you know her name?'

Mags looked anxiously at Derbhla and Kate. They nodded.

'Rourke,' said Mags. She flicked ash into her mug. 'Kelly Rourke. But don't tell her I told you. Band secret.'

'Shit,' said Diggsy. 'Who's that?'

The security lights had been triggered at the front of the house.

'It's the Guards,' said Derbhla.

'Don't panic. I got rid of all the gear,' said Mags.

I took responsibility for going to the front door. I was the only one fully dressed.

'Hello?' I asked the door. But there was no reply. I opened it. But the stone porch was vacant. A cold wind chased leaves over the gravel. I guessed that the lights must have been triggered by an animal.

'Who is it?' asked Mags, from the warmth of the hall.

'Oh, nobody. It was probably a fox.' I turned to rejoin her, but stopped. Some distance down the tree-lined drive, I could hear a car. It was the familiar, fat thrum of a car with half an exhaust.

'Karma?'

I ran for all I was worth.

I wasn't wearing shoes. Again I punished the soles of my feet, but this time on angular gravel. I ran directly into the car's headlights. They were set to full beam, preventing me from identifying the vehicle. I ducked out of the light and found the driver's door. It was the Datsun. The car looked like it had been hit. And it was empty.

At least, I thought it was. Then I saw movement in the back seat. I pressed my eyes to the glass. It was Karma. Her hair looked sticky, like she'd been tarred. I had to get her out, but the Datsun's rear doors could not be opened from the outside. The driver's door had taken the brunt of the impact. It had been powerful enough to dent the door and jam the lock, but the window remained intact. And the passenger door sat too close to a tree to be fully opened. I scrabbled around in the dirt until I found a rock big enough to smash the driver's window. I put my hand through and unsnibbed the rear door. I leaned in and pulled Karma onto the gravel.

Blood oozed from her open forehead. Her wrists were tied with a red knee sock.

'Scarlet,' she said. 'He's killed Scarlet.'

13

Karma unwrapped a needle from its sterile sheath. She threaded it with a length of suture. She held the assembly in a pair of tweezers and brought it to her head. She used my shaving mirror to locate a flap of skin just above her right eyebrow. Slowly, she stitched her own wound.

'I still reckon we should get you to hospital,' I said.

'Jay, I'm the nurse here. I'll be the judge of whether or not I need hospital treatment. I am not going to sit for seven hours in some soul-destroying casualty department. Not for a minor head wound. Not when I have my kit in the car. I can treat myself. It's only a couple of stitches. I could do it with my eyes closed.'

'I wouldn't,' I said. 'They may stay closed.'

Karma grabbed a pair of nail scissors and nipped the suture. 'There we are,' she said, proud of her handiwork. 'It's right along the frown line, so it shouldn't leave a scar.'

Typical Karma, I thought. Tougher than an armadillo in a flak jacket. She would have stitched her forehead with a twig and a bootlace if they had been the only materials at hand.

'Before you put your needle away,' I said, 'I've got some socks you could darn.'

She smiled, a sign she was coming round.

When I had first brought Karma into the house she was not completely lucid. I needed to know about Scarlet, but she would only repeat, *He's killed her.* She wouldn't elaborate. I tried to humour her, to win her round, but she was a closed book. I guessed it was shock. I asked the others to leave us alone while I tried to coax something out of her.

Karma wrapped the needle in cotton wool and dropped it into the kitchen bin. She swallowed a medicinal measure of the whisky I had prescribed her. She looked me in the eye. She was ready to talk.

'He's killed Scarlet, Jay. And it's all my fault.'

'No, Carmel. It's not your fault. This guy was on a mission. He followed us down here. You've got to relax and tell me what happened.'

Karma pushed her whisky glass into the middle of the table, like a child rejecting a plate of sprouts. 'I can't drink any more,' she said. 'My head's splitting. I need water.'

I rinsed the whisky from her glass and refilled it from the cold tap. Karma popped three Nurofen onto the table. She swallowed them with the water.

'I was trying to find the road out of Dalkey,' she said, 'the one that would take us back to Dublin. I knew I was heading the right way when I passed the harbour. The lifeboat was on my right. I remembered it was on our left when we followed the van here earlier. That's when the car hit me. He must have been waiting on the harbour slip. I didn't see him coming, he didn't have his headlights on. I just felt this bang to my right side and I thought I'd caught the quay wall. My head hit the steering wheel. The seat belts in the Datsun are

157

fucked.' Karma rubbed her right shoulder, at the spot where the belt would cross it.

'And Scarlet?'

'I'm trying to remember. I'd taken a knock to the forehead. I was disoriented. At first I thought the car had flipped right over. There was all this pressure in my head. I thought I was upside down.' Karma closed her eyes. 'That's right. And then I saw a figure, a man, running round the front of the car. And I knew I was the right way up. He opened the passenger door and pulled Scarlet out. He moved so quickly, I was convinced the car was on fire. I was sure it was going to explode. I thought he was very brave, pulling her free, putting his life on the line like that. But he carried her off somewhere. He was gone for some time. I started to panic. I thought, *why is he leaving me, why is he leaving me in a burning car?*' Karma opened her eyes again, allowing tears to fall out.

'Could you not get out?'

'I couldn't move my legs. I thought they'd got crushed. It was the shock, I guess. I tried to open my door, but it was jammed. And then he came back and my heart lifted. I knew I was going to be fine. He leaned across the passenger seat. I undid my seat belt and threw my arms round his neck. He was strong. He lifted me out. I was so bloody stupid. I thought he was rescuing me. I thought he had rescued us both. Stupid, stupid, stupid.'

Karma drummed her fists on her temples. They dislodged flecks of dried blood from her hairline.

'You're not stupid,' I said. 'How were you to know?'

'I actually thanked him. Can you believe that? I actually said *thank you*. And then I saw Scarlet and I knew why he had been gone such a long time. She was lying on the grassy verge, barely conscious. She was naked. And then he grabbed my wrists and bound them with her knee sock and I knew he was going to rape me too.'

'Jesus, Carmel. God, I'm so sorry. I had no idea.'

'No, Jay. He didn't touch me, at least, not straight away. He moved the passenger seat forward and forced me into the car, across the back seat. Then he disappeared again. I managed to get my head to the window. Yes, I remember. I saw him lift Scarlet and put her into his car. He reversed the car back down the slip till you couldn't see it from the road. Then his head appeared again, followed by his shoulders, his arms and his legs, walking back up the slip towards me. He had rolled his car into the water with Scarlet inside and now he was coming back for me. I pretended to be unconscious. I thought if I closed my eyes he might disappear. But he didn't. He climbed into the car and drove. And I knew he was taking me somewhere, to rape me, to kill me, God knows.'

'But he didn't. He brought you back here.' I positioned myself behind Karma and rubbed her shoulders. Even though I rubbed gently, her right shoulder recoiled. I noticed the bruising left by the seat belt.

'Why would he drive you back here?' I asked.

'I don't know, Jay. I just thank God that he did.'

The kitchen door opened, only slightly at first. Mags looked in at me. I nodded. She entered.

'Are you all right, Karma?' she asked. She assumed rubbing duties.

'I don't know about all right. But I'm alive,' said Karma.

Again, Mags looked at me. She silently mouthed: *Scarlet?*

I shook my head.

159

'Ow,' shouted Karma. 'You're hurting my shoulders.'

Mags quickly retracted her hands and used them to cover her face. Her head sank into them.

'Mags. Mags, I need your keys. I need to borrow the van,' I said.

Mags sniffed hard. She fanned her face. She nodded.

It was getting light. As I followed the road down to the harbour I could make out a squadron of seagulls suspended above the sea like a child's mobile. And then I heard their cackling and I thought of Scarlet in the water and I saw not seagulls, but vultures.

I stopped the van at the top of the slip. I stepped out and something crunched under my foot. I looked down to see chips of broken tail light ground to a fine orange powder by my boot. I was standing at the point of the impact.

The water was viscous still. It slurped at the slip, betraying nothing of its hidden gluttony. But I knew what lay in its belly. And I knew I had to go in. There was nothing I could do to save Scarlet. I had arrived too late for any heroics. But I was determined to pull her out of there, to spare her the bloated indignity of a watery grave.

I hoisted myself onto the quay wall and removed my boots and socks. I stepped out of my jeans and folded them on top. I made my way down the cobbled slip, my feet fighting to gain purchase on the slick seaweed that clung to its runners. The seaweed was wet for a good eight or nine feet, an indication that the tide was on its way out. Perhaps I needn't go in, I thought. If I waited for the water to retreat, the car would slowly reveal itself.

No. No, that would only prolong the horror. I had to go in.

I stood in the water, numbed to the knees. Should I dive straight in? Or should I acclimatize myself by degrees, walking in and out, a little deeper each time? Again, I decided not to delay the inevitable. I braced myself. I inhaled a tankful of sea air. I aimed my hands at a spot three feet in front of me and jammed my eyes shut. I called the Lord's name and, abandoning all logic and reason, I walked straight back out of the water.

It took me four further attempts before my shoulders were submerged. I trod water, kicking my legs wildly beneath me in the hope they'd locate the roof of the car. And then I heard an engine. I turned to confront the sound and my momentum sucked me under the water. I stayed under for as long as I could, fearing that if I brought my head up, it would find a propeller. But my lungs quickly wrung themselves of air. I surfaced to see the first trawler of the day puttering out to sea, some distance away. I hacked and spat the salt from my mouth. Now fully baptized, the decision to dive was an easy one.

My first recce yielded nothing. I groped blindly underwater, trying to pluck something from the murky ether – an aerial, a wing mirror, a pair of fluffy dice. I made three more dives at different points parallel to the slip. They proved equally fruitless. Perhaps I wasn't going deep enough. I knew we were in a harbour, so the seabed couldn't be that far down. But perhaps I had underestimated it.

I allowed myself to hyperventilate, emptying my lungs of air and refilling them with slightly more each time, until both chambers were full. It forced me to consider two things. One, how fortunate I was not to be a smoker. And two, how stupid it is that people say *breathe in* on entering a packed elevator, when doing so actually increases your body mass.

I dived again, deeper this time. It was hard work. The lungs that allowed me to stay under for longer, were also preventing me from sinking any further. Like Scarlet's horny gobbler I had to fight their urge to float me to the surface. And the deeper I went the stronger the current became and the more my body got sidetracked.

And then I touched something. I ran my hand all over it, trying to ascertain what it was. It felt like a panel, cold and smooth as a car door. I traced my hand down its side, trying to find a handle. But the surface became uneven and pitted. I felt a knobbly mass that had stuck itself to the side of the door. It cut the tips of my fingers. I realized I had grabbed at some mussel shells. And this was no car door they were clinging to. How could it be? The car had gone under barely an hour ago, not long enough to be colonized by crustaceans. I dived down another few feet and hit sand. It only confirmed that the object I had found was not a car. I guessed it was a groyne, one of many that were bedded into the sand to act as a breakwater to the harbour. I remembered seeing them the previous morning when the tide was out, when we first drove into Dalkey.

I called off my search. I retrieved my dry clothes from the quay wall. I sat in the van, naked and dripping, with the heating turned up full blast.

There was no car in the harbour waters, I was sure of that. So had Karma been lying? Or had the knock disoriented her to the extent that she had hallucinated? I looked down the slip. Only the top half was visible from where I was sitting. I quickly realized that Karma hadn't lied. She had said that the car reversed down the slip until she lost sight of it. But she also said that the driver rolled it into the sea. How could she be sure, if she couldn't see the car? What if her attacker had simply parked the car at the foot of the slip to mask it from the road? What if he'd driven Karma back up to the house with the intention of going back for Scarlet? If he had, Scarlet might still be alive. But where had he taken her and what did he intend to do to her? She needed to get to a hospital. She was in a bad way. Karma had said her condition could be fatal.

I didn't get it. If Scarlet's stalker had intended to abduct her, why didn't he just drive off with her straight away? Why did he drive Karma back to the house?

My legs were sufficiently dry to slip back un-hindered into my jeans. I zipped myself into a fleece I had found in the passenger footwell. I figured it must have belonged to Mags. None of the other girls were my size.

I slammed my door and turned the ignition. I drove three feet and immediately stopped. There, in my headlights, lay Scarlet's clothes. The ripped red material adorned the ground like roadkill.

I collected it all up, her boots, her skirt, her button-less shirt. I retrieved her other knee sock and those forlorn red panties with their cream trim. I felt sick. The whisky, the salt in my throat, the lack of sleep, they all contributed to my nausea. But they weren't the root cause of it. I pulled a carrier bag from the glove compartment and filled it with Scarlet's effects. I had never felt more wretched.

I headed back to the house. I tried to cheer myself with the thought that she might still be alive. But what comfort was that, knowing she was with *him*? I couldn't stop myself from imagining the horrors he was subjecting her to. For the second time in as many hours I found myself hoping that the drugs had claimed her.

I swung the Mercedes into the trees and up the gravel path. Karma's car remained halfway up it, partially blocking my way. I slowed the van and rolled my offside wheels into a low ditch, squeezing myself between the blackthorn and the bashed-up Datsun. And a strange thing happened. Or rather, it didn't happen. The security lights at the front of the house did not come on.

I manoeuvred the van back onto the path and stopped. I was now sitting closer to the house than Karma's car and I still hadn't triggered the lights. I got out and walked the rest of the way. I got to within twenty feet of the porch before I was blinded by urgent white light. Whoever had driven Karma back to the house had got this close to it. Closer, perhaps. Christ. Had he got inside the house?

The girls.

I ran up the steps. I ignored the bell and banged my fists on the door.

'Karma! . . . Mags! . . .'

The door opened. Diggsy stood behind it in a T-shirt and nothing else.

'Jesus, man,' he said. 'You've got sand in your hair.'

'Is everyone here? Are the girls all right?'

'Aye, everyone's fine. Come in. I'll get Maggie to run you a bath.'

'Aye. Aye, I will. Just give us a minute, will you? I need to bring the van up.'

Diggsy ran up the stairs giving me a more than generous view of the penis I had earlier done well to avoid. I stood on the porch. I looked back down the drive. I was sure that Karma's driver – Scarlet's stalker

164

and abductor – had triggered the lights. But I had been stupid to think he was in the house, for hadn't he gone back down to the harbour for his car? It still didn't explain why he would drive here in the first place, or why he would walk up to the front door.

The door. I examined it. There were no signs that it had been forced. There wasn't so much as a chip or a crack in the thick green gloss. The brass knocker remained at rest, undimmed by fingerprints. And the letter box was . . . open. I ran into the hall to see if anything had been put through. There was nothing on the carpet. It was only when I shut the door behind me that I noticed a basket screwed to the inside of the letter box. It contained a postcard.

I removed the card. It wasn't a postcard at all. It was a photograph. Diggsy had taken this picture. It had been printed up from his stolen film. It was Scarlet, in her bikini and sarong, sucking on a Sea Breeze. Her face had been completely obliterated by the frenzied lacerations of a red biro. In the bottom right corner of the picture, the artist had added his signature: *PIRA*.

14

'Hello?'

'This is Big Jessie. 0152 394552. I need to speak to Steeky.'

'Sorry?'

'Steeky. Tell him it's Big Jessie. 0152 394552.'

'You want to speak to Steeky?'

'Oh, for God's sake. It's Jay Black. I need your Chief Constable to call me back. The Provisionals have murdered my . . . my . . . Just get me fuckin' Meeks, all right.'

'I'm sorry, sir, I won't tolerate language like that. Not in my restaurant. I'm afraid we're fully booked.'

'Is this not 02890 465683?'

'No, sir. This is the Jasmine Palace, 02890 465863.'

'Shit.' I killed the receiver.

I knew this would happen. I had warned Meeks that I would forget his number. I had told him I should write it down on a piece of paper. I had even promised to swallow it when all of this blew over. But oh no, he had made me repeat it over and over and over again, so that wherever I was, at whatever time of day, no matter how extreme the circumstances, I would always be able to pick up a phone and order Kung Po chicken with water chestnuts.

I dialled again.

'Hello, this is Big Jessie. 0152 394552. Get me Steeky.'

'Will do.'

The phone went dead. I hung up. I waited.

The sun was up but I wasn't in the mood. I flicked my sunglasses forward, letting them fall off my head and onto the bridge of my nose. In truth, they weren't my sunglasses. They were Karma's. She had also lent me her car. I had parked the bashed Datsun beside the phone box.

The Dundalk locals had immediately endeared themselves to me. The moment I got out of the car, two passing teenagers had kindly offered to check my tyre pressure. As I waited for Meeks to call me back, I watched them assess the rear tyres first, kicking the rubber as hard as they could. Each kick was preceded by a name – 'Kilbane!' *Kick*. 'Keano!' *Kick*. 'Quinnie!' *Kick*.

'Here, lads, pack it in, you'll wreck the car.'

'Jays, mistor, it's already fecked. We're savin' you the bother of takin' her to the knacker's yard. *Cascarino!*' He volleyed the tyre again.

'Just leave the tyres alone.'

'Mistor, your wheels need adjostin'. I'll take a feckin' look at them.'

One of the lads knelt down and prised off a hubcap. I had imagined he would produce some implement with which to carry out the repair, a jack, a spanner, or suchlike. But no. He tucked the hubcap under his Louth shirt and the two of them ran like Croke Park finalists.

I hadn't the energy to chase them. I hadn't slept. I

hadn't eaten. My head hurt. And I had to stay by the phone.

I had earlier gathered Karma, Diggsy, Mags, Kate and Derbhla into the drawing room of the Dalkey mansion. I did not tell them of Scarlet's murder. They would only have insisted on calling in the Garda and I couldn't have that. The guards would want to take statements. They would examine the photograph. They would want to know why the Provisional IRA had murdered Scarlet and why they had posted their calling card to me. I would have to tell them she'd been murdered as a warning to me to lay off O'Hanlon. The whole thing would get messy. I mean, where was my proof? The photograph had been taken by Diggsy. Any of us could have defaced it. And until they had Scarlet's body, they had no murder. They would haul me in for questioning. It would take time, and time was something I didn't have. I needed to get to Dundalk and I needed to get to O'Hanlon.

I wasn't doing this for Meeks any more. I was doing it for Scarlet. I had something on O'Hanlon, at least I had a hunch it was something. It remained in my inside breast pocket, tucked securely into the pages of a Toni Morrison novel. I was going to use it, but not to secure O'Hanlon's abdication from the ministerial election or to force his hand on decommissioning. I was going to use it to get Scarlet back. He could either tell me where his Provo lackeys had dumped her body, or he could face a humiliation that would send him into political oblivion.

Scarlet had been murdered because of me. It was now my responsibility to find her. Without a body, her killers could never be brought to justice. I owed it to Scarlet to ensure she didn't become one of Northern Ireland's many vanished. I owed it to her parents, that they might give their daughter a proper burial. Without a body they would be condemned to a life of abject uncertainty, unable to grieve for their daughter until a decade, maybe two decades later, when her remains would be discovered by some man out walking his dog, or she would be unearthed by some farmer's JCB. And that's if they got lucky. So many mothers, fathers, wives and husbands are stuck in this limbo, waiting for a phone call or a knock at the door, praying for good news, praying for bad. Grief is one thing, but it is a far more terrible thing not to be able to grieve.

I had to get her back.

So I lied to Diggsy and the girls. I told them Scarlet had been kidnapped. I hid the photograph from them. Instead, I went out to the van and hastily faked a ransom note. I made them believe that her kidnappers wanted a slice of her father's whisky profits, to the tune of IR£200,000. I told Mags to drive everyone back to Belfast as I feared for their safety in Dalkey. I asked Karma to leave me her car. I promised that I would hold the fort until Scarlet's parents returned from New York. I would be on hand to negotiate with the kidnappers, should they contact the house.

Harry Clegg and Stephen Meeks were the only people who knew I was in Dundalk. I had a fair idea that the IRA knew too.

I had no idea why Sinn Fein were in Dundalk, however, and in December of all months. Their annual party conference, the Ard Fheis, was more commonly held in Dublin some time in October. Perhaps this year, like an Olympic committee, they had invited Irish towns and villages to submit their bids to host the 2001 conference. Dundalk might well have beaten off serious competition from the likes of Carrickmacross

169

(which offers the discerning Sinn Fein delegate limit-
less opportunities to purchase quality lace), Spiddal
(where the keen Republican can polish up his Irish
while enjoying deep-sea fishing off some of the finest
coastline in Ireland), and Muff (where reformed
terrorists are invited to mingle freely with young local
beauties, contestants in the annual 'Miss Teenage
Muff' pageant).

I knew The Corrs hailed from Dundalk. I knew that the
sister of Robert Burns was buried in one of its grave-
yards. And I knew that it was a renowned centre of shoe
manufacturing. But I failed to see how this recommended the town to the Sinn Fein executive, unless they
were fans of bad Scottish verse or bland Celtic AOR.
Perhaps O'Hanlon had decided to award the conference
to Dundalk when the heels fell off his brogues.

Then I recalled 1998 and the vote on the Good Friday
Agreement. An astounding 81 per cent of the people in
Northern Ireland had cast their vote in the referendum,
71 per cent of them voting 'Yes' to the accord. I remembered the returning officer being drowned out by the
cheering, the clapping, and the loud refrains of *Here we
go*, voiced as much out of relief as celebration. This
was supposed to be it, the way forward, the way out of
the violent abyss. And I remembered that within hours
of the result, the Garda intercepted two cars loaded
with bomb-making equipment – in Dundalk.

Prrrrrreeep, prrrrrreeep . . . prrrrrree—

I grabbed the phone. 'Hello?'

'Big Jessie?'

'Steeky?'

'It's me, Black. What can I do you for?'

'Jesus, you took your time. I've had to stand here
like a stewed prune while some wee lads stripped the
wheels off my car.'

'It's Saturday morning, Black. I play golf on a Saturday morning. They eventually got hold of me on the fourteenth green. You made me miss a putt to beat the Chairman of the Ulster Bank, five and four. So this better be good.'

'Well, I do apologize. It's just, something's come up. The IRA are onto me. They know I'm after O'Hanlon. They've told me in no uncertain terms to back off. They've murdered my . . . my . . . this girl I know . . . knew.'

What *was* Scarlet to me? She wasn't my girlfriend – we hadn't been lovers. She wasn't my friend – we had only recently met. She wasn't a colleague or an associate. Did that mean she was nothing to me? Impossible. It felt like she was everything. She had been everything to me in those last few days of her life. And she continued to occupy my every waking thought, even in death. My feelings for her had only become stronger. Yet there was no word, or set of words, to describe what she was to me. How can language let you down like that? The injustice of it. For it wasn't just death that had robbed Scarlet and me of a relationship – *words* would forever prohibit us from establishing one.

'Relax, Black. I've got two officers watching you as we speak. Take a look across the road. Do you see that little café, The Singing Kettle?'

I looked, I did.

'Yes,' I said.

'Well, those two big lads there in the window . . . see? The ones stuffing potato bread into their faces? I've had a word with them. They'll make sure you're not harmed.'

One of the fat men in the window cocked a buttered knife in my direction.

171

'Gee, I feel so much better,' I said.

'You should, Black. It's costing me two grand a day to watch your ass.'

'Well, sorry if I sound just a little pissed off, *Stephen*, but someone very close to me has just been abducted and shot by the paramilitaries. Where were the Two Fat Ladies last night, when I really needed them? Eh? And who was *watching my ass* yesterday morning at the border? If an IRA gunman had aimed his high-calibre rifle a foot to the left, I wouldn't have an ass to watch.'

'Calm down, Jay. Please. I'm sorry. Look, I . . . *we* didn't think the Provos would be onto our little operation so quickly. I can't bring the wee girl back, but I can make sure you're safe. But time's running out. I want O'Hanlon's balls delivered on a silver platter, and I want them in the next four days. I want him to stand down from the election and I want him to kick-start decommissioning. The IRA still have enough guns and explosives in their caches to mobilize a small guerrilla army. They're concealed too deep for my boys to detect them. And they're protected from the elements, they won't rust away in the thatch like they once did.'

I didn't need to listen to his rhetoric. I wasn't doing this for him any more. I didn't give a shit whether the Provos gave up their guns. I just wanted Scarlet back.

'Stephen, have you not heard the news? This morning, the parochial wing of the IRA issued a statement. They say they're hanging on to their cudgels, but they've offered to put their pitchforks beyond use. What do you think? It's a start, isn't it?'

'Enough, Black. I understand you're a bit shaken, but fuckin' snap out of it. So somebody's murdered some wee doll. Big fuckin' deal. There are bigger

172

issues at stake here. I'm not just talking about decommissioning. I'm talking about the future of my police force, the future of Northern Ireland. So here's what's going to happen. You are going to go into that conference and confront O'Hanlon with this Kate Owen thing. And then you're going to call me. And if I don't like what I hear, I will instruct the *Two Fat Ladies,* as you affectionately call them, to haul your ass back up to Belfast, where I will formally charge you with the manslaughter of former Northern Ireland goalkeeper Miles Huggins. Is that clear?'

'Steeky?'

'Yes?'

'You can stick Huggins up your hole.'

15

The conference wasn't scheduled to kick off until midday. I had an hour to kill. I left the car where it was, even though I knew it was at the mercy of the local kids. They would undoubtedly strip it like hyenas round a fallen impala.

I found a road that led off the main street and down to the Castletown River. A couple of anglers stared in jaundiced silence at their dormant floats. They were dressed head to foot in so much rubber, you would have sworn the river was contaminated with uranium. Their fluorescent sinkers sat perfectly still in the water, like two cherries in a jelly. It struck me that the anglers weren't staring at their floats at all, they were lost in the inverted reflection of the Cooley Mountains that butterflied across the surface of the glassy river. For perhaps the first time in my life I understood the appeal of fishing. It had nothing to do with the fish. As I passed, one of the men greeted me with a solemn, almost imperceptible nod of the head. His friend toasted me with a maggot.

'Nice day for it,' I said.

'Aye, but they're not biting. And me up since four, soaking my bait in Guinness.' The maggot wriggled and writhed between his finger and thumb like it had enjoyed a skinful.

My guts were performing similar contortions. I was nervous about meeting O'Hanlon. He was a powerful man. I was sure he was just as intimidating in a shirt and tie as he had once been in a balaclava. His intellect was equally ferocious. O'Hanlon had spent a long time holed up in Long Kesh during internment. He had used the time to read prodigiously, going through books like they were contraband fags. His first and longest prison term was served in 1974, not long after he left Queen's. Even from inside the compound, he continued to write for a paper – *The Republican* – under the pen name Scallion. In his column he laid down the ideological and strategic foundation for the Provisional IRA for the next twenty years. O'Hanlon was championed by Republicans as a prisoner of war. His experience in Long Kesh only hardened his resolve. Twenty-seven years on and despite the radical image makeover and his transformation into all-round man of the people, his eyes, with their bottomless black pupils, could still put the fear of God into you.

I arrived at a bridge and sat on a bench cut into its stone. I took the novel from my pocket and removed the centrefold stolen from *Gown*. I opened it up. I examined the photographs again, the pictures taken at the 1967 Queen's University PolySoc Ball. 1967 – the days before O'Hanlon had killed. The days before violence had taken hold of Northern Ireland like a dose of malaria. Once it got into her bloodstream, she seemed unable to get rid of it.

I shielded the page from the sunlight. I examined the young woman's face, just to be sure. I checked the names under the photographs, to corroborate my hunch. Martin O'Hanlon and Kate Rogers – co-editors of *Gown*. Martin O'Hanlon and Kate Rogers – an item. Martin O'Hanlon and Kate Rogers – the latter now known to voters as Kate Owen, Labour's Secretary of State for Northern Ireland and wife of Party Chairman Geraint Owen.

The Secretary of State and the Sinn Fein leader, the beauty and the beast, it was a story worthy of Walt Disney. But Walt wasnae getting it. Jay Black was penning this one. And though the tale of Marty and Kate probably merited a feature-length animation with a Phil Collins soundtrack, or a dramatization on ice, the front page of the *News Letter* would more than suffice.

Once it got out that O'Hanlon had enjoyed a relationship with Kate Owen, his credibility would be destroyed. The two of them could not have been more diametrically opposed. Everything that O'Hanlon stood for would be compromised. He'd be a laughing stock at Stormont. His position as Sinn Fein party leader, never mind as prospective First Minister, would become completely untenable. And that's just for starters. I could only imagine what his wife and daughter would think.

I folded the page back into the book. I was about to enter the hornet's nest. I was nervous, yet excited. I was apprehensive, yet focused. I knew what I had to do and I drew all my resolve from Scarlet.

I made my way back towards Dundalk Town Hall, the venue for the Ard Fheis. I passed the impressive courthouse, its Doric columns recognizable by the design that topped them, a wedge of Cheddar sitting on a digestive biscuit. Green bunting fluttered from everything – trees, telegraph poles, traffic lights, small dogs. The crowd siphoning into the hall was larger than I had expected. Catching a few accents I judged that a fair proportion of the Dundalk locals were attending. This seemed strange, as the Sinn Fein party conference is a notoriously guarded affair. I searched the crowd for those people wielding cameras, mobiles and spiral-bound notepads, and took my place among the press pack.

A brute of a man stopped me as I got to the door. He had a face on him like a pug licking piss off a thistle.

'Pass.'

'That's awful nice of you,' I said and made to go by him.

He stopped me with a stiff arm, raising it like a car-park barrier.

'I said, *pass*. You need one to get in.'

'Oh, right you are.' I produced my laminated press pass.

'*Ulster News Letter*,' said the doorman, a little too loudly. The other journalists immediately glared at me. Many tutted and several crossed themselves.

The doorman grudgingly let me through.

I took my allotted seat in front of a dais at the far end of the hall. A long wooden table was positioned across the stage, with seven pens, seven pads and seven glasses of water placed equidistantly along it. Yet there wasn't a dwarf in sight. And I was disappointed with the backdrop. I had expected Sinn Fein to push the boat out for their annual conference and dress the stage with a Mount Rushmore-sized effigy of O'Hanlon's beardy face, or a slapdash mural of a hunger striker shunning a pasty supper. But alas, all that adorned the wood-panelled wall behind the long table was a square of green silk curtain with a gold rope attached to one corner.

The hall was full, even if the stage wasn't. The last person to seat herself was headed for the chair next to me. She was young, in her late twenties, and she looked flustered. She carried a coat, a pile of papers and one of those old mono tape recorders with the clunky buttons. She forced my entire row onto our feet as she squeezed past, apologizing all the way. None of the men seemed to mind. If she had been a bloke, they'd have broken her shins.

'Hello there,' she said. 'Could you hold these for me a wee second?'

She offloaded onto my lap coats, papers, tape recorder, fondue set, face sauna, hostess trolley, crystal decanter and cuddly toy. Didn't she do well?

She filled the vacant seat beside me. She rooted around in her bag and produced a brush. She ran it quickly through her long auburn hair. She picked stray hairs off the brush and wrapped them in a tissue, which she then returned to her bag. She applied a bit of lippy and opened a button on her blouse.

'Right so, that's me presentable,' she said. She offered me her hands. 'Nuala Fitzgerald, *Dundalk Argus*. Thanks for minding my stuff.'

I returned her belongings.

'Jay Black. *Ulster News Letter*.'

She looked shocked. 'And they let you in?' she asked. 'Ah well, I suppose Dundalk *is* the gateway of Ireland. We've witnessed the passing of many an army of Celt, Norseman, Norman, Jacobite and Williamite. I suppose we can make room for the *Ulster News Letter*, so.'

She attached a bulbous microphone to her antique tape recorder.

'I suppose you must be chuffed,' I said. 'It's a bit of a coup for your town, staging the Sinn Fein Ard Fheis.'

'I can't say you'll see many of us celebrating,' she said. 'The twentieth of December is a solemn day for us Dundalk folk. But we are honoured that Mr O'Hanlon saw fit to mark it.'

'I don't understand,' I said.

'Today is the twenty-fifth anniversary of the Kelly's Bombing. Sinn Fein kindly moved their conference so they could honour our dead. Jaysus, he calls himself a *jornalist*. You need to do your homework, so. Be a bit more professional. One, two, buckle moi shoe . . .' She had spoken into the microphone. She stopped the tape and ejected it. She rewound it by sticking a biro through one of its spools. She reinserted the cassette and pressed play: '. . . more professional. One, two, buckle moi shoe *clunk*.'

'That's me ready,' she said. 'Ready to rumble.' She raised her microphone, jabbing it into the well-groomed head of the guy from the *Irish Independent* who was seated in front of her.

Suddenly, the amplifiers either side of the stage buzzed into life, spewing out a bass-heavy version of *Things Can Only Get Better*. The crowd around me rose to their feet and began clapping and whistling and dancing like dads at a wedding as the grinning ex-terrorist, Martin O'Hanlon, took to the stage. He paused momentarily to wave his hand around the hall, as if he was blessing it. He was joined by his deputy, Seamus Keane, the Aughnacloy Assassin. Three men, all in their early fifties, filed onto the stage behind them: Paddy Feeney, Gerard McCann and Michael Condit, the Bann Street Butchers, every one of them on early release from the Maze under the terms of the Good Friday Agreement. The Infamous Five did a lap of the stage, a deadly conga line. I expected the music to abruptly switch and see Marty and his hoodlums lead us in that famous holiday dance: *Agadubh-dubh-dubh, pull a trigger, shoot PC, Agadubh-dubh-dubh, set a timer, blow a street.*

Instead, the CD jumped. O'Hanlon remained unfazed

by the repetitive glitch. He approached the microphone.

'Would somebody shut that up. I don't care how you do it,' he said. He made a gun with his fingers and aimed it at one of the speakers. As he 'fired', the speaker emitted a sound like a broken zip and the music stopped. O'Hanlon blew on his fingertips. It drew laughter from the gallery.

'Isn't he wonderful, so,' said Nuala Fitzgerald. 'Such a showman.' A tear climbed out of her eye.

O'Hanlon struggled with the microphone. A young guy ran onto the stage and adjusted its height, drawing it level with the leader's beard. As he did so, two people I did not recognize – a man and a woman, both in their late forties – took the chairs to the immediate left and right of the Sinn Fein leader.

O'Hanlon was the only person in the hall left standing.

'Party members, fellow Republicans, ladies, gentlemen, members of the associated press.' O'Hanlon took a sip of his water before continuing. 'The twentieth of December 1976 will forever remain ingrained in the memories of the citizens of Dundalk, who welcome us here today. For at twelve twenty-two on that dreadful afternoon a Loyalist car bomb exploded outside Kelly's Tavern, killing four and injuring seventeen. I have, sitting either side of me, the children of two men who lost their lives in that cowardly attack.'

O'Hanlon put his hands on the shoulders of both relatives.

'Deirdre Cullen was a week away from her wedding when she received word that her father, Cormac, was a victim of this atrocity. And Brian Lowney was only a young man of nineteen when he lost his father, Dermot, in the Loyalist bombing. I know that both of them would like to say a few words.'

O'Hanlon invited Deirdre Cullen to the microphone.

180

She seemed unsure of herself, her unease compounded by the barrage of flashguns. She slowly spoke, her quiet words finding their own resonance in the hushed hall.

'My daddy, Cormac Cullen, ran the butcher's in Francis Street, which still has his name on it today. We had been really busy in the run-up to Christmas. That Saturday, Daddy was so busy that Mum sent me up to the shop with his packed lunch. He asked me to stay and mind the place while he took a couple of turkeys up to Kelly's Tavern on Crowe Street. As we all know, every year Kelly's lays on a Christmas dinner for all those lonely souls who don't have any family to spend it with. And every year Daddy gave them two free turkeys as a gesture of goodwill. I can remember hearing the bomb from the butcher's, it near blew the meat off the bones. But I had no idea Daddy was anywhere near it. We were . . . told . . . I'm sorry.' Deirdre reached for her water. O'Hanlon asked if she was OK to continue. She nodded.

'My mother . . . Mammy told us he died instantly. I was due to be married the following week, on Boxing Day. My daddy was supposed to take me down the aisle. I remember him saying that he didn't want to give me away. Not when he could get a good price for me at the cattle auctions.'

I couldn't tell whether Deirdre Cullen had started to laugh or cry, or both, but she couldn't go on. O'Hanlon helped her into her seat.

'Brian?' he asked, offering the mike to the man on his left.

Brian Lowney stood too close to the microphone. It popped and whistled as he spoke. 'I have been through what Deirdre has been through. I have known her pain. My father, Dermot Lowney, was a decent, hard-working man. He used to call on most of you, selling you logs and peat from his van. He had started work that Saturday at seven a.m. and was finished, as usual, by lunchtime. He would normally go for a drink in the Sceptre before going home, but a chance meeting dragged him over to the other side of the town. Dad had been making his way to his usual pub when he ran into a lady who was laden with parcels and Christmas cards that she needed to post. Dermot Lowney, being the decent man that he was, wouldn't have any of it. He insisted on carrying her parcels up to the post office for her. On his way back, he popped into nearby Kelly's for that drink. My father was pronounced dead at Louth County Hospital five days later. He had hung on till Christmas Day.'

O'Hanlon took Deirdre Cullen by the hand and walked her over to the small green curtain. Brian followed, handing O'Hanlon the mike.

'Brian, Deirdre, I can feel your sadness,' he said. 'Your fathers were good people, decent people, the kind of people who provide the backbone to community life in Ireland. It is tragic that these men lost their lives in such a meaningless fashion. But it is even more galling that their Loyalist killers have never been brought to justice, even though, as it is now widely known, they have long been identified. We know who these evil-doers are. And we have damning and irrefutable evidence that the RUC colluded with the perpetrators of these murderous strikes into the Irish State. And still the guilty roam free. The continuing peace in the North and in the border counties gives me hope for the future. But let me promise you this, as First Minister elect, I will not rest until the RUC is dismantled and your fathers' murderers are brought to justice. Let this commemorative plaque be the first step towards ensuring that these men will never be forgotten.'

O'Hanlon forced Deirdre's hand and Brian's hand on top of his own. Together, they tugged the rope. The green curtains parted to reveal a bronze plaque in the shape of a Celtic cross, engraved with four names. They held their pose for the benefit of the cameras. They were forced to close the curtains and repeat the unveiling for a UTV news crew who had been down the pub and had arrived a fraction late.

O'Hanlon then moved to the front of the stage.

'Can I have everybody's attention? In five minutes, at twelve twenty-two precisely, the bells of St Patrick's Church will be tolled as a mark of respect. The church is on Crowe Street, directly opposite, so could you all make your way out of the hall? Tea and sticky buns will be served in the vestry. Sinn Fein delegates are asked to reconvene back here at two o'clock when we shall press on with party business.'

This was my chance to get close to O'Hanlon. This was my chance to confront him about Kate Owen, over a sugary tea and a slice of baklava. His bodyguards wouldn't be able to touch me. Not when he's surrounded by a grieving public and an eager press. And not when he's standing in a place of worship. This was my chance to get him one to one.

'Right so,' said Nuala. 'Let's grab ourselves something hot and wet and you can tell me all about Belfast.' She forced me to carry her tape recorder. 'I believe Tescos are opening stores all over the North,' she continued. 'Is it true they've issued their staff with bullet-proof tabards?'

Nuala followed me across the road and into the church. She remained glued to my side as the bells tolled. When I joined in with the singing of a hymn to remember the dead, Nuala provided the close harmonies to my faltering alto. Inside the vestry, she made me look after her stuff while she got us a tea. I honestly feared she would return with one cup and two straws. Clingy? They could've used her skin to wrap sandwiches.

'So, Jay, you're here to report on the conference?'

'No, I'm actually a music journalist. I'm here to threaten Martin O'Hanlon. Last night he had a rock star murdered. He instructed his IRA henchmen to abduct her, strip her and shoot her. Her body is buried in an unmarked grave and I want O'Hanlon to tell me where it is.' I sucked tea out of my freshly dunked ginger snap.

Nuala shook her head. 'I don't know. You Belfast people and your *bleck* humour,' she laughed. She slapped my arm, spilling hot tea over my hand.

'Uch, I'm sorry. Let me find you a paper towel.'

She tried to force her way to the front of the bun table but her arms were ripped from their sockets by two sweet-toothed pensioners. The old dears directed her to the back of the queue. Nuala shrugged at me and took her place. I wasn't going to wait for her. I had spotted O'Hanlon. He had walked out of the vestry and into the gardens to answer his mobile phone while his bodyguards fought over the last French fancy.

I stuffed Nuala's belongings behind a lectern. I considered taking her tape recorder out to the gardens to record my conversation with O'Hanlon, in the hope he might incriminate himself. But how could I conceal such a brute? I couldn't exactly Sellotape it to my chest – it just might give the game away. So I dumped it with the rest of her junk. But not before I pressed 'record' and spoke into the attached mike, repeating '*Smoke marijuana*' over and over again in a devil voice.

I made for the gardens.

O'Hanlon stood by a large rhododendron bush, yelling angrily into his phone. I had no idea who he was talking to, or what he was saying, for he was shouting in Gaelic. I feigned an interest in pyracantha, azalea and cotoneaster, as I waited for him to finish. I felt like I was waiting to be caned by the headmaster.

Marty returned his mobile to a pouch on his belt. How appropriate, I thought. He wore his phone like a gun.

He moved towards the church door but I blocked his path.

'O'Hanlon. Martin O'Hanlon,' I said.

'Well, my face is on every telegraph pole in the North of Ireland, so I suppose there's no point in denying it. Yes, I am Martin O'Hanlon.'

'I'm Jay Black. *Ulster News Letter*. Ring any bells?'

'I know who you are.'

'Of course you do. You murdered my girlfriend.'

O'Hanlon looked irritated. He darted his eyes over each of my shoulders in turn, calling, 'Seamie? . . . Mal?'

'Your babysitters are inside, Marty. They've got their eyes on a Mr Kipling. Now, are you going to be exceedingly good and tell me where you've dumped Scarlet?'

'I'm no murderer, Black. I'm a man of peace.'

'Cut the crap. That little speech you made, over the road, you may be able to fool your fawning public but you don't fool me. All that stuff about *feeling their sadness*, about *lives lost in a meaningless fashion*, how *murderers should be brought to justice*. A bit rich coming from a man who was an active and willing participant in IRA murders for over a decade, a man who provided photographs and details of potential victims, and who carried out surveillance on them using electoral rolls to verify their addresses. Shit, you even drew nice little maps of their homes, in coloured felt-tip, so your gunmen could plan their murders.

And you're still at it. Last night you instructed them to kill Scarlet.'

O'Hanlon grabbed my arm and hauled me round the blind side of the rhododendron.

'I'd watch what you're saying, son. Those sort of accusations have a way of coming back on you. My past has been well documented. I don't deny it. I was fighting a war. But now that war is over. The days of campaigning with a ballot box in one hand and an Armalite in the other are well behind us. My election as First Minister will only prove that.'

'You're right, Marty. But not about your election. Your chances of becoming First Minister are slimmer than none. You see, the past *can* come back to haunt you. And your past *is* well documented. Take a look at this.'

I reached into my breast pocket.

'Fuck, a gun,' shouted O'Hanlon. He pushed me into the bush.

'Relax,' I said. I held up the Toni Morrison novel. 'It's only a book. It's not going to kill you. It may emancipate you, but I assure you it's no tool of execution.'

I pulled myself up and smacked the soil from the seat of my jeans. I opened the book.

'What is this?' asked O'Hanlon. 'Are you going to read me a story?'

'Aye, I've got a story for you. But I'm not going to read it to you. It's a photostory. A love story. The story of how a young Republican fell hook, line and sinker for a doe-eyed English girl. He worshipped the ground she walked on and the hot pants she wiggled in. But the story ends in tragedy when the girl's religion, her politics and her love of David Cassidy eventually drive a wedge between the young lovers.'

I handed O'Hanlon the *Gown* centre spread. I had expected him to spit blood, to beat his chest, to fall on his knees and decry the gods that mocked him. At the very least, I expected a 'Fuck!' or a frown. But, as he pored over the pictures, they roused a smile that had been hibernating somewhere in the thick undergrowth of his beard.

'Jeez, this takes me back,' he said.

'So you admit it, then. You and Kate Owen, née Rogers, the Secretary of State, you were getting it on.'

'The PolySoc Ball 1967. God, I was slim back then. You wouldn't get me into that suit now.'

'Oh, I dunno, flares are coming back in,' I said. 'I hope you're enjoying the nostalgia trip because, once this gets out, it'll set you back years.'

'You're a confident wee gobshite, aren't you?' He flicked the laminate that hung round my neck. '*Ulster News Letter*. Do they still employ you? Jeez, how do they get the stories at your place, do they just give monkeys like you a typewriter and see what you can concoct? So you have pictures of me kissing a young girl at a university function. Big deal. Kate and I did not have a relationship, if that's what you're trying to suggest. Look at her . . .' He jabbed his finger at one of the pictures, smudging the ink. 'She was pissed. Look at the other pictures. She's kissing other lads. And so is yer woman, Aisling Coyles, Kate's best friend. As I remember, the pair of them were collecting kisses to see who could get the most. Everyone knew Kate and I didn't get along. Politics wasn't the only thing we disagreed on. Still, as co-editors, it made for a balanced paper.' O'Hanlon laughed ruefully at the thought, momentarily hopping back on the nostalgia bus. Or camper van. 'Whatever, your pictures are harmless. Aisling had dared Kate to make a play for

187

me, simply because she knew how much the two of us hated each other. I only went along with it because I have never been a spoilsport.'

'Not even when you tossed that grenade over the wall of the Oval during the 1973 Irish Cup final?'

O'Hanlon looked right into me, as if with one look he could ascertain everything about me. He filed the information away in some dark part of his brain, away with all the photographs, the felt-tip drawings and the electoral rolls.

'What have I told you about making wild accusations, son? I'm going to do you a favour and ignore what you've just said. And as for this . . .' He held the paper up to my face. 'This is laughable. If you're lucky, one of the nationals might give you half a grand for the pictures. You should consider it, because you'll get nothing from me.'

O'Hanlon pressed the paper into my chest. I let it fall to the ground. I wasn't going to let him get away. I reached into the back pocket of my jeans and produced the mutilated photograph of Scarlet.

'How much will one of *the nationals* give me for this, then? This was Scarlet. She fronted a band. She was due to headline a gig in Dublin this evening. All *the nationals* were on the guest list. But her fellow band members have had to cancel the gig. The official reason is that Scarlet has come down with a bug and it's affected her throat. The Provisionals' reason is that they've murdered her. And you gave them the nod. This was your warning to me. You knew I was onto you. You knew that Chief Constable Meeks had instructed me to do whatever I could to bring you down. You had Scarlet shot so I'd stay away. But I'm here, Marty. I am right here, right in your beardy little face and I will stay in your beardy little face

188

until you tell me where you've dumped Scarlet's body.'

'Meeks? What does that precocious little shit want?'

'You know what he wants, Marty. He wants decommissioning. He wants you to withdraw from Thursday's election. And he wants me to strong-arm you into it.'

O'Hanlon laughed.

'Strong-arm, he says. Jesus, where do I start? Let's take decommissioning first. How does Meeks propose that I can secure decommissioning? I am the leader of Sinn Fein. I hold no sway with the IRA. And anyway, Meeks knows that there is no clause in the Good Friday Agreement to say that the IRA must decommission its arms. And there is nothing to say that my party will be excluded from the Executive unless they do so.'

O'Hanlon buttoned his jacket. He adopted the soapbox posturing of the politician. He gave me the full sermon.

'Let me draw your attention to paragraph twenty-five of the Agreement, in the section concerning the Executive. *Those who hold office should only use democratic, non-violent means, and those who do not should be excluded or removed from office under these provisions.* Sinn Fein is a non-violent, legitimate political party. It cannot be excluded from office and I will not be withdrawing from the election. On the other hand, the Agreement *does* include a commitment to reforming the RUC. So you go and you tell Meeks that when I do become First Minister, I will tear the crown from his green cap and I will disband his corrupt little organization.'

'I'm not going anywhere and I'm not telling anybody anything until you tell me where you dumped this girl.' I made him look at the picture. I made him see the life he had stolen.

'You've got an overactive imagination, son. So this is your girlfriend, you say?' O'Hanlon grabbed the photograph off me. He gently shook his head as he studied it. 'Don't know what she sees in a streak of piss like you.' He bit his lip. He rubbed his thumb on the squall of red that had obliterated Scarlet's face, until he had worn a hole clean through the picture. 'Mind you,' he added, 'she seems your type. I can't see the face but she definitely dresses like a cheap tart.' The photograph disappeared into his clenched fist.

I saw red.

I aimed a punch.

He caught my wrist before it connected.

'You have just come to within an inch of your life, Black. One inch. If your hand had got one inch closer to my face, my security would be hosing your bullet-riddled body off this grass. Now be a good little boy and get the fuck out of Dundalk.'

190

16

O'Hanlon had his security escort me to Dundalk train station. I made him believe I had a return ticket to Belfast. I didn't want his cronies walking me to Karma's car. They would've only laughed at me the moment they clapped eyes on the Datsun. More crucially, they would've noted her registration. Karma normally parked her car in west Belfast, in the grounds of the Royal Victoria Hospital. I didn't want the IRA thinking I was on their manor, spying on them. And I didn't want Karma to turn the key in her ignition and be blown to smithereens.

Unfortunately, Seamie and Mal stayed with me on the platform to see me safely onto the Dublin to Belfast train. I told them not to be silly, to go on back to their conference. I said that I hated tearful goodbyes and promised to write. But they were having none of it. We stood on the platform in a kind of Mexican stand-off until the long orange train rattled in. I climbed aboard. I took a window seat and blew them a kiss as I pulled out of the station. I waited till the train had curved round an embankment before I jumped off. The doors were the sort you opened yourself, such are the advantages of Ireland's primitive rolling stock.

I landed on a circular carpet of ash where there had recently been a trackside fire. The dead embers were littered with scorched bottles – Bulmer's, Smirnoff, Night Nurse. I picked myself up and dusted the ash from my jacket and jeans. I climbed up the embankment and found the town, looking like one of the walking dead.

If you ignored the dented driver's door, the smashed window and the missing hubcaps, the car was immaculate. A flyer flapped from under the wiper blade. Unfortunately, the wiper blade rested on the roof, having been snapped off by the person distributing the leaflets on his first attempt at securing one to my car. The flyer advertised a local artist. He was selling prints of his pencil portrait of Martin O'Hanlon. For an extra IR£25 you could get your own portrait sketched with your arm round the Sinn Fein leader, provided you supplied the artist with a recent photograph. I considered phoning him and asking him to quote on a portrait of me with my arm round O'Hanlon, holding him in a headlock, my fingers ripping the beard from his scabrous chin.

I started the car, a minor miracle. I found the M1 and headed north.

I had been stupid to confront O'Hanlon, armed with so little. He had been right. The PolySoc photos were nothing. If they leaked out he would only laugh it off, 'the innocence of youth' and all that. Far from being scandalous, the pictures might actually have boosted his popularity. They would humanize, not demonize him. People would see a normal, red-blooded male enjoying student life to the full, a far cry from the icy, impenetrable killer that he became not three years after the pictures were taken. Moreover, evidence of his romantic dalliances and his illicit flings would only enhance O'Hanlon's sex appeal. Women all over

192

Ireland would be clogging confession booths and demanding absolution from their impure thoughts.

I wanted more than ever to hurt him. But how could I when I had nothing to hurt him with? I was back at square one, do not pass Go, do not collect O'Hanlon's balls on a silver platter. Or was I? The way O'Hanlon had looked at those pictures of Kate Rogers only convinced me that there was more to his relationship with the glowing blonde than he was prepared to divulge. Yes, his face had been filled with nostalgia and reminiscence, but his brow had tightened, his eyes had lacquered over and his tone had become rueful. Such expression was not consistent with a man flippantly dismissing his past. Had I exhumed some buried feelings for an old flame? I couldn't be sure. A furrowed brow, a watery eye and an embittered voice hardly amounted to damning, indefatigable evidence of an affair. And in no way would it be enough to satisfy Meeks. I needed more. Thankfully, without realizing it, O'Hanlon had given me more. He had given me a name: Aisling Coyles.

I waited until I had crossed the border into County Down before I called Harry. He was in a typically jovial mood.

'Davey, turn that fuckin' racket down, I'm on the fuckin' phone.' (Harry adopts posh accent:) 'Hello, *Ulster News Letter*, Harry Clegg speaking.'

'Harry, it's Jay.'

'Jay? Is that a car I can hear? Aren't you supposed to be at the Sinn Fein hooley?'

'Aye, I am. I mean, I was. I'm on my way back. I've got what I need.'

'So, did Ronan Keating show up? Or perhaps Gary fuckin' Barlow did a duet with O'Hanlon – "Relight my incendiary device"?'

193

'Nothing quite so exciting, Harry.'

'Well you'd better have something. I didn't give you that press pass for the good of my fuckin' health. I've got a newspaper to fill.'

'Relax. I'll have a story for you. I just need a bit more info. That's why I'm calling. I need your help. Have you heard of Aisling Coyles?'

'Aisling Coyles. As in the novelist Aisling Coyles?'

'That's what I'm thinking,' I said.

'She writes all those fuckin' bodice-rippers. The wife's a big fan. I don't read them myself, though I did buy the wife the video of *The Dingle Bride*, but only cos Kate Winslet gets her duds out. Course, I can't fuckin' watch it now. The tracking's gone funny at that point in the tape.'

'Harry, I need to get hold of Aisling Coyles. I need a phone number or an address and I need it pronto.'

'Jesus fuckin' H., Jay. What has an Irish romantic novelist got to do with Sinn Fein? Next you'll be telling me Maeve Binchy's gunrunning for the fuckin' 'Ra.'

'Just get me Aisling Coyles, Harry, and I'll get you your story.'

'Jay?'

'Yes, Harry?'

'If you're still south of the border could you bring us back a Tiffin bar? We can't get them up here. They're fuckin' gorgeous.'

'Anything else, Harry? I mean, I've only been threatened with a grisly execution if I don't get out of the country. But don't worry, I'll stop and grab you your chocolate. While I'm at it, shall I do you a line on the Lotto? Perhaps I could go visit the Blarney Stone and make you a fucking wish?'

'Jay, son. What's up? What have you been saying at

that conference? I told you not to go getting yourself into anything that you couldn't get out of.'

'Aye, well, you just get me Aisling Coyles and I'll worry about how I'm going to get out of this.'

I ended the call before Harry had a chance to redirect me to Belleek to buy him some pottery.

The gauge on the dashboard alerted me to the fact I was running out of petrol. I pressed on regardless, testing the theory that a car will always keep going so long as you never stop. My mind raced up the road ahead of me. Where was Scarlet? Was she in a ditch, in a makeshift grave, or lying on some refuse tip with the magpies fighting over her eyeballs? When would her parents return from New York? What would I tell them? And what would I tell Meeks? He had asked me to call him straight after I'd confronted O'Hanlon. But I had nothing to tell him. At least, nothing as yet. Time was running out faster than four-star from a Datsun, but there was no way I was phoning him. Not until I'd spoken to Aisling Coyles.

O'Hanlon had said that Kate Rogers and Aisling Coyles were best friends at university. If O'Hanlon and Rogers had been carrying on, I presumed that Aisling would know about it. Whether she would talk about it was an altogether different matter. But what other option did I have? Aisling was my only hope.

My mobile started to buzz across the dashboard.

'Hello, Harry.'

'You're in luck, Jay. I've got an address for that Coyles woman. She rents bicycles from a cottage in Portaferry. The address is one, The Shambles, Portaferry. That's all I've got.'

'That's all I need. Cheers, mate.'

'Oh, and Jay . . .'

'No, Harry, I don't have time to bring you back some Portavogie scampi.'

195

'You know I can't eat fuckin' shellfish, Jay. The potassium's bad for my eczema. No, I was just going to tell you to tread carefully with Aisling Coyles. It seems she's a bit of a recluse. A dozen cats and a cottage falling on top of her. The last journalist that tried to speak to her was a guy from *The Times Literary Supplement*. She sliced his arm open with a rusty tin of Sheba. She cut his fuckin' artery.'

'How can she be a recluse if she rents out bicycles?'

'Oh, she has no problem with tourists, Jay. It's just fuckin' journalists that she stabs with cat food.'

'Well, I'm all right then. Sure, aren't you always telling me that I'm not a *proper fuckin' journalist*.'

'That's bollocks, Jay. You're the best this paper's ever had. It's just, well, sometimes you go too fuckin' far. You get yourself in these situations and . . . how many times have I defended you, eh? I'm the reason you still have a job. But you agreed to keep your head down. No more scandal. Jeez, it was your decision to retire to a two-day week and be put out to graze on the entertainment page. I'd have you back on the juicy stuff tomorrow.'

'I appreciate it, Harry, but don't get your hopes up. I'm coming out of retirement on this one, but it's this one only. And I wouldn't pursue this story if I didn't have a gun to my head. After Christmas I'll be back to my gigs, back to reviewing all those bands with ridiculous names and no tunes who just aren't Sinatra.'

'Aye, well, you never did do it *my way*.'

'And I'm not about to, Harry.'

I turned the car off the motorway and headed up the Down coast.

17

Portaferry sits at the bottom of the Ards Peninsula. To get to it, I had to take the car ferry from Strangford across the narrowest point of Strangford Lough. If the Ards Peninsula is shaped like a finger with Portaferry at its tip, the opposing Strangford coastline resembles a stubby thumb. Where the two villages meet, they appear to pinch the Irish Sea on the behind.

The late afternoon sun made a concerted effort to hold its head above the waterline, resisting the polar drag. Slick rugs of seaweed popped and burbled on the surface of the lough as the ferry churned it up. An inquisitive seal flitted round our bow, checking us out.

I was the only car passenger on the ferry. Two male cyclists sponsored by North Face fanned their water-proof map open and let it flap like a sail in the breeze. The air tasted of sea salt and petrol. Over the persistent belching of the ferry engine I managed to ascertain that the cyclists were Scandinavian. Not that I could deter-mine whether they were Swedes, Danes, Finns or Norwegians, I merely recognized a bouncy lilt in their accents that was characteristic of the region. They seemed to be having difficulty with the map, so I offered to help them out.

'Er . . . hello. Me *Jay*.' I pointed to myself. 'I help *you*?' I pointed to them. 'With your *map*?' I pointed to their map.

The pair of them looked at me like I'd shaken off my care worker.

'Um . . . it OK, I not *dangerous*.' I stabbed them with an imaginary knife while shaking my head in the negative. 'Me from *Northern Ireland*.' I pulled an imaginary balaclava over my head and fired an imaginary gun over an imaginary coffin. No, I didn't. I pointed to the surrounding hills and the truly absorbing, sheep-flecked fields. 'Are you from *Norway*?' I asked. I stroked the imaginary horns on my imaginary Viking helmet.

They looked at each other and smirked. I tried again.

'You *Sweden*?' I had never been much of a singer, but I gave it a go: '*Gimme, gimme, gimme a man after midnight*?'

Their reaction to my warbling killed any ambitions I had to pursue an alternative career singing swing tunes on cruise ships. The two of them were convulsing.

'We not Sweden,' said the Scandinavian who was shedding the fewest tears. He added, 'We from Swansea.'

The ferry journey was only fifteen minutes, but it felt like an hour. I walked to the starboard side of the boat, as far away from the Welsh cyclists as I was able, but I could not escape their pant-wetting cackles, occasionally punctuated by Abba classics sung in deep-voiced close harmony.

By the time the ferry docked I was already sitting in Karma's car. The barrier was let down to form a bridge onto the slip. I started the car. Or rather, I turned the key in the ignition and waited for something to happen. Not a murmur. I had run out of petrol, luck, or both. The Datsun had given up on me. You could only push a car so far and Karma's old banger had endured enough. It had finally thrown in the chamois leather.

The local ferryman and his cross-eyed son helped me to push the car onto land, but not before offering to do me a favour and push her off the other end of the boat and into the water. I had seen *Deliverance* so I thought it safer not to argue with them, lest I ended up squealing like a piggy. We rolled the Datsun up into one of the six empty spaces in the small harbour car park. I offered the ferryman a tenner for his trouble, to have a couple of Guinness on me. He declined the money, saying he didn't drink Guinness. Of course, I thought, he probably distilled his own illicit moonshine up in the hills, from local spuds. I offered him the money again, telling him to put it towards his son's banjo lessons. But he waved it away with a six-fingered hand.

I rescued what few valuables I had from the car and made my way into the village on foot.

Portaferry has all the simple, familiar components of the traditional Irish village – a bakery, a butcher's, a greengrocer, a post office, a fire station, seventeen pubs and an internationally celebrated aquarium. It also has a castle; at least, it has the remnants of a castle. I walked past it as I ascended a steep road that curved into the village, away from the coast. A clamour of rooks had made their nests in the castle's ruined tower. Untidy beards of vegetation sprouted from every nook in the stone. A sign informed me that from March to September I could pay £8 to enter the ruin and cavort round its bedraggled ramparts. But this was December and the gates were heavily padlocked. The old granary next to the

199

castle was open, but you could no longer enjoy the smells of malt and grain and freshly baked soda farls that had once infused the Portaferry air. The old building had been turned into a clumsy arcade filled with gift and craft shops. I made my way inside, however, to enquire about their most famous local resident.

The shop was stocked with all the usual suspects – assorted shillelaghs, inflatable shamrocks, a leprechaun's laughter captured in a miniature whisky bottle. You could even buy a CD recording of the ambient sounds of Strangford Lough. Presumably you could lie back in bed and relax to the gentle claps of lapping water, the plaintive *coor-li* that gives the curlew its name, and the distant coughs of seals, before the relentless industrial thrashing of a ferryboat kicked in and woke your neighbours.

I ignored the tat and made straight for the books. I found a carousel totally devoted to the novels of Aisling Coyles. I spun it round and examined the covers, all illustrated in watercolour and all by the same artist. Each one depicted a beautiful young colleen dressed in tight-fitting, turn-of-the-century peasant attire, deferring herself into the arms of some square-jawed, sideburned and uniformed man. Each couple stood under an oppressive sky on some exposed stretch of Ireland, a beach, a bog or a brooding hillside. The name AISLING COYLES was always dominant and embossed, and the titles underneath it were printed in a gold typeface so exuberant and swirling that, if you stared at it too long, it could induce a fit.

Aisling was a prolific writer, for I counted at least twenty different titles and each book was thick enough to inflict a serious pelvic injury should you inadvertently drop it on your lap. I grabbed three of the slimmest novels, but even they were substantial enough to rock the old granary to its foundations as I thumped them onto the counter. The girl standing behind it eyed me up and down. With similar scrutiny her laser gun scanned the barcodes.

'So, you don't look like an Aisling Coyles fan,' she said. 'They're usually twice your age, American and on hormone replacement.'

'The books are a Christmas present,' I said.

'Three books? Aren't you the generous son. You must really love your mother.'

'They're for my dad. I've bought my mum some tungsten drill bits for her Black & Decker.'

The girl shook her head. She was quite attractive in a rustic sort of way, though I suspected her ruddy hue had less to do with an enviable life spent on a bracing, windblown shoreline than with the Aran polo neck that she insisted on wearing in a hotly air-conditioned gift shop.

'That's twenty pounds ninety-seven. Do you want a bag?'

'What, to put over my head? Aye, it's probably best. I don't want anyone thinking I read gushing tragi-romances.'

'Nobody here will think ill of you. Are you in the village for long?'

'Just for the day. Actually, I lied about the books. They're not presents at all. I'm a journalist. I'm researching a biography of Aisling Coyles and I'm here to interview her. I don't suppose you could point me in the direction of the Shambles?'

'Sure. You walk up to the Square and cross it. The Shambles is the road running down to the shore from Craigan's Bar. Aisling Coyles lives in the blue cottage right at the very end of it. But I'll say this for nothing, she doesn't take kindly to inquisitive souls. The last boy who went up there with a notebook and pen came back with the arm hanging off him.' She slipped my books into a paper bag and tossed in a free bookmark. As she handed me my change, she let her hand linger on mine for a beat. 'If Ms Coyles doesn't eat you alive, perhaps I'll see you in the Drop Inn, opposite the Cornstore, at around eightish?'

'Perhaps,' I said. Jesus, I thought, they're not backward in coming forward around these parts.

'The name's Ciara.'

'And I'm Jay. Cheers, Ciara.'

The light had begun to fade as I crossed the Square. I watched the sun slip lazily into a kink in the hills, a copper penny dropping into a slot. By the time I reached the blue cottage it was indistinguishable from the cobalt night save for one window which flickered with the light from a fire. A broken white picket fence surrounded the garden like a jaw of rotten teeth. It couldn't keep the plants in or the cats out.

I hovered in the space where once there was a gate, wondering how I should play this. I removed one of the novels from my paper bag and checked the author's picture on the inside reverse of the sleeve. I wanted to get some idea of the ogre I was about to confront. The picture eased my pulse. Far from looking intimidating, Aisling Coyles had the assured smile of a woman who has just been offered six figures for the film rights to her ninth novel. Even her hair looked confident – dark, jagged curls zigzagged from solid silver roots. This was an engaging lady. She did not look like the sort of woman who would stab you if she took a dislike to you. But then, that sort of woman never does.

The photograph was copyrighted 1996, so she could not have changed much. I didn't think I had anything

202

to worry about, but, as I had received two warnings about Aisling in as many hours, I decided to approach the cottage with caution.

The front door was shrouded in dense ivy that had crept up on it from the unkempt garden. Indeed, it was hard to tell where the garden ended and the cottage began. There appeared to be no knocker or bell, so I sought admission with my knuckles. They slid dully off an oily scum that coated the door.

There wasn't a sound from within. Nobody was answering. I felt sure Aisling was at home, though. She was known to be a recluse and anyway, who in their right mind would go out and leave an unguarded fire burning in their living room? She mustn't have heard the knock. I tried again, harder this time, my wrists jarring with each short, sharp rap.

On the third knock something attached itself to my head. A loud hissing filled my ears. I grabbed fur. An animal had landed on me from the ivy above. It dug its claws into my scalp, using my skull as a pincushion. The pain was excruciating. I tried to find the back of its neck with my hands but only succeeded in finding its mouth. I felt the rasp of its tongue and the points of its teeth. A cat, I guessed. I pitched forward into the door, my full weight forcing a loud boom through the cottage. It seemed to do the trick, for although the cat's crampons adhered resolutely to the cliff face that was my forehead, the door was quickly answered.

'Jasper! Put the man down!'

Aisling Coyles made a grab for her pet, but it leapt out of the way allowing her hand to smack my ear.

'Christ, that hurt,' I said. I had recovered my vision enough to notice two puncture wounds to my right hand. I sucked at the holes and spat out the blood, like cats were venomous in this part of the world.

'I'm sorry about Jasper. I've just had him neutered and now he goes for any male he sees. I guess he's a little crotchety.' Aisling rested her hand on my back. 'Please don't report this. They'll make me put him down.'

'Don't panic. I think I can forgive your cat. I'd be crotchety if someone snipped my balls off.'

'Wait there,' she said. She walked back into the hallway and closed the door behind her.

I remained on the step with Jasper rubbing his flanks on my shins. He was purring contentedly, right up until the point when I kicked him into a hawthorn. When Aisling reopened the door, he was inside like a shot.

'Here, wipe this on those cuts,' she said. She handed me a damp and pungent sponge. 'It's tea tree oil. It's a natural antiseptic.'

I dabbed the sponge round my crown of thorns and onto the stigmata that bled from my hand. The tea tree oil was napalm. It ignited my head. Aisling prodded another sponge onto my ear. She was trying to be nice, but I found the action irritating, like your granny licking a tissue and wiping her lipstick off your cheek.

'So, what can I do for you?' she asked.

'Call an ambulance,' I said.

'Oh, come on now, don't be a big baby. You'll survive.'

'You sound like someone I know,' I said.

Aisling hadn't changed in the last five years. Well, the hair was almost totally silver now and she looked less assured as a nurse than a novelist, but she was still recognizable as the woman on the book jacket. Her eyes even hinted at the girl from the PolySoc Ball.

'Did you want to rent a bicycle?' she asked.

She was being friendly and warm and I wanted it to continue.

'Yes,' I said. 'I need a bicycle. My car's given up the ghost.'

'You don't sound like a tourist,' she said. 'Is that a Belfast accent?'

'It is. But in a way, I am a tourist. I figured that I've lived on this island for thirty-four years, yet I don't really know the place. So I'm touring the coast of Ireland, stopping at places beginning with the letter D. Ow!'

'Keep your head still,' scolded Aisling as she dabbed and prodded some more. 'So, why would you only stop at places beginning with D?'

'Well, it seems that these days you need a gimmick to tour Ireland. Like that bloke with the fridge, and yer man who stopped at every bar with his name on it – McCarthy, you call him. So I started my journey down in Dalkey, then went on to Dublin and Dundalk. And from here I'll go up to Donaghadee, Dunmurry, Derry and Donegal. I'm writing a book about it.'

'But why stop in Portaferry? It doesn't begin with D.'

'As I said, my car conked out. I had no choice but to stop. And anyway, it sort of begins with D. It's the Down Coast, after all.'

'Well, I suppose the least I can do is get you a bike then. Come on. Follow me.'

Aisling rammed her hands into the pockets of her densely crocheted cardigan and hugged the wool round her hips. She led me back through the invisible gate and across the road. We stopped at a lopsided barn. She lifted the latch.

'You should keep it locked,' I said. 'Someone might want to steal your bikes.'

'You obviously haven't seen my bikes,' she said.

The barn had no electricity, but Aisling unhooked a torch from one of the rafters. She moved it around the barn, catching the eyes of what I took to be rats. They immediately disappeared into the black.

'Take your pick,' she said, handing me the torch.

I dragged the torchlight over the bicycles, the moths fighting for centre stage in its beam. I picked out plenty of bicycle parts, but few complete bicycles. Those that were in reasonable working order were closer to the penny-farthing than the alloy mountain bike in the great chronology of two-wheeled propulsion. The names that I did recognize were all dated Raleighs – Tomahawks, Choppers, Boxers and an RSW with its puffy white tyres. In the end I plumped for a Triumph Twenty. It was the only one big enough to carry me that didn't have a basket or a horn attached to its handlebars.

'I'll take that one,' I said, fixing the Triumph Twenty in my night sight.

'But it's a girl's bike,' said Aisling.

'I know,' I said. 'But I'm comfortable with my sexuality.'

'Your choice. But I'll warn you, the young farmers here don't take too kindly to gays. Wheel her out, then.' Aisling secured the barn door behind me. 'And listen, you can have her for free. Keep her for as long as it takes you to get round Ireland and write that book.'

'No, please, let me give you something.' I reached into my back pocket.

'Uch, put it away,' said Aisling, dismissing me with a face so sour you'd have sworn she'd swallowed a lime. 'It's the least I can do after Jasper assaulted you. If you must give me something, you can give me a mention in your book.'

I felt awful. She had shown me so much goodwill

that I could no longer keep up the pretence. Aisling was no ogre. She was a considerate woman who valued her privacy. I knew she would help me, but the longer my lies went on, and the bigger they got, the less likely it was that she'd talk to me about O'Hanlon. I walked her back to the cottage before I came clean.

'I haven't been entirely honest with you, Aisling.'

Her face dropped. 'How did you know my name? Uch, don't tell me you're another bloody fan. Well, I'm not signing anything, if that's what you're after.'

'No, I'm not a fan.'

'Well, thank you.'

'No, I didn't mean it like that. Look.' I opened my paper bag. 'I've bought three of your novels but I've yet to read them. Perhaps I'll become a fan. For now I'm just a two-bit hack that wants a bit of information.'

'You're a journalist? Well, of all the despicable, underhand ruses ... Give me that bike.' Aisling wrested the handlebars from my grip. 'I don't talk to journalists. I never talk about my writing. *Never.*'

'I don't want to talk about your writing.'

Aisling wheeled the bicycle up her garden path, ripping its wheels through the tatty weeds. She propped it against the door and fought with her cardigan for the key.

'I want to talk about Kate Rogers.'

She turned and looked directly at me, the moon catching her corneas like a rat in torchlight.

'I want to talk to you about Kate Rogers and Martin O'Hanlon and 1967.'

Aisling rattled the key in the door. She opened it, allowing Jasper to shoot through her ankles. She slammed the door behind her.

The surrounding hills reverberated to the beautiful sound of a Triumph Twenty landing on a cat.

18

The Drop Inn proved more difficult to find than I had imagined. I followed Ciara's directions but found myself standing in front of a faceless grey terrace. There was no sign to indicate the boozer, no Day-Glo posters and no giant, wall-mounted, backlit pint of Guinness. I only knew for sure that there was a pub among the long line of duplicate housing when a drunken eejit fell onto the street through one of the brightly painted doors. I sought confirmation from the man.

'Excuse me, is this The Drop Inn?'

'My eyes!' he screamed. He staggered down the street, blindfolding himself with his hands.

I made my way into the pub. It was brightly lit by strip lighting that flickered intermittently like poor man's disco. The plastic casing that housed the long white tubes was littered with the dried-out husks of wasps, flies, spiders, and what appeared to be a condom. They formed ghoulish silhouettes and in some way contributed to the curious smell about the place. It smelt like a dead man's waistcoat – a blend of tobacco, stale soap and vinegar. The regulars were of such an advanced average age I decided the pub should be renamed The Drop Dead.

As I made my way to the bar, a few of the auld fellas kept a tight hold of their pints and gave me that steely, you're-not-from-around-here look. I ordered a Kilkenny, convinced I was in the wrong bar. Surely a young lass like Ciara wouldn't spend her quality drinking time in a hole like this? It was only after I paid for my pint that I saw a door to the right of the bar that led to an annexe. I walked through and the traditional Oirish Come-All-Ye's that had been bleating over the tinny speakers in the front bar were immediately replaced by the more contemporary, antiseptic strains of David Gray.

A younger crowd populated the annexe and all of them were engaged in a game of Killer on the pool table. It had gone 'eightish' but there was no sign of Ciara. Not that I particularly wanted to see her, but she was a friendly face and I'd seen precious few of those since my arrival in Portaferry. Ciara also seemed to know a little bit about Aisling, so perhaps she could advise me on another way of approaching the recalcitrant recluse. I found a sticky table and supped my warm beer.

When the Winter Olympics are screened, I sometimes catch myself staying up till four in the morning engrossed in the quarter-finals of the curling, or lifting the phone off the hook while the Nordic skiing unfolds. In the same pointless way, I quickly became absorbed in the game of Killer being enacted before me. A dozen of the young locals were sharing the same cue, at least the same broken half of a cue. A guy in a cheap replica Manchester United shirt (sponsored by 'Vodkafone') was using the same stick of school chalk on the cue that he used to score the lives on the small blackboard. The pool table was so threadbare they were playing 'preferred lies'. The game had to be interrupted at one point while they squeegeed cider and blackcurrant off the 'D'. One of the girls deliberately tugged back her boyfriend's arm as he tried to address the cueball. He then threatened to put the ball in his sock and 'bate her round the head' with it. I watched all this in the sure and profound knowledge that Sky Sports could make a fortune screening it.

I spotted a payphone in the small hallway that connected the annexe to the main bar. I considered phoning Meeks to update him on my whereabouts. I even got as far as placing my pint on top of the phone and sorting my loose change. I called the number but hung up the moment it was answered. It had suddenly dawned on me how stupid I was being. Meeks didn't give a shit about Scarlet and he didn't give a shit about me. All he wanted was O'Hanlon and I couldn't deliver him. I was expendable in his grand scheme. He was probably at this moment issuing a warrant for my arrest in connection with the suspected manslaughter of Miles Huggins. He was reopening one of my many old wounds but I no longer cared. And because I didn't care, I was liberated from the Chief Constable's blackmail. He no longer owned me.

Scarlet was dead and I wanted to bring her killers to justice. That was all that mattered. The IRA were onto me and the RUC had probably been instructed to haul me in. I was effectively on the run. I had to elude all of them until I got something on O'Hanlon. He was going to tell me where Scarlet was dumped.

Without a body, there was no murder. The press would be billing Scarlet as the next Richey Manic, one of rock's great disappeared. She was on medication, she was unstable, she was scared of her impending fame and so she opted out, that's what they'd be saying. Stupid boys would be filling the letter pages of *NME* and *Melody Maker* with sightings of Scarlet in their local ASDA, or they'd be claming they bumped into her while backpacking in Thailand. They'd say she looked drugged, had her head shaved and was living in a cave.

Without a body the book could never be closed.

Ironically, if I could get something on O'Hanlon – something that was sufficiently humiliating for him to tell me where Scarlet was, in return for my silence – it would inherently be humiliating enough to force him to stand down in the election, make a move on de-commissioning and get Meeks off my back. I could kill two birds. Trouble was, my only hope of getting such information in such a short time resided with Aisling Coyles. And she was staying schtum. To get her to talk, I had to find a way of appealing to her better sensibilities. And to do that, I had to understand the woman.

'So how did you find Ms Coyles?'

It was Ciara. I didn't have time to lift the novels off the crowded table, so she was forced to balance her drink on top of the pulpy stack. She pulled a stool under her bottom.

'How did I find Aisling? I followed your directions,' I said.

'No, I mean, how was she with you?'

'She was nice. Quite sweet, really.'

'She stabbed you repeatedly with her crochet needle and you think that's *quite sweet, really*? Christ, what does it take to piss you off?'

'Sorry, Ciara, what are you talking about?'

'Your head. Look at it. It's like a friggin' colander. And your skin's gone yellow.'

I stood up and checked my head in the Jameson's

mirror. It explained the severe looks I had received on entering the bar.

'Oh, shit. I forgot. Her cat attacked me. The yellow stuff is tea tree oil.'

'Her cat attacked you with tea tree oil?'

'No. He'd just been neutered. He was a bit prickly.'

'Neutered? What did you do, slam his balls between two of those books I sold you? No wonder he went for you.'

Ciara hoisted her Aran sweater over her head. I watched her breasts rise and fall in her white cotton T-shirt and I swear I heard Scarlet scolding me. Ciara slipped an elasticated band off her wrist and stuffed it into her teeth. She scooped her hair to the back of her head and twisted the band over it to make the dinkiest ponytail. She repositioned herself on the stool, allowing her chest to dip forward slightly. She let her knees touch mine. And though she was clearly an attractive girl, I felt no spark, no magic, no electricity or chemistry, none of those things you're supposed to feel when you make a connection. I felt only guilt and emptiness and I wondered whether I would ever be able to make a connection again.

I defaulted to journalist mode.

'So, Ciara, what do you know about Aisling Coyles? I mean, apart from the novels and the psychopathic predisposition towards journalists.'

'Jeez, that's a big dictionary you've swallowed. The biggest word I know is phloccinoccinihilipilification. I think it's somewhere in Wales.'

'Seriously. How long has Aisling been living in Portaferry? Does she get on with the locals? Has she ever had a male friend, or a husband? And how come she's living in a rundown cottage renting clapped-out bicycles to tourists, when she's clearly worth millions?'

Ciara counted on her fingers as she rattled off the answers. 'Since I was born. Keeps herself to herself. I don't think so and definitely not. And I haven't the foggiest.'

'Is that it?' I asked.

'Listen, Jase—'

'Jay.'

'Jay. I don't make it my business to know everything about the woman. You're her biographer. *You're* supposed to be telling people like *me* about Aisling Coyles.'

She had a point.

'Now,' she said. 'Are you going to buy me another drink, or are you going to sit there with your head buried in her bloody novels?' She picked up the top book – *The Cross in the Sand* – and tossed it at the fruit machine. It fluttered to the ground, more of a brick than a butterfly.

'That's it,' I said. 'That's what I should do.'

'Great. I'll have a Southern Comfort and lime.'

'No, not that. I should read one of Aisling's books. She won't let me into her cottage, but I can still get inside her head.'

'You can what?'

'If I read one of her books, I'll at least get a sense of how the woman thinks. And if I know how she thinks, I'll know how to get a response from her. I'll be able to get her to see things my way. I'll get her to talk.'

'You're forgetting one thing, Jay.'

'What's that?'

'Her books are fiction. They're made-up stories. They're lies. How can you read someone's mind when all they tell is lies?'

'Ciara, if I can get into the darkest, loneliest recesses of someone's brain by rooting through their dustbin, I can do it by rummaging through their prose. Now, if you don't mind, I'm going to find myself a bed and I'm going to curl up with a good book.'

I retrieved the novel from the gummy carpet and slid it back into the paper bag beside its sisters. I necked my dregs and made for the front bar.

'Oi, what about my Southern Comfort and lime?' shouted Ciara.

I ran my hands along one of the cushions on the pool table, scooping up a fistful of twenty pees. I handed them to Ciara and beat a hasty exit.

It was cold out. One solitary beer provided little in the way of insulation. I began to trawl the streets in search of a guest house, but they had camouflaged themselves even more successfully than the pubs. I spotted a pinkish blur of neon in the distance and walked towards it in the hope that it would come into focus as the word 'Vacancy'. I wasn't too disappointed that it eventually read 'Chips, Peas & Gravy'. I hadn't eaten since the Sinn Fein tea party.

In the length of time it takes to eat a cod with curry sauce, I found a guest house. The Narrows it was called, possibly a reference to the size of its rooms. I had gone forty hours without sleep, so frankly I didn't care. I would've paid good plastic to bed down in their washing machine if it had a 'Do Not Disturb' sign on the door.

My room wasn't lavishly appointed, but it had all the requisites necessary to satisfy the experienced bed-time reader. It had a bed, a light and a floor. I stripped down to my boxers and got under the covers. I folded the pillow in three and stuffed it behind my head to create at least the illusion of comfort. I had kept the plastic fork from my curried cod and I set it beside me. If I caught myself nodding off, I could jab it into my thigh.

I tipped the chunky Aisling Coyles novels onto the bed and one of the legs collapsed. It didn't, but if it had, I could have used the two spare books to prop the bed up. This raised the question: which book do I actually read – *The Dingle Bride*, *The Cross in the Sand*, or *The Rose of Inishowen*? If I judged them by their covers, which you're never supposed to do, I would have said that they were all shameless retreads of exactly the same story with a few names and hair colours changed. No, I had to use other criteria. I considered going for the shortest one, but even that came in at 723 pages and, as my intention was to skim read, the length didn't really matter. In the end I let Ciara make the decision for me. I chose the book that she had thrown to the floor of the bar – *The Cross in the Sand*. I ignored the curly hairs stuck to its cover and I soon grew accustomed to the smell of stale ale and vomit as I started to read.

The Cross in the Sand by Aisling Coyles is the story of two young women – best friends – and a long hot summer in Gweedore, County Donegal. One of the women – Aoibhinn – falls in love with the son of a wealthy landowner, a local rebel named Michael O'Hare. Their fledgling romance drives a wedge between Aoibhinn and her best friend, Catherine. Catherine is jealous of Aoibhinn and Michael. She envies the time the couple spend together, their long afternoons lost in the dunes. And even though Catherine believes that she is the woman for Michael, she begins to display an irrational hatred towards the handsome young buck.

Sadly, when the unforgiving Donegal winter sets in, Aoibhinn falls ill with suspected consumption. Catherine is forced to forego her differences with

Michael as they both tend to the stricken girl. In a moment alone with Aoibhinn, Michael promises to marry her if she pulls through. Miraculously, she begins to regain some strength and it seems that the worst is over. But Catherine begins to panic. She had been eavesdropping on Michael's proposal. If Aoibhinn marries Michael, Catherine will lose her best friend for ever. More crucially, she will lose any chance she has of ever becoming Michael's bride. She will not let that happen.

Catherine turns coquette and sets about performing the ultimate in treachery by seducing Michael. The local community is holding a night of festivities to herald the shortest day of the year. Aoibhinn is still too frail to attend, but she urges Michael to leave her bedside and go with her best friend. As they bask in the wobbling heat from a burning effigy, Catherine plies Michael with a flagon of seaweed cider. He succumbs to her advances and on this dark and fateful night, Michael O'Hare deflowers Catherine.

A month passes and Aoibhinn makes a full recovery. But, while she plans her wedding, her maid of honour (Catherine) is telling her fiancé (Michael) that she is with child. Michael rides out to the shore and berates the gods. They, in turn, rain their thunder and lightning down on him, soaking his shirt and providing an enduring image for all female viewers of the resulting BBC adaptation.

Michael visits Aoibhinn and delivers the news that, even though he loves her, he must stand by Catherine and his child. Aoibhinn takes to the hills in her wedding dress. Her frozen corpse is discovered some days later by a local turf-cutter.

Michael is distraught. His heart has been ripped from his rain-soaked chest. At Aoibhinn's wake he publicly blames Catherine for the death of his true love. He will not support her, nor will he provide for the bastard child she bears.

The novel ends with Catherine giving birth alone on the wide expanse of Carrickfinn beach, in the throes of a tempestuous Atlantic storm. The baby – a boy – is stillborn. Catherine buries him in the sand and marks the grave with a small cross, fashioned from driftwood and seagrass. She walks into the roaring ocean and is never seen again.

It's a black comedy.

I also suspected that *The Cross in the Sand* was a flimsily disguised autobiography.

I dressed.

There were no signs of life by the time I walked down to the blue cottage. Aoibhinn had extinguished her fire. A glance at my watch told me it was 2.22 a.m. The book had taken longer to skim read than I had anticipated. I took a pen from my pocket and wrote on its cover. The novel was too big to be squeezed through her letter box so I propped it against the foot of her door, secured by the weight of a broken roof tile.

How was I to know I was being watched?

I righted the fallen Triumph Twenty, quietly untangling it from the ivy. I cycled back to the Narrows, convinced that Aoibhinn would talk.

19

> '*I am the ancient one,*
> *I am the Sea.*
> *They call me the Irish Sea,*
> *a shallow and narrow sea.*
> *You have come to visit me.*
> *Your fathers and their fathers feared me*
> *in all my moods and movements,*
> *for I am the giver*
> *and the taker.*'

I stood in a pitch black room in Portaferry's Exploris Aquarium watching a video installation that cut from crashing breakers to waves the size of houses, to pin-prick trawlers being juggled unmercifully by a heaving grey mass of Irish water. I exited before my breakfast moved northwards.

It was 10.38. Aisling was eight minutes late. The first waves of doubt crashed through me. What if she hadn't got my message? She could be having a lie-in. Or perhaps she had opened her front door to let the cat out or bring the milk in and the book had fallen face down, obscuring my hastily penned message and my request to meet her in the aquarium. She might have picked it up and tossed it in the bin, thinking it was merely from a desperate fan seeking her signature.

But what if she *had* read my message and still refused to come? Surely she wouldn't, not when she read my interpretation of *The Cross in the Sand*. She wouldn't be able to resist it. If I was wrong about the book, she would want to tell me I was wrong. See, I was beginning to understand the woman. Aisling didn't talk to journalists because journalists were full of speculation. They would take her words and misrepresent them. At least as a novelist, sitting at her typewriter, she was in control of her words. If I was wrong about the subtext to *The Cross in the Sand*, she would feel compelled to put me right. She wouldn't want me to go speculating all over the newspapers.

And if I was right about the book . . . well.

The aquarium wasn't busy. I had the free run of its dark tunnels. They took me on an underwater journey from Strangford Lough to the depths of the Irish Sea, their luminescent tanks brimming with all forms of sea life native to Ulster's shores. The only other human I passed was a student dressed as Neil the Seal. He assured me I was 'as close as you get, without getting wet!'

If their names were anything to go by, Northern Ireland had some seriously hard-done-by marine life – the poor cod, the brittle star, the lesser octopus, the thick-lipped mullet, the pouting and the small fry. Presumably the latter native could also be referred to as the Ulster fry.

I felt suddenly hungry. The yellow tang, the mandarin fish and the sea gooseberries weren't helping. I wanted to squeeze a lemon over half the exhibits. A large Dublin Bay prawn was looking particularly vulnerable. He retreated behind his rock.

219

A bloated coral that grew in one of the tanks was *Alcyonium Digitatum*, or dead man's fingers. The fish that exfoliated themselves against it were triggerfish. The irony did not escape me. Only in the Northern Irish aquarium would the fingers be on the triggers. An adjacent wave tank further educated me about my homeland. For Northern Ireland isn't merely comprised of a Protestant community and a Catholic community, it appears we're also home to a thriving kelp community.

I made my way into the central hub of the Exploris complex. Eight large tanks formed the outer perimeter of this circular room. I stopped by one of the windows and stared unblinkingly at what I thought was a shark. It was four foot long and it patrolled its water like a cold-blooded sentinel. A nameplate reliably informed me I was looking at a harmless bull huss. Whatever, I wasn't about to slice a knife across my calf muscle and paddle in on my lilo to find out.

In the centre of this room sat an open octagonal touch tank, filled with crabs, urchins, starfish and 'friendly rays'. An old fella dressed in the Exploris uniform was cleaning one of the tank's eight glass panels. I had a question for him.

'Excuse me, why are they called *friendly* rays?'

He didn't look up. He sprayed Windolene onto the reinforced pane and continued to wipe it down. I tried again.

'In what way are the rays friendly?' I asked. 'Do they insist on getting the first round in? Can you always count on them in a crisis?'

Still he ignored me. I tapped him on the shoulder. He turned to face me, revealing the hearing aid on the other side of his head. I spoke slowly, shaping my words deliberately, so he could read my lips.

'Why are they called friendly rays?'

'EASY!' he shouted. 'RAYS ARE COVERED IN SENSORY ORGANS, SO THEY'RE INQUISITIVE BUGGERS, ALWAYS CHECKING OUT WHAT'S HAPPENING ON THE WATER SURFACE. THEY'LL COME RIGHT UP TO YOU AND LET YOU STROKE THEM. GO ON, STICK YOUR HAND IN.'

'No thanks. I was just asking.'

'GO ON, STICK YOUR HAND IN. THEY LOVE IT.'

'No, I really—'

'GO ON.'

'OK, OK.' I dipped my hand in the water and stroked the friendliest ray. Anything to shut him up. The old fella that is, not the ray.

'Having fun?'

Aisling had caught me with my elbow in the water.

'No, I'm just selecting my lunch. I've had skate wing before, but never ray.' I removed my arm from the tank and wiped it dry on my thigh. I offered Aisling my hand. 'Thank you for coming. I was beginning to think you were going to stand me up.'

'I gave it serious consideration,' she said. 'Yours, I believe.' She handed me the copy of *The Cross in the Sand*, the one I had defaced. 'It makes interesting reading,' she added.

'Well, you would say that. You wrote it.'

'I'm talking about the foreword that you so rudely scribbled over the cover.'

'Yes, I apologize for that. I had nothing else to write on.'

'That's another thing I dislike about you journalists. You're so uncouth. You have no respect for the written word. You'll write your misguided musings and your idiotic insinuations on anything at hand – beer mats, matchboxes, napkins. Rather appropriate I suppose.

221

The quality of the prose is directly proportional to the quality of the medium it is written on. Might I suggest you carry a pen and a toilet roll everywhere you go, in case inspiration grabs you.'

Bingo, I thought. I had touched a nerve. I had got to Aisling Coyles. She was standing in front of me and she was talking. I decided to come right out with it.

'So I'm right about your book, then. Kate Rogers and Martin O'Hanlon had a child, didn't they? It's all there in *The Cross in the Sand*. The two best friends – Aoibhinn and Catherine – they're Aisling and Kate. And the *handsome young rebel* Michael O'Hare, he's Martin O'Hanlon.'

Aisling nodded. She dipped the tip of her little finger into the water and trailed a wake through its meniscus.

'Marty . . .' she said. 'Martin and I were together back then, you know, as a couple, a regular item.' She cleared her throat. 'Listen, this is ridiculous. I don't think I should be talking about this. I've kept quiet all these years. Why should I suddenly go blabbing to you? I don't even know you.' She walked towards the exit.

'Wait. I'll tell you why you should talk to me. Martin O'Hanlon had my girlfriend murdered. He's killed the woman I love.'

Aisling looked horrified. She nodded towards the old boy cleaning the glass.

'That's OK. He can't hear a thing. He's deaf.' For some reason I mouthed the last two words without actually speaking them. Like he could hear me.

Aisling then did a strange thing. She put her hands to her mouth and shouted, 'FIRE!'

The old fella didn't blink. He squirted, sprayed, smeared and sponged.

Aisling shrugged and rejoined me at the touch tank. 'Marty O'Hanlon killed the woman you love?' she repeated, with some incredulity.

I knew that would hook her. I had appealed to the novelist's romantic sensibilities and now I only had to reel her in.

'Yes. He killed Scarlet and he's hidden her body. I just want to get her back. That's why you need to talk to me. I need to know about Martin O'Hanlon and Kate Rogers. I need to threaten him into giving Scarlet up. If what you say is true, and Martin and Kate had a child, I need to know about it. I need to know every detail, to give credence to my threat. If I leak this story, the embarrassment will destroy O'Hanlon. I need some clout. So talk to me, Aisling. Tell me everything.'

Aisling was still eyeing the cleaner with some degree of uncertainty, but slowly she found her voice.

'Like I said, Martin and I were boyfriend and girlfriend. We were inseparable. I had a room in the Queen's Elms, you know, the halls of residence. Marty and I would skip lectures and sit in my room smoking Gallaghers and listening to the Kinks. He could talk for hours, about anything. He had a frightful intellect even as a teenager. He was a wonderful lover, too. Very patient. Marty had such a gentle way about him. Hard to believe it of him now.'

Aisling let her woolly sleeves fall down over her hands. She scrunched them into her pockets and rubbed the bottom of her cardigan about her waist to generate warmth.

'He proposed to me, you know. We had a date set and everything, eighth of July 1967. Course, by then Kate Rogers was pregnant by him. None of us knew. Kate and Marty . . . they were so different. They could never agree on anything, whether it was politics,

223

religion, or how many tea bags you should stick in a pot. It was strange though, because even though she seemed to actively hate Marty, Kate wanted to spend more and more time with him. She was always dragging him out of my room to work on that blasted paper. Well, I now know what she was up to.'

'And what was that?' I asked, feigning naivety.

'Kate was fascinated by Marty. He was dangerous and she craved danger. Throughout her childhood Kate had everything handed to her on a plate – the cheerleader looks, the private education, the typically cosy upbringing in the Home Counties. Her father was a top-ranking officer in the British army. Her mother was the first female lawyer in Britain to command a six-figure salary. But this wasn't enough for Kate. She had to rebel. And boy, did she pick the right guy to rebel with. Martin O'Hanlon. The Wild One. The Irish Rover.'

There was a sudden commotion in the water. The rays were disturbed by something. They rippled their fins, unsettling the sediment and turning the water orange. Aisling seemed to clam up. I produced the pictures from the PolySoc Ball, to see if they would jar her. The page quickly blistered with drops of salt water. I assumed they were generated by the flapping rays. Then I saw Aisling's eyes.

'I'm sorry,' she said. 'It's just, I think that that was the night.'

'What night?'

'*The* night. The Queen's PolySoc Ball. Fifth of May, 1967. That was the night Kate slept with Marty. I had to go home early, I wasn't well. I don't know whether it was the drink, the food, or some bug that I'd picked up. Marty and Kate both offered to take me back to halls, but I insisted they stay on and enjoy the party.

They'd paid three pounds each for their tickets, which was a lot of money back then, especially when you're trying to live off a grant. I told the pair of them to stay and get their money's worth. Ha!' Aisling was shaking her head. 'They certainly did. And they got more than they bargained for when Marty's condom split.'

'Martin O'Hanlon wore condoms? He's a God-fearing Catholic. I didn't think he believed in the things.'

'Well, he doesn't believe in them now. Not after he got Kate up the stick.'

Aisling seemed to cheer herself with the thought.

'So, Kate was pregnant with Martin's child. Did she have an abortion?'

Aisling shook her head. This was getting better by the minute. If the bastard offspring of the Sinn Fein leader and the Secretary of State was alive and well and willing to take a DNA test, Scarlet would get her justice and Meeks would be kissing my boots.

'So where is he? I'm assuming the baby was a boy, like the one in your book?'

'Yes, they had a little boy. But I don't know where he is . . . Heaven, Hell, who can tell.'

'I don't understand.'

'You said you read my book. Think about it.'

I played dumb even though I knew what was coming. I needed to hear her say it. I needed to know every detail. Aisling duly obliged.

'Kate confessed to me that she had slept with my fiancé and his child was growing inside her. But she told me not to cancel the wedding. She had decided to have an abortion. Well, abortion was illegal in Northern Ireland, still is, so Kate planned to head back to England. She begged me not to tell Marty that she was pregnant. Abortion went against everything he believed in.'

225

'So he was opposed to abortion, but he believed in condoms. What cock-eyed form of Catholicism did Martin O'Hanlon practise?'

'Let me finish,' insisted Aisling. 'I could have kept quiet and married Marty and he would have been none the wiser. But I'm not one of those gormless doormats on the covers of my books. I wasn't going to wear the pretty dress and play the kept woman. I wanted to hurt him. So, when I ended our relationship, I told Marty that Kate was pregnant. Well, he went spare. He pleaded with Kate to have his child. For weeks he wouldn't let her out of his sight, afraid she'd hop on a boat. But Kate was determined to have that abortion. Unfortunately, she had no money. Marty wasn't going to give it to her. And she could hardly turn to her parents. Imagine it, the daughter of a British officer impregnated by an Irish hooligan. They'd have dis-inherited her. So Kate skipped her end-of-year exams and took a job in the Ulster Museum. But by the time she'd raised the cash to get herself back to England, no clinic would take her. She was too far gone.'

'So she *did* have the kid.'

'She did. She fell straight back into Martin O'Hanlon's arms for the remainder of the pregnancy. I honestly believe she tried to make a real go of their relationship. And who knows what would have happened had the baby survived. It might have changed the course of Irish history.'

'But it was stillborn, wasn't it? Like the child in your book.'

'Not a breath in him. Nothing but a little blue bag of skin and bone. Martin was beside himself. It destroyed him. Believe me, that child's death was the ruin of Martin O'Hanlon. As far as he was concerned, Kate Rogers had killed his wee boy. This woman, this

English woman, had murdered his child. It's all very sad. Marty used to place such great value on the sanctity of human life, but from that day on, and for decades after that, he exhibited such a wilful disregard for it. The baby came into this world and died the same day in 1968. It couldn't have happened at a worse time. Marty was heavily involved in the whole Civil Rights thing and, you know, some of that lot weren't too civil. He had a grievance and a cause and well, the rest is . . . tragic. So bloody tragic.'

A party of primary schoolchildren filed into the circular room. Aisling kept her face away from them and clapped her palms on the water. The teacher counted heads, and once the number tallied with the one on his clipboard, he led them away from us, down one of the dark corridors.

'What did Kate do? In your book, Catherine walks into the sea and isn't seen again.'

'Kate buried the child in Northern Ireland. Martin had disowned her by that stage, and she couldn't afford a funeral, but the nurses up at the Royal all clubbed together and helped her out. Kate went back home, across the Irish Sea and, like Catherine, I never saw her again. Not in the flesh, anyhow. But some years later I switched on my television and there she stood, delivering a speech about family values to delegates at the Labour Party conference. Talk about double standards. She married Labour's young hotshot Geraint Owen and, well, you know the rest. No doubt her education in the North of Ireland helped her secure her present ministerial post.' Aisling looked me dead in the eye. 'I will never forgive her for coming between Marty and me.'

A meaty crack.

Aisling's windpipe burst out of her neck.

I wiped her blood from my eyes.

The deaf cleaner stood behind her with a hot gun in his hand.

Aisling's weight pulled her into the touch tank, the mass of her body displacing an equal quantity of water. It was enough to distract the gunman. I ducked down behind one of the thick glass panels before he had time to discharge another shot.

We remained like that for ten, maybe twenty seconds. I was crouched down behind one of the eight reinforced panels, with Aisling's killer on one of the opposite sides. If the water had been clear, it would have been easy to tell which panel he hid behind. I had earlier been able to see right through the octagonal tank. But the water was seething with sediment and blood and unfriendly rays.

I could hear a scuffing sound. I sensed that the gunman was crawling round the tank towards me. But from which direction was he coming?

I chose to go left.

I chose wrong.

He fired again.

He missed.

I lunged at him, but he threw me off with frightening ease, like he was brushing a hair from his lapel. The guy had the strength of someone twenty years younger.

He aimed his gun at me.

But something seemed to distract him. I followed his eyes to see a small frosty circle spouting water and quickly cobwebbing across the glass window on one of the large tanks in the perimeter wall. His errant bullet must have caught it. The glass let out a resigned groan before its full force exploded over us.

I felt like a cat in a washing machine. All the lights went out. I only saw what a surfer must see when he's swallowed by a tube. Except that the water that took me was one part coral and two parts glass. It cut me. It winded me. It grabbed me by the hair and repeatedly smacked my head on the floor. Then it dispersed itself down the various corridors that led off the circular room. I felt like the victim of a punishment beating watching his assailants escaping down the back alleys. The water ran away and left me for dead.

Then I remembered the old fella, the cleaner, the killer. Where was he? Was he about to finish me off?

I tried to get my bearings, but I could only open one eye. The other was stung by salt. The water had deposited me in a different part of the room to the one I'd been crouching in. The central octagonal tank remained intact, with Aisling floating face down in the crimson murk. The scene around it was madness itself, like the Provos had targeted Atlantis. There was none of the familiar debris associated with a terror bombing – no broken masonry, no contorted car parts, no innocent shoppers lying dead and undignified with the clothes blown from their bloody bodies. The devastation that surrounded me was bizarre – a lot of glass, a lot of water and a lot of flick-flacking fish.

I caught sight of the gun. Its owner was hauling himself along the floor towards it. His Exploris uniform was soaked through. His head was bleeding. He had lost all his grey hair. The water had swapped his wig for a healthy clot of dark hair that clung to his forehead like seaweed to a pier wall. His moustache, too, had disappeared with the flotsam and jetsam. His hearing aid was another bit of disguise lost at sea.

He got his hand to the gun.

He threaded his finger through it.

He formed a fist around it.

He swung it towards me till the little black hole at the end of the barrel was in perfect alignment with the little black hole in my one open eye.

He closed one of his own.

He grimaced.

He dropped the gun.

A four-foot bull huss had locked its jaws round his wrist. The guy was flapping like landed salmon.

I needed to get the gun but it was slow progress. I hadn't got my wind back. My ribs were corset-sore.

He fought with the fish but it stayed attached to his hand – Jaws meets Punch and Judy. His weapon sat in an inch of water. I had never touched a gun before and I held it with all the amateurishness of a child who finds an unexploded Second World War grenade washed up in a rock pool. The guy saw what I was going. His eyes grew perceptibly wider and he thrashed the huss all the harder.

I aimed the gun at his head. The gun that had so recently killed; the hunk of fat metal that had so nearly claimed me. But the bastard was squirming like live-bait and I couldn't get a fix on him. I moved the gun to his chest.

I couldn't do it.

I heard crying. I turned to the source. Two of the young schoolchildren had got separated from their party. They stood at the entrance to the room. They clawed at their jumpers, trying not to let go of each other. One of the wee boys had wet his shorts. They looked at me with faces that could have been painted by Munch.

I realized they weren't looking at me at all. Their eyes mistook me for a killer. They were in the presence of a murderer who was hovering his gun over one of the aquarium staff. And they could see my first victim floating in a tankful of her own blood.

It was all too terrible.

I wanted to explain the situation to the wee lads. I wanted to tell them that everything was not as it seemed. I needed to convince them that I was one of the good guys. I would never be able to stop them having nightmares about the hell that confronted them, but I could at least ensure that I wasn't the demon.

But there wasn't time.

I told the boys to go get their teacher. I had to say it three times. They seemed afraid to turn their backs on me, like I might put a bullet in each of them. I tried not to let it get to me, that they should think I was capable of such a thing. I tried not to take it personally. I had to keep telling myself that they didn't fear *me* as such; they feared the *idea* of me. They feared all the gunmen they saw painted on gable walls. They feared the soldiers their parents had told them about, the ones who used to carry rifles round the streets. And they feared the guns they saw on TV. They might have witnessed tragedies like Columbine on *Newsround*. They would have known that, occasionally, schoolkids got shot.

No, they didn't fear me. They feared the world they lived in. And that world had suddenly become all too real.

It didn't stop me feeling like utter scum.

I had to get out.

I left the bull huss choking on a terrorist. I buttoned the gun into my jacket and doubled back towards the entrance. It was quicker that way. If I'd followed the exit signs I would have had to negotiate the entire warren of tunnels, taking me past more schoolchildren, a presentation on seal rehabilitation and

231

endless tanks silently occupied by everything from jellyfish to John Dory.

I hurdled the three-pronged barrier, and left a line of wet shoe prints on the carpet. Had anyone been pursuing me they would have been able to follow my feet out the door.

I had left the Triumph Twenty unlocked, testing Aisling's theory that none of her bikes were worth stealing. Thankfully, she had been right. I threw my leg over the saddle and pedalled towards the guest house.

It was only when I brought my rusty wheels round the third bend that I realized a car was tailing me. I abruptly changed course and freewheeled downhill towards the lough. This forced the car into a three-point turn, which the driver performed with pit-stop precision. His front bumper was biting at my rear wheel in no time. This guy was either a pro or a maniac.

I pounded the pedals again as I hit the flat harbour road. The wind had got up and was blowing directly into my face. I felt like I was cycling through syrup. The old Triumph Twenty was doing her best, but I couldn't help cursing Aisling for not stocking her barn with titanium racers, or one of those BMXs that lifts off the ground and carries you and your alien, in silhouette, across the moon.

The more I pedalled, the more futile it seemed. I was never going to outpace the car no matter what bike I was riding. And I had reached the long straight stretch of the road that follows the sea wall out of the village. There wasn't another turning off it till you hit Ballyquintin Point.

I zigged and zagged the bike, not in some audacious attempt to shake off Colin McRae behind me, but because I had to avoid the perilous mats of seaweed that had been tossed over the sea wall and onto the road by the choppy lough.

And then I remembered. There *was* a turning off this road. Of sorts. And I was approaching it. I threw all my weight to the left and turned the bike onto the ferry slip. The car wasn't fooled by my sudden change of direction. It skidded sharply, righting itself behind me. It was eating up the yards between us. There was only one way to get rid of the bugger. I had no choice.

I launched myself at the water.

I cleared a distance of perhaps six feet before my front wheel smacked the ferry deck. The wheel buckled and the bike somersaulted forward, wedging itself under a lorry. Mercifully, I had been thrown clear by the initial impact.

I picked myself up. There were holes in my trousers where the knees had been. My legs were blancmanges. When the little bridge at the rear of the boat came to rest in the vertical position, I propped myself against it.

The lunatic driver had managed to brake just short of the water. I watched as he attempted to reverse his car back up the slip. But he was having no joy. His wheels couldn't get purchase on the galeblown seaweed. His rear tyres became Catherine wheels, green smoke whizzing round the arches.

The driver opened his door. He managed to undo his seat belt and step out before his car slid dopily into the sea.

I retrieved the mangled Triumph Twenty from under the lorry.

I walked it past the two Welsh cyclists I had met the

233

previous afternoon. They sat astride their gleaming road bikes. They sang:

Mama Mia,
there he goes again,
my-my,
how can you resist him?

20

Aren't you supposed to feel happy when you escape from a potentially fatal situation with your life intact?

Aren't you supposed to experience an adrenaline rush, a corporeal euphoria, as every nerve and sensor in your body is simultaneously switched back on again, like some joyous and extravagant Christmas illuminations? Don't your senses become alive to new possibilities – can't you suddenly taste air, touch the sky and hear angels? Do you not reappraise your entire belief system in a matter of seconds – reprioritizing your life in an eyeblink, with 'Money', 'House' and 'Job' somewhere near the bottom of the list, and 'Family', 'Friends' and 'Base-jumping off an Active Volcano for a Cancer Charity' right up there at the top?

And is it not true that somewhere in the midst of this epiphany you can find your God?

Either I was a heathen or my God had deserted me, for I experienced none of the above. I was angry and more than a little world-weary. My muscles had started to burn from the cycling as the lactic acid flooded into them. My wet denim had become ice-brittle on the exposed deck. Death was stalking me. Death had touched my rear wheel. Strangford Lough might as well have been the River Styx, for its ferry commuted me from hell.

The forces that conspired against me were darker than I had imagined. This wasn't Cowboys and Indians. This was the IRA. They had no qualms about murdering Scarlet. It was a ruthless and calculated act. More chilling, however, was the murder of Aisling Coyles. That was pure evil. If Aisling's story was true – and a bullet had been despatched to silence her, suggesting it was – then Martin O'Hanlon had once been in love with her. In fact, if it hadn't been for one erroneous shag with Kate Rogers, O'Hanlon would have made Aisling Coyles his wife. Thirty-four years later and O'Hanlon is prepared to blow a hole in Aisling's neck – the same neck he had once stroked, kissed, nuzzled and licked – just to protect his fragile ego.

Pure evil.

O'Hanlon must have ordered his men to follow me from Dundalk. Both the gunman and his driver were IRA, I was sure of that. They would've been acting under his instruction. The Sinn Fein leader knew I was onto him, though he also knew I had little evidence to support my accusation. However, knowing O'Hanlon, he wouldn't have let a small matter like that mitigate my fate. While I remained free to run around and dig the dirt he would not have been able to relax. He had too much to lose. So he'd despatched his gunmen to make sure I didn't get that evidence.

Unfortunately for Aisling, she was my evidence. I had led the Provos to her door. They had been watching me. They would have found the book on her doorstep. They would have known where and when I was to meet her. Their disguised gunman was in position by the time I reached the aquarium. He hadn't needed his hearing aid to tune in to Aisling's damning tale. He had listened in with two perfectly good ears and he hadn't liked what he heard: the story of Martin O'Hanlon, the Secretary of State and their dead bastard love child. O'Hanlon's gunman had taken the decision there and then that nobody else should hear such a story. He shot Aisling. He then tried to shoot me, so the story would die with me.

Unfortunately for me, he missed.

See, I had escaped with my life and I should have been elated, but no, I wasn't stupid. Aisling had passed her story on to me like a relay runner handing over a lit stick of dynamite. The longer I carried that story, the more my life was in danger. I now had no choice. If I wanted to retain any hope of staying alive, I had to tell it to someone. I could go straight back to the paper and type it into tomorrow's front page, but that would involve Harry and questions and anyway, the IRA knew where I worked. O'Hanlon had seen my press pass. There was no way they were going to let me get to my PC.

There was only one thing for it. I would pay Meeks a visit and let him arrest me. An RUC cell was the safest place for me, probably the only place in Ireland where the Provos couldn't get to me (though you could never bet against it). I would be able to tell Meeks everything I knew. I would hand him the dynamite.

The ferry seemed to be taking an age. Even the seals looked at their watches.

Though I blamed O'Hanlon for the murders of Aisling and Scarlet, guilt was nibbling at me. These women were innocent bystanders whose only crime was to know me. The tragic irony was that, initially, neither woman had wanted anything to do with me. Aisling had slammed a door in my face but I had eventually compelled her to talk to me. And Scarlet hadn't asked me to board her tour bus and follow her to Dublin. I had thrust myself upon her. These women were dead by association. It was like I'd been walking in the calm eye of some invisible twister and the second these women got too close to me, a violent force had removed them.

I threw the bicycle's broken reflector into the sea, cursing myself. I should never have put the phone down the previous evening in the Drop Inn. I should have let Meeks know where I was. He would have despatched his men to arrest me, but at least Aisling would have been spared.

Hold on . . . I wasn't mad at myself at all. I was mad at Meeks. If he had kept his word then none of this would have happened. He had promised me that the RUC would back me up all the way in my pursuit of O'Hanlon. If they'd been doing their jobs properly, they would have known I was in Portaferry. They would have stepped in and hauled me back to a Belfast cell long before I stroked a ray, before I watched a film explaining *How Waves Work*, and before I got a novelist's oesophagus blown over my face.

The ferry arced into dock at Strangford. I was angry, wet and sore. I must have smelt of fish, for a squadron of insistent terns snapped their yolk-yellow beaks at me. They didn't know I had a gun in my pocket. I might have used it on them had the one lorry on board not started its engine, dispersing the birds from the deck.

It occurred to me that I had no transport. How would I get to Meeks? My bike was mangled – the Triumph had turned to disaster. Not that I was about to cycle the fifty or so miles to Belfast. I would have rather nailed my tongue to the mast of a sinking ship.

A taxi wasn't an option as I had no money – my wallet sat on an unmade bed in a two-bit, two-star Portaferry guest house. All I had on me was a novel and a gun. I could use it to hijack the lorry, I thought. I could jump in and threaten to narrate *The Cross in the Sand* to the driver unless he took me to Belfast. But I didn't have the nerve. I put the book away and threatened him with the gun instead, figuring it might be just as persuasive.

The lorry driver was in his thirties and thickset, with tight curly brown hair covering his head, neck and chin. He looked like one of those circus freaks that sport a Beard O' Bees. He also looked like your typical lorry driver, the sort of bloke who could direct you to the decomposing bodies of Norwegian hitchhikers dotted up and down Britain, from Dover to Stranraer.

I climbed into his cab and pointed the gun at his midriff, keeping it well below the level of the lorry windows. No need to alarm the citizens of Strangford.

'Listen, mate, I apologize for the gun, but I really need to get to Belfast.'

He seemed more irritated than scared. 'Jeez, biy, cyud ye not have got yerself a wee bit ay cyardboard and wrote Belfast on it?'

He was what is known in the trade as a culchie.

'I don't have a pen,' I said.

'Sure, why didn't ye say? I've got loads o' the critters.' He opened his glove compartment. Among the porn, petrol receipts and powdery travel sweets there must have been two dozen pens. They were all printed with the name of a company: Ahoghill Agricure Ltd.

'But I spose ye won't be needin' a pen if ye've got yerself a gyun. Gyood thing ye do, cyoz all them pens is useless. I cyan't write with any o' them.'

'Did your company get them from a dud supplier?'

'No. I cyan't write with any o' them cyoz I cyan't write.'

The lorry's air brakes sharply exhaled. The ferryman waved us off the boat.

'So, biy, where in Belfast will ye be wantin' te go?' asked my driver.

'Cultra.'

'Cyultra?'

'No. Cultra.'

I kept the gun on him. I knew what he was trying to do. He was pretending to be my friend. He was playing the innocent fool to make me feel superior. He was trying to elicit my confidence. Then, when my guard was down, he would pounce. But I was onto his game. He didn't fool me for a second. Behind those gobstopper eyes and that buckeejit expression worked the brain of a cool and calculating man.

'Hey, biy, dyee mind if I put on one o' me cyassettes?' he asked. He indicated a tray in front of his gearstick, stuffed with scuffed plastic tape boxes.

'Go on then,' I said, quickly scanning the titles. 'You can stick anything on, as long as it's not Garth Brooks.'

'Oh. Right you are, then.'

He kept his eyes on the road and his tapes in their tray.

'Are you serious? You only listen to Garth Brooks?'

'Gyarth's the Kying o' Cyuntry.'

I rested the gun on my lap. I had nothing to fear from this man.

'Biy, if ye don't mind me askin', how cyome yer clothes is soaked through?'

'I was at the Portaferry Aquarium.'

'Jeez, were ye an exhibit?'

'Nearly. Neil the Seal promised me I was *as close as you get without getting wet*. I'm going to sue him. He'll

240

be down to his last herring by the time I'm through with him.'

'You cyan't bate a nice bit o' fish, biy. A nice byattered cyod. Cyourse, it's Christmas now. I won't be eatin' fish for a gyood while. The next few weeks it'll be tyurkey sandwiches, tyurkey cyasserole, tyurkey cyurry, and tyurkey loaf.'

'Turkey loaf? I've never heard of turkey loaf.'

'Gyood thing ye haven't. The wife makes it. Gyod-awful it is, too. Tastes like an Arab's armpit. It's like meat loaf, but I don't eat red meat, see.'

This did surprise me. He was a country boy, a yokel. I thought that to survive, his kind had to chase their dinner across muddy fields and rugby tackle it.

'But you're not a vegetarian, are you? Not if you eat turkey and fish.'

'I have a simple rule. I don't eat anything that I cyan't take out with one punch. That means no cyows, no sheep, but I'll have the odd bit o' bacon. It depends on the size o' the pig.'

We were stuck behind a tractor, an occupational hazard of driving on Northern Ireland's roads.

'Biy, I've got te ask, are you one o' them tyerrorist fellas? And if so, are ye Cyathlic or Laylist?'

'I'm no terrorist. I'm a journalist. Though I suppose there's not much difference between the two. We're both scum. We both have the power to destroy people's lives. But if you're a terrorist you get a bigger turnout at your funeral.'

'So, if yer not into the vilence, why dyee cyarry a gyun?'

'There's a simple explanation. The IRA have killed a rock star, a girl I cared about very much. They've also assassinated Ireland's best-selling novelist. They tried to shoot me, but the bullet got a shark instead. In the

241

confusion, I grabbed this gun. I want you to drive me to Cultra, to the home of the RUC Chief Constable, where I will tell him that the Sinn Fein leader has fathered a love child by the Secretary of State for Northern Ireland. The Chief will try and use that information to secure peace in our troubled land. But not before he arrests me for the manslaughter of the Northern Ireland goalkeeper some five years ago, even though I'm not strictly guilty. But enough about me, let's hear about you. What's the fuel consumption like on this baby?'

'Biy, ye cyan put yer gyun away. I'll get ye te Cyultra pronto. This is the most exciting thing that's happened te me since I gyot me hand cyaught in a thresher.' My driver raised his right forearm. The skin was a matt, salmon-coloured prosthetic. 'I had to cyut it off with me own penknife or I would've been sucked through the mechyanism. They'd have been using me as pigswill.'

He pressed his plastic hand on his horn. The sound forced the tractor off the road.

'By the way, I'm Brendan,' he said. 'What name did yer mother give ye?'

'Jessie. But friends call me Jay.'

'Well, Jay, I'll help ye get peace in Ireland. But it'll have to wait a cyouple o' minutes. I need te stop fer petrol and a bag o' peat brickettes.'

Brendan put his foot to the floor. I hoped that it wasn't made of plastic too.

'Aye, this is powerful exciting stuff,' he added. 'I cyan't wait till the next Young Farmers' night. I'll be kyept in Gyuinness for years on this one.'

By Northern Ireland's standards, the police earned good money. Some officers were known to clock up

£80,000 with overtime. Their prosperity, and the need for tight security, enabled RUC officers to live in safe, comfortable, middle-class ghettos in the Greater Belfast area. Cultra – a small knot in the ribbon of road that connects Belfast to Bangor – is one such ghetto. Aided by generous rent allowances, several RUC officers were known to have bought nice homes in Cultra, overlooking Belfast Lough.

Stephen Meeks boasted the biggest and most intimidating pad of all. Despite its size, his house was rendered invisible from the road, screened off by conifers, and secured by a portcullis of a gate. It was reputed to be a fortress, bristling with armed security and sophisticated electronic protection.

Brendan eased his lorry up to the gate. I hid the gun in the glove compartment. A guard dressed in a thickly padded jacket set down his girly magazine – *Amazons and Armalites* – and approached the driver's window. He had the walk of a bodybuilder, his arms hanging out from his sides like he was carrying two rolled-up carpets. He made circles with his finger and Brendan responded to the gesture by winding down the window.

'Afternoon,' said Brendan. 'I've gyot a fella here wants to see the Chief Cyonstable.'

The guard looked from Brendan to me, then back to Brendan again. He spat his gum into the air and volleyed it with a polished boot onto the road. He stared back at Brendan. He shucked snot from his nose into his throat and swallowed.

'No,' he said.

'No?' I said. I leaned across Brendan's knees and craned my head to the window. 'Is that it? You're not going to ask who I am? You don't want to know my business with Constable Meeks?'

243

'No,' he said. He put his hands on the side of the lorry and pushed hard, stretching his calves, like a runner before a marathon. He straightened and turned his upper body left, then right, then left. 'I need you to back this vehicle away from the gate,' he added.

'Excuse me,' I said. 'When you've finished your aerobics could you get on your intercom and tell Meeks that Big Jessie is outside. He'll know who I am.'

'What can you bench?' asked the guard.

'What do you mean, what can I bench?'

'See these arms.' The guard held them out like he was performing a battery lift. 'These babies can press two fifty Ks.'

'How many gyoats is that?' asked Brendan. 'I cyan lift a pregnant gyoat over a drystone wall.'

I gave him a dig on the shin. 'Brendan, would you shut the fuck up,' I whispered. 'Try and remember that you're being hijacked. Let me do the talking.' I spoke again to the guard. 'Listen, mate, I'm really not interested in your gym routine. But I am interested in speaking to the Chief Constable. Just tell him Big Jessie's here and it's urgent.'

'See these thighs,' he said, adopting a John Wayne stance. 'Each one's thicker than my girlfriend's waist. And these abs . . .' he punched himself in the stomach, '. . . like tungsten.'

'And what's your point?' I asked.

'My point is that if you don't back up this lorry in the next ten seconds, I am perfectly capable of pulling it onto the main road with my teeth.'

I didn't doubt him. His neck was so thick that if you sliced it open you'd be able to age him from the concentric rings.

'Right, Jay, what're we gyoin' te do?' asked Brendan. 'Are ye gyoin' te waste him with yer gyun?'

He was really getting into the role. I couldn't share his enthusiasm.

'No, Brendan. We're not *wasting* anyone. You'll have to back her up. You can drop me off at a payphone. Thanks anyway.'

'But what about those gyirls that the 'Ra kyilled? What about the Sinn Fein leader and his illiterate kyid?'

'His illegitimate kyid,' I corrected. 'Don't you worry about all that, Brendan. Just get me to a payphone and I'll handle the rest myself. Actually, if you could spare us twenty pee, I'd be grateful.'

'No,' said Brendan. 'I won't do it.'

'Jesus, it's only twenty pee,' I said.

'No,' said Brendan. 'I mean, I'm not drivin' away from here till we've seen the Chief Cyonstable. We're not beaten yet.'

The guard slapped the driver's door. 'Oi, I told you to back her up.'

'Will do,' said Brendan.

He released the air brakes. He used his real hand to hook his gearstick into reverse. He checked his mirrors and slowly drew the lorry backwards. Then he stopped. He crunched the gears again. He revved the engine.

The guard sensed what was coming. He scrambled to withdraw his gun from his hip.

'No, Brendan. Don't do it.'

He looked at me with his mad culchie eyes and whooped, 'Houl on te yer briches!'

He released the clutch. The lorry lurched forward, into the gate. It made little impression.

'Brendan, stop this. There's no need for you to get involved.'

'Nonsense,' he shouted. 'It's powerful craic.'

Again he reversed the lorry and charged it at the gate. I heard a gunshot. Then another. Then the lorry listed to the right.

'He's shot your tyres. This is crazy. You've got to stop.'

'Uch, dry yer eyes, biy. Gyive me one more crack at the gyates and I'll have them open.'

He reversed for the third time. The guard positioned himself between the lorry and the buckled gate. He aimed his gun at our windscreen.

'Duck,' shouted Brendan.

A bullet zipped cleanly through the glass. Brendan's topless calendar fluttered onto our lowered heads. Jo Guest had been shot in the left tit. The ricochet had obliterated the driver's window.

Brendan hit the accelerator and launched us at the guard and the gate.

The lorry faltered. Its wheels locked.

'Christ, Brendan, you've gone over him.'

'Well, he shouldn'ta bin standin' in front o' me like an eejit.'

The lorry lurched forward again. We brought our heads up. We were skeeting up the Chief Constable's tree-lined drive, two tyres down, sparks flying.

'Relax, biy, we went over the gyate not the gyard. I told you we weren't beaten.'

A shot rang after us. Another ricochet. A peacock was strutting on the lawn. Its head exploded.

Brendan cut the final corner, tearing the lorry across the grass. We were within sight of Meeks's front door. It was open. Two uniformed officers had positioned themselves behind a marble gryphon that guarded the steps. Their arms were outstretched. Their hands jumped in time to the crack of their guns.

'Fuck's sake, Brendan. Stop the lorry. They're going to kill us.'

'Aye, but what a way te gyo.'

'You're not serious. Think of your wife. Think of Christmas. Think of her turkey loaf. Actually, don't think of that.'

Brendan jumped on the brake. The lorry skidded to a halt, spitting gravel up the steps, through the open door and onto Mrs Meeks's pristine hall carpet. Brendan killed the engine. The shooting stopped.

Everything was silent, save for the softly piped mew of a newly widowed peahen.

'STEP OUT OF THE VEHICLE WITH YOUR HANDS ON YOUR HEADS,' came the unequivocal instruction from the marble gryphon.

'No more, Brendan. We're going to do as he says. Now listen to me. When we get out there, they're going to be rough. But if you keep your mouth shut, I can get you out of this, OK?'

Brendan scratched his forehead with his plastic hand. 'Okey dokey,' he said.

I opened my door and jumped onto the gravel. I walked round the front of the lorry. I kept my hands on my head. The two officers moved out from behind their statue and walked towards us. Rather, they walked towards me. Brendan remained in the van.

'DRIVER, STEP OUT OF THE VEHICLE. I WILL COUNT TO FIVE. THEN I WILL SHOOT.'

'Do it, Brendan,' I shouted. 'I *allow* you.' I turned to the officers. 'This has nothing to do with him.'

'ONE.'

'I hijacked his lorry.'

'TWO.'

'I forced him to drive through the gates.'

'THREE.'

'Honestly, he wouldn't hurt a fly.'

'FOUR.'

'Brendan, for fuck's sake come out.'

'FIV— Jesus!'

The officers were blown clean off their feet.

A solid jet of brown liquid powered into them from a vent on the side of the lorry. The smell was 100 per cent unadulterated country. It appeared that Ahoghill Agricure Ltd dealt in fertilizer. My first hijack and I'd commandeered a muck-spreader. The glamour of it.

The officers didn't know what had hit them. I used the time to remove my hands from my head and gesticulate wildly at Brendan.

'Jesus, Brendan, turn it off.'

The jet subsided. Brendan opened his door and hopped out.

'Sorry, biy, I cyouldn't stop meself.'

'Do you have any idea how much shit you're in?'

'Shouldn't ye be askin' them officers the same question?'

'Big Jessie.' Stephen Meeks was standing at his door with a gun in one hand and an orange juice in the other. 'This had better be good.'

'It is. But please, just let this fella go. He means no harm. I forced him to do this. It was the only way I could get to you.'

One of the shit-covered officers aimed his gun. 'HANDS ABOVE YOUR HEADS.'

We both did exactly as the officer said and placed our hands on our heads, except Brendan whose hand fell to the ground.

'I told you, Steeky. He's an invalid. I threatened to cut his other hand off unless he drove me here.'

Meeks supped his juice. He let his gun arm fall to his side.

'All right,' he said. 'Driver, pick your hand up and get that ruddy lorry off my property. Boys, follow him down. And for Christ's sake, make sure he stays on the driveway this time. That grass cost a bloody fortune. The guy who laid it seeds the greens at the Belfry.'

Brendan offered me his hand. The real one.

'Gyood luck,' he said. 'And remember, I'm expecting peace.'

'I'll see what I can do.'

The officers bullied him away.

Meeks motioned his head, inviting me into his house.

21

The Chief Constable's hallway was lined with framed photographs of himself shaking hands and exchanging playful punches with a veritable Who's Who of politics, religion and royalty. All the heavyweights were on view – Margaret Thatcher, Bill Clinton, Lady Di, Tony Blair, Ariel Sharon, Desmond Tutu and Jimmy Tarbuck.

'Jesus, Steeky, you're not going to tell me that Tarbie had some role in the peace process. Did you hope we could laugh all our troubles away?'

Meeks stared fondly at the photograph of himself and the gap-toothed Liverpudlian. 'No,' he said. 'I played golf with Jim in a Pro-Am at Royal Portrush. We were in a four-ball with Darren Clarke and Ronnie Corbett. You should have seen Ronnie on the first tee. He did the funniest thing. He reached into his bag for his driver, but pulled out a three-foot plastic club, a kid's toy. He addressed the ball with it and everything. He had us in stitches. You see, Jay, *that's* comedy. Not like these so-called alternative comedians with their blue humour and their cheap digs at authority.' Meeks straightened a plaque commemorating his investiture as Chief Constable of the RUC.

A young boy came running up the hall. He was carrying a plastic gun. He tugged at the crease in Meeks's trouser leg.

'Daddy, Daddy. Is this the IRA man? Are you going to shoot him?' The boy pointed his pistol at me and mimicked the sound of rapid gunfire, showering me in spittle.

'No, Billy. This isn't the IRA man.'

'You have him well trained,' I said.

'A future Chief Constable,' said his proud father. 'Either that, or an Open Champion. When Caroline was pregnant, I took her into Eastwoods and asked them to give me odds on my unborn son winning a Major by 2030. They took one look at her swollen belly and offered me two hundred to one, which gives you some idea of the promise Billy showed, even as a foetus. The same bookie was prepared to offer fifteen hundred to one on a Mars landing by 2030, and four thousand to one on a united Ireland by the same year.'

Meeks rubbed his son's head.

'Daddy, the man smells of fish. Is he a Catholic?' The young boy had unsheathed a plastic dagger and was jabbing it into my knee.

'No, Billy. The man isn't a Catholic,' said Dad.

'Does that mean he's a prostitute?' asked Billy.

'Yes, son. He's a *Protestant.*'

The boy returned his dagger to his belt. He ran up the stairs shouting, 'Mummy, Daddy's got a prostitute who smells of fish.'

Meeks allowed himself a chuckle. 'He's a smart cookie. At the last parents' night, his teacher complained that he'd been bullying some of the other kids. She said it like Billy had some serious behavioural disorder. I explained to her that if he was bullying the other kids it was because her classes weren't engaging

251

him. He's got a high IQ. He needs to be challenged. It's not William's fault that his classmates are slow.'

'Bullying kids, was he? I wonder who he gets it from,' I said.

'Oh, come on, Jessie. What are you trying to insinuate? I was never a bully. I was doing you a favour back then. I was preparing you for life's knocks.' Meeks balled his fist and slammed it into his opened palm. 'Only the strong survive out in the big bad world. The weak are quickly picked off. Don't tell me you haven't become a stronger person as a result of our banter.'

'*Banter*? You call getting Huggins and McClaren to hold me down while you removed my trousers and set fire to my pubic hair, *banter*? And connecting one end of a Bunsen pipe to a gas tap and inserting the other up my backside, was that *banter*? And remember when my mum appeared in the *Telegraph* presenting a cheque from her bridge club to Seahill Hospice? You cut her face out and stuck it onto the body of a woman getting fucked by an Alsatian, and then you photocopied the picture and pasted it to every telegraph pole in East Belfast. Was that *banter*, Stephen? Was that supposed to be *character-building*? I wanted to kill you for that. I really would have killed you if my mother hadn't stopped me. She said she could take the embarrassment of a dirty picture but no way could she cope with the shame of a son going to prison.'

Meeks shepherded me into his living room and gently clicked the door shut.

'OK, OK. Keep your voice down. What do you want me to say? I'm sorry? I was only a kid, Jessie. Kirk McClaren, Miles Huggins and I, we were only having a laugh. Shit, that's what boys *do*. It's part of growing up. I do feel bad about your mum, I can see that now.

When you're young you don't think. You act first and ask questions later. But Christ, can you not let it lie? This insane obsession you have with going after us all, trying to exact some pathetic sort of revenge. You're targeting the wrong people. We've all become grown men. We aren't the kids we once were. They're the ones you should have gone after. If you'd wanted to even the score you should have done it years ago, when those kids were still around. I would have respected you more if you'd stood up to me at the time. Who knows, we may even have become good friends.'

'I seriously doubt it,' I said.

'See, you're still bitter,' said Meeks. 'You're still looking at me like I've got horns. I've put the past behind me, why can't you?'

'That's just it, Steeky. You haven't put the past behind you. At least, not *my* past. You're still using the Huggins thing to coerce me into doing your dirty work for you. So let's strike a deal. You forget about Miles Huggins and I'll forget that the three of you, including McClaren, made my life an unbearable fucking misery.'

'You know I can't do that,' said Meeks. 'The stakes are too high.' He opened the living-room door. 'Now get those clothes off and take a bloody shower. William was right. You smell like a Harry Ramsden's.' He arched his head round the door, and yelled, 'Caroline, my friend Jay would like to take a shower. Can you grab him a towel from the hot press?' He directed me to the bottom of the thickly carpeted stairs. 'I'll get the wife to leave some clean clothes outside the wetroom. I'll be in the garden playing football with Billy. When you're done, you can join us. You can tell me what you've got. And perhaps you will also explain to my son why his pet peacock is missing its head.'

I had thought that my penthouse was plush, but even it lacked a wetroom. The Chief Constable's shower was housed in such a room, a watertight room with a tiled floor, a tiled ceiling and four tiled walls. A channel cut into the floor was designed to siphon the water away. If I were into dismembering and disposing of bodies, this would be the room for me.

You needed a Masters in Engineering to operate the shower. A confusing array of knobs, dials, switches, funnels and gauges were set into the wall beneath the shower head. I managed to get the thing working, but not before I'd filled the entire room with hot, mentholated steam from the aforementioned funnels.

I sucked on the moist and minty mist, drawing it deep inside me. I threw my head back and let the water clatter over my shoulders, chest and legs. It blasted the scabs from my body and replaced them with new, pink skin. I peed where I stood. My piss, my blood, my salt and my dirt were flushed down the gutter. It felt good.

As did the hand on my penis.

Caroline Meeks was standing beside me, her naked body sequinned in condensed steam. She took my hand and pressed it between her legs. It was a strange sensation: she was completely shaved. She moved my fingers in slow circles, encouraging me to rub the slick, stubbled skin.

'Jesus, what are you doing?'

Caroline kept her eyes closed.

'It's called foreplay. It's what you do before you fuck.'

'No . . . no, this isn't right. I can't.'

254

'Oh, I think you can,' she said, jiggling my un-apologetic erection.

'But Steeky . . . Stephen . . . your husband?'

Caroline opened her eyes. 'He's in the garden. I told him I've gone to lie down. He won't bother us.'

'Well, he's bothering me. If he catches you in here he'll shoooot—'

Caroline had sunk to her knees. She was devouring me whole.

'Caroline, can I please have my cock back?'

I tried to ease myself out of her mouth, but she pinched her teeth.

'Christ, do they not feed you in this house? Caroline? Caroline?'

She didn't respond. This woman had manners. She didn't like to talk with her mouth full. She licked and sucked and munched and chomped like she was eating a hot buttered corncob, and even though the sensation was undeniably pleasant, I could only feel angry. Who did she think she was, attacking me like this? What right had she to assume that I'd want this? She wasn't unattractive, but that wasn't the point.

My skin started to prickle in the heat. I made a grab for the dial to switch the shower off, but only succeeded in turning the solid jet into short, sharp pulses of scalding water. I put my hands on Caroline's busy head and tried to force her off me, but her jaw tightened and her teeth again threatened castration. What could I do?

I heard Scarlet's voice. I caught myself humming one of her songs.

Caroline came up for air. I still couldn't prise myself away from her, however. She had dug her nails into my balls, grabbing them like they owed her money.

'Listen, fella. I haven't had a prick inside me since

Billy was born. So you are going to fuck me, whether you like it or not. And if you don't, I will scream for my husband. And when he's done with you, you'll be using your dick as a loofah. So do me a favour and at least pretend to enjoy it.'

She reeked of alcohol. Her breath was 40 per cent proof.

She returned to her knees.

It occurred to me that there was only one way out of this.

I closed my eyes. I mentally thumbed through the Littlewoods catalogue till I arrived at Ladies Hosiery. *Nope*. I imagined synchronized swimmers flicking towels at each other in the changing rooms. *Nada*. I pictured novice nuns playing strip Twister. *Eureka*. I came in the mouth of the wife of the Chief Constable of the RUC.

She immediately recoiled. She hawked and spat. My sperm marbled the tiles.

'Bastard,' she howled.

My erection was already dwindling.

'I'd love to have sex with you, Caroline. I really would. But I don't think I'm up to it.'

'Bastard,' she repeated. She remained on her knees. And then she did an unexpected thing. She started to cry.

'Bastard won't go near me,' she said. 'Not since Billy. I've tried everything, the fancy knickers, the videos, the toys . . . when we first dated, he liked me to shave myself. I've tried that too, but he won't even hold me. I must really disgust him.'

She cut a pathetic figure, naked, drunk and hunched on the tiles. Her tears fell in time with the pulsing water. She sniffed sharply. A sticky thread clung to her upper lip. It was hard to tell whether it originated from her nose or my balls. I felt sick, like I'd somehow assaulted her, even though it was she who had forced herself onto me.

I took her hands.

'I disgust my own husband,' she said.

'Come here, Caroline.' I hauled her to her feet. I put my arms round her. We stayed like that till her crying stopped, till the skin on my fingertips started to pucker.

I walked her through to the changing cubicle and gave her my towel.

'I'm sorry,' she said, as if suddenly sober.

'So am I,' I said.

'Do I disgust you?' she asked.

'Do I disgust you?'

'Don't be silly,' she said.

'Ditto.'

Caroline hastily dressed, her damp feet jamming in the legs of her jeans. She left the wetroom and returned some moments later with a neatly folded stack of clothes. They were her husband's: a custard-coloured V-neck, a cotton shirt, and a pair of slacks with creases so regimental I suspected that Meeks's iron had a built-in spirit level. I didn't complain. I was just relieved not to find a pair of his jockey pants in the pile. The idea of wearing the Chief's whips did not appeal.

I was surprised to find Meeks in the living room and not the garden. Surprised and worried. Had he been privy to what had just gone on between his wife and me? Was he about to pull a gun from his slacks?

'I'm disappointed in the outfit,' I said. I pulled my collar over the V of the borrowed jumper. 'I was hoping you'd let me wear your bulletproof vest.'

'Shush,' urged Meeks.

257

He turned up the volume on his TV. He was watching the ITN evening news. Poirot's brother – John Suchet – was reading it.

'*A more serious setback was the news that the Ulster Freedom Fighters, the largest Loyalist paramilitary group, are withdrawing their support for the Good Friday Agreement. And the Progressive Unionists have removed themselves from talks until, they say, there is progress. The British and Irish governments have until Thursday – when George McCrea must be re-elected or a new First Minister appointed – to forge a deal on arms and other issues. The favourite to succeed McCrea as First Minister is Sinn Fein leader Martin O'Hanlon. He remained unequivocal at yesterday's Sinn Fein party conference in the border town of Dundalk.*'

The broadcast cut to footage of many black and bulbous microphones gathering round Martin O'Hanlon's beard like penguins at feeding time. He shielded his eyes from the epileptic flashguns. He said: '*We Republicans hold the line that the IRA will honour its commitments on decommissioning so long as the British side of the bargain – demilitarization and police reform – is implemented. Police reform will be high on my agenda as First Minister. The RUC is the most discredited police force in Europe.*'

The picture consumed itself as Meeks hit the 'off' button. The veins were raised on his greying temples.

'Would you listen to him, Jay. *The most discredited police force in Europe,* he says. The record of awards to the RUC for bravery and gallantry is unequalled in war and peace by any other police force. Does he mention that? And can you believe that British television is giving prime airtime to a terrorist, just so he

258

can undermine my men and women? That's what I'm up against, Jay. That's why, whatever you have, it better be fucking apocalyptic.'

Meeks removed two heavy-looking glasses from his sideboard and decanted Drambuie into both. He handed one to me.

I took a tentative sip, more out of courtesy than out of a love for sweet liquor.

I handed him the stick of dynamite.

I told him everything: the border shooting, Scarlet's murder, the IRA's calling card, the murder of Aisling Coyles and the subsequent attempt on my life. I said I had further revelations concerning O'Hanlon's relationship with Kate Owen, née Rogers. I relayed Aisling's story, the one on which she based *The Cross in the Sand*.

Meeks drummed his fingers on his glass and listened with an almost childlike diligence.

'So there you have it. The Sinn Fein supremo and our Secretary of State had a child. Apocalyptic enough for you?'

Meeks said nothing. I took this as a good sign. He was plotting his next move.

'Now, if you'll just arrange a police escort to take me down to the *News Letter* offices, I'll type the story up as a provisional front page. Then we can contact O'Hanlon and demand a move on decommissioning and his withdrawal from the election. In return, we won't publish our revelations, allowing him to retain some shred of credibility. You'll have your police force back, I'll have my freedom and we can all live happily ever after.'

'I don't think so,' said Meeks.

'You *don't think so*? What do you mean, *you don't think so*? This is huge. If it wasn't huge, why did the

IRA try to silence me? Why do you think I arrived at your front door in a fucking muck-spreader? It's not my preferred mode of transport. I hijacked it. I'm on the run. O'Hanlon has ordered a bullet for me and you stand there and say *I don't think so.*'

'Calm down, will you? I don't deny that this is pretty weighty stuff, but don't you know the first rule of policing – support the charge with evidence. As far as I can see, Sonny Jim, you ain't got no evidence. You claim O'Hanlon had this Scarlet girl murdered. So where's the body? And why hasn't anyone reported her missing? No worried relatives? No concerned friends? Some might question whether she even exists.'

'She exists,' I said. She's in this room right now. She hasn't left my side since the night she was stolen away. Not that you'd understand that, Stephen. You don't know what it's like to want someone so badly it makes you ill. You'll never know that feeling because you're emotionally impotent. You're a selfish man and a lousy husband. And how do I know this? Your alcoholic wife just told me. After she'd taken my cock out of her mouth.

'I believe you, Jessie. But we need the evidence. We need her folks to report her missing before we can investigate. Aisling Coyles, on the other hand, I *do* know about. We had a 999 from the aquarium. Our boys are down there as we speak. From what I gather they have yet to recover a gun. So once again, Jessie, we have no evidence. As for the whole O'Hanlon and Kate Owen shebang – well, where's your proof? All you have is the say-so of some batty, reclusive novelist, and her body's getting stiffer by the minute. The RUC would look a bit stupid waving a copy of *The Cross in the Sand* in O'Hanlon's face and demanding peace in Northern Ireland.'

'What about the baby?' I asked.

'Well, even if we could prove that Kate Owen had a baby back then, we couldn't prove that O'Hanlon was the father. If we had the kid, things would be different. We could take a sample of his blood and prove O'Hanlon's paternity.'

'We could find the grave,' I said.

'And what would that prove?'

'We could exhume the body and extract DNA.'

'Jesus Christ, Jessie. Are you right in the head? On what grounds could the RUC start digging up dead babies? It's not our business to go round emptying graves.'

'Even if it's O'Hanlon's business to go round filling them?'

The door shucked open. The draught agitated the Christmas cards that hung on strings attached to the picture rails. Caroline entered the room, carrying a tray of tea.

'I thought you boys would like something hot inside you,' she said. Then, as if conscious of the double entendre, she added, 'It's . . . it's cold outside.'

'I didn't know you'd gone out,' said her husband. 'Your hair's wet. Is it raining?'

You could have toasted marshmallows on the back of my neck.

Caroline said nothing. She used her foot to pull a small table out from its nest.

'Answer me, woman,' said Meeks, raising his voice. 'Why were you outside? I thought you weren't feeling well. You said you were off to bed. How *is* the migraine?'

Caroline didn't set the tray down. She dropped it onto the tabletop. She couldn't look at me. She couldn't look at either of us.

'I wasn't out. I had a soak in the bath . . . cleared my sinuses.'

She took our empty glasses and closed the door behind her. Again, the Christmas cards grumbled.

'I apologize for my wife,' said Meeks. 'Sometimes I just don't know what goes on in that tiny wee head of hers.'

He fixed himself a tea. No milk. No sugar. He took it across to the bay window.

'You've made a right bloody mess of my lawn, you know. When I saw that lorry careering up the drive I had prepared myself for a mortar attack. It does nothing for my nerves.'

Meeks stirred his tea with a spoon, for some unfathomable reason. I better understood his abstinence from milk and sugar. Got to keep that heart in A1 condition. Never know when it'll go into overdrive.

'Your idiot guard wouldn't let me in,' I explained.

'That's what he's there for,' said Meeks. He stared a while longer at the swaying conifers. Then he said, 'I'll need something concrete on O'Hanlon.'

'What . . . like a breeze block?'

'The clock's ticking down, Jay.'

'But what about Scarlet? She's dead. That bastard had her killed.'

Meeks gave me the same bitter-lemon look he'd earlier cast at his wife. 'At this precise moment, the wee girl doesn't concern me. What does concern me is that over the course of the Troubles, eight thousand of my officers have been injured and two hundred and sixty killed. And seventy of those have been suicides. It's a stressful job, Jessie. I want a better deal for my men and women. The RUC is not just a name, it's a title conferred by royal charter. Very few organizations on the planet enjoy that privilege. And see that

262

woman . . .' Meeks pointed towards the chimney breast, on which was hung an oil portrait of himself accepting some token from the Queen. 'I have sworn allegiance to Our Sovereign Lady. I will do whatever it takes to protect her interest in this land.'

'You think the Queen has an interest in Northern Ireland? You think we're even on her radar? Didn't Prince Philip, on his last visit to the province, step onto the tarmac at Aldergrove, shake hands with the Mayor of Belfast and remark, *Is this where the fuzzy-wuzzies live?*'

'This is all one big joke to you, isn't it? The next thirty-six hours will have a profound effect on the future stability of the land in which we both live. The RUC have reduced violence to one tenth of what it was a decade ago, but there's still no sign of a permanent peace. The province rests on a plateau of violence. Which suits O'Hanlon. He doesn't want peace. The impasse is fine by him. He's in a great position. He's got the backing and protection of the IRA, but he can maintain a public distance from them. He's making a very nice living out of the Troubles, so he needs the IRA to exist. Ever stop to wonder where he gets his money? You don't buy Armani suits on an Assemblyman's salary. That's why he's not interested in disarming his terrorists. Donations to the IRA would dry up if they were rendered impotent by decommissioning. O'Hanlon *knows* he won't get a united Ireland, not in his lifetime. He's in this for the short term. He's in this for what he can get.'

'Surely this plateau of violence suits you too,' I said. 'It's the Troubles that keeps you and your officers in jobs.'

Meeks nodded. 'You're right. In a way. But the situation has taken a turn. I *need* peace. I need the guns to come in. It would mean a reduction in police numbers, say from thirteen thousand to ten thousand, a slight descaling of the force. But at least I'll still have a force. If the guns don't come in, George McCrea will not put himself up for re-election and Martin O'Hanlon will replace the RUC with, in his words, *three and a half thousand routinely unarmed, community-based policemen and women.* In other words, his vigilantes will still be allowed to police neighbourhoods with baseball bats and coshes while these *community officers* sit around hugging trees and singing "Kumbaya".'

An unmarked squad car was ordered by Meeks to take me back to my flat. As it whisked me up the dual carriageway past the City Airport and the dilapidated Oval football ground, I thought about what Meeks had said. Why couldn't I forget the past? Why couldn't I get on with my life instead of exhausting hours, days and months in my relentless attempts to get even with my tormentors? And wasn't that Northern Ireland's problem? We just can't forget the past. We have to get even, no matter how futile our actions. And until we can put the past behind us, we can't move forward.

After I'd caught Kirk McClaren with his trousers down, I had turned my attention to Huggins and Meeks. I had targeted Huggins first, as he was easier to get to, but I had simultaneously been doing my homework on the Chief Constable.

Back in 1996 I'd been pursuing an allegation that Meeks was accepting backhanders from Loyalist paramilitaries in exchange for allowing them free passage of drugs into the province. The allegation had been put to me by one Davey Gavin, alias 'King Rot' (short for Rottweiler), the notorious Loyalist hoodlum. He was in the Maze at the time, serving three concurrent life sentences for the brutal shooting of one of his own men – an alleged informant, Samuel Kerr. Before he murdered him, King Rot forced Kerr to watch while he put a bullet in each of his twin sons. Nice man.

To say I had been 'apprehensive' about meeting Davey Gavin was like saying I'd be 'a tad reluctant' to pop round to Dennis Nilsen's to help him unblock a drain. Thankfully, it was from behind reinforced glass that he went on record to say that Meeks had turned a blind eye to UVF drug-trafficking, in return for a cut on their profits. Of course, he could have been lying. Davey Gavin was a manipulative bastard. It would be easy to think his testimony was motivated by a desire to get back at the police service that banged him up. However, something happened that gave me a hunch his story was true. Not two hours after I'd been driven out of the Maze gates, Davey Gavin was killed by a prison officer in an act of self-defence.

I had known then that I had something, and I was determined to pursue it till I had the evidence that would destroy Stephen Meeks. And if it hadn't gone so tragically wrong with Miles Huggins, I might have been able to nail him.

22

March 20th 1996 was a remarkable day for Linfield goalkeeper Miles Huggins. In more ways than one.

His team had been drawn away to Bangor in the semi-final of the Bass Irish Cup. I was pursuing him at the time, so I paid my four quid and was admitted through the Clandeboye Road turnstiles. And it *was* remarkable. Over the course of the 120 minutes, penalties and subsequent sudden death, we experienced warm sunshine, sleet, hail, snow, and fire. The weather was biblical. You wouldn't have been surprised if it had rained frogs.

Huggins was in no small way responsible for the fire. One of the home fans had thrown a lit firework at his goal. This was a rare event at an Irish League game. As a consequence of the Troubles, fireworks were banned from sale in Northern Ireland. At least, you could purchase 'indoor fireworks', but let's face it, throwing a sparkler or a Bengal match onto a football pitch is hardly going to recreate the incandescent fervour of a Rome derby.

With cat-like reflexes, Huggins caught the hissing missile and drop-kicked it into Bangor's vacant Abattoir End. Unfortunately, the redundant, ramshackle stand did not comply with all of the fire and safety regulations demanded of football grounds post Bradford and Hillsborough. In truth, it didn't comply with any of them. From the enthusiasm of the resulting inferno, Bangor's dilapidated stand appeared to have been constructed from newspaper sticks, peat brickettes, magnesium ribbon, and tinder gathered from the nearby Crawfordsburn Country Park.

By that stage Linfield had won the game. Huggins was the penalty-saving, fire-starting, headline-grabbing hero. Yet it could have been so different.

In the last minute of normal time Huggins nearly lost it for his team. The score stood at 1–1 when he took the headstaggers and hared out of his box for a one-on-one with the Bangor striker, Michael Surgeon. The big keeper tried to rugby-tackle 'Surgie', who had broken Linfield's offside trap. Luckily for Huggins, he missed the jinking Bangor man, thus escaping a red card and a ban from the final. Not that Linfield were about to make the final, for Surgie lobbed the ball over the flailing keeper, sending it into his goal. The Bangor forward pulled his shirt over his head and ran Ravanelli-like towards the away fans to thoroughly goad them. The keeper's humiliation seemed complete when a beetroot-faced Bangor fan guldered, '*Huggins . . . yer an onion!*'

However, it was the celebrating Bangor striker and not the Linfield keeper who was made to look stupid. For, while the shrouded Surgie blindly danced, jumped and bared his arse to the Linfield fans, he did not see his lobbed ball stop dead on the goal line, sticking in the mud. The pitch had become a quagmire with all the bad weather. Surgie was still flicking Vs at the Linfield fans and performing somersaults with his shirt over his head when Huggins calmly

267

retrieved the ball and the referee blew for extra time.

Yes, the gods were smiling on Miles Huggins that day. Their heavenly intervention took the game to penalties, allowing 'The Big Man' – *hands like frying pans* – to justify the £2 million that had been bid for him, that same morning, by Manchester City.

See, Miles Huggins also kept goal for his country. He was the only Irish League player in Bryan Hamilton's Northern Ireland squad. But that was about to change. For Huggins had been spotted. His performances for his country were nothing short of legendary. He was a great keeper in a woeful Northern Ireland team. He consistently and single-handedly rescued our wee country from utter humiliation.

Northern Ireland had been favourites to secure second spot in a 'dream' World Cup qualifying group that consisted of Bulgaria, Iceland, Lithuania, Armenia, Narnia and Ikea. When the group was drawn, we seemed destined to make France '98, our first finals for a dozen years. But the results didn't go our way and we were sitting second from bottom. During the campaign, Northern Ireland's FIFA world ranking slipped from 85 to 102, one place above Malawi. If it hadn't been for the acrobatic antics of Miles Huggins salvaging the odd point here or there, things would have been much more embarrassing. We would have been kept out of the top 150 by St Kitts and Nevis.

But the morning of 20 March 1996, Huggins got the recognition he deserved. As he boarded a Bangor-bound bus with his Linfield teammates, the news broke of his impending transfer to Manchester's Maine Road and the giddy heights of the English First Division. The fee of £2 million was a record for an Irish League player and Linfield were set to prosper. Even before Huggins had passed his medical and signed on the dotted line, the Linfield board members had ordered their Porsches. They assured their fans that the rest of the money would be ploughed back into the team (they didn't add to the squad, but they did pick out some really nice curtains for the Players' Bar).

I remember thinking that £2 million seemed a stupidly high amount to pay for a twenty-seven-year-old part-timer. But Huggins was a goalkeeper, so I supposed that he still had a good ten years in him. Still, I thought, £2 million for a part-timer? Well, he *was* an international and there were rumours that Newcastle United wanted to poach him from under City's noses.

However, something still didn't click.

I remembered that Huggins suffered from a heart condition at school. And he was an asthmatic. He never took part in games or PE classes. So how could he have passed a rigorous medical? And how could he play top-flight football?

A hole in the heart would not prevent you playing in the Irish League, such is the standard. You'd need to be wearing calipers or missing a limb to get 'found out' on an Irish League pitch (even then, you'd probably make the subs bench at Ards). And true, Miles Huggins was a goalkeeper. His position did not demand the stamina of an outfield player. His heart could cope.

But why would a big English club want to shell out £2 million for a guy with a dodgy ticker?

The answer is, they wouldn't. Not if they knew about it. And Manchester City clearly didn't know about it.

I went to work. I found the name and address of the doctor who had performed the medical on Miles Huggins. I boarded a flight to Manchester.

Dr James Cowan was performing reductive surgery on a Brie and grape baguette when I was eventually admitted to his office. I confronted him with what I knew of the medical history of Miles Huggins. I demanded to know why he'd overlooked the hole in the goalkeeper's heart.

He threatened to have me thrown out of the building.

I threatened to have him struck off.

Cowan threw his lunch in the bin. He produced an unfiltered cigarette from his inside breast pocket. He dragged a match across the rough, bronchial cross-section of a model lung that sat on his desk. Through a pungent fug, he told me that Linfield FC had got to him before he carried out the medical. £2 million was a lot of money, too much for the club to lose. They had offered the good doctor £50,000 to 'overlook' anything that might compromise the transfer.

'But you were performing the medical on behalf of Manchester City,' I said. 'You were supposed to be protecting their interests, not selling your soul for fifty grand.'

'I sold my soul long before that call,' said Cowan. 'What you don't realize, because I've lost the accent, is that I'm a Coleraine boy, born and bred. And I'm a dyed-in-the-wool Northern Ireland supporter. I sold my heart and soul to the green shirt long before my parents emigrated to England in '76. So you see, Linfield didn't need to buy my silence. There was no way I was going to tell anyone that Miles Huggins was unfit to play top-class competitive football, because that would mean he'd never play for our country again. And Huggins is the only thing stopping us becoming the whipping boys of European football.'

'In what year did Northern Ireland win the last ever Home Championships?'

'Sorry?' asked the doctor.

'Come on. You must know, being the big Northern Ireland fan. I'll give you a clue. England announced their withdrawal from the competition the same year, citing lack of serious competition, despite Northern Ireland beating them to the title. To this day, we're reigning British Champions. You must know.'

'Of course I do,' said Cowan. He killed his fag in a flask of urine. '1984,' he said, throwing his hands behind his head.

'Wrong. The answer on my card is 1981. So we have established two things. One, you're no son of Ulster. And two, you can be bought for five figures.'

'I can't be bought,' he shouted. He slammed his hands on his blotting pad. His eyes were pink.

'OK. OK. So you didn't accept the bribe. Are you going to tell me the real reason you faked Huggins's medical?'

The good doctor lifted himself out of his chair.

'I turned the money down. But Linfield, or at least, the man who was phoning on their behalf, said two things that compelled me to act in their interests and not City's.'

'What did he say?'

'He said that my daughters, Ellen and Hayley, attended Radcliffe Primary School. He also said that my wife was a nurse who left her VW Beetle unlocked in bay twenty-three of Salford Infirmary.'

'Ah,' I said. 'I suspect the guy who contacted you was more LVF than LFC.'

'Funny,' said Cowan. 'I suspected the same thing.'

I had what I wanted. I had confirmation from the

doctor that he had lied. And I had the power to get back at Huggins.

I chose my moment very deliberately. I doorstepped Northern Ireland's No. 1 on the eve of his supposed transfer. I told him his move to City had been scuppered. I said he could read all about it in the next morning's *News Letter*.

He collapsed right there in his hallway, clutching his arm.

Pathetic, I thought. I hadn't seen such hammy acting since my father's memorable performance in Sydenham Amateur Dramatic Society's production of *Hello Dolly*. Dad had entered stage, taken one deep breath to belt out the signature number and immediately inhaled his false moustache. As my father fussed and flailed, choking to death, the audience were in stitches, marvelling at his exquisite comic timing. It was only when he turned blue and an off-yellow foam began to seep from the corners of his mouth that anyone took him seriously.

I was glad I had attended that show, for when Miles Huggins began to display the same symptoms from the discomfort of his hall carpet, I knew he wasn't faking it. Either he'd swallowed his sideburns or he was experiencing a very real seizure.

I keyed three nines into my mobile, but Huggins was kicking my shin and shaking his head. Between snatches of breath he asked me to get his pills from the bathroom cabinet. They were prescribed, he said. They were the reason he was able to manage his heart condition.

I did as he directed and ran up the stairs. When I returned, he'd barely an ounce of air in him. I unscrewed the cap on the pill bottle.

'How many?' I asked.

He held up four fingers.

I tipped seven or eight into my palm. I was frantic.

He took them from me and laughed. The man was having a heart attack and he laughed. He slapped the pills between lips that were dry and grey. They sat on his colourless face like two slugs in salt.

'You're still a Big fuckin' Jessie,' he said.

You're still a Big fuckin' Jessie.

The last words of Miles Huggins.

He died barely a heartbeat before the ambulance pulled up outside his pebble-dashed semi.

When the RUC arrived they asked me to go over everything that had happened. I explained that I was a journalist on the *News Letter* and that I had been interviewing the goalkeeper on the eve of his big money move across the water. I told them that he just collapsed. No rhyme or reason. I explained that I had done everything I could. I had given Huggins his pills. I had called the ambulance.

A paramedic snatched the pill bottle out of my hand. She took one look at the label and branded me an idiot. The pills had been prescribed to a Mrs G. Huggins. And they were Clomifene, she said, a drug used to treat female infertility. Miles and his wife had been trying for kids.

The paramedic explained some side effects associated with Clomifene. It can cause hot flushes, haemorrhaging and convulsions. 'In other words,' she told the police, 'you don't give seven or eight of the fuckers to a man experiencing a heart attack.'

Huggins's club and agent went ballistic. Well, they would, wouldn't they? Two million Manchester pounds had slipped through their fingers. They informed the police that I had not been granted an interview with the dead star. Geraldine Huggins told the police that I had been hounding her husband for months.

The RUC hauled me in.

And that was when I came face to face with my old head boy Stephen Meeks for the first time since school. There wasn't time to reminisce, however. Meeks cut to the chase. He asked me why I had killed Miles Huggins. He said that my prints were on the pill bottle. He pointed out that as I could read the label, I would have known what it contained, whom it was prescribed to, and the recommended dosage.

'You killed him, Jessie. That's the long and the short of it.'

'The guy was having a fucking heart attack,' I protested. 'He asked for the pills. I didn't stop to analyse the label. And he took them. All of them. I assumed I'd done the right thing.'

'Huggins was in no position to ascertain whether the tablets you gave him were the correct ones. As you rightly point out, he was having a fucking heart attack,' said Meeks. 'And we've got to ask ourselves, why did he have that heart attack in the first instance? What brought it on? It wouldn't have anything to do with your ongoing attempt to destroy his life, would it?'

Meeks held up a faxed layout of my intended *News Letter* front page.

'Look,' I said, 'when I called at his house, it was to prepare him for tomorrow's revelations. But Miles had a weak heart. It could have gone any time. It could have gone during his first game for City. And if it had, would you have been accusing Dr James Cowan of killing him? It was he who faked the medical, not me. I'm a journalist. I was only reporting the truth.'

'Bollocks,' said Meeks. 'You make it sound so noble.

Truth is, you destroyed this man's life because of some skewed belief that he destroyed yours. I'm onto you, Jessie. I know what you're up to. And I know you're trying to do to me what you did to Miles. But I'm a reasonable man, so I'll cut you a deal.'

Meeks folded the faxed article and slipped it inside a blue cardboard sheath, the cover of which displayed my neatly typed name. The file was surprisingly thick considering my lack of previous criminal convictions and given the fact that I'd only recently been hauled in. I guessed that Meeks had been keeping an eye on me for some time.

'I want you to give me everything you got from your little tête-à-tête with the late Davey Gavin,' he continued, corroborating my hunch. 'Tapes, transcripts, everything with my name in it. You can make it easy and tell me where this *research* is, or I can direct my boys round to your flat to do some research of their own. But, as I said, I'm a reasonable man. In return for your co-operation on this, I will not charge you with the manslaughter of Miles Huggins.'

And from that moment, Meeks owned me.

Although the death of Miles Huggins had featured prominently in the next day's *News Letter*, my revelations about his condition, the faked medical and Linfield FC's links with unsavoury organizations did not.

I'd had enough. I offered Harry Clegg my resignation. He told me not to be so fuckin' ridiculous, no fuckin' way was he fuckin' accepting it. I took this as a no and agreed to stay on at the paper in some unobtrusive capacity. I settled for semi-retirement, a two-day week and the innocent pastures of the Entertainment page. My pay was slashed, but I didn't need the money. I had no mortgage on my million-pound penthouse.

Look where all this had got me, though. I only wanted a quiet life. I only wanted to keep my head down. But five years on and I'm reviewing some band and their lead singer winds up murdered by the para-militaries. And it's all because of me, because of my history with that bastard Meeks. Scarlet was dead because Meeks had me over a barrel. He would charge me with manslaughter if I didn't bring O'Hanlon down.

I wanted her back.

And I wanted my quiet life back. But how?

Even if I got more on O'Hanlon, enough to satisfy Meeks, would that be the end of it? Would Meeks leave me alone to live happily ever after?

Not while he had the Huggins file in his top drawer.

Then again, Meeks wasn't the only one holding back incriminating information. I remembered giving him the Davey Gavin Tapes. But I don't think he ever received 'King Rot (live and uncut) – The Complete Boxed Set'.

23

'Why are you boiling your knickers in my saucepan?' I asked.

Karma was standing in our kitchen, trawling a wooden spoon through a thick and simmering stew of pants.

'I need to boil them to get rid of all the germs. The washing machine isn't hot enough,' she replied.

'Is that the reason you insist on ironing towels, to burn off the germs?'

'Yup. It's hygienic,' she said. 'And before you argue with me, Jay, I know what I'm talking about. I'm a nurse.'

Karma used a ladle to transfer her heavy, smoking knickers into a basin of cold water. She left the residual water to bubble away on the hob.

'Don't empty that water out,' I said. 'We could use it to make a broth. Waste not, want not, as my granny used to say.'

'Was this the same granny who stuck a fork in her sugar bowl and hung her used tea bags out to dry on the washing line?'

'She was from a different generation, Karma. She was a child of rationing.'

'Is that why she made your father wear his pants inside out to school, to get an extra couple of days out of them?'

'Christ, how did you know that?'

'You told me, Jay. You're forgetting that we go back a long way. After a dozen years sharing bottles of supermarket cider in parks, propping each other up in bar snugs, and climbing into each other's beds on Sunday mornings to eat burnt toast and set the world to rights, I'd say I know everything about you.'

'You don't know *everything*,' I said.

'Try me,' she replied. She pulled a pair of sopping knickers out of the basin, wrung the life out of them, flapped them open and draped them over the top rung of the clothes horse, like she was drying dulse. A dozen identical pairs of black knickers were subjected to the same unblinking treatment – twist, flap, drape, twist, flap, drape.

'What's my favourite album?' I said.

'*Joy* by Ultra Vivid Scene. And your favourite song of all time is "Nightporter" by Japan. *Play it again Sam* is your favourite film, on those few occasions when *Manhattan* isn't. You hate it when people say "lickerish" instead of "liquorice" and "Febuary" instead of "February". And you absolutely *detest* it when they unnecessarily put the word "The" in front of band names – "*The* Eurythmics", "*The* Cocteau Twins".'

'Well, why do people do that? It's "Eurythmics". You wouldn't say "*The* The The", would you?'

Karma wasn't listening. She had heard it all before. She continued to tell me how well she knew me, pausing only to bin a pair of knickers that had four holes in them instead of the usual three.

'I know you lost your virginity on the eve of your

eighteenth birthday,' she said. 'To Karen Johnson. It was one minute to midnight when you entered her, so, technically, you were still seventeen. And when you were done, a whole three minutes later, you had become a man of eighteen. You're still telling people that you had sex that lasted a year. And I know this wasn't the first time you tried to shag Karen. The previous Saturday you forced me to buy you some condoms because you were too embarrassed. You intended to use them that night at a house party I was throwing. Only, you never got Karen into my parents' bed. The party came and went and so did your chance of losing your cherry. Karen's mum appeared at my front door, in her dressing gown and curlers, and whisked her daughter home before you could violate the poor girl. I remember the two of us clearing away the sour lager bottles and stale ashtrays and you complaining that the condoms had been a complete waste of money. As I remember, you then stuck your hand down the front of your trousers, pulled your condom off and scrunched it into a beer can. You'd been wearing it all night. You had put it on before the party even started. I mean, how did you pee? Did you keep taking it off and putting it on again? And can you imagine if Karen and you *had* got as far as the bedroom? Don't you think that when you whipped your boxers off, she might have thought you were being a tad presumptuous? God, I loved you to bits for that, Jay. I just wanted to bundle you up.' Karma pinched my nose with a wet finger and thumb and tugged it. She returned to her laundry.

'OK, so you know *a lot* about me, but you don't know everything.'

'I know you're missing Scarlet and it's cutting you up. I know that you're in some sort of trouble. And I know that you suffer from social anxiety disorder, but you won't admit to it.'

'Social anxiety disorder? What's that when it's at home?'

Karma propped her bottom against the washing machine.

'It's an intense fear of social performance, resulting in an avoidance of certain social situations,' she said. 'That's why you went through puberty doing silly things like putting a condom on four hours before sex. You were too embarrassed to do it in front of the girl. And that's why, more recently, you never got round to telling Scarlet how you felt about her. You've always been afraid of failure, Jay. You're not nearly as bad as you used to be, but you still worry yourself sick. I mean, look at the state of you. You've got to be stressed to start dressing like that.'

I had forgotten that I was still wearing Meeks's custard V-neck and slacks.

'I'm not stressed. I needed to borrow some clothes. It's a long story.'

'It's OK,' said Karma. 'Really. It's perfectly normal to suffer from acute embarrassment. Ten million Americans have been diagnosed with SAD.'

'Well, that's hardly surprising. I mean, if I was an overweight, opinionated loudmouth who spent all my hard-earned dollars on junk food, diet pills and telly evangelism, I'd be embarrassed.'

'That's not my point,' said Karma. 'Your condition is common. The accepted belief is that your anxiety is related to embarrassing events in your past. But that's just lazy, old-school psychology. Doctors now know that the condition is caused by an imbalance of serotonin. So all that blushing, sweating, tensing of the muscles, drying of the mouth and pounding of the heart is due to a common biological deficiency.'

'And who told you that crock of shite?'

'Dr Jason Gourley. He's been on my ward all week. He's quite dishy, actually. Sort of a blond George Clooney. Anyway, Jason says that serotonin transports the electric signals between the various nerve cells in the brain. An imbalance in the chemical affects the cell-to-cell communication and can stimulate your feelings of anxiety and embarrassment. He knows his onions, Jay. He's our top neurologist.'

'I tend not to listen to those fellas. I'm a bit of a neuro-sceptic. And anyway, why were you chatting to this Jason Clooney about me? Ever heard of patient confidentiality?'

'You're not my patient, Jay. You're my friend. My closest friend. I'm concerned about you, that's all.' Karma lifted the clothes horse out onto the balcony, to dry her underwear. It did not seem to concern her that the wind was up and that her panties could end up decorating the Christmas tree outside City Hall.

I considered her little diagnosis. I didn't like it. I had spent all these years blaming my schoolmates for my social ineptitude, yet Karma was suggesting my suffering could be attributed to some chemical (or lack of it). Was serotonin to blame for the tortures I endured growing up? Had I gone after Meeks, Huggins and McClaren unnecessarily? Surely not. It wasn't serotonin that secreted gay pornography in my schoolbag so my parents would find it. Serotonin didn't paint 'JESSIE BLACK ONLY HAS ONE BALL' on the playground walls of the girls' secondary school in six-foot magnolia letters. And serotonin didn't start the rumour that my mother had miscarried a baby girl before I was born and that she had dressed me in girls' clothes until the age of six because my sister's death had sent her doolally.

Karma shucked closed the sliding doors.

'Right,' she said. 'I've got to get into my uniform. I'm on a twelve-hour shift.'

The hospital. The Royal Victoria Hospital. Of course. Aisling Coyles had mentioned it shortly before she was shot. She had said that after Kate Rogers had given birth to her dead son, the nurses at the Royal had organized a whip-round to help pay for a funeral. The son of Kate Rogers and Martin O'Hanlon had been born at the Royal Victoria Hospital. There would be a record of the birth. There would be proof of their liaison.

'Karma, let me come with you,' I said.

'To the hospital?'

'Please. You were right, I *am* in trouble. Serious trouble. And I need your help. I need you to get me into the maternity ward.'

'The maternity ward? Are you sure it's you that's in trouble? Or have you got a girl into trouble?'

'Yeah, yeah. I told her parents she was smoking. Seriously, Karma. This is important.'

'OK, but you're paying for a taxi. I'm already running late and, thanks to you, I no longer have a car.'

'I said I was sorry about that.'

'Whatever,' said Karma. She grabbed a pair of tights from the wash basket, sniffed them, shrugged, and took them into the bathroom. She passed Diggsy on the way. He entered the kitchen and immediately handed me a wet photograph.

'I've just developed the roll I took on the way down to Dublin . . . the one that wasn't stolen,' he said. 'I thought you might like to keep that particular pic.'

I examined the picture: Scarlet, eyes closed and

earphones in, her red body warmer balled up between her soft cheek and the window of the Mercedes van.

I wondered, did she look as peaceful in death?

'Thanks, Diggs. Thanks, man.'

I slid the picture into my back pocket, while Diggsy unwittingly plopped some brittle noodles into Karma's bubbling knicker water.

I hate the smell of hospitals. It is a dense, antiseptic odour that resides when all other smells have been stripped away. It's a non-smell, one that dredges up restless memories of starched bed sheets, sweat-soaked pyjamas, flat Lucozade and fevered sleep.

'These places make me ill,' I said.

'They're supposed to have the opposite effect,' said Nurse Carmel McCaffrey.

We were walking through one of the general men's wards. Our every step resounded off a floor that had been polished so enthusiastically you could have played curling on it. We were on our way to the Maternity Unit, having already enjoyed a tour of Paediatrics. It was Christmas and, as they did every year, the Royal had drafted in a top celebrity to do the rounds and lift the spirits of those poor kids who wouldn't make it home to unwrap their presents. This year the honour had been bestowed on Damien Day from local boy band Boyz-A-Daizy.

According to Karma, all had been going well until Damien approached the bedside of one wee fella who had suffered full-thickness burns to his chest and arms (he had been standing too close to the stolen Astra he and his brothers had just torched). As the nurses changed the wee lad's dressings for the third time in eight hours, Damien Day offered to give him a fire-man's lift. 'And later,' added Karma, 'they had to forcibly escort Damien off the ward when he tried to pick a young girl up by her ankles and swing her between his legs.'

'What's wrong with that?' I asked. 'It's just a bit of innocent horseplay. My dad used to do that to me.'

'Yes, but you weren't suffering from brittle bones,' said Karma.

'Ah.'

Karma stopped me and smiled. 'You know, Jay, that white coat actually suits you.'

'Thanks, but I'm not convinced. I mean, do I look like a doctor?'

'No, but if anyone asks I'll say you're a student medic and I'm giving you the tour. Now, are you going to tell me why I'm smuggling you into Maternity?'

'I can't.'

'Jay, I'm putting my job on the line. Don't I at least deserve to know why?'

'It's complicated. Too difficult to explain.'

'I'll bet it's not as complicated as reconstructing a knee. And you're forgetting that, only last week, I had to tell a mother her son had been crucified and had died in resus as a result of his injuries. Crucified, Jay. Nailed to a fucking door. Compared to that, nothing is too difficult to explain.'

'OK, OK. You did ask, so here goes.' I pulled Karma behind a set of screens that stood redundant in the corridor. 'Scarlet hasn't been kidnapped. She's not being held to ransom, like I said. She's been murdered by the Provos. They sent their calling card to the house in Dalkey the morning after she went missing. I didn't tell you because I didn't want to alarm either you or the girls in the band. I'm trying to blackmail Martin O'Hanlon into telling me where her body has been dumped. I believe he ordered the killing. I've

284

been doing my research and have discovered that O'Hanlon fathered a child by the Secretary of State, Kate Owen, and that the baby was born here. I have the potential to ruin him, but I need to get access to the births records so I can prove it. Kate Owen was admitted as Kate Rogers, some time in 1968—'

Karma stopped me mid-flow, placing her hand on my arm. She didn't ask the questions that my story clearly begged. While most people would have deemed my ranting insane, Karma did not doubt me or interrogate me. She had merely stopped me so she could hug me. And she did so with all the unquestioning affection of a true friend.

The screens were swished back.

'Jeez, you two, could you not get a hotel room?' said a young nurse. Lisa, she was called, if her name badge was to be believed. 'Come on now, Doctor, put the nice nurse down, you're needed.' She jabbed her finger into my kidneys. I hoped she wasn't as brutal with a hypodermic. 'There's a bolshy git in ward four, won't let me near him,' she continued. 'Says he'll only see a male doctor.'

'But. I'm not a—'

'You'd better go . . . *Doctor*,' said Karma.

The two nurses cajoled me into a dimly lit ward, past metal beds that supported an unhealthy collection of men, their complexions myriad hues of yellow ('you find the colour, Dulux will match it'). The man in the bed closest to the corridor (and therefore the closest to death?) looked at me with far-gone eyes: eyes like pickled onions in milk. He didn't need a doctor, he needed a priest. Or an exorcist.

Lisa led Karma and me to the last-but-one bed. The man lying in it was in his late fifties/early sixties. His hair was thick and silver and resembled three Brillo

285

pads strategically positioned on his head. In marked contrast to the men in the other beds, this guy had a healthy tan, though his face was as creased as a Californian raisin. The other thing that distinguished him was the cradle that had been positioned over his bed. A system of pulleys and cables held the bed sheets a good foot above his midriff.

'A doctor,' he said. 'Thank Christ. I'm in agony.'

'What seems to be the problem?' I asked, adopting my best bedside manner. I directed the question to Karma as much as to the man himself.

'It's his penis,' barked Lisa, with the disarming frankness of a medical professional. 'Mr Kennedy has been suffering from impotence. To remedy the problem, he's been prescribed Alprostadil, which he administers by intracavernosal injection preceding intercourse.'

'I don't like the sound of this,' I said. I didn't understand a word of it, but it sounded painful all the same.

Mercifully, Karma came to my rescue. 'Dr Black is a graduate trainee. I don't think he's encountered a penile priapism before. Am I right, Doctor?'

I nodded.

'Before sex, the patient injects a drug into the penis, about five micrograms, enough to sustain an erection for one hour,' said Karma.

'Mr Kennedy got a bit *carried away*,' said Lisa, aiming the last two words directly at the man in the bed. 'He had a rush of blood to the head and gave himself eight times the recommended dose. And now all the blood has rushed to another area entirely, hasn't it, Mr Kennedy?'

'It was my anniversary,' the man protested. 'My ruby wedding. I just wanted it to be special . . . give my Pauline a night to remember.'

286

'He's suffered a priapism. We've done the initial penile aspiration using a nineteen-gauge butterfly needle inserted into the corpus cavernosum. We managed to draw fifty millilitres of blood, but it doesn't seem to have done the trick.'

I looked to Karma again.

'He has a permanent erection,' she explained.

'It looks like a black pudding,' said Mr Kennedy. 'It's the size of a baby's arm.'

'I need to examine the testes to check there's no haemorrhaging,' said Lisa. 'But he won't let me touch him. So, Dr Black, if you don't mind . . . can you do the honours?' She handed me a pair of disposable rubber gloves.

'I can't. I—'

'Course you can,' said Karma. 'You just have to feel each testicle and check that there's no abnormal change in size. It's the same as doing a self-examination, only you're looking for an overall swelling, not a lump.'

The nurses pulled the screens round the bed and waited the other side of them.

I nervously donned the gloves, jabbing my fingers into the wrong holes. I did my best to look confident, there was such hope in Mr Kennedy's eyes. I peeled the flimsy bed sheet away from the cradle. This created a delicate waft of air around his engorged manhood. The way Mr Kennedy squealed you would have sworn I had slammed a car door on it.

'Stop laughing, Karma. That wasn't funny,' I said.

She butted one of the swing doors that led into the Maternity Unit.

'Come on, Jay. Smile. Give your face a holiday.'

'No. I didn't appreciate that. I can't get his . . . *thing*

287

. . . out of my head. I don't think I'll ever be able to muster an erection again. I'll get flashbacks. The size of a baby's arm, he said. I assume he was referring to a baby elephant.'

'Jeez, you wouldn't last two minutes in this hospital. That was wee buttons compared to some of the things you see.'

'Right now, the only thing I want to see is a birth certificate that names Martin O'Hanlon as the father of Kate Rogers's child.'

'Well, if we've kept such a record, it'll be in here.'

Karma showed me into a cavernous room that was sandwiched between two of the delivery theatres. There appeared to be no heating. The room was icy. Its walls were rendered invisible by row upon row of dog-eared files that were stacked, floor to ceiling, on metal shelves. I assumed that these were the records of every baby that had been delivered at the hospital. Such a primitive filing system came as a shock to me. This was the twenty-first century. I had assumed I would be able to access the file I was after by simply clicking a mouse.

'Surely the hospital could have got someone to transfer all these files onto disk?'

'That would take time. And time is money. And money is something the NHS hasn't got,' said Karma. 'You're just going to have to get your hands dirty.'

I noticed that the shelves were new. There were little stacks of fine plaster dust at regular intervals on the floor. The uprights had been recently drilled to the wall. I also noticed that boxes of files had been stacked on top of a permanent marble monolith in the middle of the room. There was guttering cut into the floor around it.

'This room wasn't always the records room, was it?' I asked.

'No,' said Karma. 'We moved all the files in here in October. The room had ceased to become viable for its original designated purpose. At least, that's what it said on the official memo.'

'It had ceased to become viable? How can a room stop being viable?'

'The nurses refuse to come in here. It used to be the mortuary. This is where they brought the babies that didn't make it. They conducted the post-mortems in here. There's another tiny room behind that locked door where families could say their goodbyes to their children.'

'And why won't the nurses come in here?'

'Have you not noticed how cold it is?' asked Karma.

'Yes. But that's hardly a reason to shut the room down. You just need someone to fix the thermostat.'

Karma grabbed my hand and walked me across the room. She placed my palm on top of a radiator. It was hot as toast.

'I don't understand,' I said.

'The room's . . . and I can't believe I'm using the word . . . it's haunted.'

'Wise up, Karma. You've been watching too much Scooby Doo. Don't you think you've pulled my leg enough this evening?'

'I'm serious, Jay. We had the priests in to bless the place, but the nurses were still seeing and hearing things.' Karma pointed to a soap dispenser on one of the few patches of exposed wall. 'I've seen that thing squirting soap all by itself. I've heard babies crying in here, when the place has been empty.'

'Are you saying you believe in ghosts?'

'No. But strange things go on in hospitals. You just,

I dunno, *accept* them. I was on the Geriatric ward one night when I heard a bell, a patient calling me to their bed. Perfectly normal, I thought, and responded to the call. Thing was, the bell came from a bed that was in a redundant section of the ward. It was behind a door that had been locked for several months. When I eventually found the key to get in, the ward was completely dark. Except for one bed. The light above it was switched on. I can't explain it. I don't try to. You just have to accept that this sort of thing happens in a building that has been the theatre for so much death.' Karma opened the door. 'Now, if you don't mind, I'll have to leave you to it.'

'You're leaving me alone in here?'

'Jay, I've got a job to do.'

'But what if someone comes in and sees me rifling through the records?'

'Trust me,' said Karma. 'Nobody will come into this room.'

'That makes me feel a whole lot better.'

I didn't know where to start. The files had not been alphabetized. Nor were they strictly chronological. One wall moved encouragingly from 1962 to 1965, then immediately jumped to 1974, as though England's World Cup win and Neil Armstrong's giant leap had never happened. When I eventually found 1968 my heart sank. There must have been a baby boom that year, for if the files for 1968 were stacked side by side they would have touched both ends of an Olympic swimming pool.

I flicked through the sandy-coloured envelopes, their corners soft with age. The year 1968 was filed by month, but how was I to know the day Kate Rogers had her baby? I had resigned myself to having to plough through every record, when I remembered that Aisling

Coyles claimed that Kate Rogers had slept with O'Hanlon on the night of the PolySoc Ball. That was May 1967. Add nine months . . . equals February 1968. I flicked my fingers along the top of the files, their pulpy gills fanning dust into my face. Feb 68 . . . Feb 68 . . . *got it*. Strangely, once I'd located the month, the chronology was abandoned and the files reverted to alphabetical order. Emerson, Fletcher, Gilmour, Girvan, Hudson, Kipling, Larmour, Law, Longmore, Murphy, McBride, McCrystal, McIlroy, McKee, O'Connor, Patterson, Price . . . Rogers.

Bingo.

I slipped my hand into the envelope and removed two pieces of paper and a square of card.

The first sheet of paper was a copy of the birth certificate. Kate Rogers was named, but there was no mention of the father. Damn. I couldn't escape the feeling that O'Hanlon was a charmed man. The botched attempts on his life, the lawyers that had consistently failed to bring him to justice, his rise to the Sinn Fein leadership and, perhaps, to the position of First Minister – and now this. How did he do it? The bastard was unstoppable.

Somewhat deflated, I turned my attention to the other bit of paper. It was the baby's death certificate. There was an annotation on the reverse of the document indicating that his body had been transferred to Rosemount Crematorium. But again, no mention of O'Hanlon.

I examined the square of card. It had a tiny black footprint and an even daintier handprint inked onto it. I presumed these prints belonged to the dead boy.

Perhaps O'Hanlon wasn't so charmed. Some of the baby's sweat or skin cells would have impregnated the ink. I felt sure that it wouldn't be too hard for a

police scientist to isolate these cells and extract the
genetic code that would pin paternity on the Sinn Fein
leader.

'I'm not sure they can obtain DNA from footprints,'
said Karma.

I had waited until we were out in the hospital car
park before I showed her the card.

'Maybe not,' I said. 'But O'Hanlon doesn't know
that.'

24

Jessie Black, you have twenty-four hours to save the world.

That was what it felt like as I was whisked along the empty Westlink carriageway in the back of a black cab, at twenty to midnight, with an RVH file clamped firmly under my arm.

I understood the folly of getting a black cab while trying to avoid the IRA (the black cab was the terrorist's equivalent of a company car). But there was nothing else I could do. The Royal Victoria Hospital sits in West Belfast, an area in which any taxi other than a black one is either lost or stolen.

I had what I needed on O'Hanlon but, once again, I was faced with the problem of confronting him with the evidence. How was I going to get near him? This time I did not have the luxury of a press pass to one of his conferences. And I was sure that O'Hanlon's men had twice tried to gun me down. There would be a 'shoot to kill' policy if I came within the ten-mile exclusion zone that had been placed round his beard.

Nor could I just pick up the phone and call him. Martin O'Hanlon, quite sensibly, was not listed in the telephone directory. At least, not *the* Martin O'Hanlon.

I pitied his namesakes, though. A crank call or an unordered pizza was the least of their worries. In one unfortunate incident, a Martin O'Hanlon from Newtownards had his home firebombed by a particularly dumb group of local Loyalist dissidents (the 'Ulster Volunteer Farce', as the *Irish Times* called them). Mind you, this sort of stupidity was not confined to Northern Ireland. With the publication of the paedophile register, paediatricians all over England were waking up to find they'd been barricaded into their homes by groups of gravel-voiced, bleach-blonde mothers, demanding their immediate castration.

The answer to the problem of how I could get access to O'Hanlon came from an unexpected source. It was written in two-foot letters on posters that lined both sides of the dual carriageway.

JINGLE STRINGS

a Yuletide celebration starring

Edel O'Hanlon

"THE GIRL WITH THE EMERALD HARP"

DECEMBER 23RD – WATERFRONT HALL – £25-£50

sponsored by imagine2008

Edel O'Hanlon. The Girl with the Emerald Harp. Martin O'Hanlon's daughter and Ireland's very own Vanessa-Mae. Only Edel couldn't play the violin. And she was a decent, clean-living Irish rose who would never be pictured knee-deep in the Singaporean surf wearing a see-thru bikini while furiously plucking her instrument.

I knew a bit about her from my work on the Entertainment page. In her twenty-three years, the prodigious harpist had recorded a string of hit albums (no pun intended). They were contemporary inter-pretations of traditional Irish folk classics, played on her famous emerald-studded harp and then given the full techno/drum'n'bass makeover by some overpaid Ibizan producer. The gig at the Waterfront Hall was designed to promote her *Jingle Strings* Christmas album.

I realized I could access O'Hanlon through his daughter. I figured that Edel would be thrilled to know she had a half-brother, even if he had been committed to the earth a decade before she was born. She would want to interrogate her father. He would want to know who had told her about his son and what proof they had of the child's existence.

Edel O'Hanlon was my way in.

The security that surrounded her was legendary. Not only was she the daughter of prominent politician and (ex?) terrorist Martin O'Hanlon, she was one of Ireland's biggest exports, her album sales accounting for one third of the island's Gross Domestic Product. She was a valuable commodity, as was her jewel-encrusted harp. She was almost as untouchable as her father.

Thankfully, I had one thing working in my favour. I was a music journalist.

Her show opened the following evening, so I knew she'd have to be at the Waterfront Hall that afternoon to do her soundcheck. I would get Harry Clegg to fix me up with an interview. Edel's people would jump at it. After all, she had an album and a concert to promote.

I turned to my driver. 'Listen, mate, on second

thoughts, I won't be going home. Can you drop me out at the *News Letter* building, Boucher Road?'

My foul-mouthed editor would still be at the office, putting the paper to bed.

Harry fed an A3 sheet of newsprint through two spinning cylinders, coating the back of the paper in hot wax adhesive. The sheet listed the day's Births, Marriages and Deaths. He fanned it in the air and slapped it onto the angled rubber cutting mat. He steadied his metal ruler and used his scalpel to slice the sheet into five equal columns, literally dissecting people's lives. Three fingers on his left hand were capped with puckered sticking plaster, testament to Harry's erratic command of a scalpel blade. He positioned the long strips of newsprint onto a page proof, trimming the bottom off any column that was too long and carrying it over to the top of the next. As usual, there were too many Births, Marriages and Deaths to be contained within the page. Harry's solution was simple. The last surplus inch or two of print was binned. If your surname happened to be Wilson or Young, your demise was likely to remain unannounced and your funeral would be poorly attended.

Harry didn't see me slink into the office. He had been concentrating too hard on keeping his fingers.

'Aha, the prodigal returns,' he shouted, when he finally looked up.

I ignored him and fired up my PC.

'We've a crackin' fuckin' leader tomorrow, Jay. That novelist I gave you the address of, Aisling Coyles, she's only been shot in the fuckin' aquarium.'

'Is that anywhere near the sternum?' I asked.

'You tell me,' said Harry. 'You were in the vicinity.

You wouldn't happen to know who fired the shot?'

'Ask me no questions, Harry, I tell you no lies.'

He shook his head and held his hands up in a gesture of surrender.

I didn't have time to indulge him. I had some research to do. If I was going to lend credibility to an interview with Edel O'Hanlon, I figured I had better find out a bit more about her.

I went online.

There was surprisingly little by way of new information on the harpist. Her official website made no mention of her family or her upbringing. There were a couple interviews with her (guardianunlimited.com/thetimes.co.uk) which I quickly scanned. But they concentrated exclusively on her music. And for an artist with multi-platinum record sales, there were surprisingly few unofficial fan sites. The handful there were told me nothing I didn't already know. Actually, I tell a lie. One informed me that Edel O'Hanlon was the proud owner of double-jointed thumbs.

This Girl with the Emerald Harp was more enigmatic than I thought.

If I couldn't research the harpist, I could at least pretend to know a bit about her instrument. I entered the domain of the harp.

The daughter of the infamous Irish Republican could not have picked a more appropriate instrument to play. The harp was resonant in more ways than one. Ireland is the only country to have a musical instrument as its national emblem. The Irish Free State adopted the harp in 1922 as 'an emblem of humanizing harmony'. The irony of it. The instrument simultaneously appears on the Free State seal, the Irish coat of arms and the presidential standard. Harps have been minted on the obverse of Irish coins from 1928 until the present (though the euro would soon consign them to history). Irish courthouses, post offices, and embassies all display a harp, as do their official documents and publications. A harp is even embossed on the front of the Irish passport. A more potent symbol of Irishness you could not find.

I found it impossible to ignore the symbolism attached to Edel's chosen instrument. I didn't believe that her dedication to the harp was entirely co-incidental, given her father's politics. This was confirmed when my line of investigation led me straight back to Martin O'Hanlon.

In the eighteenth century, the national flag of Ireland was 'the Green Flag' – a yellow harp on a flat green background. This yielded to the green, white and gold Tricolour in 1916. The Tricolour became the flag of the twenty-six counties and at the same time a partisan flag in the North. According to the final website I stumbled into, Martin O'Hanlon believed that the Green Flag 'will be the only serious candidate as the flag of Ireland, once I have reunited her'.

And there was me, wondering why O'Hanlon's daughter hadn't taken up the recorder like normal children.

I still needed Harry to fix the interview.

I found him at his desk drinking brandy from a plastic coffee cup. He smelt weird. Like a woman.

'Jeez, Harry, what's your deodorant? It smells like . . . coconuts.'

Harry adopted a Ballymena accent. 'Cyoconuts? Well, it's boun'te,' he joked. He indicated a bottle on his desk – Vaseline Dermarub with coconut oil. 'It's for my eczema,' he said. White light bounced off his freshly greased forehead and into my eyes.

'Listen, Harry, I need another favour,' I said.

'No, Jay. No more favours. Not until you start showin' me somethin' on this big fuckin' story you say you're onto. That's if there is a story. I'm beginnin' to think all this chasin' around after pop stars and authors is some elaborate fuckin' smokescreen. Or is it a red herrin'? It's probably a smoked herrin', the way you're carryin' on.'

'You'll see something in the next twenty-four hours. I promise you. But right now I need you to telephone Edel O'Hanlon's management and fix an interview for tomorrow morning. She'll be at the Waterfront Hall.'

'Edel O'Hanlon? Marty's daughter? The Girl with the Emerald Harp?'

'Aye. All three of them. The Holy Trinity.'

'Jay, I know you're a music journalist but since when were you seduced by the delicate and sonorous beauty of the fuckin' harp? The only time you ever expressed an interest in the harp, it was one pound twenty a pint in Lavery's.'

'Please, Harry. I'd normally arrange these things myself, but you know what her security is like. I need your clout.'

Harry looked at me with the face of an old man who was about to put his life savings on a greyhound just because he liked the sound of its name.

'Twenty-four hours,' he said.

'And I'll deliver you a story so huge it'll make the revelations about the Bishop of Galway look like an *and finally*.'

25

All over Northern Ireland people were waking up to the smell of fried bacon and burnt sausages ('the Cookstown sizzle'). A fair few were roused by the wholesome aroma of toasted wheaten. Not so myself. I was resuscitated by the sickly scent of orange liqueur, like someone had doused my pillow in Glayva.

I needed the bathroom.

I made my way through the living room and was surprised to find Diggsy already up and dressed. Diggsy was never up before me. True, I had slept in. The last few days had finally caught up with me. But out-sleeping Diggsy – it was unheard of. He was always the last one to rise, even when Karma was recovering from her night shift.

'Morning, Diggsy. It is morning, isn't it? Tell me my watch hasn't stopped.'

'Ten thirty-two,' he replied.

'How come you're up? Is it giro day?'

'I couldn't sleep. I was too excited. This morning *Orange Disorder* went live.'

Diggsy drew my attention to his bowl of rotting oranges. No, they weren't oranges. They were furry blues. And they explained the smell of alcopops that had permeated the flat. It was like the morning after an unsupervised children's party.

'Your oranges are dying. How can they *go live*?'

'Take a duke at this,' he said. He clicked an icon on his PC, calling up a new window on screen. It displayed a live feed from his digicam, a seemingly static shot of the six oranges rotting in their wooden bowl on the Union Jack. Underneath the image sat a logo – imagine2008 – and a purple window containing the credit:

'ORANGE DISORDER'
(A LIVING SCULPTURE)
PETER DIGGS, BELFAST

'Explain?' I asked.

'It's the imagine2008 website. They're the guys behind Belfast's bid to become European Capital of Culture in 2008. The bid has to be submitted by March 2002, in ten weeks as it happens. And as part of the whole run-up they want to showcase the work of prominent local artists. When I got back from Dalkey there was a message on the answer machine from my old college tutor. He thought I'd like to submit a piece. So I thought, *Orange Disorder*, live, on the World Wide Web. Pretty cool, eh?'

I stared for a second at the image on the screen. Then I looked at the real oranges doing nothing in front of the camera. It was like watching paint dry. Or oranges rot.

'But I thought the whole point was to time-lapse the film, speed it up so the oranges decompose while life outside our window fizzes forwards. I thought it was a video installation, not a *living sculpture*, whatever that is. Didn't you want David Holmes to show it at his gigs?'

'Aye, well, I changed my mind. The imagine2008 website means that my work can touch more people. Anyone can check up on it at any time, from anywhere in the world. A work of this magnitude demands a global audience. I only called it a living sculpture because they didn't have a category for video artists. They wanted painters, poets and sculptors.'

I wanted to take the piss. I really did. But there was a look on Diggsy's face that I had never seen before. Gone were the jaundice and the hangdog resignation. Instead, his eyes flitted up and down the screen, examining his work with real enthusiasm, before they settled on his name credit like two melons on a fruit machine slotting into a winning line. Peter Diggs, Living Sculptor, was convinced he had made his mark. His great 'statement' had been made. No way would I rob him of that.

'What happens if I bare my arse in front of the camera?' I asked.

'Don't.'

I chose to bare my arse in the shower. I had to scrub up. In just under an hour I would be interviewing Ireland's second most celebrated virgin, Edel O'Hanlon.

The Waterfront Hall was a mirage, an architectural chameleon. Its glass exterior reflected the sky around it so that, as I approached it, the entire building seemed to disappear. I expected to locate the entrance by smacking, sparrow-like, into some imperceptible glass door.

I managed to find reception without breaking my nose. I gave my name to the young woman at the desk. I explained that I worked for the *News Letter* and that I had an 11.45 with Ms O'Hanlon. She handed me a visitor's badge. She invited me to take a seat. She wondered if I would like a newspaper. She offered me coffee. Then tea. A biscuit, perhaps? A cold drink? When I declined, she asked me if I was feeling OK. Then she rooted around in her handbag and retrieved two Nurofen, popping them into my hand.

Thankfully, an ebullient blonde bounced out of the elevator and rescued me. She wore the clothes and the demeanour of a hip twenty-something, but her skin betrayed her age, hanging a little loosely round her chin, her neck and the tops of her arms, like it was two sizes too big for her frame. Early forties, at a push. She spoke with the volume turned up to eleven, introducing herself as Vanilla Ice.

'Vanilla Ice?'

'Fionnuala Rice,' she repeated. 'I'm Edel's tour manager. She's upstairs now, in one of the rehearsal rooms.' Her accent was not dissimilar to the ones I'd heard down in Louth. And her 'S's were slightly lisped. She didn't shake my hand. She shook my whole arm, wrenching it from the socket.

'Er, hello, Fionnuala, I'm J—'

'Jay Black. I know. Your editor called me last night. He says you're a big fan of the harp.'

'Does he, now?'

'So you're here to interview Edel. I suppose you'll be wanting to ask her some questions.'

'That's the plan.'

'Can I take a wee look at them?'

'A wee look at what?'

'Your questions. I need to approve them.'

'May I ask why?'

Fionnuala threw me a slightly patronizing look, one that said *you're new here, aren't you*? 'It's my responsibility,' she said, 'to safeguard the interests of Edel

303

O'Hanlon and her record company. She will only answer questions that specifically relate to her music. These interviews aren't usually granted at such short notice. Normally I'd get your questions faxed through to me a week in advance, so I can make my selections.'

'You *select* her questions?'

'It's in her interests.'

'And they all have to relate to her music? So I can't ask her about her likes and dislikes, her upbringing, her fath—'

'Certainly not. That would be inappropriate. A lot of people have invested a lot of time and effort in creating the Girl with the Emerald Harp. We have to protect our investment.'

She made it sound like Edel O'Hanlon was assembled at some top-secret facility in the bowels of a Swiss mountain, and that the whole E.D.E.L. project was financed by a consortium of unscrupulous multinationals.

'Does Edel not have a say in this?'

'Good God, no,' she laughed. 'So anyway, let's see your questions.'

'I don't usually write them down. If I wrote my questions down, I wouldn't need to attend the interview. I could just mail a questionnaire to whichever artist I was interested in and get them to fill in their answers.'

'What a great idea,' said Fionnuala.

'But it's not natural. Normal people don't interact like that. When I meet my mates down the pub, I don't post them my questions in advance so they can prepare suitable responses. I prefer a bit of spontaneity, you know, to go off-road a little. A proper, two-way conversation. I find I get more out of people that way.'

304

'Well, you won't be going *off-road* with Edel O'Hanlon. Not today. I'll sit in on the interview.'

Fionnuala took me up to the second floor. She guided me into one of the studio suites. The room was a simple box with lilac walls and a steep bank of seats, a cross between a lecture theatre and a small-screen cinema. But it contained no lectern or cinema screen. The vacant seats presided over a low stage on which sat a solitary harp. It wasn't an emerald harp. It was your regular, common or garden harp. Not that the instrument is in any way common. Or garden. You don't see many schoolkids lugging harps onto buses.

'So where's Edel?' I asked.

'She'll be out in a minute. I told her I was popping down to reception to fetch the man from the *News Letter* and she rushed off to do her make-up.'

'But I don't have my photographer with me.'

'I know, I know. But she's a woman. She wants to look her— Ah, here's my star.'

Edel O'Hanlon was taller than she looked on TV. She kept her head slightly cocked and her left eye remained hidden behind two thick twists of strawberry blond hair. Her make-up was teen naïve. She looked like the victim of a flour bomb. Her skin was powder. I guessed there was a pretty face under it all, but I couldn't be sure. One thing was certain, she looked nothing like her father. (Stick her in a balaclava, however, and she was the spit.)

Fionnuala and I took two seats in the front row and Edel positioned her stool in front of us.

'Edel, this is Jay Black. Jay, this is Edel O'Hanlon.'

'Hi,' mumbled Edel, from somewhere behind that fringe. She had adopted the posture of the shy and reluctant ingénue, Diana meets Dana. It was an image that had seduced the great Irish public. Mothers prayed that their daughters would turn out like Edel; their sons could find no better bride.

Fionnuala had created a monster.

'So, Edel,' I said. 'The harp. An expensive instrument, I imagine. Would it not have been easier *and cheaper* to take up the cymbals?'

Edel looked at Fionnuala.

Fionnuala nodded.

Edel spoke in a hushed monotone. 'You're right. A harp can cost ten thousand pounds and that's before you pay for covers, trolleys and servicing. I had the loan of one in my early teens and later, when I attended Trinity in Dublin—'

'Edel recorded a tape,' interrupted Fionnuala. 'She busked in Grafton Street, selling her tape to shoppers, hoping to raise some money to buy a harp of her own. She sold four thousand copies. It was a regular little phenomenon. Two months after she made that recording, Edel had a five-album deal with EMI and an invitation to Washington to play at Bill Clinton's birthday party.'

Edel visibly shrank while Fionnuala did all the talking.

This was going to be hard work. If I had been conducting a genuine interview it would have been difficult enough. But this wasn't a genuine interview. Not only did I have to feign an interest in Edel's music, I had to maintain the pretence under the close scrutiny of the thought police. Somehow I had to engineer an opportunity to speak to the girl, unchaperoned. Call me crazy, but I had a hunch that Fionnuala would not approve of the question: *So, Edel, did you know that you have a dead, bastard brother?*

And that was when Mercury, God of Mobile Telecommunications, answered my prayers. Fionnuala's phone began to bleat out a tinny rendering of the theme from *The Piano*.

'Arsebricks,' she said, examining the screen. 'It's London. I'll have to take it. Edel, I'll be just outside this door— *Hello, Richard . . . yes, I can talk . . .*' Fionnuala covered the phone with her hand. 'Mr Black,' she whispered, 'no off-roading.'

She exited stage left.

Edel immediately looked at the floor.

I should just spit it out. *Edel, you have a brother.* It wasn't that hard, when I thought about it. Five little words. *Say them, Jay. That's what you're here for.* But what if she takes it badly? What if she . . . goes into shock, or faints or I don't know? *She won't. She'll be delighted. This is a brother she never knew she had.* No. I can't do it. Because whatever way I phrase it, I will still be telling this girl that her brother has died. *Think of Karma. How many times has she had to deliver bad news – the worst news? It's part of her fucking day job. You've got to do this, Jay.*

Edel's eyes remained glued to the floor. Perhaps the pattern on the carpet tiles was one of those Magic Eye illusions and she was actually staring at a 3-D image of a unicorn vaulting a sandcastle.

Whatever her illusions were, I was about to shatter them.

'Edel, you have a brother,' I said.

She blew her fringe off her eye.

'What?'

'You have a brother. He died at birth. Your dad, Martin, he fathered a child by another woman, ten years before you were born.'

Edel stood up. She demonstrated the room's impressive acoustics by shouting, 'Fiiiiiiiiii!'

'Please, Edel, you have to believe me.'

'Fiiiiiiii! Fii—'

'Look!' I screamed. I handed her the white card with the two inky prints.

Fionnuala threw her head round the door. Again, her hand covered her phone.

'Edel? Was that you? Is there a problem?'

Edel held the card to her chest. 'Yes, Fi. There is a problem.' She looked directly at me. 'I'd like some water,' she said. 'But not the stuff in the cooler. I want sparkling. Can you organize some Ballygowan?'

'No worries,' said Fionnuala. 'I'll pop over to the— *No, Richard. She's fine . . . yes, she says she'd love to play with the Philharmonic . . .*' Fionnuala's voice became lost behind the supposedly soundproof door.

Edel righted her stool. She sat down and examined the card. She spread out her palm and held it above her brother's tiny handprint.

'Where did you get this?' she asked.

'The Royal Victoria Hospital. Your brother was born there in 1968. Your father was still at Queen's University. There was this girl in his politics class. They had a bit of a fling and, well . . . the baby didn't survive.'

Edel's eyes stayed hidden but I could tell she was upset. A tear fell onto the knee of her tights. She pulled her sleeve over her hand and pressed it to the hot, dark dot.

'Why are you telling me this?' she asked.

'Because I need your help. I want you to fix me a meeting with your dad. Call it an interview. There's something he has to tell me. But I need you to do it today, Edel. If I don't speak to your father today, his political life is over. The story about his illegitimate son will be splashed all over tomorrow's paper.'

Edel straightened.

'Wait. How do I know you're not a terrorist? How do I know you're not going to kill my dad? People have tried before.'

'You don't. You'll just have to trust me. Look, I'm not a terrorist. I don't want to kill your father. I just need some information, that's all. I think he knows where my . . . girlfriend . . . is buried.' I removed the photo of Scarlet from my wallet and flashed it at Edel. 'That's Scarlet. The IRA murdered her. I just want her back.'

Edel stared for some time at the photograph.

'She looks so . . . peaceful. How long had you two been an item?'

'That's the thing. It sounds odd, but we weren't *technically* an item. To tell you the truth, we weren't an item at all. But I was very fond of Scarlet. I just couldn't bring myself to tell her how fond, that's all. Because I'm a stupid prick. I've always been a stupid prick. And now she's dead because I allowed myself to be blackmailed like a stupid prick.'

Edel returned the photograph. She stole a quick breath and looked for all the world like she was about to say something, but no words came. She bit her lip.

'I'm not after your father's blood. I just want Scarlet back. Her parents are in the States. They'll be returning for Christmas. I owe it to them to recover their daughter's body. I *must* talk to your father today.'

'Why couldn't you tell this girl how much you liked her?'

'Whoa, Edel. I'm the interviewer here. I'm the one who should be asking the probing personal questions.'

'I mean, you're risking an awful lot to get her back. I'm not as naïve as you think. I know what my father is capable of. You must have liked this girl a great deal to go to all these lengths for her. And yet, you couldn't even talk to her?'

Edel pulled the hair off her eyes. Her tears had traced sticky rivulets into her powdered cheeks. But she looked at me with a new confidence. Her expression demanded an answer.

I couldn't tell Scarlet how I felt because I have a deficiency of serotonin and my brain cells don't talk to each other. Yeah, bollocks, Karma.

'I couldn't tell Scarlet how I felt because I get hopelessly embarrassed when it comes to admitting my feelings,' I said. 'I literally gag on my words. But that's nothing compared to how sick I feel without her . . . without the *possibility* of her. See. I can find the words now. But now is too late. Pathetic, isn't it? I mean, how do you tell a dead girl you love her?'

Again, Edel pinched her bottom lip with her teeth. Then she turned 180 degrees to stifle a sneeze. She rummaged in her pocket for a tissue, before discreetly dabbing her nose. When she turned back to face me, two ruby studs sat in her left nostril.

'You just did,' she said.

26

'So, do I call you Edel or Scarlet?'

We snaked through the young cherry trees that lined the grounds of Rosemount Crematorium. The trees had been planted equidistantly, each representing a loved one turned to dust.

Edel or Scarlet, or whoever she was, had asked me to bring her here. She had told Fionnuala that she needed to pee and had slipped out of the Waterfront Hall by a fire exit. She was insufficiently dressed for December. She folded her arms under the sleeves of her cardigan and walked, scrunch-eyed, into the scurrilous drizzle.

'Call me Edel. I'm Edel O'Hanlon.'

Edel had removed her make-up in the back of our cab. She had made me pop into a garage on the way, to get her some wet wipes. She went through two packets, slowly and deliberately removing each layer of powder and foundation, until her face emerged like some lost treasure being carefully excavated from the clay earth. Her hair was off her eyes now, twisted behind her ears and secured into tight pigtails. The ruby studs remained in her nose. That she wished me to call her Edel felt slightly weird, for she now looked more like Scarlet and less like the reluctant harpist.

'Won't Fionnuala wonder where her young star has got to?' I asked. 'She'll be up to high doh. After all, she's got to protect her *invethment*.' I said the last word in my best imitation of her manager's Louthian lisp.

'Fionnuala has invested nothing in me,' said Edel. 'She doesn't even work for me. She works for my father. The security that surrounds me has little to do with my fame. It's got everything to do with having a bully for a dad. My father has me watched, twenty-four seven. He won't let me out of his sight.'

Edel stopped. She glanced over her shoulder. She resumed her walking, tearing a leaf off one of the few trees that still had leaves on it. She twirled it between her thumb and finger. She seemed to be retreating into herself again. I had to keep her talking.

'So your dad's a wee bit overprotective,' I said.

'More than a wee bit,' she said. 'I suppose it's to be expected. My father was a terrorist. There were many people who wanted him dead. He was convinced that my mother and I would be targeted too. He still is. It's made him paranoid. It's not much fun being reared by a paranoid father. I was taught from an early age never to open the door to callers, or to answer the telephone. I was never to touch Daddy's gun, which was as familiar as the television in our living room, or the toys on my bed. I was rarely allowed to play with other children. And when I went to school, the kids used to tease me about my dad. They said that he killed people. When I questioned him about it, he said that kids were cruel and I should ignore them. For years he made me believe that he worked in the civil service. Can you believe it? I thought that civil servants were glamorous secret agents and that was why Dad needed all the security on the house ... the cameras ... the bars on the front door. I thought he was James Bond.'

'But you're still covering for him. You told me your dad ran his own business importing and exporting whisky.'

'That wasn't such a lie, Jay. He *was* in the import business, back in the Seventies and Eighties. Only it wasn't whisky he was importing, it was guns. My father single-handedly revitalized the IRA's campaign of terror by bringing in massive shipments of arms, ammunition and explosives from the Middle East. Jesus, I remember him testing a high-velocity rifle in our back garden. He wrapped a bulletproof jacket round a sack of spuds and fired at it. The bullet tore clean through the back of the jacket. That evening we had baked potatoes for dinner and I bagsied one with a hole in it.'

'Gives a whole new meaning to jacket spuds,' I said. Edel didn't react.

I wanted to ask her about Scarlet, but I had a feeling that she was getting to that in her own roundabout way. Besides, the journalist in me didn't want her to stop. Here was the daughter of one of Ireland's most notorious terrorists, an international star in her own right, and she was giving me her full, unexpurgated exclusive. This was gold dust. Green, white and gold dust.

'My dad disgusts me,' she said, like the thought had just occurred to her. 'When he returned from a killing, our dog would recoil from his smell. And the dog wasn't the only one. My mum wouldn't go near him. The two of them weren't getting on back then. Dad thought the solution was to pack Mum and me off to the summer house in Dalkey. I mean, how insensitive could he be? Mum hated being in that house. She said it was paid for by gun money. That house was everything she wanted to get away from. I stayed in it while I studied at Trinity, but my dad's the only one who uses the place now. Mum even insists that no family photos be displayed in the house. She's washed her hands of it.'

Edel stopped and turned round. She stared more intently at the trees, like she could see right through them. The wind clattered their branches.

'Is something the matter?' I asked.

'No,' she said. She continued her slow walk, barely lifting her feet. Her soles skidded across the sodden grass. 'It's just, well, I now know that Dad had Scarlet followed. Remember that soldier who searched me when we were stopped at the border, the guy that got his fingers blown off? One of Dad's men pulled the trigger.'

'He wasn't a stalker?'

'Huh . . . I've been stalked all my life. Edel O'Hanlon can't even sneeze without a gloved hand appearing from a bush to offer me a tissue. I wasn't wrapped in cotton wool by my father, I was wrapped in barbed wire and booby-trapped. I'm a dangerous girl to know, Jay. My dad won't let anyone near me.' Edel stopped, but this time she looked directly at me. 'That's why I created Scarlet,' she said.

'I don't understand.'

'Scarlet was a free spirit. As Scarlet, I could escape the prison of my existence. I could play the music I wanted to play. I could get a taste of the life I wanted to live. Scarlet didn't need minders, because nobody would recognize her as Martin O'Hanlon's daughter. Dad and I struck a deal. I got to live as Scarlet, as long as I continued to play my harp as Edel and promote the O'Hanlon name around the globe. I have

314

unwittingly been one of the biggest fundraisers the IRA's ever had. They get ten per cent of everything with my name on it. But a deal was a deal and I honestly believed that, as Scarlet, my dad would leave me alone.'

She folded her arms into her chest and resumed her slow walk.

'I was wrong, Jay. The first inkling I had that he was having me watched was when I met you in Bar Baca after our Belfast gig and you said that the security at the Limelight didn't belong to the venue. I had a hunch they were Dad's men. Then, when that soldier got shot at the border, I was sure Dad was behind it. And when you told me that a stalker had threatened you with a gun on the night of the Belfast gig, and that he warned you to stay away from me, I knew he was IRA. That's why I went a bit crazy in Dublin. I was depressed. I couldn't handle the gig. I wanted to hide from the lights, to run for the shadows like a bloody cockroach. He was watching me. Everyone was watching me. I was terrified. I knew that I'd never be free.'

Edel's cardigan was heavy with rain. There was a vulnerability about her that I hadn't seen since that night in Dublin. I remembered her dismissing it as pre-gig nerves and claming that she suffered from hypertension. I now realized she had been lying. What she had been experiencing back then was pure, undiluted fear. It was something that could not be remedied by beta blockers and breathing techniques.

'Is that why you tried to kill yourself . . . to be free?'

'I knew that our summer house was kitted out with CCTV. My dad was having me watched, so I decided to give him something that he could look at over and over again. I drank all his whisky, necked all my pills and threw myself into his pool. He could rewind that and play it back till the day he joined me in hell.'

'You really wanted to die?'

'I'd had enough, Jay. Of course, you and Karma had to go and spoil it all by saving my life. You have no idea how angry that made me.'

'Sorry,' I said. Though I didn't quite know what I was apologizing for.

'I regained consciousness when Karma's car crashed. One of my dad's men had deliberately driven into us. Remember, the Dalkey house had been under constant surveillance. Dad's security would have seen the little episode in the pool. But they had to stop me getting to hospital. Dad couldn't have me admitted to A and E, not in that state. They would work out who I was. Can you imagine if the story got out that Marty O'Hanlon's clean-living, harp-playing daughter, *Ireland's daughter*, was a pill-popping punk? He'd never recover from the shame and embarrassment.'

Edel had got it spot on. That was all I had to do to bring the man down. Never mind Marty's dead, illegitimate son, I could go public with the story of Edel O'Hanlon, his suicidal, drugged-up daughter. I could, if I didn't love every bone in her crazy, mixed-up body.

'The bloke who crashed into you, did he . . . Karma said he stripped you. He didn't . . . ?'

'No, Jay. He didn't. He just wanted to discard my red clothes. All he said was – *Scarlet's dead.* He had some of my more sober wardrobe in his car. He dressed me in that and drove me to Dad's hotel in Dundalk. Our family doctor was there when I arrived. So, while O'Hanlon Senior wooed the Irish public at his Ard Fheis, O'Hanlon Junior was recovering from her failed suicide in his guarded hotel room. In a way, you had it figured out correctly. My father *has* killed Scarlet. He has murdered something inside me.'

Edel picked up her pace, striding ahead of me. She continued down the grassy bank, examining the names on the tiny crosses that were pegged beneath each cherry tree.

'What's going to happen to The Harlots,' I shouted after her, 'now they don't have their front woman?'

'They'll do fine without me. It's probably the best bit of promotion the single can have. *Lead Singer Vanishes*. It's so rock'n'roll.'

'Do Mags and the girls know who you are?' I asked.

'They do. And they know that I'm fine. They won't breathe a word. They're all the daughters of IRA men and women. It was the only way Dad would allow me to form the band. He's always chosen my friends and associates very carefully. All those "uncles" and "aunts" that came through our house when I was a child, they were all IRA.'

I remembered Scarlet's reaction to the soldiers at the border.

'Are you an IRA sympathizer?'

'No, Jay. However, if you want my stance, I'll give it to you. I believe in a unified island of Ireland, but it isn't worth the life of one man. Or one child.'

Edel had stopped at a small cross, as seemingly insignificant as the hundreds of other crosses she had passed. Strangely, the raindrops that thudded into the ground around it disappeared into the soil without forming a puddle. A realization hit me. Rosemount Crematorium was built on land reclaimed from Belfast Lough. The ground beneath our feet was composed largely of silt and sand.

'The cross in the sand,' I said.

'Sorry?' asked Edel.

'It's the title of a book by one of your dad's old flames, Aisling Coyles. *The Cross in the Sand*. It's the story of how your father cheated on Aisling with her best friend, Kate Rogers, and how Kate had his child . . . your brother. Only the names are changed. And so are the outfits. In the novel, the character representing Kate gives birth on a Donegal beach. Her child doesn't survive. She buries him in the dunes, marking his grave with a cross in the sand. The cross at our feet is the one the book's title refers to. Sure, isn't half of Belfast built on sand.'

'*Béal Feirste*,' said Edel, though it was barely audible.

'I didn't catch that.'

'*Béal Feirste*. Belfast. In Gaelic it means the sandbank on the river.'

The two of us stared in silence at the small cross bearing the name MARTIN ROGERS. There was no accompanying date, but I was confident that the cherry tree that cavorted above our heads was thirty-three years old.

Edel pinched her bottom lip with her top teeth, the way Scarlet did when she sipped a drink. But there was nothing cute or flirtatious in the way Edel wore the expression. She looked pained.

'I can't believe that all these years I had a brother,' she said. 'And that bastard never told me.' She wiped a knuckle under each of her eyelids.

I wanted to console her, to put my arms round her and gather her wet head into my chest. But, as ever, my body would not respond to the signals my brain was screaming at it. My legs were concrete. My arms stayed strapped to my sides. At the very least, I could say something.

'Try not to be upset, Edel. Your father is only protective of you because he's already lost one child. He doesn't want to lose you too.'

318

'That's bollocks,' she said. The 'b' blew the spit from her lip. There was venom in it. 'My dad was a bully. A violent bully. He hit me. And now I know why. Dad's always wanted a son, someone to carry the family name. But Mum could only give him a girl before her ovaries dried up. So you see, it's bollocks that he doesn't want to lose me. He resents me being alive. His son has died and for twenty-four years he's been taking it out on me.'

She was crying now. Big, unconfined heaves that dictated the rhythm of her speech.

'I don't even *like* the fucking harp. But Dad forced me into taking lessons. I hated it. Three times I deliberately broke my fingers to avoid having to practise the thing. That really pissed him off. And once, when he asked me to play at his fortieth, I sliced a bread knife down my palm. But the blade slipped onto my wrist and shaved an artery. Sometimes, when I look back, I wish they'd just left me to bleed away.'

My limbs now moved of their own volition. My legs took two steps towards her and my arms found her shoulders. I held her for some time. Her stubby pigtails scratched at my chin as she cried.

By the time she prised herself off me, she was able to force a smile.

'I'm not even that good at the harp,' she said. 'There are a dozen people more gifted than me. I'm not stupid. My father's influence and the O'Hanlon name have contributed to my notoriety.'

'Don't be so hard on yourself,' I said. 'You're a fantastic harpist.'

'Jay, you wouldn't know a fantastic harpist if she plucked your eyebrows.'

'OK, OK. But you look good on a poster. I'm sure that hasn't harmed your record sales.'

'Yes, but I'm sick of it. I'm sick of being paraded as some delightful and inoffensive Catholic role model. Jesus, my albums get played on religious radio programmes. There's a bishop in Tyrone who claims my music can heal. I should be making the sort of records that the Church wants to burn. If only they knew, Jay. If only they knew Scarlet.'

'Perhaps they should,' I said.

I realized that I no longer needed to blackmail Martin O'Hanlon into giving up Scarlet's corpse. Her corpse stood in front of me, radiating health. To borrow a quote – rumours of her death had been greatly exaggerated.

I could now go public with the whole O'Hanlon scandal, the illegitimate son by the Secretary of State, his violence towards his daughter. I could embarrass him, humiliate him, ruin him. The bastard deserved it.

Meeks wouldn't be happy. He wanted me to hold back such revelations so he could use them to black-mail the Sinn Fein leader. But I owed it to Edel to go public. She would finally be free of her father. He wouldn't be able to lay another finger on her. OK, so Meeks might not get his decommissioning or his Nobel Peace Prize, but with O'Hanlon removed from political life I could at least allay any fears that the Chief Constable had about him becoming First Minister and reforming the RUC. O'Hanlon would be O'History.

If this wasn't good enough for Meeks, if he still threatened me with the Huggins manslaughter charge, well, I still had the Davey Gavin tapes.

Right now, O'Hanlon was my priority. It would be easy. I could get a cab back to my office and key the story into tomorrow's paper. But Edel had given me an idea. Wouldn't her father's humiliation be made more potent if the revelations came from the mouth of his own daughter, *Ireland's daughter*, 'The Girl with the Emerald Harp'? While the *News Letter* had a circulation of a few thousand, Edel's Christmas concert would be beamed to forty-one countries and an audience of millions. And what if the 'Girl' didn't have an emerald harp at all? What if she was dressed in red, with a guitar slung at her hips?

'Edel, does Scarlet know the chords to "Frosty the Snowman"?'

'What are you thinking?' she asked.

'Tonight, at the Waterfront Hall, I reckon Scarlet should make a guest appearance.'

'Have you not been listening to me? Scarlet's dead. My dad won't have it.'

'Your dad's a bully, Edel. He hits you, for Christ's sake.' I remembered Mags telling me that Scarlet's dad could be violent. I remembered the fishing net to the back of the legs. The man had to be stopped. 'This is your chance to put an end to it, Edel. You can stand up on stage and let the world know what your father's really like.'

'I can't, Jay. He'd have me killed before he'd let Scarlet get up on that stage. Besides, it's totally impractical. I'd need stuff — red hairspray, red clothes — and even if I got them, how would I smuggle them into the hall? My security searches everything. They even open up my harp to check for "devices". And they're particularly jumpy today. It's the eve of my dad's election. They're worried there could be an attack on me. Or they're afraid that some group may try and sabotage tomorrow's election by bombing Belfast's precious concert hall.'

'Just hear me out, Edel. How long is your interval?'

'I get a twenty-minute break between my traditional set and my Christmas set.'

'OK. I'll get you your red hairspray and your clothes. I'll keep them at my flat. It's only a five-minute walk from the hall. Two and a half, if we leg it. I'll meet you outside the fire doors at the interval, just like I did this afternoon.'

'Impossible. Fionnuala's not going to fall for that stunt again. She'll follow me to the toilet. There's no way I can get out of that hall.'

'Then we'll just have to try a different tactic. Listen, my editor has got me two tickets to this evening's performance. They're front row. I'll make sure Karma is sitting beside me. At the interval, you can feign a stomach cramp, faint ... whatever. The important thing is that you call for medical assistance. I'll make sure that Karma brings her nurse's ID. She'll offer to go backstage and help you out. She can insist that you get some fresh air. They'll be so anxious to get you out for the second half, they'll let her do whatever it takes. Once Karma brings you outside, I'll take you across to the flat.'

'Nice plan, Jay. But how do I get back in?'

'Karma can give you her ticket stub. You can just stroll back in the front entrance. Nobody will recognize you, because you'll be Scarlet. You can take your seat in the front row and hop up on stage when the lights dim.'

Edel looked at me and smiled. She shook her head and bit her lip again. She turned away from me towards the lough. The rain had eased off and the first flashes of sunlight gave the water the texture and luminescence of creased tinfoil.

'You're mad,' she said. 'But you're also right. I need to do this. If I don't, they'll be planning another tree here. And there'll be a cross underneath, with my name on it.'

322

My mobile started to ring. I was sure my phone disliked me, for it only chose to go off at the most inappropriate moments.

It was Harry. It seemed that I was required to *haul my fuckin' ass down to the office, pronto.* He would send a cab to pick me up.

'I'm sorry about this, Edel. I can drop you back at the hall.'

'No problem. Sure, you've got shopping to do. I'd better give you a list of what I need.'

I rooted around in my pockets for a pen and a scrap of paper.

'Jay?'

'Uhuh.'

'Did you mean what you said, back in the rehearsal room, about your feelings for Scarlet?'

I felt the heat pricking my cheeks. My face was a pincushion.

Edel spotted it.

'It's OK,' she said. She leaned forward and kissed me on the cheek, adding, 'I know.'

27

I once overheard a teenager bragging about the time he
smuggled a laser pen into Belfast Zoo. He had pointed
the pen at the penguins, dancing the red dot across the
rocks behind them. The penguins couldn't take their
eyes off it. Their heads moved in total synchronicity,
this way and that, following the dot. (I had once
achieved similar control over my old history teacher
by bouncing a shaft of sunlight off the face of my
watch and onto his blackboard.) Apparently, when
this teen aimed his laser pen at the water, two dozen
penguins dived in after it.

I was having an equally mesmeric effect on my work
colleagues. They were all eyes as I entered the office. I
had to stop and check I wasn't still wearing Meeks's
clothes. What the fuck were they staring at? It wasn't
until Nosmo King formed a gun with his fingers and
thumb and cocked it at me that I knew what was going
on.

I was about to be fired.

My mother used to say you get the face you deserve.
Her theory was that if you spent your life frowning
you'd end up with a brow like a bloodhound's.
Similarly, if you allowed yourself a smile now and

again, in your later years you'd be blessed with the face of a saint. I judged the look on Harry's face when I entered his office and guessed that he'd spent every free hour of his waking life hammering nails into his penis. He looked livid. His neck was tandoori red. (Nobody deserved a face like Harry's.)

'Ah, here he is . . . the outlaw Jesse fuckin' James. Forgot your gun?'

'Harry, I know what's coming. I said you'd have my story in twenty-four hours and I meant it. So go ahead and fire me. There are other pape—'

'I *said* . . . forgot your gun?'

Harry drew my attention to his desk.

I immediately reinterpreted Nosmo's quick-draw hand gesture. Sitting on a handkerchief on top of Harry's blotter was a handgun.

'Jesus, Harry. Sneezing guns? You want to get those sinuses seen to.'

'I'm in no fuckin' mood, Jay. Some culchie by the name of Brendan dropped the weapon in not half an hour ago. He says you left it in his muck-spreader. Which begs several questions, not least of which is – what the fuck were you doing hijacking a fuckin' muck-spreader? I know I'm tight, but I think I can extend your travel expenses to the odd taxi now and again.'

I had no choice but to come clean. I levelled with Harry.

'The gun, it's a cigarette lighter . . . a Christmas present for my dad. Brendan's the guy who makes them. Realistic, aren't they?'

'Really,' said Harry. He popped open the button on his breast pocket and removed a squashed packet of B&H. He tipped the gold box onto his mouth and injected a cigarette into his lips. He went for the gun.

'No!' I shouted. 'OK, OK. It's not a lighter. It's a murder weapon. That's the gun that killed Aisling Coyles.'

Harry lifted a box of matches off his desk. 'Go on,' he said. He lit his fag, surrounding himself in a blue haze.

'The gunman took a shot at me too, but he missed. There was a struggle and I . . . I liberated the gun. But his driver was waiting outside the aquarium. He chased after me. I had to get out of Portaferry fast, so I commandeered Brendan's truck. I was desperate. You would do the same if the IRA were trying to kill you.'

'You're wrong,' said Harry.

'Course you would.'

'No, you're wrong about the IRA tryin' to kill you. The gun doesn't belong to the Provos. It belongs to the RUC. It's standard issue. It even carries a serial number and there's been no attempt to remove it, which suggests the gun isn't stolen.'

'What are you saying?' I asked. 'The RUC are trying to kill me?'

'Looks a lot fuckin' like it,' said Harry.

I took a seat, knocking Harry's blazer off the back of it.

'But why? And why would they want to kill Aisling? I don't understand.'

'Neither do I, Jay. That's why I need you to talk to me. You appear to have got yourself into some serious fuckin' trouble here and I don't want this paper gettin' any grief because of it. I need you to tell me what's goin' on. I need to know my options.'

'So you *are* going to fire me.'

'It's an option.' Harry parked one arse cheek on the corner of his desk. 'Listen, Jay, I've always looked after you. I've always bailed you out. But this is too fuckin' hairy, even for me. I can't have boss-eyed bumpkins

326

strollin' into these offices and wavin' firearms. It's not good for staff morale.'

'So what are you going to do?' I asked.

'You tell me,' said Harry.

I wasn't sure. My world had gone skew-whiff. I had thought it was O'Hanlon trying to dispose of me and now I find out it was Meeks. Jesus, the RUC were supposed to be watching me, backing me up, not taking potshots at me. Why the turnaround? Meeks might have known I was in Portaferry. I had hung up in the Drop Inn, but 1471 would have given his intermediary the area code of the phone. And he'd instructed the Two Fat Ladies to watch me. But why instruct them to kill me? Especially when he knew I was so close to getting him proof of O'Hanlon's relationship with Kate Owen.

That could be it, though. The dead baby would be an embarrassment not only to O'Hanlon but to the British government too. It wouldn't look good, their Secretary of State for Northern Ireland having a child by the Sinn Fein party leader. The Government would lose a lot of credibility in the province, the peace process would be further jeopardized and Meeks could well lose his job. After all, he was the one who had instructed me to get hold of such a scandal in the first place. He had needed something with which he could broker decommissioning for Downing Street. Only his plan had backfired. I had uncovered more than anyone had bargained for, enough to embarrass all parties.

I tried to rewind to the shooting. The RUC gunman had worn a hearing aid. Perhaps he wasn't the only one listening in on my conversation with Aisling. What if his hearing aid was some sort of two-way bug? So when Aisling told me the truth about Kate Owen's baby, did someone, somewhere, take the executive

327

decision to stop her talking? Did they relay the instruction into the gunman's ear, to shoot Aisling through the throat? And was the same officer ordered to shoot me too, so the story would die with me? The only person who could have given such an order was Stephen Meeks. But if he wanted me dead, why didn't he kill me when I gatecrashed his house? Perhaps he didn't want blood spilt on his precious lawn. More likely, he didn't want his little boy to witness a killing.

I remembered how Meeks had been singularly unimpressed when I'd relayed the O'Hanlon story. He claimed I had no evidence. In fact, he had actively discouraged me from pursuing it. This had surprised me at the time but now it made sense. Meeks didn't want this story getting out. He didn't want the Government embarrassed. He had tried to have me killed to stop me going public.

I was now certain he'd try to kill me again. There were no two ways about it. I had to get to Meeks before Meeks got to me.

'I'll tell you what you're going to do, Harry. You're going to give me the number of your old RUC drinking buddy, Doug Ferguson. Then you're going to lock me in this office with a cassette player and a password for your PC. Anyone asks, I'm not here. Now you'll have to excuse me, I've got to grab something from my locker.'

I opened his door.

'Jay, you can't . . . this isn't . . . aw, fuck. You'll get Dougie at Bangor, treble four, treble five. And it's lillian. All lower case.'

'Your password's lillian?'

'It's the wife's name. Will she ever let me forget?'

'Cheers, Harry. I appreciate this.'

'Aye, but Rupert Aziz won't. If His Worship finds

out about the gun, I'll be the one that gets a fuckin' roasting. Still, another typical day in the life of Harry Clegg. You get bollocked at work, you go home, get bollocked by the wife, bollocked by the kids and then the dog pisses on your fuckin' foot.'

'Hi. Thanks for agreeing to talk to me. Jay Black. Ulster News Letter. *Do I call you Davey or David?'*

'King Rot, to you.'

'Oh . . . OK . . . Mr Rot.'

'King Rot.'

'Sure . . . King Rot.'

'So, Black, I believe you have something under your foreskin that I may be interested in?'

'You what?'

'Don't go all fuckin' coy on me. You've got something for me, haven't you? Jimmy's told you to wrap it and fold it under your knob.'

'I . . . I . . .'

'To get it through the prison security?'

'Um . . . I don't know how to say this, King, but I'm not sure my foreskin can accommodate a file or a pair of bolt cutters.'

I hadn't played this tape since Davey Gavin's 'accidental death'. His voice was flat and dispassionate, more chilling than I remembered, but perhaps that was because I was now listening to the voice of a ghost.

I remembered our opening exchanges without the aid of the tape. Davey had been expecting a communication from one of his UVF deputies. It was an authorization for the group to carry out the murder of a Protestant building contractor who had accepted work on a Catholic primary school in West Belfast. Davey had expected the authorization to be written on the back of a piece of cigarette foil and folded under my foreskin. At the time, this was the popular mode of message delivery in and out of the Maze. A bit like e-mail, though you wouldn't want to accumulate too much junk in your inbox. Davey had confused me with his next visitor.

I pressed the fast-forward. This wasn't the juice I was after.

I was on side two of cassette two before Davey made any mention of Meeks.

He alleged that back in 1995, Meeks had helped the UVF to purchase a yacht. They had a false deck built into it. Davey claimed that Meeks kept the yacht moored in Helen's Bay, a mile or two down the coast from his Cultra home. Meeks, he said, hired UVF men to act as his 'security' on the boat. In collusion with the then detective inspector, the paramilitaries used the yacht to smuggled drugs into the province unnoticed.

'*The yacht was called* The Beaten Carder. *Meeks chose the name*,' said the ghost of Davey Gavin.

I stopped the tape. I thought about my old history lessons again.

The Carders were a group of nineteenth-century Irish hooligans who slashed the backs of their victims with the wire brushes once used to card wool. Nice chaps. In a way they were Ireland's first sectarian murderers and their crimes were every bit as brutal as their latter-day successors. Anyone who testified against a Carder was beaten to a pulp, then stoned, then pitchforked onto a burning dungheap. When Sir Robert Peel arrived in Dublin as the new Chief Secretary of Ireland, he set up a countrywide police force to move into the disturbed rural areas and stamp out these Irish hooligans. Peel's methods created the foundations on which the Royal Ulster Constabulary was built.

Although six years my senior, Meeks would have at one time attended the same history classes. Our masters adhered rigidly to the same syllabus. He too would have remembered this particular lesson. A Protestant schoolboy is unlikely to forget a story peppered with gore and laced with a good dose of anti-Catholicism.

It now occurred to me that this chapter of Irish history had inspired Meeks the policeman, for it seemed he commemorated it in the name of his yacht – *The Beaten Carder*. But I had no proof that the yacht even existed. An unusual name and a hunch based on a history lesson would not be enough to put Meeks away. And any allegations made by the late UVF madman, King Rot, would be laughed out of court.

I keyed 'lillian' into Harry's PC and searched the *News Letter*'s database for mention of the *The Beaten Carder*.

Nothing.

There was one last resource available to me. In normal circumstances I could have called any one of a dozen RUC contacts and tapped them for information. But these weren't normal circumstances. I couldn't be sure how many of them were trying to kill me.

Not a problem, Jay. You'll just have to bring Doug Ferguson out of retirement.

I sought an outside line on Harry's phone and called his old mucker.

I got him on the first ring.

'Douglas Ferguson. What can I do for you, Mr Black?'

Bloody hell, I thought. Harry had said that Dougie was the most intuitive detective that ever donned an RUC cap, but this bordered on premonition.

'How do you know who I am?'

'Your favourite editor and mine just spoke to me. Old bastard said you'd call. Also said you're in a lot of trouble. What makes you think I can help you? I've hung up my uniform, Mr Black. Don't have the inside track any more.'

'But you did in '96.'

'RUC changed in '96. Wasn't the force I'd served in for thirty good years. We lost good men in that Chinook, top brass, four of my dearest friends.' Dougie's voice faltered. 'Men like Hugh McIlwaine were irreplaceable. And what do they do? They give his office to a jumped-up daddy's boy like Stephen Meeks. Claimed he was just the sort of firebrand who could drag us into the twenty-first century.'

'You and Meeks didn't get on?'

'I wasn't the only one. Top job should have gone to someone senior, someone with a bit of experience. There were men like me who were there when the first shots were fired in anger. Men who'd spilt blood on their green shirts while Meeks was still dribbling puréed apple onto his bib. Said as much at the time. Well, that was my card marked. Meeks wasn't interested in the old guard. Offered us all a voluntary retirement package. Nothing voluntary about it. He knew our morale was low. Wanted us out. Kid got his wish.'

'Douglas. Sorry to be brusque but I haven't got much time. I just need you to answer one question. Did Meeks ever mention *The Beaten Carder*?'

There was an audible silence on the other end of the line.

'Douglas . . . are you still with us?'

I could just make out a television, the Corrie theme.

'You know about the boat?' he asked.

A giddy rush of blood. I felt myself fall, like those

332

sudden falls you experience in half-sleep.

'I do now,' I said. This was it. I had an RUC officer who could corroborate Davey Gavin's story about the yacht.

'Tell me all you know, Doug.'

'Not much, son. But I'll never forget that name. *Beaten Carder*. Hugh McIlwaine mentioned it. He and his dear wife Sandra had invited Betty and me over to theirs the weekend before the 'copter crash. Hugh loved his port. Two of us emptied a decanter over three racks of billiards. Hugh was right off his game. Something had been bothering him, but he wouldn't elaborate. I put it down to nerves. He was about to fly off to Inverness to table a top-level meeting about securing more funding for the force. Under a lot of pressure, poor sod.'

'Sorry, Doug. This is all good, it really is, but I'm up against it here. You said the Chief Constable mentioned the yacht.'

'Yes. Yes he did. Several brandies later his tongue loosened. Hugh could put it away, mind. Never let it be said that he couldn't hold his drink. Young Meeks, he said, don't know what we're paying him, but he's got himself a boat. *The Beaten Carder*. Name made me think he'd won it on a poker hand. Told Hugh as much. He wasn't so sure. Said there'd been an allegation. Came from a grass. Something about drugs. Said he had evidence. Most difficult thing he had to do, he said. To be honest, he wasn't making much sense. Three too many. Told me he needed Meeks in Inverness and we left it at that.'

'Meeks was in Inverness?'

'Missed the flight home, though. Admitted to hospital on the morning of the crash. Always was a lucky bastard.'

I felt sick and elated. Elated, because Dougie had given me something concrete to hurl at Meeks. Sick, because I now knew how ruthless Meeks might have been in his rise to the top of the RUC.

I spent a furious hour typing out the unedited story concerning Martin O'Hanlon, Kate Owen, their son, Edel, Aisling and Meeks. I saved it to disk and slid it into an envelope together with the baby's birth certificate, the record of his death, and his footprint (I had let Edel tear off and keep his handprint). I stuffed the envelope in my locker and sought Harry. He was taping an Elastoplast to his finger.

'Can you fuckin' believe that?' he asked.

'Yes, Harry. I can. You're shit with a scalpel. Either that or it's a cry for help. You're seeking attention through self-mutilation.'

'No. Can you believe *that*?' He held his injured finger to my face.

I immediately recoiled, expecting to be presented with a bloody, carved-up digit. Instead I saw Road Runner. Harry was wearing a cartoon plaster – a child's plaster.

'Can you believe it . . . a place the size of this and I have to go borrowin' plasters off one of the wee girls in Advertisin'? Nice lass. Only seventeen and she's got a fuckin' three-year-old.'

'Harry, I need you to hold the front page. Sod it, hold the whole paper.'

Harry unpeeled Road Runner and swapped him for Tweety-Pie.

'Are you listening, Harry?'

'I'm listenin'.'

'I have to head into town. Then I'm off to the Edel O'Hanlon concert. I'll be back here at midnight to write up my exclusive. If I don't turn up on the dot, you're to go to my flat and get my locker key. Diggsy will let you in. The key will be sitting under a bowl of rotten oranges in my living room. You can use it to get into my locker and obtain a contingency version of my story. And don't forget to give me a byline.'

'Houl' on a secon—'

'Sorry, Harry. Gotta dash.'

I ran backwards to the door.

'Remember my byline,' I shouted. *'By the late Jay Black.'*

28

Night had transformed the Waterfront Hall. It stood against the black sky, illuminated from within, like a giant jellyfish patrolling the blind depths of some ocean.

Karma and I were mingling among the VIPs on one of the venue's two galleried floors. Karma had dressed to the nines in a backless, strapless number. How the dress didn't just fall to the floor I will never know, for it had no visible means of support. The top half of the dress was made of a diaphanous material and would have been totally see-through were it not for a velvet dragon that was strategically positioned to mask both breasts. The dress was not as risqué as her footwear, however. Karma struggled to stay upright in shoes with vertiginous heels and toes so pointed they could only have been designed to kill bugs in corners.

I too had been forced into my glad rags. But I hadn't dressed to the nines. I was somewhere between the fives and the sixes in a black leather jacket, a pair of black 501s, and one of my dad's old ruffled dress shirts. His bow tie secured it to my neck, turning me into a Seventies snooker player. Karma said I looked exactly like Alex Higgins would have looked when they caught him pissing on the roses outside the Crucible. I took it as a compliment.

We were both nervous, though for different reasons. I was concerned about how we could get Edel out of the venue at the interval. Karma was nervous because she had never before been surrounded by so many famous faces. These were people she only ever saw inside a 28-inch box and now she could reach out and flick their ears. I advised her not to.

Karma examined her programme and the still-wet autograph on the cover. I had tried to discourage her from asking celebrities for their signatures. I explained that we were VIPs too and we should act accordingly. This didn't stop her wobbling over to Billy Connolly in those heels and thrusting a pen into his hand. She apologized for the intrusion and explained to Billy that she was from Northern Ireland, so she didn't get out much. The Big Yin replied that he was from Glasgow and he'd come over to Belfast to get away from the Troubles.

We steadied our nerves with complimentary champagne.

'There's one thing about your plan that I still don't get,' said Karma.

'And what's that?'

'Well, if Edel feigns an illness, won't they just drag the St John's Ambulance backstage to sort her out?'

She had a point. The hall would be crawling with the part-time medics.

'In that case,' I said, 'you'll just have to get yourself into their sick bay shortly before the interval. That way, when one of Edel's people calls for assistance, you can pull rank on the St John's. You're a senior staff nurse at the Royal. They'll have to let you backstage. They'll want the best for their young star.'

'And how do I admit myself to the sick bay? If I say I'm feeling dizzy or ill, they won't let me near Edel.'

'You could pretend that you've hurt your ankle. It's not so far-fetched. You've already gone over twice in those heels.'

'I can't do that. They'll make me lay my foot up. They won't have me limping backstage and putting pressure on it. You don't even have a basic knowledge of medical procedure, do you, Jay?'

'I know you place raw steaks on nettle stings and rub dock leaves on black eyes.'

'You're not funny. Everyone should get some basic medical training. I mean, what would you do if I suddenly collapsed?'

'I'd advise you to change into sensible shoes.'

Karma hit me with her programme.

'Be sensible. I've got to think of an injury serious enough to warrant medical assistance but not so serious that it will stop me from treating Edel.'

'I've an idea.' I thought of Harry. 'You could cut yourself.'

'What with? I didn't bring my nail scissors. My purse contains a Switch card, a packet of gum, and two tampons.'

'Use your programme. Give yourself a paper cut.'

Karma rolled her eyes. She robbed a passing waiter of his last champagne.

'Look, let's not worry about it now,' I said. 'I'm sure I'll think of something by the interval.'

'I hope for your sa— oh, hold that will you?' said Karma. She handed me her glass. 'I've just spotted that Irish fella from the films.'

Karma clopped across the tiled floor to assault local Hollywood screen sensation James Fearon, star of *The Fellowship Of The Ring*. James was riding on a publicity high after playing 'Hobbit Walking Backwards With Large Cake' at Bilbo Baggins's farewell party, a remarkable performance and one that the film's editor saw fit to hold back as a reward for only those true fans who bought the extended DVD. He was attending the concert on behalf of the sponsors, Imagine2008. During the twenty-minute interval, he was to host a live presentation to bolster Belfast's bid to become European Capital of Culture. According to the programme, it would feature a skit from a local youth theatre, a specially commissioned Imagine2008 song sung by a choir from an integrated primary school, an appearance by funnyman Patrick Kielty, and a live tour of the Imagine2008 website which James would demonstrate on a big screen. The eyes of the world were on Belfast. Imagine2008 weren't sponsoring Edel's gig, they were hijacking it. The gallery was full of their contingent, the great and the good, all quaffing their bubbly and all doing their damnedest to grab a slice of the Belfast pie. They included representatives from Belfast City Council, the Arts Council for Northern Ireland, the Sports Council, the BBC, the Ulster Orchestra, the Ulster Museum and Moy Park Chickens.

The Royal Ulster Constabulary was also represented. I had spotted Stephen Meeks. He was cradling a pure orange and chatting to Eamonn Holmes. The GMTV presenter gnawed his way through three satay sticks and a king prawn tail and nodded politely as Meeks jabbered into his ear. To say Eamonn looked uninterested was an understatement. It wasn't long before he removed himself from the Chief Constable and sought the more stimulating company of a tray of mushroom vol-au-vents.

I seized the opportunity.

'Evening, Steeky,' I said. 'I didn't know you were a fan of the harp. I thought your taste in music was confined to Queen. And Country.'

'It's good to see you've still got a sense of humour, Jessie. You'll need it in prison. I'd arrest you now but I said you had until tomorrow to nail O'Hanlon and I'm a man of my word.'

'Oh, I'd arrest me now, Stephen. See, I've a sneaking feeling that tomorrow you won't have the power of arrest. I've been talking to an old friend of yours, Davey Gavin. At least, he's been talking to me.'

Meeks laughed. 'The bubbly's gone to your head. Davey's long dead.'

'I know he's dead. And we both know you had him killed because he talked to me. Thing is, back in '96 when you threatened to pin Huggins's manslaughter on me unless I gave you the Davey Gavin tapes, I didn't entirely keep my side of the bargain. I held on to some very rare, limited-edition cassettes – King Rot, live at the Maze. Davey told me about the yacht, *The Beaten Carder*. More importantly, I now know how that Chinook crashed, killing your superiors. And it's all going in tomorrow's paper. It's over, Stephen. Your only consolation is that after Edel's performance tonight, it will all be over for O'Hanlon too.'

Meeks didn't have a chance to respond. His wife had joined us. She handed him a fresh glass of orange juice.

'I got you another Fuck's Bizz,' she said. She caught a laugh in her hand. 'Did you hear that . . . I just said Buck's Fizz.' She tried to clink her glass against her husband's. It missed. She turned to me. She waited for her eyes to adjust their focal length. 'It's that nice fella in the shower. Are you not going to congratulate us, nice fella? It's our anniversary. Not that my darling husband remembered.'

'Not now, Caroline,' said Meeks. 'Not here.' He unpicked her fingers from her glass and emptied her champagne into a plant pot.

The call came out to the gallery inviting all guests into the auditorium.

'I'll speak to you later,' said Meeks. He escorted his wife to their box like he was taking a drunk to a cell.

I dragged Karma away from another local celebrity, leaving the confused lady with an RVH pen in her hand. Karma's programme now boasted the signature of 'Gloria Hun'.

We made our way into the auditorium. It comprised a circular arena with sections of red seats laid out in triangular terraces, like two pizzas placed on top of each other with their slices pulled slightly apart. It was impressive, bigger than I had imagined. We took our designated seats in the front row.

The lights immediately dimmed. The stage became illuminated in gold and green from the two concrete lighting bridges that surrounded it. There was a spontaneous and cacophonous burst of applause. I was confused. The stage remained empty. Karma gave me a dig in the ribs. She pointed up to one of the boxes. Martin O'Hanlon rose out of his seat to acknowledge his people. Tomorrow he would be their First Minister. His grin was broad. It stretched from Belfast to Beijing. Satellites beamed it across the planet.

But Marty hadn't reckoned on his daughter. And he had underestimated Scarlet.

The stage filled with dry ice. A DJ took his place behind a set of decks positioned on a gantry at the rear of the set. A noise thudded out of his speakers like someone repeatedly kicking an empty wheelie bin inside a church. Half a dozen Irish dancers appeared.

341

They locked arms and clicked their heels, cavorting round the famous Emerald Harp. A spotlight found Edel. She wore a green ballgown that hid her feet. She seemed to float across the stage to seat herself behind her instrument. The second her hands touched the strings there was more applause. It was as if her harp was strung with laser beams and she'd triggered an alarm.

She launched into a version of the Irish folk standard 'Roisin Dubh' at 120bpm. It could better be described as Roisin Dub. It walloped me in the stomach.

Throughout the performance I couldn't take my eyes off Edel's fingers and those double-jointed thumbs. They moved with an unnatural dexterity, as if her hands had gone into spasm. I was reminded of Scarlet, how she conjured sounds from her guitar by plucking it with nails of steel. It was as remarkable to watch as it was to listen to.

Edel had told me that the last number before the interval was to be 'Fairytale of New York'. Her management had agreed this as the perfect conclusion to her Irish set as it also offered a taster of the Christmas set to come. However, she had promised me that she would change it for the evening's perform-ance. She said she would tag on an extra number before the break. And although she couldn't announce it, she said the song would contain a message for me.

The Irish dancers stopped dead on the last note of the Shane MacGowan and Kirsty McColl cover. They exited the stage in their girly Santa outfits, short green skirts with fluffy white trim. The DJ lingered a little longer to milk the applause before he left Edel alone with her harp.

A single bar of red light picked her out. Her nails found the strings.

I recognized the tune as Clannad. 'Scarlet Inside'.

I got the message.

'She's pretty amazing, isn't she?' whispered Karma.

'Yes. She's both.'

When I listened to Edel, everything became clear. In the past week I had been tying myself up in knots over Meeks, O'Hanlon, Huggins, Harry, and Scarlet. But Edel was the only person who mattered. With each note she plucked, a knot unravelled and I became as straight and sure as a harp string. I was not going to lose her again.

Karma gave me a dig in the ribs. 'So, I guess this is the interval,' she said. 'Do you still want me to cut my finger? I've been sawing it with the edge of the programme but it's made no impression.'

'I was only joking about the paper cut.'

'Oh. Right,' said Karma. 'Shall I bite it?'

'What?'

'Shall I bite my finger? I reckon I could draw blood.'

'And how would you explain that to the St John's Ambulance?'

'Good point.'

Edel plucked the last two notes of the set – *plink-plink*. A respectful audience allowed the sound to dissolve completely before bursting into yet more effervescent applause. The curtain fell down and the lights went up.

'I've an idea,' said Karma. She bent double. At first I thought she was feigning a stomach cramp but she quickly straightened and I realized she had retrieved her purse from under her seat. She hoisted herself onto her heels. 'Come on.'

I followed her to a door at the right of the hall. As I did so, James Fearon appeared on stage. A giant screen descended from the rafters with the Imagine2008 logo projected onto it. The TV cameras honed in on the Tyrone actor.

'Ladies and gentlemen, fellow Europeans, citizens of the world,' he said. 'What have Milk of Magnesia, the immersion heater, superphosphate fertilizers and the pneumatic tyre got in common? Answer . . . they were all invented in Belfast.'

'Christ,' I said. 'We've blown 2008 now. All across the globe people are getting up to put their kettles on.'

Karma wasn't listening. She rearranged the top of her dress, shifting the velvet dragon and allowing her nipples to show through the transparent material.

'What are you doing?' I asked.

'Look and learn,' she said.

She criss-crossed her arms over her breasts and approached the medic who stood by the door of the sick bay.

'Er, hi. I need some assistance,' she said.

'What's the problem?' asked the medic. He noted the position of Karma's arms. 'Have you got a pain in your chest?'

'No. The problem isn't strictly a medical one.'

'Well, I'm sorry, madam. We're only here to treat emergencies.'

'But this is an emergency.' Karma removed her arms, giving the chap an eyeful. 'My dress keeps shifting. I was hoping you could give me some sticking plaster to secure it over my nipples.'

The medic didn't know where to put himself. 'Of course. Yes. Sticking plaster. You'd better come in.' He admitted us through the door.

We weren't the only ones receiving assistance. A guy in full dress suit was bent backwards across a padded bench. A nurse was holding his head still, while another medic slid a pair of tweezers up his

344

nostril. The guy was honking like a goose. He was clearly in some pain.

'What happened to him?' I asked.

'He got a fruit gum stuck up his nose,' said our medic. 'We don't ask how, we just repair the damage.'

The offending sweet was easily removed, though the part-time surgeon couldn't prevent it slipping out of his tweezers. It landed on the man's chest, depositing a perfect exclamation mark of blood on his shirt.

'Let me see,' said our medic. 'Plasters, plasters, plasters.'

I consulted the time on my mobile. I was beginning to think that Edel had lost her nerve, when Fionnuala came through the door. She opened it first. I was surprised that she did, for she thrust herself into the room with such urgency I expected to see a trail of broken wood and a Fionnuala-shaped hole in the wall behind her.

'Please, we need someone backstage. Edel's taken a turn.'

I copied fruit gum guy and held a towel to my face so she wouldn't recognize me.

'What are her symptoms?' asked Karma. She attracted strange looks from the St John's team. 'It's OK,' she assured them. 'I'm a senior nurse at the Royal.'

'She's short of breath,' said Fionnuala. 'Her hands are all clammy.'

I bit the towel, fighting the urge to shout *well, that's hardly surprising, she's been playing the bloody harp for an hour.*

'Well then,' said Karma, 'I'd better take a look at her.'

I waited until they'd gone before I made my way back into the auditorium. Patrick Kielty was tickling the worldwide audience with his impersonation of Martin O'Hanlon does Monty Python – 'the First Minister of Silly Walks'.

And to think we hoped to become Capital of Culture.

There was no time to heckle, however. I had to get back to my flat.

I took the lift to the ground floor. I tried to remain calm as I walked out the front of the building, past a group of grumbling, exiled smokers.

In retrospect, I should have known that Meeks would follow me.

29

Back at the flat, Diggsy was changing the memory card in his digicam.

'Have you seen my bra?' I shouted.

I was in the bedroom, sorting through the clothes I had bought Edel. The list she had given me included a scarlet bra (*36C*), a scarlet miniskirt, a scarlet T-shirt (*sleeveless, no slogan*), scarlet hold-ups, and scarlet boots (*size 6, Oxbloods are fine*). She had directed me to various stores where I could purchase said articles.

My first stop had been at an establishment called Hideous Kinky. The shop's interior was flooded with UV light, making me instantly paranoid about dandruff. The clothes racks reverberated to hardcore techno. They were stocked with bizarre club gear and extraordinary lingerie. I found myself drowning in a sea of frilly things, ladies' things, tiny offcuts of silk, lace and rubber that were being passed off as under-wear when they could better be described as rectal floss. If you'd been trying them on, you wouldn't have known which hole to step into. As I flicked through a few skirts I realized I was attracting giggles from the two girls staffing the shop. They were clones of each other. They sported pink and black hair extensions that touched their bottoms. They clearly had trouble getting through airports as they had everything pierced – their lips, navels, eyebrows, eyeballs, teeth. And the pair of them wore the sort of thick-soled boots that 'special' children get teased for wearing. My embarrassment was compounded when one of the girls asked if I needed any help. She had adopted a deliberately understanding tone. It quickly dawned on me that she thought I was a closet transvestite. Confirmation arrived when she asked me if I wanted to try anything on. I assured her that the skirt was for a girlfriend. *Let me guess*, the girl said, *she's about the same size as yourself?* The clones laughed in unison. I was in hell. Matters only worsened when I asked for a bra and boots in the same colour.

'You left a carrier bag in the kitchen,' said Diggsy. 'Your bra could be in there.'

'Good man.'

I found the bag. The missing garment was inside, accompanied by a can of Flame Red hairspray that I had bought from a joke shop. Edel had said that she normally used a wash-in, wash-out dye to transform herself into Scarlet. But that would have entailed her sitting in the flat for an hour with a plastic bag over her head, and we didn't have the time.

'They should be here by now.'

'Relax,' said Diggsy. 'Karma won't let you down.'

'What if she can't get Edel out of the hall? Or what if she gets her out and someone follows them?'

The sound of keys in the door.

Karma walked barefoot into the hall with her shoes in her hand.

'Where's Edel?'

'Ta-da!' said Karma.

Edel walked into the room with her ballgown

bunched up round her thighs. 'This thing's a bitch to run in,' she said.

'Never mind. You're here now,' I said. 'The new clothes are in my room. You can change in there.'

'I'm going to need a hand getting out of this dress,' said Edel.

I looked at Karma.

Karma looked at Edel.

Edel looked at me. 'Jay,' she asked, 'can you not take a hint?'

'Ah,' I said.

Edel curled her fingers through mine. They didn't feel clammy. They felt like toilet paper – soft, strong and very long. She led me to the bedroom. I closed the door behind us. Edel immediately presented me with her back and instructed me to unzip her.

'Any trouble getting out of the venue?' I asked.

'As easy as stealing candy from a baby. Or as easy as stealing a baby from a hospital, as Karma put it. She was great, Jay. Sick sense of humour, but great.'

'That's Karma.'

Edel let her dress fall round her ankles. She stepped out of it and kicked it into a corner. She wore a pair of silvery-white panties and nothing else. I concentrated my gaze on the crumpled ballgown, trying hard not to look at its former owner.

'I should leave you to it,' I said. 'My work here is done.'

'Wait,' she said. 'I have a question.'

'Fire away,' I said. *Look at the dress, look at the dress, look at the dress.*

'Who do you love – Edel or Scarlet?'

'Who do I love?' I felt a familiar rush of blood. My temples started to pulse. *Not now, Jessie. Please God, not now.*

'See. You're stalling. That means you're not sure,' she said.

My bow tie was slowly strangling me.

'Well?' she asked.

I couldn't look at her but I sensed the anxiety creeping into her voice.

'You're pathetic, Jay. You don't even know who you've fallen in love with.'

Look at the dress, look at the dress, look at the dress.

'I need to know. Scarlet or Ede . . . del?' She had taken an involuntary gulp of air. She was beginning to panic.

The dress, the dress, the dress.

'Christ Almighty. Say *something*.'

I looked at Edel. Right at her. She seemed frightened. I studied the shock of blond hair that hid one side of her face. I examined the way the low light from the bedside lamp moved over her body like a yellow oil pastel sketching out the line of her shoulders, neck and breasts. And I knew the answer to her question.

'Both of you,' I said.

'Both of me?'

'Yes. Both of you. I've fallen for both of you. Scarlet and Edel. You're the same girl. I can't tell you apart any more.'

Edel walked towards me. She put her hands either side of my head and ran her fingers through my hair, *those* fingers, like she was making music.

We kissed.

I lifted her face away from mine. She no longer looked frightened.

'I'm the same girl,' she said.

We kissed again.

'How long have I got?' she asked.

'They'll be expecting you back on stage in ten minutes.'

'Right. I'd better start transforming myself, then.' Edel pressed her lips to mine one more time.

'You may go,' she said.

The last sound I heard as I left the room was the dull clack-a-clack of a metal ball being violently agitated in a tin of red hairspray.

Karma was in the living room massaging her feet. 'How's she doing?' she asked.

'Fine. She's a little nervous.'

'Hey, I'd be nervous if I was about to stand up and tell the world that my dad beat me. You've got to admire her.'

'I do,' I said.

The doorbell rang.

'That's my Chinese,' said Diggsy. He snatched a tenner from the mantelpiece and hurdled the sofa. 'I'm Lee fuckin' Marvin,' he said as he opened the door.

'And I'm Stephen fuckin' Meeks,' said the delivery boy. He wasn't carrying a bag of Dove in Plump Sauce, Depressed Chicken and Cashew, or any other item from the poorly translated takeaway menu that sat by our phone. Instead, he raised his hand and offered Diggsy a portion of Bang Bang Gun.

'Whoa, man. Please . . . don't shoot.'

'Do you honestly think I'd waste a bullet on you?' asked Meeks. 'It's yer man I'm after.' He nodded towards me. He pushed Diggsy into the room and backheeled the door shut. 'You and the girl, I want you both to put your hands on the window, where I and the rest of Belfast can see them.'

Diggsy and Karma did as they were told.

'Steeky. I told you earlier . . . it's over. You're only making things worse,' I said.

351

'It's far from over,' said Meeks. He swung his gun in my direction. 'Jessie Black, I am arresting you for the manslaughter of Miles Huggins and the murder of Aisling Coyles.'

'Aisling Coyles? And how do you figure that one out?'

'You mean you killed the Northern Ireland goal-keeper?' asked Diggsy.

'Shut it,' shouted Meeks. 'Nobody asked you to talk.' He returned his attention to me. 'There's not much *figuring out* to do, Jessie. Two schoolboys have given us an accurate description of Aisling's murderer. The e-fit looks uncannily like someone on the end of this gun. I had no choice but to order a search of your office at eight thirty this evening. And wouldn't you know it, my boys stumbled upon the murder weapon, wrapped in a hankie in the top drawer of your editor's desk.'

'You think that Harry Clegg killed Aisling Coyles?'

'You're a cocky sod, aren't you? Of course I don't think Harry killed her. That galoot can't bring himself to fire *you*, let alone a handgun.' Meeks flicked his eyes across to Karma and Diggsy, then back to me. 'Now do as I say, Jessie. I want you to put your hands on the back of the sofa.'

I had to bend my knees a little before my hands found the cracked leather of the sofa back. I looked faintly ridiculous, rather like Stevie Wonder would look if he went to play his piano after someone had surreptitiously rearranged his furniture. I felt stupid and angry.

'So you just *assume* that I killed Aisling,' I said. 'And you think that gives you the right to waltz into my home waving a gun?'

'I'm no dactyloscopist, Jessie, but I'll bet my badge that your prints are on the murder weapon.'

'The murder weapon belonged to an RUC man, as you well know. After he shot Aisling, you instructed him to kill me.'

'You're right. The gun did belong to one of my men. And I *had* given him instructions. I'd instructed him to follow you for your own protection. Thing is, he claims that you attacked him at the aquarium and that you stole his handgun. I don't even have to take his word for it. The schoolboys, Jessie. They saw you point it at him.'

Meeks was right. It didn't look good. I was in a tight spot but I still had my Get Out Of Jail Free card.

'Nobody will believe you, Steeky. Not when they read tomorrow's paper. Not when they see what a naughty boy you've been.'

'Ah, yes. This big exposé you've been threatening me with all these years.' Again Meeks moved his eyes to Diggsy and Karma, before returning them to me. 'One of my DIs found an envelope in your locker. He says it contains a work of fiction even more implausible than an Aisling Coyles novel. He's destroyed it. Shame, really. I like a good yarn. Perhaps you could give me the gist of it.'

The bastard had me. It was a familiar scenario but that didn't make it any easier to take. After twenty-odd years, I was getting just a little sick of Stephen Meeks. No way was I about to go down quietly. Not this time. He needed to know that I'd found him out.

'OK. It goes something like this. Stop me if I leave anything out.' I was conscious that Edel could emerge from my bedroom at any moment. And though she would appear in the guise of Scarlet, the thought that a jumpy, gun-toting RUC officer might recognize her as Martin O'Hanlon's daughter was too horrible to contemplate. I decided to raise the level of my voice in an attempt to warn her. I addressed Meeks as a prosecuting counsel might address a defendant, in order that Edel might deduce who I was talking to.

'I put it to you, Chief Constable Stephen Meeks, that on the evening of the twenty-fifth of March 1996 a twin-rotored Chinook helicopter flying back to Belfast from an RUC conference in Scotland plunged into the Mull of Kintyre. The precise cause of the crash was never established. But I have discovered from an RUC source that you, Stephen Meeks, were supposed to be on board that helicopter.'

Meeks opened his mouth slightly, as though he was about to interrupt me. I didn't give him the chance.

'You missed that flight, Stephen, when you admitted yourself to Inverness Infirmary claiming chest pains. Your three immediate superiors weren't so fortunate. Chief Constable Hugh McIlwaine, his assistant chief and a detective superintendent all perished in the crash. The Inverness meeting was reportedly convened to procure increased funding for the RUC. But I have it on reputable authority that Hugh McIlwaine had called it to address allegations of corruption within the force. And you, Stephen Meeks, had been singled out.'

Meeks didn't look like he was enjoying this. I didn't want to stop.

'You were being investigated for financial irregularities. Your bosses were particularly concerned that someone on your wage, though not an insubstantial one, had been able to purchase a yacht – *The Beaten Carder*. But their investigation had uncovered something bigger than a financial scam. If our old friend Davey Gavin is to be believed, the RUC discovered a false deck on the boat and in it a quantity of hard drugs. In other words, the top brass in the RUC knew that you, Stephen Meeks, were smuggling drugs in collusion with the UVF. Once they got you back to Northern Ireland, you were to be ejected from the force and thrown to the mercy of the courts. And my guess is that they wanted to make an example of you, to preserve the integrity of the RUC. Only your superiors never made it back to the province, did they? Their helicopter went down on a clear evening with an experienced pilot at the controls. All your accusers perished, together with all the documented evidence against you. Lucky for you that you got those chest pains. Eh, Stephen? Or you wouldn't be standing here POINTING A GUN AT ME, would you?'

This last statement was directed at my bedroom door as much as it was to Meeks.

'Strange, don't you think,' I continued, 'a fit man like you, thirty-four at the time, didn't smoke, didn't drink, a man who spoons the chocolate off his cappuccino – you were hardly in the at risk category to suffer a heart attack. See, I've a hunch there was nothing wrong with you. And I'll bet that the doctors in Inverness said as much. I reckon that you faked chest pains to avoid getting on board that flight. Is it therefore possible, Stephen, that you had some sort of premonition, that you knew the helicopter would crash?'

'Let me guess,' he laughed. 'You're going to say I got someone to sabotage the flight deck.'

'You said it, Steeky.'

Meeks flicked his eyes to the window again. He took a few steps towards me, close enough to give me a taste of his aftershave.

'Even if your little story was true,' he said, 'who's going to believe you? The people of Northern Ireland aren't going to listen to the man who killed their goalkeeper, the man who slaughtered one of their most popular novelists in cold blood, right in front of innocent schoolchildren.'

My palms were wet. I was unsure if this was a reaction to the leather in my hands or the metal in Meeks's.

Large droplets clung to the Chief Constable's forehead. Sweat channelled into his eyebrows. They had metamorphosed into two slick leeches. His finger slid over the trigger.

'So big deal,' he said. 'I assisted certain people in bringing drugs into the province, but what was I supposed to do? I was only acting for the greater good. If the IRA refuse to give up their arms, the Unionists boycott elections, O'Hanlon is in and the RUC are finished. And if they do relinquish their guns, well, then we have peace. And if we have peace, there will be wholesale job losses in my police force. But not if I replace one problem with another. Since the ceasefires there has been a huge increase in the abuse of recreational and hard drugs – LSD, heroin, ecstasy. I should know, my boys get to confiscate all the good stuff. Drugs are the future, Jessie. A country with a drug problem needs the numbers to police it. The end justifies the means. I'm keeping a lot of brave, gallant police officers in gainful employment. I'm guaranteeing their futures here, even if there is a permanent peace. I'm making sure their kids get Christmas presents.'

'Bollocks, Santa Claus. You're in it for yourself.'

'Admittedly, drugs do have a high mark-up on the street. The odd backhander is a welcome perk. But there isn't a shred of evidence to corroborate your story. As of this evening, I have the remaining Davey Gavin tapes. And the rest of it went up long ago in a blaze of aviation fuel – documents, receipts, files, photographs, flesh and bone.'

'I wouldn't be so sure,' said Diggsy.

'Didn't I tell you to shut your trap?' shouted Meeks.

Diggsy found himself under the close scrutiny of Meeks's gun. He seemed unfazed by it. 'Smile,' he said. 'You're on candid camera.'

He nodded towards his tripod. The digicam no longer pointed at his putrid oranges. At some point he had swung it round. It now captured a corrupt policeman.

'I've got it all,' said Diggsy. 'Confessions of a Chief Constable.'

'Give me the film,' demanded Meeks.

'Sorry, mate. It doesn't use film. It's digital. I'd give you the memory card but it ain't going to make a pick of difference. My camera also acts as a webcam. It's connected to the Internet. At this precise moment people all over the world are sitting at their PCs watching what goes on in this room. That's a lot of witnesses.' Diggsy found the confidence to remove one hand from the windowpane. He used it to point towards his iMac.

Meeks examined the screen. In a window labelled Imagine2008 he saw a man dressed in a dinner jacket, just like himself, holding a gun, just like himself, and perspiring, just like himself. Only, this man did not look like himself. At least, Meeks barely recognized him. This man looked ten, maybe fifteen years older. He seemed confused, inconstant, unsure of himself. He was not the sort of man you'd entrust with a firearm. What's more, he lacked *presence*. He did not carry himself with the broomstick-up-the-back authority of an RUC chief constable.

This man was wild.

Behind me, the bedroom door swished open. I caught a flash of red in the corner of my eye. Then I heard Edel's voice. 'Tonight, Matthew, Edel O'Hanlon will be . . . Scarlet Harlot.'

'Edel O'Hanlon,' said Meeks, as if to himself. He looked at her like he was working her out. Then he stared back at the camera, looking right down the lens. He coughed a wet cough.

He took his gun off me temporarily, using it to wipe the sweat from his upper lip.

'You people out there say you're tired of the violence,' he told the camera. '*There's too much of it on our streets*, you say. *The RUC aren't doing enough to stamp it out*, you complain. And yet you can't get enough of it when it's up there on your screens in glorious fucking Technicolor. You're hypocrites, the lot of you. Fucking hypocrites. You don't deserve the protection of men like me. But that's fine. I know my place. I'm only here to serve you. If violence is what you're after, I'll give you what you want. A nice bloody ending.'

He looked at Edel.

He raised his gun.

'No!' she screamed.

James Fearon struggled with his mouse. It was sticking. The two-foot cursor refused to budge on the big screen.

'Technology,' he quipped.

The audience laughed a nervous laugh.

One of the technical bods ran onto the stage and fiddled with the PC.

James could hear the sound of 2,212 people clicking boiled sweets around in their mouths. Better humour them, he thought.

'Speaking of technology,' he said. *Seamless, James.*

Seamless. 'I see that Mark Dukakis, the American billionaire, has this week become the world's first space tourist. He paid fifteen million dollars to blast off on a seven-day trip round the stars. I reckon that just before he returns to Earth we should all dress up in ape suits.'

A murmur of laughter.

How could they not find that funny? thought James. He had pissed himself yesterday when his agent had e-mailed him the same joke. That was probably it, he thought. Sure, wasn't everyone hooked up to the Net these days, in their homes, in their offices, on the train to work? A decent joke could be zipped round the planet in an hour or two. You couldn't claim it for your own any more and imbue it with your own little touches (a funny accent, a comedy face, an extra character) because everyone had already heard it. Rather, they had read it in a *viral*. Appropriate name, thought James, for wasn't humour infectious? And couldn't you die laughing? Truth is, e-mail was killing the art of story-telling.

Thankfully for James, the murmuring subsided. It was replaced by an optimistic ripple of applause. The IT guy had fixed the PC. He had summoned all his years of specialist technical know-how to remedy the problem by removing the ball from inside the mouse and blowing out a wee bit of fluff.

James swirled the cursor over the imagine2008 home page.

'Now, where were we?' he said. 'That's right. Belfast is already a Capital of Culture. And there's no better way to illustrate this than to look at the work of some of our most vibrant local artists.'

James clicked a bar that read 'Sculpture'. He highlighted the name 'Peter Diggs' and clicked again.

Two thousand two hundred and twelve people inside a packed Waterfront Hall and an estimated 123 million people across the globe were immediately treated to live footage of Chief Constable Stephen Meeks blowing his brains out the back of his head.

30

'I think you should get her something in red,' said Edel.

'You would,' I replied.

We walked round the garage forecourt again. I was trying to decide on a car for Karma. It was her Christmas present, a replacement for the death trap.

The weather was bitter. The windscreens had frozen over on the vast majority of cars, obscuring their prices. I really needed some assistance but it was Christmas Eve and the staff at Isaac Agnew Motors were too busy enjoying mince pies and mulled wine in the warmth of their showroom.

From inside my coat I removed a gold envelope decorated in emerald holly and scarlet berries.

'I bet you we'd get their undivided attention if they knew what I had in here,' I said. I dipped my hand into the envelope and pulled out three grand in cash. I waved a thick fistful of notes at the showroom window. I whistled, and called, 'Here, boy! Here, boy!'

Edel laughed.

The cash had fallen into my hands that morning, wrapped in Christmas paper. It was an anonymous present in the annual 'Secret Santa' at work. I guessed it was from Harry, however, as the attached tag wished me a 'Happy fuckin' Christmas'. I approached him to query the money but he told me to think of it as a Christmas bonus. For the first time in its history, he said, an edition of the *News Letter* had been distributed throughout the island of Ireland. It had sold out. What's more, Harry had been interviewed on Sky News about my exclusive. He was over the moon, he said, but not because of his new-found fame. He was delighted because their make-up girl had recommended a great moisturizer for his eczema.

Stephen Meeks had become the seventy-first officer in the history of the RUC to commit suicide. He was the first to do it on live television.

The *News Letter* had been quick off the mark, printing the story behind the images that had shocked the world. In it, I detailed the Chief Constable's corruption and collusion, his drug-trafficking, the Mull of Kintyre murders (as they now were), the murder of Davey Gavin (as it now was) and the very recent assassination of the novelist Aisling Coyles (which could now be attributed to the RUC). I made no mention of Martin O'Hanlon in the story. I simply claimed that I had been pursuing Meeks for five years, ever since the investigation into his purchase of the yacht, and that during the course of my research I had uncovered something more sinister.

Marty O'Hanlon did get a namecheck on my Soundz page. Or pages. An exclusive interview with Edel O'Hanlon, lead singer with The Harlots, was splashed across four of them.

After Meeks had so spectacularly redecorated my flat, the police had hauled Edel and me in for questioning. When they had finished, I had taken her to a bar on the Lisburn Road to do some questioning of my own. In the resulting feature, she talked frankly about the violent abuse she had received at the hands of her father and what it was like to grow up as the daughter of a terrorist. *I could never be free*, I quoted her as saying. *This man would barge in and take control of everything I did. He ruled me by fear. I felt like occupied territory.*

Edel also announced her retirement from the harp to concentrate on her new band.

Martin O'Hanlon responded in the only way he could. He called a press conference and announced his resignation from Sinn Fein. Moreover, he said, he wished to abdicate from political life altogether and spend more time with his family. He was ashamed of the way he had treated his daughter and was determined to redeem himself by becoming the father he never had been. He received a standing ovation. Martin O'Hanlon, it seemed, could do no wrong.

George McCrea immediately called his own news conference at Stormont and reinstalled himself as First Minister. He claimed his first job would be to try and sort out the RUC scandal. He said he would appoint an independent ombudsman to set up investigation teams to deal with all allegations of police misconduct. He was adamant, he reiterated, that the RUC should *not* be disbanded. He recognized the need for restructuring and called for a rebranded 'Northern Ireland Police Service'. If that meant losing the 'Royal' title, then, in the interest of peace, he was happy to concede it. However, he cautioned, if the association with the British monarchy was to be removed, then so should any association with the Irish State. McCrea stood on the Stormont steps and raised an RUC cap in his hand. He pointed to the badge and guldered, 'If the Crown goes, the Harp goes with it!'

Cue triumphal chest-beating from the Unionist rank and file. McCrea had claimed the day as a victory for Unionism and a victory for peace.

Within an hour of his speech there were reports of a new slogan being daubed on walls throughout Republican areas – DISBAND THE NIPS.

The IRA silently polished their guns.

Edel had asked me to keep secret the revelations concerning her father's love child. She did not want to hurt her mother. And she believed that Kate Owen had suffered enough in losing her baby. What right had I to dredge the whole thing up again? Edel wanted to remember her brother privately. She did not want him being used as a political football. She did not want his memory corrupted.

I had shamed Meeks into shooting himself. Edel had shamed her father into stepping down. Both men had experienced the great corollary of embarrassment: the more stupidly you behave, the more likely that behaviour is to become public in the most humiliating way possible and at the most inopportune moment. This was the reason my mother never let me leave the house in dirty or threadbare underwear. For if I did, she believed I was certain to get hit by a bus. The doctors would have to cut my trousers off and then, when they saw my pants, what would they think of her? She did not want to bring shame on our family.

'What about this one?' asked Edel. She sat herself on the bonnet of an unremarkable-looking Corsa. She immediately slid off it. She smacked the ice off her leggings and complained of a wet bottom.

'Why that one?' I asked.

'Look at the number plate,' she said.

'I did. NHS 2911.'

364

'It's perfect for a nurse,' said Edel. She blew on her hands.

'It's spooky, that's what it is.'

'Go on,' said Edel. 'It's a sign. You have to buy it for her.'

'You don't buy a car just because you like the number plate.'

And you shouldn't bet on a greyhound just because you like its name.

'Merry Christmas, sir . . . and madam. Hot mince pie?' A young man had approached us, his sober suit accessorized by a pair of flashing reindeer antlers on his head. He offered me a loaded plate.

'No ta,' I said.

Edel waved his pies away.

'Are you interested in the Corsa?' he asked.

'No,' I said, as Edel exclaimed, 'You betcha!'

'I'm not buying the car, Edel.' I turned to the salesman. 'She only wants me to buy it because she likes the number plate.' I gave him a conspiratorial grimace, one that said, *Women . . . huh!* He was a man. He knew where I was coming from.

'Well, sir, it *is* an awfully nice number plate.'

'No,' I asserted. 'I'm not buying the car.'

'It's a great little motor, sir. There's only thirty thousand on the clock.'

'Yes, but there's five thousand on the price tag. I only have three grand in cash.'

The salesman's eyes lit up. As did his red nose and antlers. He saw his opportunity. 'It's Christmas, sir. The season of goodwill. I'll knock a grand off if you drive her away today.'

'Go on,' said Edel.

'Four thousand?' I shook my head. 'I'm not sure, Edel. It's still a bit much.'

'Go on, Jay. Don't be tight. It's for Karma. If it wasn't for her, we may never have got together.'

I looked at the car. I shook my head again.

'What are you,' goaded Edel, 'a big Jessie?'

I turned to the salesman.

'Can you wrap it?'

THE END